D0466120

PRAISE FOR MELANIE DICKERSON

"*The Goose Girl*, a little retold fairy tale, sparkles in Dickerson's hands, with endearing characters and a charming setting that will appeal to teens and adults alike."

—*RT BOOK REVIEWS*, 4½ STARS, TOP PICK! ON *THE NOBLE SERVANT*

"Dickerson is a masterful storyteller with a carefully crafted plot, richly drawn characters, and a detailed setting. The reader is easily pulled into the story. Does everything end happily ever after? Read it and see! Recommended for young adults and adults who are young at heart."

—*CHRISTIAN LIBRARY JOURNAL* ON *THE NOBLE SERVANT*

"[*The Silent Songbird*] will have you jumping out of your seat with anticipation at times. Moderate to fast-paced, you will not want this book to end. Recommended for all, especially lovers of historical romance."

—*RT BOOK REVIEWS*, 4 STARS

"A terrific YA crossover medieval romance from the author of *The Golden Braid*."

—*LIBRARY JOURNAL* ON *THE SILENT SONGBIRD*

"When it comes to happily-ever-afters, Melanie Dickerson is the undisputed queen of fairy-tale romance, and all I can say is—long live the queen! From start to finish *The Beautiful Pretender* is yet another brilliant gem in her crown, spinning a medieval love story that will steal you away—heart, soul, and sleep!"

—JULIE LESSMAN, AWARD-WINNING AUTHOR OF THE DAUGHTERS OF BOSTON, WINDS OF CHANGE, AND HEART OF SAN FRANCISCO SERIES

"I couldn't stop reading! Melanie has done what so many other historical novelists have tried and failed: she's created a heroine that is at once both smart and self-assured without seeming modern. A woman so fixed in her time and place that she is able to speak to ours as well."

—SIRI MITCHELL, AUTHOR OF *FLIRTATION WALK* AND *CHATEAU OF ECHOES*, ON *THE BEAUTIFUL PRETENDER*

"Dickerson breathes life into the age-old story of Rapunzel, blending it seamlessly with the other YA novels she has written in this time and place . . . The character development is solid, and she captures religious medieval life splendidly."

—*BOOKLIST*, ON *THE GOLDEN BRAID*

"Readers who love getting lost in a fairy-tale romance will cheer for Rapunzel's courage as she rises above her overwhelming past. The surprising way Dickerson weaves threads of this enchanting companion novel with those of her other Hagenheim stories is simply delightful. Her fans will love it."

—JILL WILLIAMSON, CHRISTY AWARD–WINNING AUTHOR OF THE BLOOD OF KINGS TRILOGY AND THE KINSMAN CHRONICLES, ON *THE GOLDEN BRAID*

"Readers will find themselves supporting the romance between the sweet yet determined Odette and the insecure but hardworking Jorgen from the beginning. Dickerson spins a retelling of Robin Hood with emotionally compelling characters, offering hope that love may indeed conquer all as they unite in a shared desire to serve both the Lord and those in need."

—*RT BOOK REVIEWS*, 4½ STARS, ON *THE HUNTRESS OF THORNBECK FOREST*

"Melanie Dickerson does it again! Full of danger, intrigue, and romance, this beautifully crafted story will transport you to another place and time."

—SARAH E. LADD, AUTHOR OF *THE CURIOSITY KEEPER* AND THE WHISPERS ON THE MOORS SERIES, ON *THE HUNTRESS OF THORNBECK FOREST*

The ORPHAN'S WISH

Other Books by Melanie Dickerson

A Medieval Fairy Tale Series

The Huntress of Thornbeck Forest
The Beautiful Pretender
The Noble Servant

Young Adult Fairy Tale Romance Series

The Healer's Apprentice
The Merchant's Daughter
The Fairest Beauty
The Captive Maiden
The Princess Spy
The Golden Braid
The Silent Songbird

Regency Spies of London Series

A Spy's Devotion
A Viscount's Proposal
A Dangerous Engagement

The
ORPHAN'S
WISH

MELANIE DICKERSON

THOMAS NELSON
Since 1798

The Orphan's Wish

Published in Nashville, Tennessee, by Thomas Nelson. Thomas Nelson is a registered trademark of HarperCollins Christian Publishing, Inc.

Thomas Nelson titles may be purchased in bulk for educational, business, fund-raising, or sales promotional use. For information, please e-mail SpecialMarkets@ThomasNelson.com.

Scripture quotations are taken from the King James Version.

Library of Congress Cataloging-in-Publication Data

Names: Dickerson, Melanie, author.
Title: The orphan's wish / Melanie Dickerson.
Description: Nashville, Tennessee : Thomas Nelson, [2018] | Summary: In medieval Hagenheim, Germany, Aladdin, a poor orphan from the Holy Land, tries to rescue and win the heart of Kirstyn, the Duke of Hagenheim's daughter, his friend since childhood who is now pursued by greedy men seeking her father's fortune.
Identifiers: LCCN 2017060978 | ISBN 9780718074838 (hard cover)
Subjects: | CYAC: Characters in literature--Fiction. | Orphans--Fiction. | Nobility--Fiction. | Social classes--Fiction. | Love--Fiction. | Middle Ages--Fiction. | Germany--History--1273-1517--Fiction.
Classification: LCC PZ7.D5575 Or 2018 | DDC [Fic]--dc23 LC record available at https://lccn.loc.gov/2017060978

33614080708778

Printed in the United States of America

18 19 20 21 22 LSC 5 4 3 2 1

Chapter One

Summer 1401
The Holy Land

Ala ad'din's mother's eyes were closed as she lay on her funeral bier.

People whispered and stared, but no one spoke to him. Just a few days ago his mother sat cross-legged on the floor while she sewed. Sometimes she would lay aside her work. He would crawl into her lap and gaze up at her as she sang to him.

There was no one to sing to him now.

Then someone walked up behind him.

"She won't wake up."

A man with wispy black hairs growing above his top lip and on his chin stared down at him. His face was bland as he squatted in front of Ala ad'din. "She won't wake up. Not ever. She's dead. Do you know what *dead* means?"

Ala ad'din nodded.

"Don't you have a father? A grandmother? Any family?"

Ala ad'din shook his head. His chest ached as tears stung his eyes.

"How old are you?"

"Five years."

Some men came and picked up the funeral bier and started carrying his mother's body away without even a glance at him.

The man put his hand on Ala ad'din's shoulder. "You should come home with me, yes? I have a bed for you. Many other children are there, children for you to play with. Come."

Ala ad'din went with him. But when they reached their destination, the bed he'd mentioned was a thin pallet on a dirt floor. He sat on it with several other children, all of them dirty, some of them smelling of urine, while several men passed out food to them. They ate fried bread and shriveled dates and then slept like puppies piled haphazardly against each other.

The next day, when the sun was high, the man with the wispy whiskers—Mustapha—took Ala ad'din and another boy, Zuhayr, out to the bazaar.

The sun was hot and bright, and the pungent smells of turmeric, cumin, cinnamon, and cloves tickled Ala ad'din's nose when he passed the spice merchant's stall. Other smells—camel dung chief among them—wafted in and surrounded the dusty, heated marketplace.

Zuhayr was a few years older than Ala ad'din. Mustapha stopped them both, holding on to Ala ad'din's arm, his fingers gripping too tightly.

"Watch," Mustapha said in a raspy voice. "Zuhayr will go and take the fat purse hanging from that merchant's belt. Do you see it?"

Ala ad'din tried to follow Mustapha's line of vision.

Zuhayr nodded and took off, running as though he would

pass by the merchant's stall with a few feet to spare. But at the last moment, he darted toward the merchant and snatched the purse, breaking it off of the leather belt it was tied to.

Zuhayr did not even slow down as the merchant yelled and gave chase. But he was much too old and heavy to catch Zuhayr, who ran like a flash of lightning.

"Stop him! Thief! Stop him!" The merchant's face seemed to swell with rage as he pointed after Zuhayr's thin figure.

Mustapha pulled Ala ad'din by his arm away from the scene, threading around shoppers and finally stopping in a narrow alley between sandstone buildings.

"Where is Zuhayr?" Ala ad'din's heart trembled at what would happen to his new friend.

Mustapha grinned. "Look! There he is."

Zuhayr hurried toward them, panting. He handed the purse to his master.

"And that is how it is done." Mustapha's thin lips twisted as he grinned down at Ala ad'din. Then his grin disappeared and he gripped Ala ad'din's arm even tighter, giving it a shake. He showed his bright-white teeth as he said in a harsh tone, "And you must do the same."

"But that is stealing. My mother told me stealing is bad."

Mustapha leaned down until his nose was almost touching Ala ad'din's. "You will do whatever I tell you or I shall turn you over to the Sultan's guards, tell them you stole this purse, and then they will cut off your head."

"My head?"

"Yes, your head. They will slice through your neck with their long, sharp scimitars." He drew his finger across his throat from one side to the other. "Do you want to lose your head?" He grinned, and it was even more frightening than his scowl.

Later that day, when Mustapha was occupied with talking with a man in the bazaar, Ala ad'din asked Zuhayr, "Will they really cut off my head for stealing?"

Zuhayr patted him on the shoulder. "They won't cut off your head, but they will cut off your hand."

Ala ad'din gasped.

"But that's only if they catch you. You have to run fast, understand?" He stared into Ala ad'din's eyes.

"But I don't want to steal."

"You must." Zuhayr's dark eyes were solemn. "If Mustapha gets angry, he'll beat you. Just do what he says and he will feed you and not hurt you."

The next day Mustapha took Zuhayr and Ala ad'din out to the marketplace again. They passed a stall of plump fruits, including clusters of purple grapes. He could almost taste their sweet, juicy insides bursting on his tongue.

Mustapha's eyes narrowed at him. "You want those grapes, don't you?"

"No."

"Liar. Steal a big bunch of them."

Ala ad'din shook his head.

He squeezed Ala ad'din's arm so hard he yelped.

"Zuhayr, you distract the vendor while Ala ad'din steals a bunch. After you take it, Ala ad'din, put it under your shirt and walk beside me."

Ala ad'din looked at Zuhayr and nodded.

Zuhayr walked over to the vendor and started asking him a question, pointing behind him at another fruit seller. Meanwhile, Mustapha walked Ala ad'din toward the stand. As they passed the grapes, Ala ad'din reached out and grabbed a large cluster and shoved it under his shirt, while Mustapha kept up his steady pace.

They walked around the corner into a small side street, and soon Zuhayr joined them.

"The little rat is good at our game." Mustapha laughed, throwing back his head. He reached under Ala ad'din's shirt and pulled out the grapes. "Eat some." He shoved them into Ala ad'din's face.

The boy picked a grape from the bunch and put it into his mouth. Tears flooded his eyes. Could his mother see him? Was she sad that he was stealing grapes? The grape turned bitter in his mouth as he crunched into a seed.

Mustapha laughed again, then held up the bunch of grapes and ate one right off the vine.

They ate all the grapes and left the stems on the ground. As they walked back out into the bazaar, Mustapha stopped them and pointed at a boy who was perhaps nine or ten years old. He walked with a merchant who wore a snowy-white turban studded with jewels and bright-red silk shoes that curled over the toes like the liripipe from a foreign pilgrim's hood, the ones the Christians wore on their way to Jerusalem.

The man rested his hand lovingly on the boy's shoulder. He wore the same style of clothing as his father, a miniature man dressed in fine fabrics.

"You see that boy? His father is rich. He will never have to steal. But you—" Mustapha pointed at Ala ad'din and then at Zuhayr. "You will never be like him. You have no father, and you will steal and run all your lives, wallowing in dirt and filth like rats until the Sultan's guards catch you and throw you in a hole to die. Unless you do as I say." He grabbed the front of Ala ad'din's shirt. "You're a thief, and you'll never be anything but a thief. And unless you want your hands chopped off, you cannot *ever* get caught. You understand?"

He let go of Ala ad'din's shirt, grabbed his arm again, and pulled him around the outskirts of the market, keeping out of sight.

Day after day Ala ad'din and Zuhayr stole for Mustapha. Other men and children resided in the large house with the dirt floor, but Ala ad'din and Zuhayr belonged to Mustapha. He took them out every day in the hot bazaar, and then one day, while they sat in a shady spot eating fried bread drizzled with honey, Mustapha suddenly slapped Zuhayr's side.

"What are you hiding there?" Mustapha roughly drew up Zuhayr's shirt. A pouch dangled on a string from the boy's shoulder. Mustapha struck Zuhayr's cheek with his open hand.

"You little rat! You were keeping back part of what you stole! How dare you?" He slapped him again.

Zuhayr raised his arms over his face, and Mustapha took the pouch and turned away from him. Zuhayr was breathing hard, the red mark of Mustapha's hand and fingers showing on his cheek.

That night, as they lay on their thin pallets, when most of the other children were asleep, Zuhayr whispered to Ala ad'din, "When you see your chance to get away from Mustapha, run. Find some kind people who will not beat you and stay with them."

"Have you found some people like that, Zuhayr?"

"No, but I am older. I can take care of myself. Before long I will go to another town, away from Mustapha, and live by my wits."

"Can I go with you?"

"No. You still have your baby fat. Someone will take you in, but no one wants me. Go to sleep now, before Mustapha hears us talking."

Ala ad'din was too tired to ponder long what Zuhayr had

said. But then he awoke the next morning to Mustapha shouting and searching through the house.

"Where is he? Where is Zuhayr?"

The other men laughed. "Your street rat has run away from you!"

Mustapha's gaze fell on Ala ad'din. "Where is he?"

"I don't know." Ala ad'din started to shake.

"You will tell me, you little rat!" Mustapha grabbed Ala ad'din's shoulder with one hand and slapped him across the face with his other.

"I don't know." A tear slid from Ala ad'din's eye.

Mustapha let go of him, drew his hands into fists, and roared with rage.

Ala ad'din knelt on the floor and covered his head with his arms.

It took Mustapha a while to stop yelling. But when he finally did, he took Ala ad'din out to the bazaar, proclaiming, "Now you'll have to steal twice as much, my little beggar." He jerked Ala ad'din's arm as they skulked around the edges of the stalls.

"There." Mustapha pointed at a Christian knight's horse and saddle. The knight's back was turned while he argued with a vendor over a price.

"Slide your hand inside that leather saddlebag." Mustapha squatted beside Ala ad'din. "I saw him drop his purse in there. Get it. Hurry." He pushed Ala ad'din forward.

Ala ad'din approached the Christian knight's horse and saddle. He jumped up on a large bag of something hard and lumpy and stood on his tiptoes to reach into the saddlebag. He drew out a small purse, heavy with coins.

"Halt!"

Ala ad'din jumped down and ran—right into a large belly.

Hands clamped around his arms. Ala ad'din struggled, kicking and lunging, but his skinny little body couldn't pull free.

The knight who had yelled strode toward them, a dark scowl on his bearded face. He snatched the purse out of Ala ad'din's hand.

Ala ad'din screamed, fearing they would cut off his hand. But even if he got away, Mustapha would beat him.

The knight, who had hair the color of sand, said something, then shook his fist at Ala ad'din.

The large man holding him laughed. The rope encircling his round belly shook, but Ala ad'din concentrated on waiting for the man's grip on his arms to loosen.

When he stopped laughing, the man, who was dressed in the robes of a Christian priest, said something to the knight. The priest bent until his face was level with Ala ad'din's. Then he spoke in a strange language Ala ad'din did not understand.

The priest seemed to be waiting for an answer, but Ala ad'din didn't give him one. Then the priest said in Arabic, "Where is your mother?"

Ala ad'din shook his head.

"You have no mother? Father?"

He shook his head again.

The knight said something in his harsh voice, his lips twisting.

"Do you have a master?" the priest asked.

Ala ad'din's gaze darted to the right, where Mustapha stood watching.

The priest and knight both followed the direction of his gaze. Mustapha turned and disappeared behind a big display of barrels of spices and bread flour.

"Where did you get those fingerprints on your cheek?" The priest's face had sobered. "Did your master strike you?"

He nodded.

The priest looked up at the knight. "We shall take him with us."

"What do you mean? He is a child, not a stray animal. Besides, his master would slit our throats if we took his little thief."

The priest raised one eyebrow. "Are you not capable of saving us from the boy's master?"

The knight scowled, then spat on the ground.

The priest turned to Ala ad'din. "Boy, what is your name?"

"Ala ad'din."

The priest tried to repeat the name, but it came out sounding like "Aladdin."

"That isn't right, but no matter. Your name shall be Aladdin, if you like it. Do you like Aladdin, boy?"

He nodded, no longer concentrating on how to get away, remembering Zuhayr's words from the night before.

"And do you wish to come with us—with Sir Meynard and me—to a place called Hagenheim, far to the north?"

Aladdin gazed into the priest's kind eyes and nodded.

The priest laughed and pulled out a small loaf of bread and handed it to him, finally releasing the boy's arm from his grip.

Aladdin bit into the bread. The priest held out his hand and Aladdin took it, and they walked away from the bazaar and away from his Arab homeland.

CHAPTER TWO

Summer 1403
Hagenheim, Lower Saxony, Holy Roman Empire

The first time Aladdin saw Lady Kirstyn, her pale-blonde hair shone in the summer sun like the gold-and-yellow stained glass of Hagenheim Cathedral, reminding him of one particularly bright angel. Was this girl an angel like the one in the window?

He was still learning the language of the Christians, so when he pulled on the sleeve of the priest's long, flowing robe, he said, "Who?" and pointed at the small girl who was laughing in the sun.

The priest stared down at him with that amused look he wore nearly all the time and shook his head. Then he bent down and said softly, "She is pretty, is she not? Only about two years younger than you, I would guess. But that is the duke's daughter, Lady Kirstyn."

Many days and weeks after that, when the priest was satisfied that Aladdin had learned enough German to understand others and make himself understood, he took him back to the place where Aladdin had seen the girl angel. They stood in the grassy yard behind a large brick building where a group of children were playing.

Priest leaned down to talk to Aladdin, and he gestured at a well-dressed woman. "That great lady there is Lady Kirstyn's mother, Lady Rose. She has invited you to come and play with the orphans every day when you finish your studies. Would you like to play with the other children?"

"Yes."

The next afternoon he joined the children as they played a game of blindman's buff in the yard at the end of the street that led to Hagenheim Castle. He kept looking for the angel girl, but she was not there. In fact, several days went by before he saw her again.

Lady Rose was standing nearby, speaking with the woman in charge of the orphanage. Aladdin kept his eye on Lady Kirstyn as the children played. She was laughing as the other children ran forward and touched the blindfolded child on the arm or shoulder or back, then stepped back or ran away. Finally Lady Kirstyn stepped forward, rather timidly compared to the others, and touched the blindfolded boy on the arm.

The boy, who was a head taller than her, reached out and grabbed her by the wrist.

Lady Kirstyn screamed.

Aladdin leapt toward the boy and reached him just as he was taking off his blindfold.

Aladdin grabbed the boy by the arm that held Kirstyn. "Let her go!"

The boy let her go and grabbed Aladdin by the throat, glaring down. "What do you think you're doing?" He drew back his fist.

Aladdin cringed, closing his eyes as he waited for the blow.

"Stop that!" A woman stood beside them, the white wimple trembling that covered her steel-gray hair. "Hanns, do not strike him. He doesn't know the game." She glowered at the boy, and he let go of Aladdin.

Lady Rose stood beside Aladdin and bent toward him. "All is well. It's only a game. I'm sorry no one explained it to you."

Lady Kirstyn stood beside her mother, staring at him with big blue eyes. "Are you the boy who came from the Holy Land with Priest and his knight protector?"

Aladdin stared back at her.

"What is your name?" the little girl asked. "How old are you?"

"My name is Aladdin. And I don't know how old I am."

She gave him a puzzled look.

The woman in charge of the children was still speaking with Hanns. Lady Rose smiled down at Aladdin and bent toward him. "Hanns was not hurting Lady Kirstyn, but thank you for coming to her aid."

The woman with the steel-gray hair said, "The child with the blindfold must try to catch one of the other children. He caught Lady Kirstyn, so now it is her turn to wear the blindfold."

Kirstyn laid a hand on his arm, her touch light like a butterfly's wings. "No one will hurt me." She smiled. "Come and play with us."

Aladdin wondered what it must be like to believe no one would hurt him. After staying with Priest at Hagenheim Cathedral, he was beginning to understand. Hagenheim was a safe place full of families who were kind to each other. And for those children who had no family, they made up their own family in a place called an orphanage.

Kirstyn was already putting the blindfold over her eyes, and her mother tied it behind her head.

Hanns seemed to have already forgotten Aladdin, and he and the other children swarmed around Lady Kirstyn. Aladdin stood back and watched as the children touched Lady Kirstyn's shoulder or arm. She smiled, her teeth showing white between her pink lips. She flailed her arms out in front of her, her small hands grasping only air. She squealed as someone touched her elbow, and she swung around.

Finally her hand grasped another girl's hand just as she came near. She called out a name, and the girl admitted it was her. Lady Kirstyn laughed and shouted in triumph, lifting the blindfold from her face.

The woman tied the blindfold around the other little girl's face, but Aladdin still watched Lady Kirstyn, the way her eyes sparkled as she talked and smiled and laughed.

His heart thumped hard against his chest, suddenly full and warm.

Spring 1406
Hagenheim Cathedral

Aladdin had been excused from his language and mathematics lessons for a week as Priest lay sick in bed. Aladdin sat nearby reading, and Priest's breaths were loud as he struggled to draw in each one. The doctor had come and gone that morning, and now Priest lay with his eyes open.

"Aladdin, come here," he rasped.

Aladdin put down his book and hurried to his bedside. "Do you need some water or wine? Shall I fetch the healer?"

"No." He drew in a noisy breath between words. "I want

you . . . to go live . . . with the children at the orphans' home. And, Aladdin . . . never forget . . . your Jesus. He saved you. Love Him. Always." He closed his eyes, as though speaking had exhausted him.

Aladdin nodded. "Of course. I shall. Anything you wish, Priest."

"Take this . . . copy . . . of the Holy Writ. It's yours now."

Aladdin had seen Priest reading that book every day, always in the morning before he broke his fast, then again in the evening. He'd been using it to teach Aladdin how to read Latin. Aladdin's eyes watered at the thought that Priest would never read it again.

Aladdin leaned over him and patted his arm. "Rest so you can get well."

"I will not . . . get well . . . this time."

Aladdin's own breath hitched and tears flooded his eyes. "I'm sorry for what I did when I was younger. I promise I'll never steal again."

"You are . . . forgiven. I shall . . . see you . . . in heaven . . . You are . . . my son . . . from the Holy Land." Priest lifted his hand and touched Aladdin's cheek with his fingertips, then let his hand drop. His eyes closed and he continued to breathe hard, his chest rising and falling beneath the large cross hanging from a chain around his neck.

After about an hour, his chest stopped rising and falling. The rasping breaths ceased.

Aladdin waited. He touched the older man's shoulder, but he still didn't open his eyes. Priest was dead.

The next two days were a blur of numbness. On the third day the whole town of Hagenheim came to see Priest's body as it lay in the polished, ornate coffin. "He's not there," Aladdin wanted to tell them. "He's waiting for me in heaven."

Everyone had come, even Duke Wilhelm and Lady Rose and all their children. They gazed down at Priest's waxy, still face. Lady Kirstyn stared at him the longest. She was still standing there when her parents and siblings had moved away.

Aladdin's tears had been sitting like a hard lump inside his chest for three days. They suddenly rose to clog his throat, then continued up until they blurred his vision, spilling onto his cheeks and flowing down his neck.

Priest had been the one who taught him to speak German. Priest had bandaged his skinned knees and patted him on the shoulder. Priest had laughed at the things he'd said, calling him "a fine boy" and "clever beyond reason" and "destined to do great things." Priest had taken him from a cruel master who forced him to steal. He'd fed him and clothed him and taught him about the One who saves all people from their sins, the Son of God who died a vicious death so men could be free from shame and guilt.

Priest was his family. Who would care about Aladdin now that Priest was gone?

He took a shuddering breath, using his hands to wipe the tears from his neck and chin. When he looked up, Lady Kirstyn was holding out a small cloth bag.

"I brought you some cake."

He took the bag, which was still warm.

Lady Rose approached him, smiling gently. "Aladdin, would you like to live with the other children at the orphans' home? Did Priest talk with you about that?"

He nodded. Kirstyn stood next to her mother, looking at him even though her siblings and nearly everyone else had left the church.

"Will you show me where you sleep? Perhaps we could gather your things, and Kirstyn and I could accompany you over there."

Aladdin walked by the coffin that held Priest's body, but he could no longer bear to look at him there.

They were both starting a new life. Priest's was certain to be good, but Aladdin was less sure about his.

CHAPTER THREE

Spring 1409

Kirstyn had purposely worn her oldest dress and sturdiest shoes. She fetched her lightest cloak from her bedchamber and ran down the stairs, out the door, and into the fresh spring air.

The sun was shining and the sky, bluer than she ever remembered it, was dotted with fluffy white clouds, whiter than the cleanest wool. She raced toward the stable and kept running to the large chestnut tree where Aladdin had agreed to meet her. He was just arriving with a smile on his face.

"Did you finish your studies early?" she asked.

"Yes."

"Are you sure you won't get in trouble?" She bit her lip. Aladdin was always so willing to do whatever she asked of him. Was he so willing that he would take a beating for her? Her stomach sank at the thought.

17

"What kind of trouble?" He tilted his head to the side.

"The stable master might be angry with you for being late. He would not punish you, would he?"

Aladdin shook his head and waved his hand as if the idea were silly. "I can simply work late instead of early."

"Then let us go!" Kirstyn giggled and started off in the direction of the gate leading out of town.

She glanced over her shoulder. "Why are you walking behind me?" Of course, she knew why. Before he could answer, she said, "You must walk beside me. We'll be at the gate in a moment."

"You are the duke's daughter. I dare not—"

"Nonsense. We are two people—a brother and a sister perhaps—making our way to our little wattle-and-daub house in the woods." She giggled again. How fun it was to pretend!

Aladdin allowed himself to catch up with Kirstyn. His heart soared at being her companion for the afternoon.

"I brought some apples and bread and cheese for us." She showed him the bag at her waist. "In case we get hungry."

Her cheeks were pink, and her teeth flashed in the sunlight. She didn't seem to have any idea how pretty she was. He was suddenly thankful she was the duke's daughter. That fact would protect her in future from lecherous eyes.

She turned toward him even as she kept hurrying along. "The weather is still a bit cool, but I simply could not wait."

"I don't mind the cool air."

As they approached the gate, Kirstyn threw the hood from

her cloak over her head, letting it hang low over her eyes. He drew closer to her side as the guards scrutinized them.

Would the guards stop them and question them? Aladdin had never passed through the gates alone before. Would they recognize Lady Kirstyn?

The guards did stare, first at Kirstyn, then at Aladdin, then glanced away as the two of them passed on by.

When they were several horse-lengths outside the gate, Kirstyn turned to him and clapped her hands. Then she veered off the road leading away from Hagenheim and ran.

Aladdin ran after her, quickly overtaking her. He stayed beside her as they traversed a meadow full of wildflowers. In the middle of it was a large tree. Kirstyn didn't stop until she reached it, then leaned her shoulder against the trunk.

She was breathing hard, but a wide smile stretched across her face. "This is fun. But I feel as if I'm doing something wrong."

"Are you?"

Her smile faltered, but then she shook her head. "No one said I could not go exploring with a friend. They only said I couldn't leave the castle courtyard alone."

He frowned a little, but he couldn't scold her.

"And I will not permit anyone to blame you if they try to punish us. I shall tell them I forced you to accompany me, that you warned me and tried to stop me. Come. Let us go explore the forest."

She pushed herself away from the trunk and strode up the gentle hill toward the edge of the dark woods. He walked beside her, listening to her chatter about the leaves and the trees and the animals who lived in the forest.

The trees were mostly beeches and oaks, with their spring leaves just sprouting—new life on limbs that stretched up to the sky.

"The ground is so soft and springy," Kirstyn said. "How many years' worth of leaves are under our feet?"

Aladdin touched the tree's bark beside him. There was something restorative about being in the woods, in the natural world, away from cobblestone streets and stone and brick and people.

"You're very quiet," Kirstyn said.

"I like how quiet it is. We haven't heard anything besides a few birds chirping."

"Yes, the forest is almost reverent, like a church."

She was so clever in how she described things, and the joy on her face created a warmth in his middle.

They walked a bit farther. "Look at these pretty flowers!" Kirstyn bent and examined the tiny purple blossoms.

"What are those called?"

"I think they're violets. I shall pick some and take them home to my mother."

A small animal scrambled out of the dead leaves and raced across the ground. Kirstyn let out a short scream.

Aladdin leapt forward, ready to defend her. Perhaps he should have brought a weapon of some sort. He did have his small knife that he carried everywhere in the pouch at his belt.

Kirstyn laughed, pressing her hand to her chest. "It was only a field mouse."

When Kirstyn had asked him to go exploring with her, Aladdin inquired of the men who worked in the stable whether dangerous animals roamed in the forest outside Hagenheim.

After teasing him about all of the wolves, poisonous adders, wild cats, and bears, one of the kinder men, Eiderholt, told him that wild animals large enough to harm a man rarely appeared anywhere near Hagenheim. They preferred the mountainous areas away from people.

Which left the adders.

Aladdin scoured the ground until he found a fallen tree and broke off a limb about six feet long. He cleaned the smaller limbs from it and gripped it. Yes, it was just the right size.

Kirstyn looked at him. "A walking stick. What a good idea."

He didn't tell her he wanted it in case they encountered a snake in the leaves.

"I want one too." She stepped to the same tree where he'd gotten his stick and, using her foot to hold it down, broke off a similar limb. Soon she had it all cleaned and was ready to go.

They walked farther into the woods and found a small footpath that led to an old house. The straw thatched roof was sagging and slipping, and the door was hanging loose on one hinge. Behind it they found a small stream.

Kirstyn sank to her knees before it, laid her stick aside, dipped her hands in the water, and brought it to her lips. "It's refreshing. Try some."

Aladdin knelt by the fast-moving stream and took a drink. The water slid down his throat and dripped from his chin. He smiled and nodded. "Good. Whoever lived here chose a favorable spot for fresh water."

"What would it be like to live in the woods, so isolated?" Kirstyn sank back on her heels and looked around. "Aladdin? What do you think?"

"It would depend on who was with you. If you had your

family around you, it would be . . . joyful." He felt a slight squeeze around his heart and glanced away from Kirstyn, who was staring intently at his face.

"Yes, exactly. But . . . it's hard to imagine not living at the castle with all our people."

By "people" she meant servants.

Aladdin had lived in the orphanage for several years now, sleeping in a room with ten other boys, but he had no trouble imagining what it would be like to live elsewhere, in a house with his own wife and children, with love and warmth and laughter.

They walked a bit farther.

"Look at this!"

Some tiny pieces of blue eggshells lay scattered on the ground. Aladdin gazed up into the tree next to them. "There must be a nest in that tree." He glanced behind them, trying to make note of anything that would help him recognize the way back.

Kirstyn sighed, standing up and turning all the way around slowly. "I love the woods, don't you?"

"They are very interesting, but if we go much farther, we could become lost. There aren't a lot of landmarks here."

"I suppose. But you did enjoy exploring with me, did you not? And will you come with me again?" Her eyes were wide and so innocent.

"I did enjoy it, and I will come again with you."

"Thank you." She reached out both hands and squeezed his arm. "I love being out here, with no one else around to interrupt or bother us in any way."

He gave her a half smile, his heart skipping as it sometimes did when she looked him in the eye. They turned back the way they came.

At the edge of the forest, Aladdin propped his walking stick against a tree so he could retrieve it on their next walk. Kirstyn propped hers next to his. "In the castle my brothers and sisters get all the attention, but the forest will be *our* place."

Chapter Four

Spring 1410

Aladdin hurried across the castle bailey. After a colder and snowier winter than usual, he and Kirstyn were finally able to go exploring in the woods again. But Master Alfred had kept him later than usual, asking him to teach a mathematics lesson to the other children.

He passed through the castle gate, and Kirstyn was already standing there. Her face lit up with a smile. She waved to him, and he ran the rest of the way.

"Sir Ruger is supposed to meet us." Kirstyn glanced over her shoulder. After the first time they'd gone walking in the woods, Kirstyn's father had forbidden them to go without a guard. They'd had a series of the duke's knights and soldiers accompany them.

Kirstyn turned her blue eyes on Aladdin and grasped his arm. "I am so glad to see you! You've grown two handsbreadth since I saw you last. Soon you will be as tall as Father."

"You've grown too."

"Not as much as you. And now that I'm twelve, Mother says I may not grow much more. But let us be off. I don't want to wait for Sir Ruger. He knows where we go, and he can catch up."

Sir Ruger was probably distracted by the baker's daughter who sometimes walked with him to the gate and lingered there.

"I think we should wait for him," Aladdin said.

"You're always afraid of getting me in trouble with my father." Kirstyn shook her head at him. "But what about you? Did you tell the stable master you would be late to work today?"

"I'm not working in the stables anymore."

She looked surprised, so he went on.

"Frau Litzer and Master Alfred decided they wanted me to help teach the younger children, and they're also training me to keep the financial records for the orphanage."

"So you're the steward for the orphanage? That's wonderful! A commendable position." Her face lit up again. "Although I'm sure you will someday advance to the highest position in the castle—my father's steward—it is a good start. The other boys must be so envious of you."

Aladdin shrugged. He didn't mention that after word spread about his promotion, Dieter and his friends had caught Aladdin behind the orphanage. They tripped him, but Aladdin's friends found them before Dieter could land the first blow. If they'd been caught fighting, they would have been punished.

"Oh, here is Sir Ruger." Kirstyn propped her hands on her hips and glared at their knight protector.

The young red-haired knight hurried toward them, his sword jostling on his back, the hilt bobbing over his shoulder. "Forgive me for being late, Lady Kirstyn." Then he nodded to Aladdin.

"Of course. Let us go." Kirstyn hastened forward.

The *Marktplatz* was more crowded than usual, as it had been cold and rainy the previous two market days. Everyone was out on the relatively warm spring day.

When they passed through the town gate, they glanced behind them. They'd already lost Sir Ruger.

"Well, I'm not waiting again for him," Kirstyn said.

"I'm sure he'll be along soon." Aladdin strained to see through the crowd of people but didn't spot the knight.

When Aladdin turned around, Kirstyn was running up the hill, just as she had done almost a year ago. Her laughter carried through the still air and seemed to lodge in his chest.

Aladdin smiled. Perhaps she was a bit too accustomed to getting her way, but how could he not want to please her when she was so full of life and innocence and playfulness?

He caught up with her before she was halfway up the hill. He opened his mouth to tell her to slow down and wait for Sir Ruger, but before he could speak, she laughed and ran even faster. Her long skirt didn't even slow her down.

Aladdin paused at the edge of the forest, watching to see if the knight would appear below them. He waited as long as he dared, lest Kirstyn lose him too, then started after her.

A scream, shrill and urgent, stopped his blood cold in his veins.

He lurched forward, running into the forest, leaping over bushes and old tree limbs in the direction of Kirstyn's scream.

A bear stood on its hind legs, its huge black body nearly blending into the murky dark of the forest. Beside the bear was a small cub. And directly in front of it stood Kirstyn.

Urgency flowed through his body and propelled his legs forward.

Did he have time to retrieve his walking stick? It was too far behind them now.

The bear let out a roar, its enormous jaws agape. Kirstyn took a step back, then another, still facing the bear and her cub.

Aladdin edged forward while Kirstyn inched backward. When Aladdin was beside Kirstyn, the bear roared again, its small black eyes shifting between Kirstyn and Aladdin.

"Keep moving backward." Aladdin tried to keep his voice soft and soothing. "Slowly."

He maneuvered his body in front of Kirstyn's. The bear came down on all four paws and roared again. "Lady Kirstyn, I want you to run."

Kirstyn grabbed his arm from behind.

"No, just run. I'll be right behind you."

He still felt her hand on his arm as the bear sprang forward and charged toward them.

Aladdin spun around. "Go!"

Kirstyn's eyes were wide and round as she turned and bolted.

Aladdin ran too, shielding her body with his. The pounding of the bear's paws on the thick layers of leaves filled his ears.

Hot, moist breath heated the back of his neck. Something slammed into his shoulders, hurtling him stomach-first onto the ground. The next moment searing pain ripped through his lower leg as the bear's teeth sank into it.

Kirstyn had reached the edge of the trees, but Aladdin was not behind her. She screamed. He was on the ground, the bear on top of him, tearing into his leg. The bear paused her rampage to roar, then her front paw slipped under Aladdin's shoulder and flipped him over. She roared in his face.

Kirstyn glanced around. Their sticks leaned against the tree just beside her. She grabbed Aladdin's stick, her blood surging through her veins, and raced forward.

The bear slashed Aladdin's shoulder with her enormous claws, and Aladdin cried out, his voice filled with agony.

Kirstyn ran faster, screaming.

The bear looked up at her just as she reached it. Kirstyn swung the stick as hard as she could into the bear's nose.

The bear roared again, this time directing her rage at Kirstyn. Her heart in her throat, Kirstyn swung again, striking the bear in the side of the head.

Another voice let out a protracted yell, drawing closer and closer.

The bear turned toward this new threat, and swinging her shaggy head, she backed away from Aladdin's prostrate body. She hesitated, shifted side to side, turned, and lumbered back toward her cub, which fell in beside its mother as they headed toward the mountains.

Kirstyn sank down beside Aladdin, barely seeing Sir Ruger running toward them with his sword drawn.

Blood reddened Aladdin's leather cape at his shoulder and across his chest, his clothing torn in long strips. His face was white and his lips ashen.

Her chest hollowed as all the breath left her. "Oh, Aladdin. Oh, God in heaven, have mercy. Mercy, O God." She took off her own cloak and pressed it to his chest and shoulder to stop the bleeding.

"I think his leg is the worst," Sir Ruger said, his voice hoarse.

Kirstyn turned to see the puddle of blood forming under his

leg. With trembling hands, she wrapped her cloak around his lower leg.

The tangy smell of blood swept over her. Her vision began to spin and grow black around the edges.

Sir Ruger knelt and nudged her aside, holding the cloak tight around Aladdin's wound. "Go get help." He looked her in the eye. "Be strong now."

Aladdin closed his mouth and swallowed. "It's not bad. I'll be well."

Kirstyn squeezed his hand and jumped to her feet. She sped off, her vision all a blur. She tripped and fell, rolling a little way down the hill, but jumped back up and kept running.

Tears were streaming down her face when she approached the gate. Openmouthed, the guards stared at her—having no doubt heard her screams, yet not allowed to leave their post unless they could see danger.

"Help me!" Her chest was still bereft of air, even as she breathed hard. "Come! Aladdin is injured. You must take him to the healer. Hurry."

She turned to lead them, but they ran so much faster and she couldn't keep up. As they hurried up the hill, she fell to her knees in the grass.

"God, please." Horror overwhelmed her as she relived the bear attacking Aladdin. "This cannot be happening." If only she could go back and stop herself from startling that bear and her cub. If only she had waited for Aladdin and Sir Ruger. What a child she was, a thoughtless, foolish child.

She was too devastated to cry any more. How could she draw attention to herself when Aladdin was hurt?

Soon the two guards carried Aladdin down the hill, moving quite fast. How much blood had he lost? How bad was his leg wound? *He must be in horrible pain. O God.* Her stomach twisted and she clasped her hands together.

Please, please, God, please don't let him die.

Aladdin lay on the small bed in the healer's chambers, his mind fogged over with anguish.

Frau Lena leaned over him, applying a thick salve to his chest and shoulder. But his leg, elevated by several blankets, gripped his attention.

"Are you ready for more tea?" Frau Lena's voice drifted through the fog and jarred his aching head. "It will help with the pain."

"Yes," he said, because it would take too much effort to nod.

Frau Lena left off dabbing at his chest wounds. When she returned a few moments later, beside her was a girl—Kirstyn—holding a cup.

He touched the blanket to make certain it was at least covering his stomach and lower body, though his chest was bare.

She approached him and slid her arm under his head while Frau Lena stuffed a feather pillow behind him, propping him up a bit. Kirstyn held the cup to his lips as their eyes met. He reached out to take the cup from her, but his hand shook and she did not let go.

He drank several swallows of the bitter herbal concoction before drawing back.

"Would you like some water?" Kirstyn's eyes focused intently on his as she leaned close.

"Yes." Getting mauled by a bear must make a person thirsty as well as dizzy and weak. Sweat tickled his forehead.

Kirstyn hurried away and came back with another cup and

held it to his lips. He drank two gulps of the cold water, then nudged the cup away as his stomach threatened to empty its contents.

He closed his eyes and lay back against the pillows. Kirstyn removed the extra pillows so he could lie flat.

"Are you feeling sick?" Kirstyn asked softly.

"Yes."

Something cool and damp touched his forehead. He opened his eyes to see her stroking his brow, then his face, with a wet cloth. The sick feeling began to subside.

He felt himself drifting away . . .

When he opened his eyes again, the light outside the window was waning. Frau Lena was closing the shutters.

"Your Grace." The healer curtsied to the man standing by his bed.

Duke Wilhelm glanced his way. "How is he?" Aladdin knew he should bow. But he was lying flat and couldn't even move.

Frau Lena spoke in a whisper. Aladdin closed his eyes and listened.

"He's lost a lot of blood, but he is strong. I'm hopeful he will recover. Pray his injuries don't become putrid or diseased."

"And his leg?"

Her voice softened so much he could no longer hear anything except, "We must pray it will not be necessary to . . ."

Aladdin strained to hear what he could, then Duke Wilhelm mentioned Kirstyn. Would he forbid her to come any more to the sickroom?

Frau Lena said, "They have a bond, even more so now."

Aladdin would have liked to hear everything they were saying, to add his own thoughts to the conversation, but the herbs were drawing him under the darkness of sleep.

Kirstyn knelt in the chapel in the southern tower of Hagenheim Castle, her hands clasped in front of her and her head bowed. When she finally looked up, her mother was kneeling beside her.

Mother's eyes were closed in prayer as well, so Kirstyn said nothing. She kept praying but glanced every so often at her mother.

Finally Mother rose from her knees, kissed the cross she wore around her neck, and gazed up at the crucifix over the chancel.

Kirstyn rose too and followed suit, making the sign of the cross over her chest and falling in behind her mother as she walked toward the doorway.

When they were both in the corridor outside the chapel, Mother turned and hugged Kirstyn. "Did you see Aladdin today?"

"I went to the sick chamber this morning, and Frau Lena said he is a little better."

"But you didn't speak to him?"

"He was sleeping."

"And you have been crying."

Her compassionate voice conjured up the tears again. Kirstyn threw her arms around her mother and pressed her forehead into Mother's shoulder.

"It was all my fault." Kirstyn sobbed at the horrible truth. It sounded almost worse spoken out loud than it did in her mind. "He wanted me to wait for Sir Ruger, but I laughed and ran ahead. I ran into the woods and I didn't see the bear until I was too close to her. She'd already seen me and must have thought I wanted to harm her cub."

"Aladdin saw you were in danger and caused the bear to attack him instead of you." Mother held her tight and rubbed her shoulder.

"Yes. So you see what a horrible, horrible thing I did."

"No. You did not do anything horrible. You were being play-ful. It's what children do—they play and hide and run and are sometimes reckless. But it was not your fault, not really. It was an accident. No one knew bears were so close to Hagenheim. They usually stay in the mountains, far away from town. You could blame Sir Ruger for not staying close to you—as your father did." She lowered her voice. "But it's not his fault either. Sometimes bad things happen . . . A man who has survived a battle gets thrown from his horse on his way home and dies, or lightning strikes a man while he's plowing his field. We don't understand it, but it is part of life. But one thing you can always depend on."

Mother seemed to be waiting to make sure Kirstyn was pay-ing attention. She held her gaze. "We can depend on the assurance that God cares about us and is always with us."

Mother's intense look seemed to demand a response, so Kirstyn nodded.

"We can pray for Aladdin, as I'm sure you were just doing, and be sure that God hears and He cares, about you and about Aladdin. And we can thank God Aladdin's injuries are not worse."

Kirstyn withdrew the handkerchief her mother always made her carry in her pocket and wiped her eyes and nose. "I hope he doesn't lose his leg or have to limp for the rest of his life." She bit her lip. She had to stop crying. "And I know it's selfish, but I hope he doesn't hate me."

"I'm sure he won't hate you. He's your friend."

She and Aladdin had been on many walks in the last year. They talked about their likes and dislikes, about their relation-ships and favorite books. Besides her mother and her sister

Margaretha, Aladdin was her best friend. She could tell him almost anything. And now he might be crippled or even die. She couldn't bear it if he did, not when he had been trying to protect her.

CHAPTER FIVE

Throbbing pain woke Aladdin from a dream that his leg was being squeezed in the blacksmith's vice. The sound of sparks from his fire turned out to be rain pattering outside the tower chamber.

Frau Lena's helper, a young woman with brown hair and a shy smile, caught his eye and asked, "Would you like something to eat?"

"Yes." He pushed himself up to sitting. Even if he was still in pain, at least his stomach was calmer. His head no longer pounded and his vision no longer spun.

The woman soon brought him some soup and bread. While he was eating, Frau Lena came in. "Feeling better?"

"Much better."

She sat on the stool beside him. "Your friends came this morning to ask about you, as did Master Alfred, Frau Litzer, even Duke Wilhelm. And Lady Kirstyn has been here almost all the time since they brought you in." She smiled. "I realize I'm caring for a very special person."

"Everyone is very kind to me." Aladdin's cheeks heated. He set his empty bowl on the tiny table beside him.

"I'm glad you're able to eat. That's an excellent sign. Now I'll just look at your leg." She flipped up the blanket covering his feet and unwrapped the bandage on his lower leg. Inside the bandage was a layer of brown moss Frau Lena had been using to stanch the flow of blood, which she removed to see the wound. The movement intensified the pain.

"I can already see some healing happening." She leaned closer to examine his leg. "There may not be any damage to the muscle or bone. Which would be a very good thing. You will have terrible scars, but we shall have to keep praying. Perhaps the outward scars will be the only lasting effect."

Let it be so, Lord. Aladdin could not lose his leg. How would he earn his fortune with only one leg? He tried to imagine his life with one leg and a picture jumped into his mind—a long-buried memory of a one-legged man in the bazaar sitting on a mat and begging for money. He had held out his hand to Mustapha, but Mustapha kicked him.

"Worthless beggar." Mustapha shook his fist at the poor man.

Aladdin shuddered.

"Do you need some more herbs to help with the pain?" Frau Lena hovered beside him.

"No, thank you." The herbal drink made him sleep, and he was tired of sleeping.

Frau Lena held a pot of the brownish salve with a cloth, then picked up the stick resting in the pot. It had a ball on the end from which she let a drop fall on the inside of her wrist. It must have been the right temperature because she drizzled the warm honey-like substance over his ripped and ragged wounds.

Aladdin clenched his teeth against the intense burning and

stabbing pains in his leg. But the application of the salve was soon over, and Frau Lena began wrapping his leg again with a clean bandage.

She brought him a cup of cool water. He drank it while the pain lessened. He closed his eyes and took deep breaths.

What were his friends doing now? Probably studying mathematics or economics. Aladdin was ahead of the other students, but he didn't want to lose this time and get behind. Perhaps someone would bring a book and some notes to him.

What was Lady Kirstyn doing? He hoped she was not too affected by the horror of the bear nearly attacking her and seeing him get attacked. No doubt Duke Wilhelm would be irate at how close his daughter came to being mauled by a bear. Were their walks and exploring over forever? His shoulders slumped at the thought.

Hushed voices came from the door behind him. He turned his head but had to use his arms to turn his whole upper body to see. Lady Rose and Lady Kirstyn stood there.

"He is much better," Frau Lena told them.

Kirstyn's gaze captured his. She smiled and hurried over to him, then knelt on the floor at his bedside.

"You mustn't. A stool's right there." Aladdin's face heated at the thought of the duchess seeing her daughter kneeling by his bed.

"I'm so glad to hear you are feeling better." She remained kneeling. "Truly, you look better—less pale. Are you in pain?"

"Not very much." How could he feel pain when she was looking at him like that, with concern on her face?

"I also wanted to tell you . . ." Her voice became hoarse, and he could barely hear her. "I'm so sorry. I should have waited for Sir Ruger. It was my fault you got injured. Please say you forgive me."

"It was not your fault." Aladdin pushed himself up higher on the pillows so he was looking down at her.

She picked up his hand, held it between both of hers, and bowed her head over it. Something wet and hot splashed on his skin.

"I just want you to know I'm sorry." Her voice cracked. "And I hope you don't hate me."

"Of course I don't hate you. I will never hate you." He was aware of her mother and Frau Lena so nearby, but he caressed her blonde head just for a moment, even as she continued to hold his other hand.

She raised her head and gazed at him with eyes made even bluer by the tears swimming in them. Then she lifted his hand and pressed the back of it against her cheek.

"You are so kind and wonderful, Aladdin. The truest friend I ever had. I would never, ever want to see you get hurt."

"You didn't hurt me." He tried to infuse his voice with enough intensity to make her believe it. "It was the bear. And I would fight ten bears to protect you." He smiled so she wouldn't be frightened by the impassioned declaration of an orphan boy.

Her smile trembled at the corners. "I'm glad you don't hate me."

As Lady Rose approached, Kirstyn let go of his hand and sniffed.

"Thank you for protecting Kirstyn, Aladdin. You are a courageous young man, and Duke Wilhelm has expressed a wish to thank you in person, when you are feeling well."

"That is gracious of him."

"Not at all. Your actions were heroic. We're grateful to you for saving our little girl." Tears glistened in Lady Rose's eyes. He prayed she wouldn't cry.

Frau Lena was standing behind Lady Rose. "He may be walking again in a week or two, if there is no damage to the leg bones."

Two weeks sounded like a long time to Aladdin, but Lady Rose looked pleased. Aladdin silently vowed to be walking within a week.

Kirstyn was still kneeling beside him, but her expression was calm and composed now, with all vestige of tears gone except for a dampness clinging to her lashes. He imagined he could still feel the soft pressure of her hands on his.

Lady Rose explained how Duke Wilhelm and his men had located the mother bear and her cub and had driven them away from Hagenheim. The duke had considered killing the bear but did not want an orphan cub on his hands. Aladdin could appreciate that.

"Duke Wilhelm and his men have been patrolling the area. He doesn't believe any other bears are nearby. You may have even saved someone else's life, someone walking alone in the forest who would have happened upon the mother bear and her cub and been attacked without anyone to help."

"Lady Kirstyn was very brave as well. Did Sir Ruger tell you? She struck the bear repeatedly with her stick, or else I wouldn't even be here."

"He did tell us." Again, Lady Rose's eyes filled with tears as she turned her gaze on her daughter for a moment. "I am very proud of her courage, and yours as well." She smiled and the moisture disappeared.

"Aladdin and I are bold and fierce." Kirstyn was smiling too as she met Aladdin's eye. "We take care of each other, don't we?"

Aladdin's heart swelled. He didn't trust himself to speak as he stared back at her.

CHAPTER SIX

Spring 1414

Kirstyn's heart was bursting. She held up her skirts and ran as fast as she could across the bailey to the stable. Aladdin was just walking out, leading his horse. He was mounting when she called out, "Aladdin!"

Everyone around—stable workers, blacksmiths, a couple of knights—turned to look.

Aladdin stared at her with his brows drawn together and his lips pressed in a straight line.

When she reached him, she took hold of the horse's saddle. "How could you leave without saying farewell?" Her throat was so tight, she sounded as if she were strangling. "How can you stare down at me in that cold way?"

"I left you a letter." He turned his head, refusing to look at her.

"A letter. You can't just leave . . . not like this." She felt the gazes of people watching them. Some of them could hear what they were saying. Perhaps her parents, her younger siblings, and her brother Valten's wife, Gisela, were watching from the window.

"I'm going with you," she said.

Aladdin opened his mouth, no doubt to tell her she could not.

"Just for a little way. I'll ride with you until you're out of town." She didn't wait for him to agree. She turned and called to one of the grooms, who was dumping a bucket of water in a trough. "You there." She waved her hand at him. "Go and saddle my horse."

Sir Sigmund strode toward her. "Lady Kirstyn, I don't think—"

"I will only ride with you until you get through town, and then I shall leave you to go on your journey."

Sir Sigmund frowned, then heaved a sigh and shrugged.

Kirstyn forced herself not to look at Aladdin while she waited for a stable boy to saddle her horse, but she could see him out of the corner of her eye.

When her horse was ready, Sir Sigmund helped her into the saddle. Then he mounted and the three of them set out.

As they made their way through the streets, Kirstyn finally ventured a glance at Aladdin. His expression was slightly apprehensive, his mouth and jaw rigid. His gaze flitted in her direction, but he seemed determined to avoid eye contact and turned his eyes forward again.

Was he angry that she was here? She could not let his letter be his final farewell. Her chest ached and her eyes stung. Memories overwhelmed her of her sister Margaretha leaving to go to England with her new husband. That had been a year ago, a day very much like today. She missed her sister so much. How could she bear to part with Aladdin too?

But she would not let him see her looking sad. She pushed back against the memories and let her deep breaths dry her unshed tears.

The town had never looked so big. The main street that wound away from the marketplace, moving south away from Hagenheim Castle, seemed to go on forever today, and people flooded nearly every foot of it. Men and women hurried or strolled, carrying baskets of food and household goods, and they stopped to talk to each other and laugh. They were oblivious to what was happening to her and to Aladdin.

Finally they exited the south gate and approached the tree-lined road that would take Aladdin . . . where? The road was suddenly deserted except for her, Aladdin, and Sir Sigmund, and her heart began to thud.

Aladdin turned and held her gaze. He sighed. "You didn't like my letter, then."

"I liked the letter, but I didn't get to say my farewells."

"I told you last week I was leaving."

"And I told you not to leave." Tears returned to her eyes, and she bit her lip and blinked them away.

He sighed again. Then he glanced over his shoulder. "Can you give us a few moments to talk?"

Looking none too pleased, Sir Sigmund stopped his horse and dismounted.

Aladdin and Kirstyn continued on a few more feet, then Aladdin halted. They were far enough away that Sir Sigmund could not hear if they spoke quietly.

"I have to leave Hagenheim, Kirstyn."

"No, you don't. If you stay you can be the duke's steward. No one will be greater than you in Hagenheim except my father."

"But I will always be just a servant, and it will never . . ." He stopped and looked away. "It will never be good enough."

The pain behind his words snatched the breath right out of her lungs. "Good enough for whom?"

"I want to make my fortune, to prove I am not just a poor orphan foreigner. I don't want to be a servant with whom your father has reluctantly allowed you to associate because you begged him and he couldn't say no."

"Don't I mean too much to you to—?" Her words choked off. What could she say? Why did her heart feel as if it were breaking in half?

Her horse became restless and sidestepped away from Aladdin. Kirstyn dismounted and took advantage of the distance from him to press a hand to her cheek and take a deep breath. But when she turned around, Aladdin was standing beside her.

"I've wanted to become a merchant and make my fortune since I was very young." He leaned down—he had grown quite tall in the last few years—trying to look into her face. His black hair swooped over his forehead and rested on his neck. His dark eyes captured hers.

What if she tried to change his mind? He might stay, but he would always regret not leaving to make his fortune. She didn't want to do that to him. And although she didn't want him to leave, her reason was purely selfish. She did not want to lose her friend.

"I understand. Thank you . . ." Her throat clogged and she had to swallow hard before going on. "For being my friend." She stood on tiptoes and kissed his cheek.

The feel of his cheek on her lips made her suddenly self-conscious. She stared at Aladdin's hand holding on to his horse's reins.

"Promise me something," she whispered. She was so close she could see the tiny nick on his jawline where he had cut himself that morning shaving, could see the way his brown eyes, as dark as they were, bore flecks of gold. She could see the way his gaze flicked back and forth from her mouth to her eyes.

"Yes?"

"Promise you will never forget about me."

His throat bobbed. "I promise."

An ache welled up inside her. She threw her arms around his shoulders.

His arms enfolded her as she pressed her cheek to his chest.

It felt so good to be in his arms. But there was so much pain inside at his leaving her. He'd always been there for her, never failing to pay attention to her when she felt insignificant. When she felt like the least of many in her large family, Aladdin made her feel special, as if she were the most important person in his life. And she believed she was.

He let go. She turned away and squeezed her eyes shut, listening to him remount his horse. Part of her wished he would tell her . . . something—anything—to make her turn around and see his eyes one last time. And part of her could not bear to look into them again.

She heard his horse's hooves start moving down the road. Soon Sir Sigmund rode past her to join him.

She leaned her forehead against her horse's neck and bit her lip. In a few moments the sounds of their horses galloping through the brush faded as they disappeared around the first bend in the road.

She felt as if she were suffocating. *Aladdin. Please don't leave me.* If she had begged him, if she had held on to him, would he have stayed?

The heaviness in her chest, along with a rumble of thunder in the distance, seemed to foretell evil happenings, to portend a long separation between her and her dearest friend. But she couldn't bear to think that she would never see him again.

As he rode farther and farther away from Hagenheim, Aladdin could still feel Kirstyn's gentle kiss on his cheek, the warmth of her throwing her arms around him. And he could still see her turning away. His chest was like a hollowed-out tree stump. If he'd pounded on it, an echo would have rung out.

He knew it would hurt to leave her, but he never realized it would hurt this much. He'd always had a dream—an impossible dream of marrying Kirstyn. He'd told himself it was a foolish child's dream and dismissed it. But it seemed to have a life of its own, unwilling to die in the face of impossibility.

They made their way on the northwesterly road toward the North Sea and the Hanseatic town of Hamburg. Sir Sigmund was good company. He told him stories he'd heard of the fighting in the holy wars and sieges of castles. Aladdin in turn told stories of living at the orphanage in Hagenheim, of the strange ways of some of the older orphans who had been living on the streets and begging and stealing their whole lives—which would have been Aladdin's fate had Priest not taken him in.

He did not, however, tell him of his own days of stealing for Mustapha. Aladdin still felt too much shame. Perhaps someday when he was wealthy and respected and secure in his position, he would be able to tell those stories.

After two days of traveling, they were bedding down under the stars again. Sir Sigmund stretched out on his blanket in the warm summer's night air. Having fried some eggs for their supper,

Aladdin snuffed out their cook fire with some dirt and rocks and lay down on the ground.

"Why are you leaving?" Sir Sigmund asked, the pale light of the stars on his upturned face.

"Why am I leaving?"

"Duke Wilhelm seemed to be grooming you to take over the steward's duties. He must like you a great deal to do that."

Aladdin traced with his finger the shapes the stars made. God knew each one's name, and it was God's good will to fling the stars into the dark expanse, just as it was His will to bring Aladdin to Hagenheim. Was it God's will that he leave? Or was that only Aladdin's?

"After all," Sir Sigmund's deep voice drawled, "you were obviously a favorite of Lady Kirstyn's. It's not often an orphan boy is so close to the family of a duke. No one wanted you to go. So why leave?"

"I need to make my fortune."

Silence stretched between them, then Aladdin heard Sir Sigmund's light snore. Aladdin had a much harder time falling asleep, as he was haunted by the look on Kirstyn's face. He couldn't seem to shake the uneasy feeling that he shouldn't have left her.

Aladdin awoke to shouts. When he sat up, Sir Sigmund was reaching for his sword and leaping to his feet. Aladdin took up his own sword, which he kept by his side, and followed after Sir Sigmund in the half-light of predawn.

The shouts grew louder as Aladdin and Sir Sigmund drew closer to a group of travelers who looked to have been bedded down a few hundred feet away—yet he had been completely unaware of them.

"We're taking everything, and if you try to stop us, we're not above killing you," a rough voice said.

Sir Sigmund crouched behind a large bush, and Aladdin knelt beside him, still clutching his sword. Aladdin could barely make out the outlines of two men facing each other. The younger one held a knife pointed at the older man's throat.

"You're a fiend," the older man said. "What did you do to my men?"

Two or three other men were scrambling through some bundles on the ground, occasionally lifting something to get a better look.

"They will be all right in a few hours. Unless we gave them too much poison."

"Monster. Help me! Someone, help! Robbers! Thieves!"

"You may as well be quiet." Then the thief actually laughed. "No one can hear you."

Several men lay on the ground, moaning and writhing in the dark.

Aladdin glanced at Sir Sigmund. "We have to save him," Aladdin whispered.

Sir Sigmund scowled. Finally he whispered, "I'll dispatch the three closest ones, and you go for the one with the old man."

Three on one? Even Sir Sigmund might not be equal to that task. But in the next moment Sir Sigmund leapt out from behind the bush and charged straight toward the men, uttering a battle cry and brandishing his sword. He slashed his blade at the first man, who screamed, stumbled over a bundle, and fell backward on the ground. The second man shrieked and cowered on his knees, his eyes big and round. The third man turned and ran.

Aladdin raised his sword at the man holding the knife at the old man's throat. "Get back! Drop your knife!"

The man with the knife turned his weapon on Aladdin. "You get back. I have men all over this forest. They will attack you from behind and kill you. At any moment now. So go." When Aladdin made no move to retreat, the man ground out through clenched teeth, "This is not your affair." Aladdin noticed he wore ragged woolens, while his hostage wore the colorful clothing of a wealthy man.

Aladdin held out his sword. "If you have taken anything from this man, you must return it to him now."

The man lunged at Aladdin with his long knife and aimed at his heart.

Aladdin jumped back as he brought down his sword. The steel struck the man's hand, and he let out a yelp and dropped his knife.

The would-be thief stumbled backward, then turned and fled.

Aladdin ran after him. Then he dropped his sword and leapt onto the man's back, tackling the miscreant to the ground. Aladdin kept the thief pinned with a knee in the middle of his back.

Aladdin glanced over his shoulder at Sir Sigmund. The knight was grinning as he cinched one of the men's hands together with some rope. He quickly moved to the second man and tied his wrists together. Then he threw some rope to Aladdin.

"I'm going to catch the weasel who ran away." Sir Sigmund hurried off into the dark woods.

Aladdin tied his captive's wrists, then wrapped his bleeding hand with a cloth from the ground nearby.

The older man with the colorful clothing stood beside Aladdin's elbow. "Sir, you saved us. How can I thank you?"

"I'm glad we were able to help." Aladdin finished up with the outlaw.

"I am Cedric Kaufmann of Lüneburg, and I am forever grateful. You saved my goods and very likely my life. Please." The man was white haired and shorter than Aladdin, and he clasped his hands in front of his chest as though pleading. "Tell me your names so I know to whom I am indebted."

The sun was starting to rise, spreading a yellow light over the small clearing where so many men lay around them—some moaning and holding their stomachs, while the evildoers were bound and motionless.

"My name is Aladdin of Hagenheim, and that man-at-arms who captured the other two men is Sir Sigmund, a noble knight in Duke Wilhelm's service."

"And you, sir? Are you a knight?"

"I was employed by Duke Wilhelm, but not as a knight."

"You are a good and brave man to come to my aid. I was a stranger to you and your knight, and I wish to repay your kindness."

"That is not necessary, Herr Kaufmann."

"Nonsense! Of course I must repay you."

Moans continued to emanate from the men on the ground.

"Isn't there anything we can do to help these men? They were poisoned, did you say?"

"With something in their wine, I'm afraid." Herr Kaufmann shook his head. "I am not a wine drinker myself, but this fiend gave my guards tainted wine last night. I do not know any remedy, but perhaps you know of something that will help them?"

"Since I do not know what he poisoned them with, it is difficult to say. They are holding their stomachs and moaning . . . Do you have any ginger root, licorice, or fennel?" Aladdin had read some of Frau Lena's books on the healing arts while he had lain in bed recovering from the bear attack.

"I have all three!" The man hurried to one of the large packs. "My ships have been to Spain to trade salt, resin, and timber for spices and other goods. I have been to Bruges to claim them. These packs you see here are a fortune in themselves, if I can manage to get them back safely to Lüneburg. I am a merchant there."

He sorted through the bundles on the ground and finally brought out a bag the size of a man's head and held it up. "Here is fennel! How shall we give it to them?"

"I will boil some water. We'll steep the herbs in hot water and let them drink it."

"There is a pot of water if you can build up the fire."

The two of them set to work. Aladdin put some sticks on the fire that was nearly burned out and then added some bigger ones to feed the flames. He suspended the blackened pot over the fire so the flames were licking its sides, and soon they had boiling water.

The older man soon found dried mint, ginger, and licorice to add to the fennel.

"Put the herbs into five cups," Aladdin instructed.

Herr Kaufmann did so, and Aladdin ladled hot water into each cup. Then they took the tea around to each of Herr Kaufmann's men.

"Ho! I caught him!" Sir Sigmund's voice boomed as he entered the clearing holding the small thief by the neck with one hand and his sword in the other. The knight proceeded to tie him up.

"You won't kill us?" the young man asked. "Please spare my life. I am my mother's only son, and she will die without me to provide for her."

Aladdin was still helping the poisoned men to sit up and drink the tea. One was so sick he wasn't able to lift his head, and Aladdin had to dribble the tea through his parted lips.

"We should make them drink poison," one man said from where he lay propped on his elbow. "And leave them here to die a slow death, the way they would have let us die."

"We do have to decide what to do with them," Sir Sigmund said to Aladdin and Herr Kaufmann. "As much as I'd like to just leave them here to rot"—he sighed—"I'll have to take them back to Hagenheim and let Duke Wilhelm deal with them."

"You cannot handle the four of them alone." Herr Kaufmann looked up from his task of helping one of his men sit up. "When my men have recovered, one or two can accompany you to take these evil brigands to Hagenheim."

Sir Sigmund grunted, kicked a small tree, and scowled at his prisoners, who were now grouped in a circle on the ground, seated with their backs to the center. No doubt the knight did not want to go back to Hagenheim so soon. Would Aladdin have to return to Hagenheim as well? His heart was still sore from leaving Kirstyn. He wasn't sure he could leave her again.

CHAPTER SEVEN

Aladdin, Sir Sigmund, and Herr Kaufmann tended the poisoned men the rest of the day. Once the men were able to fall asleep for a few hours, most of them awakened feeling almost back to normal. By evening, they were all able to eat and drink a small amount without getting sick.

That night, when everyone else was lying down to sleep, Herr Kaufmann, Sir Sigmund, and Aladdin gathered around the fire.

The wealthy merchant's small gray eyes were sad as his bushy white brows settled low. "My son was supposed to transport these goods in a convoy with some other merchants from the Hanseatic League, but when he took some of the most valuable items and deserted the group, they departed without him. I traveled to the coast to try to find him, but he did not wish to be found, no doubt. I did retrieve most of my wares, and my guards and I were on our way home when we were attacked. But the true outlaw, I'm afraid, is my son. He stole from me, and he stole from several other merchants in the convoy."

Herr Kaufmann stared up at the stars. "My son—Cedric, named after me—has stolen or gambled away every pfennig he's ever had, has drunk himself nearly to death more than once, and keeps company with the filthiest rabble a man could find. He has broken my heart many—" His breath hitched and he blinked rapidly before continuing. "Many times. But I always believed him when he said he was repentant and would not defy me again. My wife died in giving him birth, and though I adopted my brother's daughter and she is a great comfort to me, it is my son, Cedric, who gives me gray hair and dims my eyes with tears."

He cleared his throat and set his jaw. "But no more. I shall disown him and forget I ever had a son."

A ghost of a smile graced his lips as his gaze fastened on Aladdin. "I see a strong spirit in you. You were Duke Wilhelm's steward—"

"Assistant to his steward."

"At such a young age! So you must be very clever and knowledgeable of mathematics and many other matters. And you and your knight attacked those ruthless men, so I know you are brave. You risked your life for me, a stranger, so I know you are a man of integrity and compassion. Therefore, I have a proposition." Herr Kaufmann leaned closer to Aladdin.

Herr Kaufmann was an interesting-looking man, with his black felt hat set with multicolored feathers and an emerald, ruby, and sapphire brooch on the front; his long black sleeveless houppelande that hung to the ground; and the enormous red silk sleeves of the garment he wore underneath it. Even his shoes were covered in bright silks. He did not try to hide his wealth.

"While Sir Sigmund takes care of the prisoners," Herr

Kaufmann said, "will you accompany me and my men on our way to Lüneburg? You are as competent as any of my guards."

When Aladdin did not answer right away, Herr Kaufmann said, "I should very much like you to work with me and help with my business affairs in Lüneburg. Would you become one of my assistant stewards helping keep track of my accounts? Though I just met you, I believe you are as trustworthy as anyone I know."

Aladdin tried to speak, but his words stuck in his throat. He swallowed and said, "Thank you for your generous offer, but it seems wrong to leave the unpleasant task to Sir Sigmund. I'd like to talk it over with him."

"Of course, of course. I shall go check on Otto. He was still a bit unsteady on his feet." Herr Kaufmann moved away to find his guard.

Aladdin looked into Sir Sigmund's craggy face, made fiercer by the harsh firelight. "Will you be all right taking the thieves to Hagenheim with only two of Herr Kaufmann's men?"

"Of course. I could do it alone if I had to."

"Will you count it amiss if I accompany Herr Kaufmann to Lüneburg?"

"You'd be a fool not to. This man's as wealthy as King Midas." Sir Sigmund shook his head and even smiled as he stared at Aladdin. "But you are the one who has the golden touch."

"What do you mean?"

"Everything you do turns to gold, as if God's favor follows you wherever you go. You come to Hagenheim as a poor orphan boy from the Holy Land, and suddenly you are the talk of everyone at the orphanage. You are the stable master's favorite, and you even gain the favor of the duke, who puts you to work in the castle as his steward in training. You're the favorite playmate of the duke's own daughter, and when you leave to make your fortune, the first

man you meet is so impressed with you that he wants to hire you."
Sir Sigmund laughed, a low, throaty sound.

"Shh." Aladdin glanced around to see if Herr Kaufmann
might have heard what Sigmund had said, but he was talking
with one of his guards, hopefully too far away.

"Nothing like that has happened," Aladdin whispered. "I'm
still a poor man with no name or consequence." But he did hope
a position with Herr Kaufmann might be the beginning of
learning how to be a successful merchant and earning his own
fortune.

Kirstyn was standing at her bedchamber window when Sir
Sigmund rode through the castle gate with several other men,
some of whom were bound with ropes. She strained her eyes to
see, but Aladdin was not among them.

Her heart leapt into her throat.

She ran from her room, racing down the corridor and taking
the stone steps two at a time. She sprinted out the door of the
castle into the bailey and across the stable yard.

"What has happened? Where is Aladdin?" She held her
side as she tried to catch her breath, her gaze fastened on Sir
Sigmund's face.

He was barking orders to the stable workers, then to her
father's soldiers, who rushed forward to deliver his captives to
the dungeon. Finally he turned to Kirstyn. "I left Aladdin on
the road."

"What? Why? What do you mean?"

Sir Sigmund did not answer her right away. He continued
unhitching his saddlebags.

She wanted to grab him and shake him, but since he was twice her size, she decided against it. "Was Aladdin well? Where is he now?"

He hefted his saddlebag to his shoulder. "The plan was for Aladdin to accompany a man named Cedric Kaufmann of Lüneburg."

"To Lüneburg? Why?"

He had already started walking toward the soldiers' wooden barracks behind the castle. Kirstyn had to almost run to keep up with him.

"Herr Kaufmann was attacked by those four men I brought back with me, and Aladdin and I came to his aid."

"Do you mean Aladdin fought them?"

"It was a quick fight. Aladdin did well."

"He wasn't hurt?"

Sir Sigmund grunted and shook his head. "Herr Kaufmann was impressed with Aladdin and took him home with him. I imagine he will put him to work."

"What kind of work?"

They had almost reached the barracks, so Sir Sigmund stopped and looked down at her. His expression softened a bit. "Herr Kaufmann is a merchant. He took an immediate liking to Aladdin, and I have no doubt he will prove himself valuable. Do not worry about the boy. He is exactly where he wants to be."

"Oh." Kirstyn had been standing on her toes and sank back on her heels.

The knight turned to go into the barracks.

"I thank you, Sir Sigmund."

He nodded to her, then disappeared inside the dark doorway.

Aladdin was in Lüneburg. Of course he was clever and trustworthy. All would be well. He would make his fortune and then . . . Her heart squeezed at the thought that he might not come back, might marry some wealthy burgher's daughter and forget about her.

Aladdin was her best friend. That must be why it hurt so much to think of him marrying someone else. She was only sixteen, and marriage for her seemed like something far in the future.

But what if he never came back? Perhaps he would need to travel to exotic lands to secure goods. Perhaps he would encounter dangers. If something terrible happened, how would she ever find out? Herr Kaufmann would not know she was here in Hagenheim waiting to hear from Aladdin.

These were unhelpful thoughts. She should have known God would make a way for Aladdin. Had not the Lord God always taken care of him? Bringing him all the way from the land of the Saracens to Hagenheim? Making the two of them friends and giving Aladdin favor with everyone he encountered? It was Aladdin's willingness to be helpful, his kind spirit, and his desire to always do what was right that had endeared him to another powerful person.

It was good news, so why did her heart feel so heavy?

Five days later Aladdin entered Lüneburg, and he was struck with the contrasts between this city and Hagenheim's relatively small, provincial atmosphere. Where Hagenheim was warm and friendly, Lüneburg was gruff and full of strangers. Where Hagenheim was unhurried and peaceful, Lüneburg was bustling and chaotic, with vendors shouting, people jostling each other in the narrow streets.

Herr Kaufmann and Aladdin were surrounded by his guards. As they walked their horses through the press of people, he noticed the elaborately decorated doors and doorways. Hagenheim had many ornately carved half-timber buildings, but Lüneburg seemed to have an obsession with doors. Brightly colored, strangely shaped, some of them were a fantastical blue with elaborate iron scrollwork and a rounded arch above. Another was less ornate but characterized by a pointed arch with alternating colors of brick, drawing one's gaze to its uniform striping. Another door, belonging to an apothecary shop, was flanked by stone statues carved in relief, depicting women, mermaids, angels, and lions, and painted bright orange, blue, and yellow.

"My home is not far now," Herr Kaufmann said.

They made their way down a narrow, curving street, and when they emerged into a wider street, the tall, slate-gray spire of a church rose high above them, piercing the twilight sky.

"That is the Church of St. John." Herr Kaufmann quickened his step.

Along the way they encountered the sights and smells Aladdin had always associated with Hagenheim—bakeries and the aroma of hot, fresh bread, butcher shops and the scent of fresh meat, fishmongers, blacksmiths, tanneries, and breweries, each with their own distinct odors and sounds. But the unfamiliar lay of the streets, curving in strange places, the new buildings and faces, constantly reminded him that he was no longer in Hagenheim.

His stomach grumbled as they passed yet another bakery, attesting to the fact that it had been several hours since they had eaten. But Herr Kaufmann paid no heed to any of the food shops as he and his men pressed on.

After they passed another church, Aladdin caught glimpses of water between the buildings to his right. Was that a river?

Herr Kaufmann touched his arm and his face split with a huge smile. "We are home at last."

While Herr Kaufmann gave instructions to his men about the goods in their care, Aladdin took in the large house before them. It was made of a dull red brick, four stories high and in a row of other houses, with only a small space on either side of it. The long roof rose to a point. Tiny windows, bare of any ornament, studded its upper floors, while the lowest floor was a solid row of square windowpanes with a plain door in the middle. Though not decorative, it was obviously the home of someone quite prosperous.

Before they could knock, the door opened, revealing an aproned woman with a white linen wimple covering her graying hair.

"Herr Kaufmann! At last you have come!" Her round face was beaming, her cheeks pink.

"Yes, Hilde, I am come. The men will return from the storehouse shortly, and we all are famished."

"I have a fresh pot of stew, enough for everyone, but I can fry some pork and cabbage and—"

"Stew is all we need, besides bread and butter." As they made their way into the house, Herr Kaufmann added, "I have brought a new assistant. His name is Aladdin."

Hilde, whom Aladdin guessed was the head house servant, looked him full in the face. "A tall, dark, handsome fellow, if I may say so."

She smiled, but Aladdin could see from the wariness in her eyes that he would have to earn her trust. What was the reason she felt the need to protect her master? Aladdin had been called a Saracen and scorned by a few of the boys at the orphanage because of his dark skin and hair. But he sensed her caution had less to do with him and more to do with Herr Kaufmann's troubles with his wayward son.

Aladdin awoke to the early-morning sun filtering through the thin silk curtains. It was the first time he had slept in a room alone since before he came to live in the orphanage. With no other boys stirring in their beds or the snoring of other male servants, he'd slept all night without waking once.

Throwing back the coverlet, he walked to the window, unlatched it, and opened the glass panes. He leaned out.

The river lay below, its waters lapping against the foundation stones of the house.

A small boat manned only by a boy of about seven or eight years floated by. The boy stared up at Aladdin. He used his oar to slow the boat. His mouth hanging open, he looked as if he wanted to ask a question.

"Greetings," Aladdin called.

"Who are you?" The boy squinted up at him.

"Aladdin of Hagenheim."

"Are you a Saracen like me?"

The boy's black hair and dark skin were very similar to his own. Aladdin's heart quickened at the kinship he felt for this boy, the first Saracen he had met outside of his homeland.

"I am from the Holy Land," Aladdin said, "but I was raised a Christian since I was little." He took in the boy's ragged gray shirt and loose gray hose. "What is your name?"

"Abu. Does Herr Kaufmann know you are in his house? He is to return very soon."

"Indeed. He has already returned, just last night, and brought me with him."

Abu's mouth formed an O and he nodded.

He reminded Aladdin of himself when he had been a poor orphan with no one to care for him—a child who hardly understood what it meant to be a child. Aladdin couldn't help simultaneously admiring Abu's happy, lively spirit and wanting to take him in and feed him.

"I shall come round soon, then. Farewell, Saracen Aladdin of Hagenheim."

Aladdin wanted to ask Abu how he came to be in Lüneburg in the German regions of the Holy Roman Empire, where he was going, and what he was doing, but he was already floating down the river, steering his boat with the oar.

Aladdin dressed quickly and left his room, making his way down the stairs. When he was nearly to the ground floor, he met a servant girl coming up.

"Are you . . . Aladdin?" She pronounced his name hesitantly.

"I am."

"Herr Kaufmann is waiting for you in the dining hall. I'll show you the way."

"Thank you."

They weaved their way through a few short corridors to a large room with a long table and several chairs. One long side of the room was lined with windows facing the river. Herr Kaufmann sat at the head of the table, and beside him was a young woman.

"*Guten Tag.*"

"Aladdin! Come and greet my daughter, Grethel. Come, Aladdin. Sit."

A servant set a cup of steaming, frothy milk in front of him, along with fruit pasties and bread, with plenty of butter and sugared berries to spread on the bread.

"How did you sleep? I hope the bed was to your liking."

"The most comfortable bed I've ever slept on," Aladdin said. "Thank you, Herr Kaufmann. It is very kind of you to—"

"Nonsense! Nothing is too good. Grethel, this dear boy saved me and my men and my entire shipment of goods, saved us all from evil robbers. What do you think? Shall we not kill the fatted calf and put a robe on him and rings on his fingers?"

Grethel smiled and patted her father's arm. "He certainly deserves to be rewarded for his kindness and bravery." She met Aladdin's gaze before glancing away as Herr Kaufmann patted her cheek.

"She worries about me when I'm away." Herr Kaufmann focused again on Aladdin. "I cannot turn my business affairs over to Cedric. He refuses to grow up. No responsibility, no integrity, no—"

"Father, please don't upset yourself." Grethel's admonishment held an edge, as if they'd had this conversation many times.

Herr Kaufmann's face slowly grew less red, and Grethel and Aladdin began to eat.

The older man sighed. He suddenly sat up straighter, as if trying to change his mood along with his posture. "Those gooseberry preserves are heavenly, are they not? Hilde makes the best fruit pasties and the best boiled fruit. How do you like the bread? It's made from the finest wheat in Germany."

"It's the tastiest bread and gooseberry preserves I have eaten. My best compliments to Hilde and the cooks." Aladdin had always eaten very well in Hagenheim, but he sensed that few kings in the world ate as well as Herr Kaufmann.

"Do you see that vase over there?" His host pointed to a large, intricately painted vase with fantastical scenes in red and black in the corner. "That was once owned by the Yongle emperor of China. And do you see that tapestry? It once hung in the palace of an Ottoman sultan."

He turned to his daughter. "Grethel, did I tell you that Duke Wilhelm was grooming Aladdin to take over as steward, but he wished to see the world?" Once again he faced Aladdin. "Tell us about the duke and his family. Did you know his oldest son, the Earl of Hamlin?"

"Yes." Aladdin thought back on the interactions he'd had with Valten. "He is a quiet man, very brave and confident, but when I asked him, he trained me to fight with a sword. Duke Wilhelm relies on him very much, especially in matters of safety and security. I have no doubt he will be a great leader, just as his father has been. The people of Hagenheim are greatly blessed in them."

"That is fortunate. As you know, Lüneburg forced out our princes, who were not so full of integrity as the Duke of Hagenheim, and several years ago we were granted the status of free imperial town. This has allowed our citizens to reap the benefits of our rich saltworks. One result has been our newest church, St. Nicholas' Church, which was just finished, oh . . ." He tilted his white head and stared up at the colorful fresco on the ceiling of his dining hall. "Seven years ago. Grethel and I shall take you there on Sunday."

Aladdin chanced a glance at Herr Kaufmann's daughter. She was pretty, he supposed, but not as beautiful as Kirstyn. Her hair was brown and smooth, her brown eyes and mouth rather small and delicate. He couldn't help comparing her to Kirstyn's pale-blonde hair, full lips, and large blue eyes. Kirstyn was also taller than Grethel.

An ache stabbed his chest. When would he see Kirstyn again? But he could not dwell on that. He would have to endure the ache a few years, at least.

Chapter Eight

Aladdin followed Herr Kaufmann around for the first week. He met the clerks and the sellers, the carters and the guards. He met the men who worked at the warehouse and the market. Herr Kaufmann taught him the way he had always accounted for the buying and selling. He also showed him around the Lüneburg Saltworks, explaining that he was the owner of two salt pans, which made him part of the *Sülzbegüterte*.

"It cost me nearly everything I had to buy out the previous owners, but I knew it was a great opportunity to buy into the salt gentry. In turn, I lease the pans to those who have boiling rights, and I receive 50 percent of the revenue."

"That is a very good percentage of profit for you."

"Indeed it is. Having salt to trade with merchants from other lands is a great source of wealth for our town. All other countries must have salt to preserve their food, their fish, their meat. Salt is as valuable as gold." He smiled, showing off a full set of front teeth, with only one chipped one.

Aladdin taught Herr Kaufmann a better way of accounting

for his buying and selling and the remainder of goods in his warehouse, which he had learned in Hagenheim.

"My dear boy! Is there no end to your talents and education? With you here, I shall prosper like King Solomon."

Soon Herr Kaufmann put Aladdin in charge of his finances. Within two months, all the sellers were answering to Aladdin and bringing him their numbers and inventory at the end of each day. Aladdin also put in order the household accounts, setting up a system for Hilde to give him the lists of items bought and consumed. Each night he discussed with Herr Kaufmann the risks and potential benefits of trading with various ports and regions. Of course, being members of the Hanseatic League made travel and trade safer, but they discussed how to increase profits.

"Our items of greatest value are the expensive silks and manufactured goods shipped to England, but lately I've lost whole shipments due to foul weather."

"We should look at the profit margins. Perhaps less expensive goods—flax, wheat, honey, and resin—traded in greater bulk will bring in more revenue."

So they looked at the numbers and came up with more profitable plans.

"Are there ever any more salt pans available for you to buy?" Aladdin asked. "If so, I encourage you to buy them. The salt pans afford you the greatest profit margins by far."

Herr Kaufmann began asking around and found that one owner, who had previously owned four salt pans, had died and had no heirs. Herr Kaufmann quickly made arrangements to buy the four salt pans, thus making him a "master salter."

"How fortunate that you suggested that, Aladdin. If you had not, I would have missed a great chance to increase our revenues. You are brilliant. Blessed indeed."

Herr Kaufmann showered him with praise, calling him "dear boy" and "my godsend, Aladdin" and "my right hand."

One evening Aladdin was up late and came to the kitchen for a small repast. When he had finished his bread and cheese, he stood from his stool at the rustic wooden table. As he walked through the kitchen doorway, Grethel met him coming in and nearly bumped into him.

"Still awake?" she asked. "I couldn't sleep either."

"I was just going up to bed."

"Stay a moment." She leaned against the door frame. "I wanted to tell you how much I appreciate how you've rejuvenated my father. He's more joyous and content than I have ever seen him."

"I'm pleased to hear that."

"He trusts you, and he is elated you are so interested in the business and increasing its success."

Unsure how to reply, Aladdin shifted his feet and leaned against the support beam beside him.

"He is so fond of you—the way he was once fond of Cedric and other stewards and clerks in the past, many of whom ended up taking advantage of him. That is why Hilde and I were a bit wary of you in the beginning. I hope you will forgive me for that."

"There is nothing to forgive. I was a stranger your father encountered on the road and brought home. I would have felt the same way in your position."

"But I want you to know that I realize I was wrong about you. You are a good man." She met his gaze, then looked away, staring down at her clasped hands.

"I am pleased to have gained your trust. It is an honor to serve your father, and I enjoy the work."

"Thank you for dealing honestly with him." She smiled up

at Aladdin, and he realized . . . she was standing quite close. She placed her hand on his arm, stood on tiptoes, and kissed his cheek.

Aladdin tried to step away from her, but he stumbled into the large beam he had propped his shoulder against.

She smiled as though amused. "*Gute Nacht*, Aladdin." She moved past him into the kitchen, and he went up the stairs.

His blood pounded through his veins and made a rushing sound in his ears. He couldn't stop remembering Kirstyn, the look in her eyes the last day he saw her, when she wanted him to stay with her in Hagenheim, when she kissed his cheek just as Grethel had done. He stumbled into his bedchamber. He shut the door and went down onto his knees.

A knife seemed to stab his chest. *Oh Kirstyn, I miss you so much.*

She was the closest thing to family he'd had when he lived in the orphanage. It hurt so much to think of her marrying and forgetting about him.

He could never forget her. She was the only person who seemed to understand him. Once when they had planned to go for a walk, she waited for him while he finished his French language lesson with Margaretha. Kirstyn crossed her arms and said, "Aren't you finished yet?"

When they were finally passing through the town gate on their way to the forest, Kirstyn had said, "Sometimes I envy you."

"Me?" He raised his brows at her.

"Because you are so clever. You do all your lessons well—I've heard Frau Litzer and Master Alfred tell Mother many times. You know what you want to do, and you're very talented. Sometimes I think everyone is talented in my family except me."

"Why would you ever think that?"

"It's true. All my brothers and sisters are good at something. And they're all louder than me too."

"Louder?"

"Yes, and I'm so quiet." Kirstyn gazed at the ground. "Sometimes I think you are the only person who listens to me."

Aladdin's heart had thumped hard against his chest.

"I will always listen to you, whenever you need me. And I like quiet people. They are my favorite."

"Truly? You always say the nicest things. Sometimes I think you are too serious and that you're always trying so hard to be perfect and to make everyone like you."

The truth of her words struck him. It felt good to be understood—that she saw how hard he was trying—but it also hurt that he had fallen so short of the mark. He had done bad things in the past when he was with Mustapha, and he often thought wrong thoughts, but he didn't like anyone to know about those.

"What is it?"

He hesitated, then said, "I'm not perfect. But I wish I was."

Aladdin and Herr Kaufmann walked toward the office in the warehouse. The early-morning sun glinted off the water of the River Ilmenau alongside them.

It was late November and the first snow had fallen the night before. A light dusting of white covered the ground.

"Well, my boy," Herr Kaufmann said as they crossed the bridge that spanned the river, "you have now been in Lüneburg for six months. Did you know it had been that long?"

Aladdin smiled and nodded. "I was thinking about that last

night." He had received a letter from Kirstyn a few days before. She had filled him in on all her family's news: Her brother Gabe's wife, Sophie, was having another baby, as was Valten's wife, Gisela, and Gabe and Sophie had visited Hagenheim Castle on their way from visiting their sister Rapunzel and her husband, Sir Gerek.

But it was the ending he liked the most, the part where she mentioned her little brother Toby. She'd written, *I've had to take Toby and one of the servants walking with me. He enjoys it, but I miss my dearest friend. I miss the talks we used to have among the trees, climbing up the rock to see the stork and her nest, which has been empty ever since you left. Please tell me all your news.*

Aladdin had begun a letter to her. Tonight he would finish it, though doing so would be difficult. He almost felt as if he were lying by writing insipid things about his work and life in Lüneburg. At times he considered writing her that he feared that making his fortune would not make him happy, that he missed her and loved her too much.

But of course he could not tell her that. Besides, loving her was foolish. He'd only be devastated when he discovered she'd married someone else, the son of a duke or an earl.

His mind traveled back to a couple of years before. Aladdin had been studying with Kirstyn and Margaretha and their tutor, Herr Vortmann, in the castle. But when the day's lessons were over, Kirstyn grabbed his arm and pulled him toward the door.

"Aladdin and I are going for a walk," she said over her shoulder.

They made their way through the castle corridor, then suddenly encountered the duke leading several strangers, one of whom was dressed in a silver-and-gold-stitched cloak.

The duke glanced at Kirstyn and then said to the richly dressed man, "You may meet Margaretha's younger sister. Kirstyn, this is the Duke of Sandziwogia's son, Lord Gregor. Lord Gregor, this is Lady Kirstyn."

She curtsied to the whey-faced man with pale-blond hair. The young lord bowed to her, his eyes very keen on her face.

"And this is Aladdin, my assistant steward."

Lord Gregor gave Aladdin a disdainful glance and moved past him.

Kirstyn glared at the duke's son, even as Aladdin felt the sting as his face grew warm.

"One of Margaretha's stuffy suitors." Kirstyn wrinkled her nose as they continued down the steps. "Your dark skin and black hair are much more appealing than these men with their pale skin and blond hair."

But Aladdin continued to feel the sting of the young lord's haughtiness. It showed the great gulf between Lady Margaretha's suitors and himself, the same gulf between Aladdin and whom-ever Kirstyn would be expected to marry.

"And what do you think of our town?" Herr Kaufmann drew his attention back to the present. "Prosperous, independent, and strong, we answer to no one and share our wealth with no one. God gave us the saltworks, and this whole part of the world depends on us for their salt supply. No more perfect place on earth. Wouldn't you agree?"

"It is a great town. You—and it—have been very good to me." *No more perfect place on earth?* Aladdin's thoughts flew to Hagenheim, to all the people he loved there—to one person in particular. But he forced her face from his mind and conjured up the *Rathous*, the fountain, the *Marktplatz* with its gener-ous cobblestone area where people bought and sold goods, but also stood and talked and laughed, meeting up with friends at the fountain while their children splashed each other with cold water. A sudden longing nearly overwhelmed him, snatching the breath from his lungs with a sharp pinch.

"Yes, we have it very good here," Herr Kaufmann went on. "And with you guiding the business, we shall be the most prosperous merchants in all the *Hanse*." He clapped Aladdin on the shoulder and made the "ah" sounds that Aladdin had grown so accustomed to. It was always easy to tell when Herr Kaufmann was pleased.

His approval, so often written on his face, in his smile and his eyes, and evident in his words to Aladdin, touched a place inside him. All his life he'd worked harder than anyone else, and he'd earned the approval of Priest, the teaching masters at the orphanage, and later, the teachers at Hagenheim Castle, the stable master, and even Duke Wilhelm. Their approval had assuaged something deep inside him that echoed with absence, a void, but the balm had felt somehow . . . inadequate. But Herr Kaufmann's approval was different. He treated Aladdin like a son, a member of his family, with concern and affection.

So it was due more to Herr Kaufmann's kindness and approval that Aladdin was content to stay in Lüneburg than to the town itself, though it was an amiable town, with its magnificent and artistic architecture, its prosperity and independent spirit.

Herr Kaufmann halted and looked down, holding up his houppelande to inspect his feet. "My shoe has come undone." He bent down.

"Shall I fix it for you?"

"No, no, I have it. I have not grown so old I cannot buckle my own shoe." He grunted as he fumbled with the buckle on the leather that came just above his ankle. The shoe's toe was so long it curled upward and also wrapped around his ankle. Aladdin had admonished him, more than once, that the fashionable shoes were not practical and would someday trip him and cause him to injure himself, but Herr Kaufmann wouldn't hear of casting fashion aside.

"People expect the prosperous to be fashionable," he would always say.

While Aladdin waited, he glanced down a narrow alley between two houses. An unusual shape caught his eye. It was a small boat wedged between two buildings with something lying inside it. The boat seemed familiar, so Aladdin went to investigate.

As he drew closer, he could see a face visible around a sea of rags and clothing and ragged blankets. It was the same little boy he'd seen floating down the river the first morning after he arrived in Lüneburg—the boy who called himself Abu.

His eyes opened a crack, his mouth opened to yawn, and arms emerged from the mass of makeshift blankets to rise high. But in midyawn, he caught sight of Aladdin and sat straight up, snapping his mouth closed.

"I didn't mean to startle you," Aladdin said. "You are Abu."

"You are Aladdin, Herr Kaufmann's adopted son."

Adopted son? Was that what people were calling him? Warmth flooded his chest.

Aladdin noticed the layer of snow covering the boy's boat-bed. "Is this where you sleep?"

"Of course." Abu wrapped his arms around himself and shivered before reaching for a torn and stained wool cape. He threw it over his shoulders and stood up.

"Why don't you come with me to the market and I'll buy you breakfast."

Abu quickly took in Aladdin's person from head to toe, then said, "I will go with you."

"Hello there, Abu." Herr Kaufmann walked toward them.

"It was a cold night to sleep out of doors. You can rest in the kitchen at Kaufmann House anytime you please."

"Thank you, Herr Kaufmann, but I like staying with my boat. It's not too cold for me."

"Very well."

The three of them fell into step as they headed toward the town center.

"So, Abu, how did you come to be in Lüneburg?"

"Herr Stenngle—he's a merchant—brought my father and me here from Palestine. But my father died of a fever, and Herr Stenngle released me from his service, and now I fish with my little pole and come and go as I please. I am no one's servant. I have a better life than anyone in Lüneburg—even Herr Kaufmann." With that observation, he laughed quite raucously.

Herr Kaufmann frowned. "What do you mean? You are an orphan with no one to feed you, and I am one of the wealthiest men in town."

"Yes, but you must get up early every morning and worry about this and that cargo ship, or this and that worker, or this and that thief who stole your money. Me? I have no ships or workers or money. I have no problems."

His gleeful smile was infectious. Aladdin laughed.

"Ach. Don't encourage his nonsense," Herr Kaufmann scowled. "The little imp has no concept of what life is supposed to be."

But when Aladdin looked down at Abu, he was still grinning. "I am the boss of me, and of my lice and fleas too. I sleep very well in my little boat. How do you sleep, Herr Kaufmann?"

"Be quiet, boy. I know for a fact that Hilde slips you bread rolls and even cheese out the back door five days out of seven."

Abu's smile finally dimmed a bit. "Yes, Hilde is very kind."

Herr Kaufmann grunted.

"As are you, Herr Kaufmann," Abu said contritely. "A man among men." He became more animated. "Truly, you will be in charge of this town someday." Abu winked up at Aladdin.

"Not I. Aladdin here. He is the wise one. He shall be running my business—and this town! Someday, you watch. Richer than all the other merchants combined."

Aladdin began, "Herr Kaufmann, I—"

"Never you mind refusing the praise. It is no more than you deserve. And here we are at the market. I shall go on and see you at our desk."

Aladdin stepped aside and bought Abu some fruit pasties and late apples, which the boy put in the stained and faded woolen bag he carried over his shoulder.

Abu drew out one of the fruit pasties and took a big bite. "Thank you, sir." His voice was muffled by the food in his mouth. "If you need any messages delivered, just ask me."

"You can call me Aladdin, and you're most welcome. I hope you will come to Herr Kaufmann's home or office if you're ever hungry or in trouble. And if you need help, ask for me."

Abu drew himself up to his full height, the top of his head reaching almost to Aladdin's chest.

Abu swallowed the bite of fruit pasty and shook his head. "I'm not a beggar. I am my own man, and I prefer to work for pay. I deliver messages for the merchants in town. I work for the butcher sometimes, cleaning behind his shop and delivering meat, and I don't ask for help. But Hilde worries about me if I don't come by very often. She says she cannot sleep if she hasn't seen me lately. But I am not an infant who cannot take care of himself."

"Of course not. You are right. I only meant if you wanted some work or you knew of someone else, a friend of yours, who might need help for some reason. I can see that you are a very capable young man."

Abu nodded slowly with a serious look. "Thank you. And I shall keep that in mind."

"Very good."

"Perhaps I shall see you sometime, Aladdin."

"Take care of yourself, Abu."

The little boy, with his long, scraggly black hair and ragged cloak, turned and walked away.

What would Aladdin's life have been like if he'd been living on the street—or in a boat—like this boy? What had happened to his old companion Zuhayr? What if Aladdin had not grown up in the Hagenheim orphanage? He never would have met Lady Kirstyn, and he might not have learned about Jesus and God's redemption.

Aladdin hurried to the office inside the warehouse where Herr Kaufmann conducted most of his business affairs. Herr Kaufmann was arguing with the man who captained the boat that conveyed his goods down the Stecknitz Canal to the port in Hamburg.

"I can no longer work for that price," the man, Orloft, said.

Aladdin stepped in and asked the man how much he wanted. The boat captain named a price that was much more than the other captains he had heard of.

"Herr Kaufmann cannot pay you that."

"Cannot or will not?"

"Will not." Aladdin met his eye and was determined not to blink. "We can offer you a bit more." Aladdin named a price that was a fair wage, as high as the highest price he knew of for making the slow, twenty-day trip down the canal between Lüneburg and Hamburg.

"*Ach* so. I will take it."

Aladdin took a coin out of the pouch at his waist and added it to the wages Herr Kaufmann had already given him. Orloft grunted. "I shall return in forty-one days."

"With the cargo from my ship, the *Wassernixe*, do not forget." Herr Kaufmann shook his finger in the air.

Orloft grunted again and nodded. "I shall bring it."

After Orloft left, Aladdin pondered the way the cog captain had reacted to what was said to him, his facial expressions, and decided to send one of Herr Kaufmann's loyal guards with him on this journey. But instead of raising Herr Kaufmann's anxiety, he went and saw to it himself.

If Orloft was stealing from Herr Kaufmann, the guard would either discover it or deter it. Either way, Aladdin could report the incident to Herr Kaufmann when it was all over.

Herr Kaufmann handed Aladdin the reports the sellers at the market had brought the evening before. Together they went over the numbers and the inventory lists.

"Profits are up quite a bit from this time last year," Herr Kaufmann remarked. "I sleep much better than I have in years." Herr Kaufmann gazed across the desk at Aladdin. His expression was warm and gentle. "You are the best thing that has ever happened to my business—besides, perhaps, the overthrow of the ruling princes and the remanding of the town government to the people."

Aladdin couldn't help an amused smile at Herr Kaufmann's mention of his favorite event in the history of his beloved town.

"But you are also like a son to me, Aladdin." Herr Kaufmann's eyes misted with tears. "I couldn't ask for a better one."

Just then, another of Herr Kaufmann's workers burst into the office. When he finished his business and departed, Herr Kaufmann turned back to Aladdin.

"I have something I wish to say to you, a question—a request, truly—and I should like to make that request . . . Tomorrow is Sunday, yes? I should like to speak with you before the church service. Will you attend with me early? Grethel can come later. The servants will escort her."

"Of course. I will do my best to grant whatever you wish, Herr Kaufmann."

"You mustn't say that until you hear the request." The older man gave Aladdin an inscrutable smile.

A prickling sensation skittered up Aladdin's spine, traveling up to his neck, where it stayed, along with a premonition of something unpleasant.

CHAPTER NINE

Sunday morning Aladdin walked beside Herr Kaufmann toward the church. The sun was shining, though the air was rather cold, giving a rosy hue to Herr Kaufmann's nose and cheeks. Aladdin's own skin had always been too dark to react so readily, but it rather fascinated him to see the effect of the elements on the pale faces of everyone he knew. Were they equally fascinated with his darker skin? Kirstyn had once told him, "Your skin is so warm looking. I think it's part of what calms me whenever I see you."

His heart swelled just thinking about that.

Herr Kaufmann was pointing out some of the buildings around them, as he often did, and telling him this or that memory associated with each one.

"My wife and I were married at *Johanniskirche*, which you have attended many times. Grethel prefers *Nicholaikirche*, and it is a beauty, another testament to how prosperous a town can be when its residents are free and independent—we were able to build a new church."

Aladdin smiled at the man's oft-spoken assertion. But they

had nearly arrived at the church, so he interrupted him. "Herr Kaufmann, you said there was a question you wanted to ask me."

"Patience, my boy."

Aladdin followed him through the front door of the church. They both touched the holy water just inside, crossed themselves, and genuflected before the crucifix. Then Herr Kaufmann led him to a small bench against the wall.

No one was near. A few people were kneeling at the chancel amid some lit candles, their heads bowed in prayer, but they were too far away to eavesdrop. A hush hovered in this beautiful, high-ceilinged nave made out of brick, plaster, and stained glass, similar to the hush at Hildesheim Cathedral. It was a holy feeling that permeated his chest and reminded him that God was bigger than he was.

"As I was saying yesterday . . ." Herr Kaufmann slumped slightly forward, speaking softly while looking into Aladdin's eyes. "You are like a son to me, a son who is loyal and trustworthy, wise and intelligent, with a great head for numbers and business. I could not ask for a better young man to come into my family. And that is why I wish . . . My dear boy, I wish you to be my son in name as well as in my heart, and for you to take on my surname and to inherit my business when I am gone—or when I'm too old to make wise decisions. And as I wish the very best for my precious daughter, Grethel, it is also the desire of my heart for the two of you to wed."

Aladdin's stomach tied itself into a knot. He sent a silent, incoherent plea to God for the right words.

"Herr Kaufmann, you must know how much it pleases me to work with you, how much I enjoy the business, and how you are like a father to me. And for someone who grew up without a father, that is a wonderful thing I do not take for granted. It is also my wish to stay with you and help grow your business. You know I have ideas to build it up and make it even more profitable."

"Yes, yes. So why do you look so grim? Grethel is a lovely girl. Many men have asked to marry her. And you must not have the notion that romantic love must come before marriage, for it absolutely comes after the wedding. You both are loving people. I am sure you will come to love each other."

"Herr Kaufmann, please. Let me explain. I care for Grethel very much, but as a sister, as your daughter, and as a . . . a sweet and lovely girl. But I . . . I do not wish to think of her as a wife." Kirstyn's face rushed unbidden into his mind. Perhaps if he told Herr Kaufmann he had already given his heart to another, that he was in love with Duke Wilhelm's daughter, Lady Kirstyn, he would understand. But how could he admit that to Herr Kaufmann when he hardly allowed himself to think about it? He couldn't love Kirstyn. It had always been his secret wish to marry her, but it was a foolish one.

A herd of wild red deer charging through his stomach could not have made him more unsettled.

"It pains me to say no to anything you wish."

Herr Kaufmann reached out and patted Aladdin's arm. "Do not upset yourself. I am sad that it cannot be, but I had to try. To join the two people I care for most in this world . . . to ensure my daughter's future . . ." He heaved a sigh. "At least I still have you as my partner in the business. I plan to have my clerks draw up the legal papers entitling you to half the Kaufmann property and profits. Equal partners we shall always be, and upon my death the business shall be inherited by you, as long as you promise to give my house to Grethel and to take care of her financially."

"Of course. And I shall sign any document saying so. You are being incredibly generous, Herr Kaufmann."

"Nonsense. You deserve it. I am the one who has been blessed, ever since the moment God brought you into my life—to save me from robbers and to soothe an old man's broken heart over his wayward son." A shadow came over the man's face, as it always did at the mention of his son.

"And I have been equally blessed," Aladdin said softly, "since the night I first met you. God has given me more than I could have asked or imagined in such a short time—a business partner, friend, and the very model of a kind father." At this admission, tears stung the back of his eyes.

"Well, you are easy to be a kind father to, Aladdin." Herr Kaufmann patted his arm again, then a smile crept over his face. "And one never knows what the future holds. But I shall say no more. We will not tell God what will be, but we shall pray and ask God to guide our future, then meet it when it comes. That is a good plan, is it not, my boy?"

"Yes. It is a good plan."

Aladdin glanced up. A tall, thin man with dark, greasy hair and a shrewd look in his black eyes stood crouched in a dark corner near them, as if he'd been there for some time, listening to their conversation. But as soon as Aladdin met his eye, the man turned and walked toward the door.

Aladdin got a sick feeling in his stomach. He turned to point out the man to Herr Kaufmann, but Herr Kaufmann was already staring after him, his eyes narrowing.

"Do you know that man?" Aladdin asked.

"He was one of Cedric's friends. I always suspected he was helping Cedric steal from me, but it was never proven."

"I think he was listening to us."

Herr Kaufmann shook his head. "We shall just have to pray nothing evil comes of it."

Winter was well under way a few weeks later. No people sat outside any of the many breweries in town drinking ale as they had every day since he came to Lüneburg.

Aladdin kept his head down as he walked, the stiff wind swirling the snow around his feet. His woolen cloak, normally so warm, felt like the thinnest linen, so little did it block the sting of the bitter wind.

Aladdin braved the wind alone on his way to the warehouse, glad Herr Kaufmann was warm at home. He wanted to go over the accounts, in spite of Herr Kaufmann saying it was too cold to conduct business.

Aladdin took a different route from his usual walk along the river. Perhaps the buildings would block some of the wind. He turned down a narrow street, then down a wider one. Few people were about. He saw no one at all for a few minutes, but then he heard someone coughing. It was a very insistent cough, and it seemed to be coming from a narrow alleyway.

What was a sick person with a terrible cough doing out in this weather?

Aladdin stepped toward the sound. The alley was rather dark, even with the morning sun shining. As he approached he realized Abu's small wooden boat was wedged in between the buildings. The makeshift blankets in the boat shook with every cough.

"Abu? Is that you?"

The blankets moved some more, and Abu's face emerged

as he raised his head and shoulders above the mound of ragged blankets and clothes.

Abu's eyelids were heavy and drooped over red-rimmed eyes, and his face was blotchy and puffy. Aladdin knelt beside the boat. "You don't look well. Are you in pain?"

Abu seemed to make a great effort to breathe. "My chest." He took another labored breath amid a rattling sound. "I think I'm dying . . . just like my father."

"I'm taking you to Herr Kaufmann's house."

Abu's shoulders drooped. He tried to stand, but it was obvious he was too weak.

Aladdin scooped him up with his blankets on top of him, and Abu did not protest. Aladdin carried him down the street, drawing some curious looks from the few people who were out in the cold. Once he reached Herr Kaufmann's home, he deposited him on the extra bed in a tiny room on the street level.

"Aladdin? Who is that? What is amiss?" Hilde followed them into the room.

"It's Abu. He's very sick. Can you send someone to fetch Herr Kaufmann's physician?" Aladdin glanced back at Hilde. Her face showed great concern.

"I will."

Aladdin heard her telling one of the other servants to fetch Herr Monnik as soon as possible, then she was back in the room, hovering over Abu.

The boy's eyes were closed and he coughed again, arching his back as he wheezed in. The coughs racked his small body, and he reclined against the pillow as if exhausted.

"Oh dear." Hilde set her hand on the boy's forehead. "He's burning up with fever. I shall fetch him some feverfew and . . ." Hilde's voice trailed off as she hurried out of the room.

Aladdin felt helpless watching Abu struggle to breathe, obviously in pain. He fell to his knees beside the boy's bed and began to pray quietly.

Soon Hilde came back with a cup. "You must drink this." She sat on a stool by Abu's side and held the cup to his lips. "Aladdin, can you hold him steady?"

Aladdin eased him forward, then sat behind him, bracing Abu's back against his chest and his thin shoulders between his hands. Hilde managed to get several swallows into him before the coughing racked his body again. But as soon as he stopped, Hilde poured the liquid in through his parted lips. After a couple more coughing fits, Hilde had given him the entire contents of the cup, and Abu lay unmoving.

Was he still alive? Aladdin touched his head. Still warm.

He carefully slid off the bed, setting Abu back, but he and Hilde propped him up on pillows so he was not lying flat. Abu slept on, his chest rattling and rasping with every breath.

Abu was awake and coughing again by the time the physician arrived. He took one look at Abu and his step faltered, his face freezing. Aladdin's spine stiffened and heat rose inside him at the physician's reaction. Was his objection to treating a homeless orphan? Or to treating a dark-skinned Saracen?

Herr Kaufmann was lurking in the corridor outside. He had a fear of sickness and bad humors. The physician took a step back, turned on his heel, and went to talk to Herr Kaufmann.

Aladdin's stomach churned. Would the physician refuse to care for Abu?

"I shall pay you the same as I would for any sick servant of my household." Herr Kaufmann's voice rose precipitously. "He is not an animal, after all. You do treat human children, do you not?" His voice contained an angry edge Aladdin had never heard before.

Moments later the physician reentered the room, a sheepish look on his face. He put down his bag and knelt beside Abu. He picked up Abu's limp hand, pressing his fingertips to the underside of Abu's wrist, then pulled on the skin underneath Abu's left eye, then his right.

"His humors are unbalanced—too much cold and wet, and too much phlegm in the body. He needs this room to stay warm and dry. To flush out his body, he will need to drink a lot of warm liquids. He must cough out all the phlegm in his lungs, but do not allow him to lie on his back or he will drown in it."

The physician rummaged around in his bag and brought out a tiny cloth bundle. He handed it to Hilde. "Here is some dried *Lungenkraut*. Give it to him in hot water or perhaps some watered-down wine—no milk."

"Yes, Herr Monnik."

"It is also possible the illness is caused by a demon spirit. In that case, only God can save him."

Herr Monnik nodded to Aladdin, closed and hefted his bag, and left.

Soon Hilde returned with a cup of the physician's dried lungwort steeped in hot water. She and Aladdin waited for Abu to awaken, and it didn't take long before he started coughing again, too hard to remain asleep.

Hilde took the opportunity to pour some of the warm lungwort drink into his mouth. Then she swung his feet off the bed and placed them in a pan of very warm water on the floor.

"My mother swore that soaking a child's feet in hot water would take away any fever."

Poor Abu was letting them move him around and do anything to him, and he remained mostly unconscious through most of it.

Soon after she put his feet in the hot water, Abu began to sweat. Sweat beaded on his entire face.

"Is that a good sign or bad?" Aladdin turned to Hilde. He had seldom been sick himself, besides when he'd been injured in the bear attack.

"Oh, sweating is a very good thing." Hilde leaned over Abu, then dabbed at his face with a cloth. "It means the fever is leaving him. That prideful physician might say his humors are balancing out."

"His breathing doesn't sound quite as bad as it did."

Hilde listened. "Not as much rattling. And the color in his cheeks is getting better."

After Abu sweated out the rest of his fever, he fell into a deeper sleep. His coughing grew much less frequent and less violent. As Aladdin sat beside his bed, he prayed, *God, thank You for sparing his life. I know You are no respecter of persons, not like that physician. Abu is just as precious to You as a prince would be.*

When Aladdin looked up from his prayer, Abu was staring at him with tired but clear eyes. "Thank you," he said softly.

"Feeling better?"

"Yes, but I'm very sleepy."

"Sleep, then. When you wake again, you'll be much stronger."

Abu nodded and turned over onto his side. Soon his breathing was steady and even, but without any of the rattling from before.

Abu was from the Holy Land, from Palestine, the same as Aladdin. But unlike Aladdin, Abu still remembered his father. The only thing Aladdin could remember was a blurry image of his mother's face as she lay dead and a vague feeling of heat, spices, and the sandy color of the buildings. And unlike Aladdin,

Abu had been living on his own for at least a year or two. What did a child, on his own, learn about life? That he had to take care of himself, that he could not trust others—this was clear from the few times Aladdin had spoken to him.

A heaviness filled Aladdin's heart, but then he remembered something Kirstyn had said a few years ago on one of their walks in the woods.

"I may not have a particular talent or any extraordinary skills—"

"That's not true. You *are* talented and extraordinary."

Her eyes were big and solemn and seemed to see into his heart. Could she tell how much he cared for her—how she was the loveliest, dearest, safest person in his life?

"I may not be as extraordinary as the rest of my siblings," she went on, "but someday I want to get married and adopt ten orphans, at least."

"Ten? Are you so eager to be a mother?"

"I just can't bear to think of a child feeling insignificant and unwanted. Every child should have a mother. And that is what I want—to adopt orphans as my mother and father adopted Toby. He was alone and mistreated, and now he is a joyful little boy. It hurts my heart to think of what his life would have been like if Margaretha had not brought him home."

A lump formed in Aladdin's throat. Her words seemed to melt inside of him, filling in the holes that the absence of a family had left.

He swallowed and said, "You will be a wonderful mother, and your children will adore you."

She smiled that gentle smile of hers. "Thank you, Aladdin. I don't know what I'd do without you. You are the best friend I've ever had."

His heart had leapt inside him—and the very next moment crashed against his chest. He was getting older. Being her best friend would not always be enough, he knew, but . . . anything more was impossible. Besides, she obviously only thought of him as a friend.

He made an effort to push the memories away as he watched Abu sleep, his face relaxed and no longer flushed.

Abu slept for a few hours, and when he awoke, he was ravenous, eating everything Hilde brought to him—thick pea-and-bean porridge, a hefty portion of pheasant, a large bread roll, and a fruit pasty. But when she tried to give him more of the lungwort tea, he clamped his lips closed and turned his head.

"Why do you want to be so obstinate? This herbal drink is what the doctor ordered for you. Will you refuse to listen to a learned man like him?"

But Abu only scrunched up his face more, lowering his brows and pulling his lips in so they were no longer visible.

"His cough is much better," Aladdin said, trying to hide his smile from the plump, motherly servant. "He doesn't need it anymore, perhaps."

Hilde huffed. "Boys are such stubborn creatures." Shaking her kerchief-covered head at both of them, she left the room.

Aladdin pulled up a stool and sat beside Abu. "Feeling better?"

"*Ja*, much better." He laid his head back on the pillow, obviously still a bit weak.

"You must listen to Frau Hilde. She has taken good care of sick children before, including Herr Kaufmann's and others she told me about. And she is very kind."

Abu frowned a bit on one side of his mouth. "She is kind,

and you . . . Thank you, Aladdin. I thought I was dying." He spoke softly, but his eyes were big and round and sincere as he gazed up at Aladdin.

"I'm glad I found you and could bring you here. Herr Kaufmann is a good soul."

"He is not a cruel man, not like some, but he would not have brought me here the way you did. He loves you. He took care of me because of you. And as soon as I am well, I shall leave."

"Perhaps you are right, but perhaps not." Aladdin shook his head. "Herr Kaufmann was constantly asking after you. He sent for the town's most expensive physician and—" He was about to say, "He hotly rebuked the physician for not wanting to treat a poor orphan from Palestine." But he said instead, "I think you would be surprised how softhearted Herr Kaufmann truly is."

Abu stared down at the blanket covering him. "I'm sorry. Please give Herr Kaufmann my thanks."

"Of course, but you may tell him yourself a bit later. And I hope you will consider staying here with us. You won't want to sleep outside in this cold, not after how sick you got."

Abu again stared down without meeting Aladdin's gaze. "I will think about it, if you want me, and if Herr Kaufmann doesn't mind me staying here."

"He won't mind." And Aladdin would make sure Herr Kaufmann told Abu so himself. He couldn't bear to think of Abu spending another night outdoors in the cold.

Abu reminded him so much of himself and Zuhayr, his friend from so long ago. If Aladdin could keep Abu safe and warm, perhaps it would give him a sense of power over those painful memories of his early childhood. It would help him imagine someone rescuing Zuhayr from the streets as well, the way Priest had rescued Aladdin, and the way he would now rescue Abu.

Kirstyn had said she wanted to adopt ten orphans. Perhaps she and he . . . But he should not be thinking that.

Chapter Ten

It was a sunny but cold day as Kirstyn and her mother were on their way to visit the orphans. She was imagining running an orphanage of her own or living in an enormous house that she would fill with her own orphans. How she would love them, wipe their tears, kiss their cheeks, tell them stories, and tuck them in at night. She'd listen to the horrors that had happened to them before they came to live with her, then reassure them that nothing like that would ever happen to them again.

She also thought often of Aladdin, of some of the things he had told her, how Priest and Sir Meynard had caught him trying to steal from them. Her heart squeezed as she thought of him, uncared for, so young and ragged, without a mother to hug him and kiss him.

"Lady Kirstyn!" Anna, one of the older orphans, waved at Kirstyn as she and Mother made their way toward the grassy area where the children played their games, the place where Kirstyn had first seen Aladdin.

Since Aladdin had gone and Kirstyn had begun visiting the orphanage more often, Anna approached Kirstyn as soon as she saw her. Anna was a pretty, brown-haired, green-eyed girl who had come to the orphanage after her mother died when Anna was thirteen.

"Lady Kirstyn, Frau Litzer said I am her most improved student."

"That is wonderful, Anna." Kirstyn squeezed the girl's arm and smiled. "I know you are proud of yourself, and Frau Litzer and Master Alfred are too."

"I told them it was because of your influence. You make me feel as if I can do anything."

"Me?"

"Of course. You are so beautiful and clever, and you are the first person who has ever made me feel as if I could be something besides just an orphan."

"Of course you'll be something besides an orphan. You already are. You're getting an education. You already know how to sew and spin—valuable skills—and you can add and subtract and multiply, and so you could be a shopkeeper or a seller in the market."

"That's very kind of you to say." Anna shook her head. "But I never imagined myself doing any of those things. I had always hoped I'd be a wife and mother."

"And I'm sure you will be. When you're older."

The other children were starting to go back into the large house where they lived.

"I'll be fifteen in a few weeks. And since you're sixteen, we are very close in age, you see. And just as you found your true love at a young age . . ." She gave Kirstyn a look from beneath lowered lashes. "Have you heard from your sweetheart, Aladdin?"

"Whoever said he was my sweetheart?" Kirstyn's breath shallowed, as it always did when someone mentioned Aladdin.

"Everyone knows that, if you will pardon me for saying so."

Kirstyn's cheeks warmed as she imagined Aladdin and her doing the things sweethearts did. "We actually were not, and are not, sweethearts. We care about each other, and we have always been close friends."

She pictured his dear face, the way he looked at her, how he always made her feel special, how he always listened to her. Her mind took her back to a conversation she'd had with her parents not long after the bear had attacked Aladdin.

"Now that you and Aladdin are growing older," her mother had said, "things might begin to become awkward between you."

"Why?" Kirstyn didn't like the way Mother and Father were looking at her.

"Because he is nearly a man," her father said. "He . . . well, he may begin treating you differently. Boys and girls simply don't stay only friends when they grow up."

"Oh, Father, that's ridiculous." She folded her arms over her chest. "Aladdin will always be my friend."

"But one day you will get married, and Aladdin will also wish to marry. He may . . . he may wish to marry you."

Kirstyn's stomach twisted. Why must Father speak of such things? "Aladdin doesn't think about marrying me. Besides, marriage is far in the future. I'm only twelve years old, and Aladdin . . . well, he's around fourteen, but he's still just a boy. He loves me as he would a sister."

"Perhaps it is too soon to speak of marriage." Mother placed her hand discreetly on Father's arm. "But we wanted to warn you that Aladdin may develop feelings for you that are not consistent with those of a brother or friend. He may care for you in a different way."

"I don't like this conversation." Kirstyn glared first at her father, then her mother. Her breath was coming fast and shallow as she became desperate to make her parents listen to her and stop this uncomfortable talk.

"Aladdin is a good boy. And I am a good girl! We are friends, and we enjoy exploring the forest and talking about a lot of things—innocent things!"

"We know you are good children. And we love you both. You are our precious daughter, and Aladdin is one of our own precious orphans. Priest entrusted him to our care, and he is an exceptional boy. Your father wants him to work in the castle as the assistant steward."

"Then I don't understand why you wanted to warn me about him. He treats me better than anyone. He is kinder to me than any of my brothers."

"Do your brothers mistreat you?" Mother asked.

"No, but Steffan and Wolfgang tease Margaretha a lot, and it hurts her."

"I shall speak to them about that," Father said.

"But Aladdin would never treat me in an untoward manner."

"I am glad to hear that." Mother smiled.

But Kirstyn remembered wondering why she and Aladdin couldn't stay children forever. She didn't want her friendship with him ever to change. But . . . she'd been having different feelings for Aladdin, especially since he left and she had kissed him on the cheek, but she had not wanted to admit them. Did Aladdin feel the same way?

When she was feeling sad after Aladdin left, Father had told her, "A man wants to make his own way. Aladdin wants to be his own man and prove himself."

Of course, her father didn't suspect she loved Aladdin. He

just thought she was missing her best friend, and she was. But she was really annoyed when Valten told her, "Men are repulsed by women who make it too clear that they love them."

But perhaps it was time to admit that the way she felt about Aladdin was no longer the same way she felt when she was twelve. But it was still annoying to think that people had assumed they were sweethearts.

Kirstyn and Anna were nearly to the building when Kirstyn realized she hadn't been listening to Anna. But now she forced herself to pay attention.

"I don't like mathematics or reading very much. What I really would like to do is serve inside Hagenheim Castle. Do you think you might mention to your mother that I would be a good worker, that I can clean and cook and do any kind of work they might wish me to? Would you please ask her?"

Anna's green eyes were wide and hopeful as she tucked a strand of brown hair behind her ear.

"Of course I can ask her. But she might think you a bit young to enter full-time service."

"Oh, I would work as much or as little as she needed me. I could work only one day a week, or I could work a few hours every evening after our studies are finished. Truly, I would love to leave the orphanage now and work for your family. Please? Just ask her. Will you?"

The look on Anna's face seemed desperate.

"Is someone mistreating you at the orphanage, Anna? Is something wrong?"

"Oh no, nothing like that." She took a step away and shook her head. "I only want to serve and do something important. I like being active, not sitting around with books all day. Thank you, Lady Kirstyn. You are so kind." Anna clasped Kirstyn's hand and smiled, that desperate light still shining in her eyes. Then she turned and followed after the rest of the orphans entering the dining hall to have their midday meal.

Winter had been quite cold at Hagenheim Castle. The stone walls kept out the wind, but the cold itself seemed undeterred as the old year ended and a new year began. Snow made everything white, clinging even to the steep roofs on the castle's five towers. Kirstyn spent a lot of her time wrapped in a wool blanket while sitting in her favorite window seat in the castle solar.

But spring had begun to brighten the view from her window. Bright-green new leaves were bursting out everywhere, and today was a sunny, warm April day. Kirstyn sat at the window staring out after reading one of Aladdin's letters. She bent to read it again.

My dearest friend Kirstyn,

I was glad to receive your letter. A letter from you is more welcome to me than anything else except actually being in your presence.

I am well here in Lüneburg and thankful God has provided me with work. The weather has finally warmed, but it was so cold that even Abu didn't venture out in February and March. I wonder if it was as cold in Hagenheim. I know how much you love the snow. I imagine you looking out the window at the way it covers the trees and roofs. You once said, "The snow is God's blanket when He gets tired of the brown grass and dead leaves." I always think about that when it snows.

Kirstyn pressed the letter to her chest and closed her eyes. No one else had ever quoted her words back to her.

A memory swept over her, of a time when she had suggested they find a stork nest.

"That's pretty far," Aladdin said. "Are you up for such a long walk?"

"Of course!" She turned and hurried through the thick leaves, then stepped over a dead moss-covered tree.

Kirstyn soon slowed her pace, and they trekked through the brush and trees, crossed a stream, and headed toward the rocky hill where the stork built her nest every year. They hoped her eggs might have hatched.

Finally they reached the rocky outcropping where the huge nest of sticks sat on top.

Kirstyn began climbing the giant rock. Aladdin was right behind her.

"Be careful," he said softly. "The mama bird won't like us getting too close."

Kirstyn climbed to a higher part of the rocky slope, having to hitch up her skirt and tie it with her belt to keep herself from stepping on it. She looked down on the nest from behind a bush, and Aladdin crouched beside her.

The nest, with twigs poking out in all directions, was four feet wide and very deep, and inside four chicks huddled together.

As they watched them, Sir Conrad signaled with his hand, then pointed several feet away where the trees and bushes were thick, probably intending to go relieve himself. Aladdin nodded, and Sir Conrad headed for the trees.

"Aren't the baby birds beautiful?" Kirstyn whispered.

"They are."

"Storks are always faithful to their mates, or so the stories

all say." Kirstyn turned and sat down so she was no longer looking at the birds but facing Aladdin. "Did you know that Father
forgot it was my birthday? He came very late to my birthday
feast."

It was her fifteenth birthday. She'd felt so hurt but didn't
want to tell her father so. While she waited for Aladdin to speak,
she started picking at a tuft of grass that had sprouted through
a crack in the rock.

"Are you angry with him?" Aladdin asked.

"He said he was sorry, that he got caught a long way from
home trying to settle a dispute between two landowners. I couldn't
be angry with him, but . . . it hurt."

Kirstyn's chin trembled, and she pressed her lips together
to try to stop it. "He always spends time with Valten." A tear
dripped from one eye, then the other. Her voice hitched as
she continued to pick at the grass, her face turned down. She
hoped Aladdin couldn't see her tears. "He and Valten go places
together all the time. They talk about things they don't share
with the rest of us. And Father teaches Wolfgang and Steffan
things like sword fighting and archery. I know my father loves
me, but sometimes I just feel so unextraordinary. It's as if no one
even sees me."

Aladdin laid his hand on her shoulder. "I see you."

She lifted her face and stared at him with watery eyes. "You
never ignore me or tease me. You make me feel as if you care
about me, as if I'm the only person in the room."

She couldn't remember exactly what happened after that, but
she was sure Aladdin had made her smile and forget all about her
father nearly missing her birthday.

If she disappeared, she didn't think her brothers would even
notice, but Aladdin wrote her long letters and remembered her

exact words. Aladdin soothed an ache in her heart, and she longed for him so much.

His letter went on to describe Lüneburg and all the friends he had made there, as Kirstyn had asked him to, and she could hear his voice as she read the words.

The door opened and Anna entered the solar wearing her servant's garb—a blue kirtle, white underdress, and white kerchief. She'd finally gotten what she wanted—a job at the castle working three afternoons out of seven.

Kirstyn folded her letter and greeted Anna.

Anna's eyes were wide and alert, her lips parted.

"What is it? Is something wrong?"

"No, something good. I have just heard that Duke Wilhelm is having some Meistersingers and traveling minstrels play in the *Marktplatz* tomorrow. Will you come? There will be dancing and food."

"That sounds delightful."

"You will be there, then?"

"Of course."

"Do you know what time you shall arrive?"

"I shall have to speak with my parents."

It seemed a bit strange that Anna knew about the May Day celebration before she did.

Later as they sat in the Great Hall having their evening meal, Kirstyn managed to get her parents' attention.

"Anna says a group of Meistersingers will be playing in the Marktplatz tomorrow."

Father nodded. "They were in town and asked if I'd like them to play and sing for May Day, so I agreed." He winked at Mother. "Your mother and I enjoy dancing together."

Mother smiled back at Father. "The children from the

orphanage are all attending. Would you like to help watch them?"

"Of course. It's strange that Anna knew about the Meistersingers and the May Day celebration."

"Anna? How did she know?" Mother looked confused, but then Adela was pulling on Mother's sleeve, and Mother turned her full attention on her little sister.

"She must have heard me speaking to them when they came to the castle," Father said.

"It will be fun to have music and dancing tomorrow. I only hope—"

"Father!" Steffan yelled. "Wolfgang is throwing food on the floor."

"Wolfgang, I told you that only makes the dogs try to force their way in."

While Father lectured her immature brothers, Kirstyn finished her sentence, even though no one was listening. "I only hope it doesn't rain."

The sun was shining brightly the next morning, and though everyone was dressed warmly, those dancing in the open space of the town center soon found themselves peeling off their outer clothing.

Kirstyn held one of the youngest orphans on her hip, bouncing her up and down and making her laugh as the music lightened her spirits. Everywhere people were smiling and laughing.

Guards were nearby and interspersed among the crowd. Kirstyn never quite got used to them watching her during festivals and celebrations. But they were enjoying themselves as well.

In fact, several of them had gone to buy food from some of the vendors.

One of the orphanage workers, Heike, came and took the little girl from Kirstyn's arms.

"It's time for her nap. I'll take her back to the orphanage with the other little ones."

Kirstyn kissed the child's rosy cheek as her eyes began to droop.

Shouting came from the other end of the cobblestone square. It grew louder, swelling until several voices had joined in, but the commotion was too far away for Kirstyn to see what was happening. The guards began to make their way in that direction.

"Lady Kirstyn." Anna ran up to her. "Come and help me get Hanns."

"Hanns?"

"Yes. Come." Anna motioned with her hand. "He went down an alley following a dog, and now I'm afraid he will get lost. It should only take a few moments."

Kirstyn followed Anna, who moved quite fast, obviously worried about the little boy who had only come to the orphanage in the last few days.

Anna turned down a narrow street between two buildings. Kirstyn followed her and soon found herself barely able to see where she was going. The two buildings on either side of them blocked out the sun.

She stopped. Something was not right.

"Anna, I'm going back. I'll fetch a guard." Kirstyn backed up a few steps, then turned and started hurrying. She was still several feet from the open street when a cart rolled up and blocked her way. A man jumped down from the cart and approached her.

Fear seeped into every part of her body. Her hands tingled. "Get out of the way."

The man did not answer her but froze in place. The look on his face made her breath quicken. Should she turn around and run? Or should she scream for help?

Kirstyn spun around. Anna was nowhere in sight, but another man was just behind her. He lunged and grabbed her arm. Something slammed into the back of her head and the world went black.

Kirstyn opened her eyes, an intense pain radiating from the back of her skull. Where was she?

Something was tied around her eyes and her mouth. She could only breathe through her nose. The floor underneath her was cold and hard, and it was lurching and swaying like a cart being pulled down the road.

She tried to remove the blindfold, but her hands were tied behind her back. Her heart pounded in time with her head. Who had struck her and tied her up? Where were they taking her? Would they kill her? Her father and one of his knights had taught Kirstyn and her sisters how to fight in the happenstance of someone trying to attack or kidnap them, but he'd never told her what to do if she actually *was* kidnapped. He'd only said they should stay alive and wait for him to rescue them. Most likely anyone who captured them would want a ransom and would not seriously harm them. But these men had already struck her.

Had they taken Anna too? Kirstyn tried to remember where Anna had been just before the men abducted her. There were two of them. Hopefully Anna was able to escape and tell Kirstyn's father that she had been taken. Or if she'd not seen the two men, she could at least tell her father where she had last seen Kirstyn.

She prayed for a quick deliverance and pushed back against her terror and panic. God would help her father find her and all would be well. Her father would never let anyone get away with harming her.

But as the cart rattled on and on, despair hung over her like a dark thundercloud, threatening to descend as she waited and waited but heard no voices. The only sounds were horses' bridles, the creak of the cart, and the clopping of horse hooves.

She faded in and out of consciousness a few times, probably because of the blow to her head and the exhaustion of terror. She tried moving around to see if she could get someone's attention, but she was wedged in between something so she could move no more than an inch or two to each side. She was also covered with a blanket, which must have kept her hidden.

Finally the cart came to a halt. She felt the covering being lifted from her body, then she was pulled slowly until someone's fingers untied the rag around her eyes and tugged it off.

Kirstyn blinked but could see nothing. It must be night. A candle came into view, along with three figures surrounding her.

Kirstyn wanted to demand they tell her where she was, but the binding around her mouth prevented her from speaking. Perhaps she should negotiate with them instead, if she was ever given the opportunity, should tell them her father would pay their ransom if they would return her to Hagenheim.

She did her best to focus on the three figures, but she could only see the man holding the candle, and he did not look familiar.

"We'll stand you up," one man said, "and you will walk. There is no use trying to get away, you should know. No one is nearby. We're in the middle of the forest."

They slid her body the rest of the way down the cart, pulled her up to a sitting position, and her feet touched the ground. The man took her arm and walked her around the side of the cart.

Two men came into focus. She tried to memorize their faces so she could describe them to her father. The two brown-haired men seemed rather nondescript, but the larger one had a crooked nose and the smaller one had a long red scar, rather fresh looking, on his forehead.

"If you do what we say," said the smaller one, a cold, hard expression on his face, "we won't hurt you. Cooperate and you can go home."

Kirstyn tried to think. Perhaps they were telling her the truth, and perhaps not, but what good would it do to try to fight them? She had no weapon. She would have to watch for a chance to escape.

They entered a small structure of some sort. It was so dark.

The smaller man pulled the gag around her mouth down to her neck, then untied it.

"What do you want?" she asked, her voice croaking because her throat was so dry.

"We have written a letter to your father. If he fills this box with gold and silver coins, we will let you go home. But you must write something at the bottom letting him know you are alive. It must be in your handwriting."

"Very well."

The smaller man left and returned with a stool. He set it down a couple of feet from her, while the larger man worked at cutting the rope around her wrists. When her bonds fell off, she rubbed her wrists, tears pricking her eyes at the indignities these evil men had inflicted on her.

"Here is the paper." The leader took a rolled-up piece of

paper and a small bottle of ink from his pocket. Then he handed her a flat wooden board. "Sit down, Lady Kirstyn."

Slowly she moved to the stool and sat down. She accepted the paper on the piece of wood, then the quill he dipped in ink.

"Down at the bottom of the paper." He told her what to write.

A chill snaked over her shoulders. She took the pen and wrote, *Father, I am well, but these men will kill me if you do not pay them what they ask. Your loving daughter, Kirstyn.*

She handed the pen and paper back to the man. He held the candle close to the paper, examining it, then a smile spread over his face. "Very good."

"What will you do with me?" Kirstyn stood.

The smaller man tied a new rope around her wrists and then tied the other end to a large beam in the middle of the room.

"You will stay here. We will deliver the letter to Hagenheim Castle. Now you have only to pray that your father will give us what we ask. If all goes well, we won't kill you."

What if all did not go well? Icicles stabbed her stomach. What would happen to her poor mother? She'd be devastated, struck down with grief. She did not deserve that. And her father would be crushed if anything happened to her. She could not bear to think of their anguish and pain.

The two men closed the door, leaving her in darkness, and yet she was fairly certain the third person was there, somewhere in the dark.

"Is someone here?" Kirstyn asked.

No one spoke for a moment, then a woman said, "Lie down. There are some blankets on the floor beside you. No more talking."

Kirstyn pulled on the rope around her wrists. It was fastened tightly, giving her just enough length so when she sat on the floor, her hand could touch the dirt beneath her.

Darkness closed in on her like an oppressive cloud. Which way was the door? She wouldn't be able to reach it anyway. Her foot bumped into something hard. It was the stool she had sat on earlier. From the stool she tried to discern where the door would be. She felt the blankets on the floor and lay down on them.

Why wasn't she crying? This was the worst thing that had ever happened to her, the most terrifying and dangerous, even worse than when Lord Claybrook had tried to take over Hagenheim Castle two years ago. At least then she had been with her mother and siblings. Her mother had kept them all thinking hopefully, praying and believing that everything would turn out well. But now that Kirstyn was completely alone . . . she was too terrified to pray. And too overwhelmed to cry.

There were probably no windows in this tiny structure, though she had not thought to look for one when she'd had the light of the villains' candle. Would her father give the men the treasure they wanted? And then would the men let her go home?

Surely they only wanted the gold and silver. They had no reason to hurt her or keep her. She would be freed tomorrow. So she only had to be strong and wait for a while longer. She could do that.

Feeling more hopeful, she prayed silently until she fell asleep.

CHAPTER ELEVEN

Kirstyn awoke again for the fiftieth time. Surely it couldn't still be nighttime. But as she lay on the uncomfortable makeshift bed, which seemed to grow harder and harder the longer she lay on it, a crack of light became visible near her.

She guessed it was morning. Perhaps she would have to wait only a little while. But she was so thirsty.

"Please? May I have some water?" Was the woman she had heard earlier still there? Kirstyn looked all around for her, but it was still too dark to make out anything more than shapes. Finally, over in the corner, a lump on the floor moved. Then it was still again.

"Can you hear me? I'm desperately thirsty. Can you give me some water?"

"There is water on the floor beside you," the voice said. Was it her imagination, or had she heard that voice before? She'd been too upset to notice last night.

Kirstyn finally found the small copper cup and a bread roll on the floor next to her. She reached over and picked up the cup and sniffed it, then took a sip. It tasted like water, so she drank it all.

The person in the corner still had her back to Kirstyn and wasn't moving. Kirstyn said, "May I have some more water, please?"

"No."

Kirstyn clenched her teeth, thinking of all the things she might say. Wasn't it enough they had hit her and seized her and tied her up? Would they refuse her a second cup of water too? Cruel, evil, hateful . . .

"I'm not allowed to let you go outside to relieve yourself, so it's best if you don't drink too much."

The panic rose inside her again. "When will those men be back?"

"Soon."

Kirstyn picked up the bread roll and broke it in half. It was stale, just like the water, but she ate it anyway. Perhaps it would quell the queasiness in her stomach.

What would everyone say when she was finally back home? Her brothers would not tease her anymore. She hoped Steffan and Wolfgang were in the chapel right now praying for her and repenting for every trick they had played on her and every time they ever teased. Mother would be overjoyed and would cry tears of joy. Father would have tears in his eyes too and hug her for a very long time.

And Aladdin . . . It seemed too hard that she would have to write to him about her ordeal. Would he return home, just to see her, when he discovered she'd been taken and mistreated and held for ransom? Did he care about her that much?

It must have been two or three hours later, the sun coming through the cracks in the walls and the ceiling, when the woman finally roused herself and sat up. Her brown hair flowed down her back, but Kirstyn still couldn't see her face.

Just then the door opened and she was suddenly face-to-face with one of her captors, the smaller one with the scar on his forehead. He was not much taller than she was, with a thin frame and face. His eyes were rather bloodshot and hollow, reminding her of the men who sat outside the brewery day after day. Her brother had told her they were men who got drunk instead of working.

"Did you get your ransom? Will you let me go now?" Kirstyn tamped down her anger and tried to look and sound humble and cooperative.

The leader's expression was sullen, but then he smirked. "It doesn't work that quickly. I left my partner in Hagenheim to await the delivery of the ransom. I'm going to sleep."

"Can I go outside to relieve myself now?"

He looked askance at her. Then he turned toward the woman in the corner. "Take her out," he ordered.

The woman turned around and Kirstyn gasped. "Anna! What are you doing here?" A sick feeling invaded her stomach.

Anna looked a bit sheepish for a moment, but her expression quickly changed to a smug smile as she crossed the room to press herself to the man's side.

"I'm with Michael."

So the smaller man's name was Michael. He stepped forward, put his arm around Anna, and kissed her cheek. Anna's smile grew even bigger.

Kirstyn went numb. The pain inside might overwhelm her if she let herself think about it, but she couldn't help asking, "You helped them kidnap me?"

"Michael said it was my chance to never have to serve anyone for the rest of my life. Besides, I would do anything for Michael. He's the first person who ever cared about me."

"I cared about you. My mother cared about you. And she trusted you." Kirstyn lost the ability to speak as she thought of how much pain her mother must be in, and how Anna had caused it by betraying them.

Michael laughed and Anna followed suit. He disentangled his arms from Anna. "Go on and take her out. I'll be standing in the doorway in case she tries to run." He untied the end of Kirstyn's rope that was tied to the support beam, then fastened it to Anna's wrist.

Anna let out a cry of dismay.

Michael laughed. "She's not strong enough to drag you away with her. Now get on with it."

They hurried outside. There were plenty of bushes and trees, and soon after, they were back inside the house. Michael untied Anna and tied Kirstyn back to the pole. Then Michael lay down and went to sleep.

Should Kirstyn try to convince Anna to help her escape? She wasn't sure she could be calm, she was still so angry. Besides that, she didn't want Michael to hear her. So she sat down and leaned against the wooden beam.

It's all right. Just a little more time. Maybe one extra day. I can wait. But tears stung her eyes and her lips trembled.

She sucked in a deep breath. She could not afford to let despair close in on her along with the darkness of this room.

Anna went outside and came back in carrying a bucket of water and a loaf of bread. She poured Kirstyn some more to drink and handed her a chunk of bread.

Forcing back the tears, Kirstyn ate a few bites of bread, which was fresh and tasted like home and sunshine. *I will not despair. And I will do my best to escape so I will have no regrets.*

"What is happening?" Kirstyn opened her eyes. A candle hovered over her. Cold fingers bit into her arm and yanked her up.

"Get up." Michael's hard face was only visible for a moment before someone took his candle. He put something over her eyes and tied it tightly behind her head. Next he bound her hands together at the wrists, but in the front this time.

"Are you taking me to my father?" Kirstyn's stomach churned as her heart beat hard and fast.

The next thing she knew, someone shoved a cloth in her mouth and tied it behind her neck.

Feelings of helplessness, anger, and fear overwhelmed her. Would she smother? She could still breathe out of her nose, but her heart was pounding, making her breath come so fast, she feared she would faint.

Tears again stung her eyes, but she concentrated on breathing in and out. *Jesus.* She brought to mind the ancient crucifix she'd seen a thousand times in the chapel inside Hagenheim Castle. She focused her mind on that image, on all the thoughts and feelings she'd ever had while praying and meditating on Jesus' sacrifice for her, on His suffering and His love.

Her breathing slowed and her heart stopped pounding. She was pulled forward by her bound hands, and as she walked, an overwhelming sense of peace replaced the panic and darkness.

"Watch your step," Anna said as she held Kirstyn's arm. Even though she was still furious with Anna, it was somewhat comforting to know a woman was beside her. Meanwhile, the feeling of peace kept her moving as her feet found the steps and went up, as if it were not frightening to be led, blindfolded and gagged, by the people who had kidnapped her.

Thank You, God, for this peace.

"You have to get into a cart now," Anna said.

Someone picked her up by her waist and placed her on a hard, flat surface.

"Lie down," Michael said.

Kirstyn lay on her side and brought her knees up, then felt herself being covered by a heavy tarp. She held up her hands to make sure the cloth did not cling to her face so there would be a pocket of air around her nose.

Still, the sense of peace persisted.

The cart jolted forward. She was aware of the cool night air, but she was warm enough underneath the covering.

She got the impression it was nighttime by the way the air had felt just before they placed her in the cart. As the cart lumbered along, she soon fell asleep.

Aladdin and Abu walked through town to the marketplace. Spring was turning to summer as the weather became warm. Aladdin purchased two rolled wafers from an old woman, one for Abu and one for himself, filled with sour cream and sugared currants, preserved raspberries, and cherries.

Abu ate the entire rolled wafer before Aladdin was half finished with his. "May I have another?"

Aladdin laughed, walked back, and bought him another one.

"Tell me again how you got that scar on your leg," Abu said between bites.

"You don't want to hear that story again, do you?" Aladdin couldn't help smiling at Abu's fascination with the violent incident. He didn't tell Abu that his leg still occasionally pained him.

"Just once more." Abu's mouth was ringed with red fruit stains.

Aladdin glanced up and noticed a large bird soaring overhead. Then Abu saw it too and pointed. "What kind of bird is that?"

Aladdin's stomach flipped. "It's a white stork." Exactly like the one he and Kirstyn used to watch. Once he had promised he would think of her every time he saw one. That was an easy promise to keep—impossible to break, even.

"It's the biggest bird I've ever seen." Abu followed it with his eyes as it continued to soar out of sight.

Foreboding stirred inside Aladdin's chest. It was as if the stork was a sign for him to pray for Kirstyn.

He prayed for Kirstyn every day, and it didn't take a stork to remind him.

But it was foolish to think something was wrong. Her father loved her, and he was the powerful Duke of Hagenheim. He would never allow any harm to befall her.

Still, Aladdin said a quick prayer for her under his breath and headed toward Nikolaikirche.

"Abu, you don't mind if we go inside the church and say a few prayers, do you?"

Abu shook his head.

Aladdin would let Abu light some candles, and then he would teach him a bit about prayer. Aladdin could pray for Kirstyn, and then surely this feeling of dread would go away.

CHAPTER TWELVE

Kirstyn was running. A dark figure was chasing her through an empty building. She ran up the stairs and could hear footsteps pounding up after her. Fear gripped her throat, making it hard to breathe. She went to a window, stepped onto the ledge, and looked down. It was a very long way, but Aladdin was on the ground looking up. He held out his arms and smiled.

"Jump! I'll catch you."

The person behind her yelled and she jumped.

She fell, but very slowly, and Aladdin seemed to get farther away instead of closer. Her body began to drift, floating forward instead of down, and soon she drifted over some treetops, obscuring Aladdin from view.

She used her arms and legs to try to change direction, to "swim" back to where Aladdin was still calling her, but to no avail. Her arms and legs were so heavy, and no amount of effort made any difference. She was sailing farther and farther away from the safety of her precious friend.

Her whole body shook with a violent jolt, and she opened her eyes. She was in the cart and had been dreaming.

Someone jerked the tarp from her body. "Get out, *Mädchen*."

Would he now pretend not to know her name? Would he call her "girl" to try to make her feel unimportant, as if she were not worthy of a name? Heat rose inside her, but a rush of cold quickly replaced it. Had he decided not to take her home?

She sat up, her hands still bound, eyes still blindfolded, and mouth still gagged. She scooted to the end of the short cart and someone helped her stand, then touched the back of her head. The blindfold came off, then the gag. She lifted her bound hands to rub her face.

Trees were thick around them, making it dark, but she was certain the sun was up. How far from Hagenheim had they traveled?

Michael and Anna were unloading bundles from the cart. Should Kirstyn try to run for help? But they seemed to be in the middle of the forest again. They must have stopped here because the cart could go no farther on the narrow path.

Michael unhitched the horse from the cart. Then he came back. "Get up the trail. There's an old house in the woods where we will stay while I decide what to do."

Anna took Kirstyn by the elbow and started toward the dirt trail that led into the thickest part of the trees. Kirstyn's blood boiled at the girl's touch. How could Anna do this? How could she have given herself to this criminal? Kirstyn jerked her arm out of Anna's grasp and kept walking, her eyes focused ahead of her.

Somehow she would get away from them. She would wait for them both to fall asleep and then she'd run. She'd find this path and follow it back to the road. And if possible, she would steal their horse and ride it home to Hagenheim. It shouldn't be too hard to find her way, should it? And if she was unsure of the direction, she would simply ask someone, whomever she encountered on the road. She might even tell them she was Duke Wilhelm's daughter, if they seemed trustworthy, and they'd no doubt take her straight to Hagenheim.

God would be with her. Wasn't God always with the righteous?

They reached the house, which was quite dilapidated, with even bigger cracks in the wattle-and-daub walls than in the last house. When her two kidnappers came inside, they all sat around a fire and ate some cold meat and cheese and bread. It was the only food she'd had besides the bread she'd been given the day before, in the two days—or was it three?—since Michael and the other man had taken her.

Michael and Anna talked a bit with each other, ignoring Kirstyn. But Michael had barely spoken, sometimes answering Anna with only a grunt, his brows drawn together. She flitted around him like a moth to a candle flame, as though trying to change his foul mood. Something about his plans must have gone wrong.

"Where is the other man?" Kirstyn asked. "The larger one who was with you before?"

Michael glared at her while Anna stared with wide eyes, her mouth hanging open. Michael's eyes were red rimmed and a bit crazed. After glaring at her for several moments, he snatched up a knife from the dirt floor beside him and pointed it at Kirstyn.

"She doesn't know any better, Michael," was Anna's feeble attempt to deflect his anger.

He shook the knife at Kirstyn. "You have no right to speak here. You are not a duke's daughter. Here you are nothing. Understand?"

Kirstyn stared back at him, unflinching, as that now-familiar sense of peace came over her. "I understand that you have kidnapped me for ransom, have wrongfully taken me from my family, and can now murder me if you like."

"I did not take you only for the ransom." His voice was cold. "Imagine my surprise when someone told me that my father had given my share of the family business to an outsider—a Saracen named Aladdin."

At the mention of Aladdin's name, Kirstyn straightened, her breath quickening.

"This usurper has insinuated himself into my gullible father's affections. Not only that, but my father even hopes to give him Grethel in marriage. This little orphan thinks he can take everything that is rightfully mine."

What did he mean that his father hoped to give Grethel to Aladdin in marriage? Was this Aladdin's intention? Who was Grethel?

"But Anna and other people I spoke to in Hagenheim said that Aladdin was in love with you." He pointed his knife at her again. "If I hurt you, I can hurt him. I can use you to force him to give up his share of my father's business, to give up everything he's worked for to set you free." He sneered. "I never planned to give you back to your father."

She had been kidnapped because this man wanted to hurt Aladdin?

"What will you do, then?"

He studied the knife, ignoring her. "Perhaps I will kill you and throw your body at the Saracen's feet, then plunge my blade into his heart."

Kirstyn's stomach roiled. Poor Aladdin!

Michael laughed, an ugly sound. Anna looked frightened until Michael sat back and put down the knife.

Kirstyn glared at him. *Aladdin would never let you hurt him. He's far too clever to allow that. And I will fight you with every bit of life in me before I let you harm either me or Aladdin.*

Anna started rubbing Michael's shoulders. "You didn't sleep at all last night. You should sleep now and I will make sure she doesn't escape."

His eyes became even darker. He turned and shoved Anna so hard she fell back on her elbow, her head nearly hitting the floor.

"You don't tell me what to do!" He leaned over Anna, his finger in her face. "I'm sick of you telling me what to do. I tell you what to do and you do it, do you understand?"

"Yes, Michael." Anna shrank away from him, her shoulders and head bowed. "I'm sorry."

He made a scornful sound in the back of his throat and turned away from her. He stalked to the bag he had brought inside and took out a piece of rope. Then he came toward Kirstyn. Without looking her in the eye, he took her arm and tied the new piece of rope to the rope that bound her wrists. Then he tied the other end to a large timber supporting the roof.

Without a word he stalked through a doorway at the back, presumably to another room in the small house.

Kirstyn's heart was still beating extra fast after the fit of rage she had witnessed. Anna sat on the floor, her arms wrapped around herself, as she stared at the doorway where Michael had disappeared.

"Where has he gone?" Kirstyn whispered.

Anna's expression was sullen. She did not look at Kirstyn. "To sleep."

Kirstyn eyed the knife on the floor where Michael had left it. Then she checked the rope that tethered her. It was not long enough, only about two feet long. The knife must be at least six feet away.

She couldn't bear the thought that this man wanted to use her to hurt Aladdin. She wouldn't let him do it. Might she be able to pull the timber up out of the ground? Or maybe she would not have to. Maybe Anna would help her and they could escape together.

"He is a frightening man," Kirstyn whispered. "A very bad temper. Does he beat you?" She had heard of such relationships before.

"He is only upset just now. His partner stole the money your father paid for your ransom. But he would not wish for me to talk to you."

"Anna, please. You don't have to be with someone like him. If you help me escape, I promise you won't be punished. Come back with me to Hagenheim. This man will only hurt you."

Anna narrowed her eyes at Kirstyn and pierced her with a steely glare. "You, with your perfect life and perfect family, the daughter of a duke." Anna's voice was raspy and quiet. "You have nothing to offer me. Michael is the only person who has ever loved me. He may not be as perfect as everyone you know, not like your father and your brothers and your perfect Aladdin. But I know Michael will take care of me, and he's the man I want. I love him. You don't understand him as I do."

Kirstyn's thoughts were spinning. What sort of madness was this?

"No, I don't understand. I don't understand anything except that I have been attacked and taken against my will, held for ransom by this man." How could Anna claim to love such a vile person? Kirstyn had always thought Anna a sweet girl. Her mother had hired her to serve at the castle even though she rarely hired anyone that young, but she had done it because Anna's pleas had softened her.

Anna turned away.

Surely if Kirstyn kept talking to her, Anna would see the truth of her situation. Surely she couldn't be so heartless as not to help her. But Kirstyn's words would have to be wise.

Aladdin found Herr Kaufmann looking over the ledgers when he stepped into the warehouse office.

"Aladdin!" Herr Kaufmann's smile was wider than usual. "Come and sit with me."

Aladdin sat, his mind running to the tasks he had planned for the rest of the day. But he focused on Herr Kaufmann's pleasant face—his rosy cheeks, broad forehead, large nose, and long chin. A little wrinkled from his sixty years of life, but it was one of the dearest faces he had ever known.

"Aladdin, my son." He leaned closer, looking intently into Aladdin's eyes. "Since you have been working with me, profits have doubled. The salt pans you encouraged me to purchase will bring in great wealth for the rest of our lives, and with very little effort of our own. We have added ships and workers, yet still our profits rise. The men all love you, and I happen to know the women who run our stalls and shops all plot to have you marry their daughters. You don't cheat anyone. Your integrity is well known."

Aladdin shifted uncomfortably.

"My point is that you are set to be the wealthiest man in Lüneburg when I am gone. How many orphans can say that? But you do not look pleased. Is something wrong?"

"I am quite pleased. It's everything I dreamed and hoped for, but it is not only due to my efforts. You are the reason for my standing, and I do not enjoy hearing you speak of when you'll be gone."

Herr Kaufmann patted his arm. "So kind of you to say that, and I trust your sincerity." He sat up straighter. "That is all. I wanted to make certain you understand that you have made your fortune. Your future is secure. Now that it's summer and the weather is warm, I thought you might wish to start planning your trip to Hagenheim to ask a certain duke if you might marry his daughter."

Aladdin's heart quickened and he cleared his throat. "What makes you say such a thing?"

"Come now. After the way I have heard you speak of Lady Kirstyn? It is clear you think very highly of her. You've said you were dear friends, and you write to her more often than to anyone else."

The thought of going to Duke Wilhelm and declaring that he loved Kirstyn and wished to bring her back to Lüneburg with him made him lose his breath. But he did love her, and it would feel wonderful to be able to admit it.

Was his impossible dream of marrying Kirstyn actually possible now?

However . . . his last two letters to Kirstyn had gone unanswered. She might have forgotten him, or perhaps she was planning to marry someone else. He swallowed past the lump in his throat.

"Perhaps I will consider it," he said. "Thank you . . . for everything."

Herr Kaufmann's smile was gentle. "Live your life and be glad, my boy."

Two days later Aladdin had made a list of what he would take with him on his journey to Hagenheim. Already he had arranged which servants and guards to take with him. He had to go and see her for himself, to see if she had forgotten him. And perhaps, if she seemed as favorable to him as she had on the day he had left . . . he would ask her to marry him. He would pledge his love to her, and if she said yes, he would without a doubt be the happiest man in the Holy Roman Empire.

These were the kind of thoughts that raced through his mind on his long walks in the evenings. His mind couldn't seem to rest. To think that Kirstyn might love him, might actually marry him, and that they might start a family together. It was almost too much. But then his mind would go to the possibility that she did not love him and would not be pleased to hear his proposal of marriage. So he walked.

The next day he and Herr Kaufmann were on their way home for the midday meal when someone called their names. They both looked ahead and saw Herr Kaufmann's servant Otto running toward them. He stopped and spoke between breaths.

"Master Kaufmann. Aladdin. Duke Wilhelm is come. He wishes to speak with Aladdin."

"Duke Wilhelm? Here in Lüneburg?" Herr Kaufmann stared with his brows raised.

"Yes. He was at the house when I left just now."

No one spoke for a moment. Finally Herr Kaufmann said, "Let us go and see what he wants with you."

Aladdin outstripped Herr Kaufmann's slow pace as he nearly ran all the way. Sir Sigmund and Sir Conrad stood outside the front door, and they nodded to Aladdin. But the grim expressions on the knights' faces kept Aladdin from returning their greeting. His heart thudded in his ears as he went inside.

Duke Wilhelm stood in the middle of the room. He strode toward Aladdin and embraced him. He remained with his arms around Aladdin for a length of time that could only mean that he was fighting emotion. When he let go and stepped back, tears were swimming in his eyes.

Aladdin's stomach sank to his toes while blood drained from his head, making him dizzy. "What has happened? Not Kirstyn."

Duke Wilhelm's lips parted, and his whole body looked weighed down. But he reached out and took hold of Aladdin's shoulder. "She was kidnapped."

"Wh-when?" His breath shallowed.

"Two and a half months ago."

How could this have happened? How could he have not felt in his spirit that she was in danger? Then he remembered the day he'd seen the stork and had gone into the church to pray.

"How?" He became aware that both he and Duke Wilhelm were sitting, facing each other. The duke had not shaved for some time. His head and shoulders were stooped, as if he had grown old in the ten months since Aladdin had seen him.

"We believe one of our servants, a young girl from the orphan-age named Anna, was helping the kidnappers. There were two of them. They . . . they snatched her from the Marktplatz during the May Day celebration."

Pain twisted like a knife in Aladdin's chest.

"I received a ransom note. My men and I brought the ransom as instructed, but only one of the kidnappers, a man named Rutgher, was at the meeting place. He did not bring Kirstyn with him. He took the money and ran. We tracked him for several weeks, but he never led us to Kirstyn. We captured him, and he is now in the dungeon at Hagenheim Castle. We think Rutgher tricked his partner, a man named Michael. He took all the money for himself, and when Michael realized it, he took Kirstyn, and . . . no one knows where they have gone. We have been looking for her, but . . ." He shook his head.

The pain never left Aladdin's chest, but gradually his thinking became clear.

Kirstyn was in danger.

"What can I do? Surely I can help you find her. There must be some way to track them."

"Only a few days after she was taken, we found her scarf in an abandoned house in the woods, and there was blood on it. We think . . . we think he may have killed her." His voice was raspy.

"But you don't know that. You don't know. Perhaps . . . perhaps it was someone else, someone else's blood." She couldn't be dead. He would have felt it in his spirit if she had died. "She is not dead. You must keep looking."

"We have searched every place we know of. We have turned up no other sign of her. No one has seen her. It's as if she disappeared—she and Anna and the kidnapper. But Rutgher recently revealed that Michael was born in Lüneburg. We thought perhaps he had come here."

"I shall organize a search." Aladdin stood up, blood surging through his limbs. "If she is in Lüneburg, I shall find her."

Hope seemed to bloom in Duke Wilhelm's expression. "You know a lot of people in Lüneburg, then?"

"Herr Kaufmann and I know nearly everyone in town. And those we do not know shall help us as well."

"My knights and I shall follow your lead."

Aladdin and Herr Kaufmann spread the word among their guards that they were searching for a man of rather short stature named Michael, with a scar on his forehead and in the company of two women. They gave a description of both Anna and Kirstyn and offered a substantial reward to whomever might find them.

Aladdin organized the search, assigning men to every section of town. He even instructed them to offer bribes for any information that would lead them to Kirstyn. When the men began coming in with various leads, he sent them off to whatever town or village the information might guide them to. And he himself listened to every lead that came in, often staying up very late at night and rising very early.

After a few weeks, Aladdin gazed down at his ledger while Duke Wilhelm sat wearily on a bench in the dining hall.

"There are still a few men who have not reported in," Aladdin said. "The two guards who went to Hamburg returned last night to report that the Michael there is not the right one. But the knight we sent to Osnabruck has not had time to return, and we're still waiting to hear from the knights we sent to Bremen and Braunschweig."

Duke Wilhelm rubbed his hand over his eyes and down his cheek. "I don't want to stop looking." His voice was gruff. "But we have looked and looked and . . . we're running out of leads. I don't know where else we could search . . . what else to do."

O God, please help us. When her father, the powerful Duke of Hagenheim, could not find her, what hope was there? And yet something inside him just did not believe she could be dead. His heart could still feel her.

CHAPTER THIRTEEN

Kirstyn put one foot in front of the other, her mind numb and her body sore. They'd been walking in the dark for hours.

It had been weeks, she wasn't sure how many, since she had been taken from the Marktplatz in Hagenheim. When they traveled at night, Kirstyn was allowed to walk. When they traveled in the daytime, she was forced to lie under the tarp in the horse-drawn cart. And every minute Kirstyn was searching for a way to escape. She had tried many times, but Michael always hauled her back before she could get far enough away to hide, before she could find someone to help her.

Finally, when dawn was breaking, Michael found a place in the woods for them to stop. They forced Kirstyn to help them drag their pallet from the cart to a sheltered spot among the trees. Then Michael tossed Kirstyn two thin, torn, moth-eaten blankets—one to lie on and one to keep her warm. He took the rope tied to her wrist and tied the other end to the cart.

Exhausted as she was, Kirstyn lay awake, waiting for Michael and Anna to fall asleep. The rope around her wrist had become loose over the last two days. She held her hand with the fingers compressed, her thumb against her palm, and worked at the rope.

Her wrist was nearly always bloody, having to endure the almost-constant pull of the rope. Now it was a series of scars and scabs. As she pushed the rope over her hand, she dislodged a scab, causing a dribble of blood on her arm. She smeared the blood over the skin on the back of her hand to help the rope slide. After a few more moments, the rope slipped off.

Kirstyn lay still, listening. Were Michael and Anna asleep? She couldn't see their faces from where she was lying, and she didn't hear anything. *God, please let them be asleep.*

Kirstyn stood and crept around the cart, trying to make as little noise as possible as she stepped on the dried leaves and sticks on the ground. She kept the cart between her and her captors and hurried toward the road they had just left.

The sun was nearly up, spreading its light on the world and leading her toward the opening ahead. When she emerged from the trees, she ran on the hard-packed, rutted road. All she had to do was find people who would help her.

Soon her steps slowed as her breathing grew labored. She was too tired to run very far.

She must have been walking for at least an hour, weary but buoyed by the hope that she was finally free. She couldn't let herself think about her mother and father, who must be searching and worried. Nor could she let herself dwell on Aladdin or wonder if she'd ever see him again. Did he think about her as much as she thought about him? His face was embedded in her memory, but it had grown fuzzy over the past year since she'd said good-bye to him.

No, she couldn't think of Aladdin now. She had to focus on finding safety and shelter. Perhaps there was a village just ahead.

A horse's hooves sounded on the road behind her. Surely this was someone who would help her. Someone with a horse riding that quickly must be either a knight—possibly even one of her father's knights!—or someone who lived nearby who would take her in, hide her, and help her get back to Hagenheim.

She moved to the side of the road as the rider came into view.

No. Her heart sank. Michael.

She jumped from the road and fled into the trees. The horse crashed through the brush behind her, getting closer. She doubled back, darting between trees and under limbs. Her only hope was if someone were to come along the road now, at this moment.

She ran back onto the road just as Michael reached her. He leapt from the horse's back and yanked her arm, and she fell back, her hip striking the ground so hard it jarred her teeth together. She jumped to her feet, but Michael held on and jerked her into his bony chest.

She screamed, squeezing her eyes closed. Michael clamped his hand over her mouth. She found herself staring into his beady black eyes.

"If you don't shut up, I'll smother you right now, sell your hair and clothes, and leave you to rot."

He took the horse's bridle in one hand, grabbed a handful of Kirstyn's hair in his other hand, and led them both off the road into the trees.

As they walked back, Kirstyn heard someone coming on the road. She opened her mouth and cried, "Hel—"

Michael clamped his hand over her mouth until the person had passed, all the while cursing and threatening her under his breath.

By the time they had gotten back to where the cart and

Anna were in the woods, Kirstyn's neck was hurting from all the times Michael had yanked her hair.

Anna rose from her pallet and approached them. Her eye was blackened and the abrasion on her cheekbone red. Michael must have punished Anna for Kirstyn's escape.

Anna shot a sullen glance at Michael, then Kirstyn, before saying, "So you beat me but not her? She's the one who ran away, not me. What kind of love is this? You're a liar."

He closed the distance between himself and Anna, dragging Kirstyn behind him. "So I'm a liar? Nothing is ever good enough for you, is it? You ungrateful little . . . All you do is complain. Who else is going to put up with you? Without me you have nothing and nobody. If I have to listen to your griping and accusations for one more day . . . You *deserve* to be beaten." He raised his hand and Anna flinched, jerking away from him.

"I hate you," she rasped. "I was better off at the orphanage. I'm leaving." As she picked up her clothing and stuffed it into a cloth bag, she started sobbing. But she kept stuffing things in the bag.

Michael stood and watched her. Then he stepped toward her and put a hand on her shoulder. "Wait."

Anna stopped but kept her back to him. She continued to sob but more softly now. He came around in front of Anna, still holding Kirstyn's arm.

"You know I can't hit her. I'm hoping to get a lot of money for her, and I won't get as much if I beat her like she deserves. Don't leave me, Anna. I need you. After what Rutgher did to me, stabbing me in the back and taking all the ransom money . . . I'd planned to use that ransom to take care of you. What will I do without you? Nobody understands me the way you do." He caressed the back of her neck.

Kirstyn's stomach roiled to watch for the third time the same scene acted out. Anna was softening, starting to turn toward him as she let the bag slip from her hand.

"Don't be a fool, Anna," Kirstyn said. "Get away from him. You know he will only strike you again."

"Shut up!" Michael turned on Kirstyn, reminding her of a wild boar she had once seen running through the streets of Hagenheim.

Kirstyn met him stare for stare but said no more.

Anna's face was red, and tear tracks stained her face. She sniffed and her sad, pleading expression turned once again to sullenness. "You promise not to hit me again?"

He smiled and shrugged. "You know I only hit you when you complain and make me mad. But you're my *liebling*. I've loved you since the first time I saw you."

"Don't listen to him, Anna. You can find a better life than this. He doesn't treat you well, and he's lying when he says—"

Kirstyn saw the fist coming, but she couldn't raise her hands in time. Pain exploded in her face, and the back of her head slammed into the ground.

Her vision went dark except for a few points of light, which gradually faded to Anna's face, hovering a foot above her. Anna looked at her for a moment, then stood and faced Michael. "You could have killed her."

"It's her fault," Michael said in a high-pitched voice. "She wouldn't keep quiet. I can't think when stupid women won't shut up."

They moved away from Kirstyn, Michael with his hands on Anna's back and neck. He talked so quietly Kirstyn couldn't make out what he was saying. Her teeth ached where Michael had struck her, and she tasted blood from her torn lip.

Michael hunched over to look into Anna's eyes, holding his palm up to her, obviously trying to gain her compliance. Anna was crying again, and then Michael caressed her cheek. She set her hand over his, and then they were kissing.

Kirstyn closed her eyes to block out the disheartening sight. She lifted her head, thinking now would be a good time to try to get away again, but when she sat up, the ground started spinning and she felt as if she was about to vomit.

She closed her eyes and imagined her mother holding her, her arms warm around her. If only she *could* feel Mother's arms. Hear Mother's voice, her wise advice. She had once told Kirstyn, *"We can depend on the assurance that God cares about us and is always with us."*

She could usually feel God's peace, but today that peace was less tangible. So she cried a few tears of her own and fell asleep.

Herr Kaufmann insisted Duke Wilhelm and his knights stay at his house during the search. Aladdin continued to direct the search, but after two weeks, Herr Kaufmann invited him into his library and shut the door.

"Aladdin, my boy, sit down." He motioned him to a chair and they sat facing each other.

"I understand why you want to help Duke Wilhelm and why you are so set on finding Lady Kirstyn, but . . ." His gaze lowered to the floor. He sighed and shook his head. "It doesn't seem as if all this searching and striving is accomplishing anything. Lady Kirstyn is still missing and . . . well, I hate to say it, Aladdin—you know I feel great compassion for Duke Wilhelm's pain at losing his daughter and you losing your friend whom you loved—but you have not done your job for two weeks, and the business is suffering.

"You weren't there to set the prices for the new shipment of goods, and some expensive silks were sold for less than what I paid for them. We lost a lot of money there. Everyone has grown accustomed to taking direction from you, and now everything has been thrown into confusion. You wouldn't think they would have forgotten everything in the past year since you've been here, but they have, it seems. I sent a message to Schwartz and Hartmann that they should wait and ask you how much resin the Lithuanians had purchased, but the message was delayed, and . . ." He lifted his hands and expelled a breath. "More money lost."

"I am sorry, Herr Kaufmann, I truly am, but I cannot stop looking for Kirstyn. She is alive and being held against her will. I cannot stop searching."

Would Herr Kaufmann understand? Or would he throw him out, disowning him for putting Kirstyn above his business?

Herr Kaufmann sighed again, his shoulders slumping. He lifted his gaze to Aladdin's. "How do you know she's alive? She couldn't be anywhere near here or you would have found her. Perhaps it is time to accept that, if she is alive, you may have to wait for the news of her to reach you." He lowered his voice, his eyes drooping. "There may actually be nothing you can do to find her."

Aladdin's chest rose and fell more quickly as Herr Kaufmann's doubt crept into his heart. No, he wouldn't believe she was dead. She was alive, and he would not give up on her, even if he lost the makeshift family he had found.

"Even Abu accompanies Duke Wilhelm's men all over Lüneburg, searching for any sign of Kirstyn and her captors. You and I, who know practically everyone in town, have questioned more people than I can count. We've thoroughly investigated every possible sighting, as well as any unusual activity, but every bit of information, every hope, has proven false."

"That does not mean she isn't nearby. She and her captor could simply be well hidden."

But Herr Kaufmann's look was changing from pity to annoyance.

Aladdin couldn't stop believing she was alive. To do so was unthinkable. He loved her. Why else had he felt so raw and hollowed out when he left Hagenheim, when he had to leave Kirstyn standing there in the road? He'd always loved her, and if he hadn't been so determined to make his fortune, he might have realized he had everything he wanted in Hagenheim.

Herr Kaufmann left the room, and Aladdin suddenly was overwhelmed with the memory of Kirstyn's eleventh birthday, when her parents had set up her celebration dinner in the play yard of the orphanage. He was around thirteen years old, and he felt himself grow a head taller as Kirstyn turned her smile on him. He was still shorter and smaller than the other boys his age, but Kirstyn never looked at them the way she looked at him.

"What do you think of the subtlety, Aladdin?" Her eyes had focused on his face.

"I like it very much. It looks exactly like a rose."

They both turned to gaze at the giant confection in the middle of the table. It was surrounded by flowers and vines—decorations for Kirstyn's birthday feast—and all of her favorite foods.

"Your cook must be an artist. Does she sculpt other things?"

"Not that I know of."

"Will you keep the subtlety? Perhaps put it in your room?"

She laughed. "It would spoil. Besides, we will eat it when the children return from their game."

"Eat it?" It seemed wrong to eat something so beautiful.

"Of course. I shall cut off a small piece now so you can taste it." She slipped from her seat on the bench and picked up a long knife. She sliced off a piece of a petal the size of her little finger and handed it to him.

He broke the almond paste and gave half to her. She popped it into her mouth and chewed. "Mmm."

He bit off half of his piece. It was mildly sweet and tasted of almonds and vanilla.

"Do you like it?" She raised her brows hopefully.

"Very much."

"It's not as good as cake, but my family always eats it on holy days and birthdays." A wistful look came over her face, and she gazed past him into the open meadow where the children were playing. She turned and looked past the town wall, beyond which lay the forest and the edge of the Harz Mountains.

"Aladdin, have you ever seen the mountains?"

"Only the peak over there." He nodded at the only tree-covered peak visible from Hagenheim.

"Have you ever wanted to explore that forest?"

Had he? He'd been too busy trying to excel at all his studies, to impress his teachers and the master at the stable where he worked two hours a day with the older orphan boys. Too busy thinking of ways he might impress Lady Kirstyn and her father, the Duke of Hagenheim—too busy trying to forget he had ever been a poor orphan in a foreign land, stealing for Mustapha.

"I have always wanted to go there. Mother used to walk there a lot when she was my age. She grew up in those woods—her adoptive father was a woodcutter. And if she once walked there, why can't I?"

"Is it safe? Did your mother give you permission?"

Kirstyn frowned. "She said I could go sometime if my father went with me, but Father is always so busy." She turned toward him with an intense look, her blue eyes pleading and expectant. "Would you go with me, Aladdin?"

He blinked. She was still staring at him.

"Yes."

"Oh, thank you!"

Her face glowed like a sunbeam as she clasped her hands together. He was so fascinated by her expression he couldn't look away, even when the other children ran back to the table, herded by Frau Litzer, Lady Rose, and Duke Wilhelm himself.

"But don't tell anyone," she whispered, leaning close to him. "It will be our secret."

"When will we go?"

"Someday when the weather is warm. I shall come to you, when you're finished with your studies, and we shall sneak away."

Would she get in trouble? Would he be punished for shirking his duties at the stable? And if anyone discovered he'd been with the duke's daughter, doing something neither of them had permission to do . . .

But to see the joy on Kirstyn's face and know he had a part in it would be worth it. She made him feel as if she needed him—even though she had a large, loving family and he had no one. She had insisted on having her birthday feast with the orphans because she truly cared about making them feel loved. She had confessed to him that she wanted to adopt ten orphans because she couldn't bear to think of them alone and without anyone to love them, even though she often felt overlooked because of her more demanding siblings.

How he had needed her—then and now! He had been afraid to tell her that, too afraid of destroying the special bond they shared. They were the closest of friends, like brother and sister, and he needed that, needed her to be his family. But the older he got, the more he loved her as more than a friend, something more than a brother. And perhaps that was part of the reason he'd left. He was too afraid of her rejecting him as a husband—and of her father rejecting him as a suitor.

But oh, how he loved her. And as much as he needed her when they were children, he needed her even more now. And she needed him—to find her.

After a month of sending out guards and knights and continuing to question people, the information had all dried up and produced nothing.

"There's nothing left to do," Duke Wilhelm said, unable to look Aladdin in the eye.

An hour later Aladdin watched the duke and his knights ride away toward Lüneburg Heath, south of town on their way back to Hagenheim.

As Aladdin wandered through town, unable to concentrate on ledgers or numbers or the price of salt and silk and resin, the boulder inside his chest grew so heavy he could hardly catch his breath. Was Kirstyn out there somewhere, needing help? Or was the one person he loved more than anyone else gone forever? He remembered the look in Duke Wilhelm's eyes and the expressions on his knights' faces, and he knew that was exactly what they believed.

Somehow Aladdin made it to the Church of St. John. He stumbled inside and knelt to pray. He could not stop the tears as he poured out the deepest pleas of his heart.

"God," he whispered, "please let Duke Wilhelm find Kirstyn alive. No matter what has happened to her, it changes nothing, God, nothing in my heart or my mind. I will love her even more tenderly if she has been abused. O God in heaven, I vow to you that I . . ." His tears choked off his voice, so he continued to pray silently.

I will love her and treat her well all the days of my life, if only You will let her be alive and let us find her.

He prayed until all his words were spent, then finally went home, as exhausted as if he'd been running all day without stopping.

Aladdin watched the river below his bedchamber window, its slow-moving current occasionally carrying something unusual, like a shoe or a hat or a tree limb. It never seemed to slow down or speed up, never got tired. It just kept carrying itself and whatever else happened to have fallen in, on its way to join the Elbe River.

A knock came at his door. It was an effort just to draw in enough breath to say, "Come in."

"Cook made your favorite." Grethel's face appeared in his doorway.

"That is very kind of her." Aladdin turned away from the window toward Grethel.

She came to him. She was wearing gemstone earrings and her hair was down around her shoulders, only partially covered by a veil. She smiled.

"What are you thinking, standing there like that?" She touched his arm. She was such a tiny thing, at least a head shorter. Her fingers, resting on his forearm, were like a child's, tapered and trimmed, obviously the hands of a wealthy person unaccustomed to work.

"Do you want to know the truth?" Aladdin asked her.

She looked into his eyes without flinching or glancing away. "I do."

He took a deep breath and let it out slowly. "I was trying to remember every detail of the last time I saw Lady Kirstyn. I thought I'd always remember it, every detail, every word, and every look, but . . . I no longer do." It hurt so much, this feeling of being disloyal to her. She deserved to be remembered.

A memory of one of their walks came to him. They'd sat down beside a tiny spring where water bubbled up. A tree lay beside them, its trunk broken, its leaves touching the ground, but flowers still bloomed on its branches.

Aladdin pointed to the place where its slender trunk was shattered but still holding together. "Strange that it can be so broken but still so alive." Just like him.

Grethel squeezed his arm, bringing him out of his thoughts. "You mustn't feel bad about that. And I know how you feel, much more than you know."

"You do?"

"I do, because I had a sweetheart once. Father did not approve of him. Johann's father died not long after he was born, and his mother did the best she could, but she never remarried, so they were very poor. Johann was an artist who wanted to paint portraits. He left to study in Florence. He didn't know if he would ever return. I never saw him again."

"When did he leave?"

"Five years ago. I was fifteen; he was seventeen. I was heart-broken, especially when the months and years went by and he never wrote to me. It seems if he had truly loved me he would have written to me."

Another stab of pain pierced Aladdin's heart. He never told Kirstyn that he loved her. Did she know? Even in his letters, he was afraid to tell her, and when he said farewell to her on the day he left, he'd been too determined to accomplish his goal of making his fortune to make her any promises, to even admit to himself how much she meant to him.

But they were speaking of Grethel.

"I'm so sorry for your heartbreak, Grethel. I think it is only God and His Spirit that can . . . soothe a broken heart." He almost said "heal a broken heart," but he wasn't sure it was possible to heal this pain. Sometimes he did feel a measure of comfort when he prayed, sensing God's presence.

"And the passing of time helps too, I think." She smiled. "I have more experience than you do at heartbreak."

He had been glancing out the window, but she continued to gaze intently into his face.

"Poor Abu has been nearly as sad as you have been. He asked Father yesterday if you would be sad forever."

He opened his mouth to say something, but she held up a hand to stop him. "I know it has only been a few days since Duke Wilhelm departed, but Abu is a child. He doesn't understand."

"I don't want him to be sad. Perhaps we could do something to cheer us all, some sort of outing."

"We should go to Lüneburg Heath." Grethel's eyes were alight now. She could be quite pretty when her eyes widened with interest. But noticing that only made him long to see Kirstyn. His heart squeezed with pain.

"Lüneburg Heath?"

"It is beautiful this time of year. Well, in a week or two it will be beautiful. The heather blooms again in autumn."

"We should take Abu."

"Abu could bring a few friends, and they could play games. The Heath is very flat, and there's lots of space for a young boy to run. We can take a picnic."

Aladdin let Grethel talk on about a picnic to the Lüneburg Heath, and by that evening, she'd planned it all.

Meanwhile, business began to capture his attention again. If he didn't attend to it, all that he had done up until now, including being able to hire more people to work for Herr Kaufmann, would be for naught. So he bought and sold and transported and made sure people got what they wanted. And Aladdin and Herr Kaufmann were experts at getting the things people wanted and giving them to them—at a fair price too.

But Kirstyn was never far from his thoughts. He still occasionally sent out men to seek Kirstyn. He also wrote to Duke Wilhelm about once a week, asking if any more had been discovered about Kirstyn or her kidnapper, but the letters he received back were short and to the point: it was as if Kirstyn and her kidnapper had vanished.

The day arrived for them to take their little trip to the Heath. The heather was purple, like a Turkish carpet of all one color but with lots of texture. Abu and a few of his friends, some boys his age with whom he went to school in town, were already whooping and running and leaping through the heather, chasing a hare, then a butterfly, then each other.

Grethel and two male servants and a young maidservant rounded out the rest of their party, as Herr Kaufmann had stayed home to rest due to a head cold.

"What do you think of it?" Grethel asked.

"I like it. The flowers look pretty, and Abu and the boys are enjoying the room to run around and play." They were starting a game of blindman's buff, reminding him of his childhood at the Hagenheim orphanage.

The servants were busy spreading out a blanket and displaying the food they had brought. Soon Aladdin sat down and Grethel joined him. He remembered the games he and the other orphans used to play and how Kirstyn used to join in, her golden hair glowing in the sun. How pretty she was. He never failed to notice, even as a child. Why had God allowed her to be taken from him, her family, and everyone who loved her? Had she suffered very much? Was she truly gone?

"Aladdin, I . . ." Grethel was leaning close to him.

He hadn't realized how close she was sitting. The servants were suddenly nowhere to be seen. Had they gone back to town?

"If you ever need to talk to someone, I hope you will come to me."

Aladdin stared at Grethel. "I don't want to hurt you, Grethel, because I respect you, and also because of my great respect and affection for Herr Kaufmann. For now, I cannot think of any woman besides Lady Kirstyn. Please understand."

Grethel sat up straighter, moving away from him. "I hope you do not think I was suggesting anything . . . immoral between us."

"No, of course not. Forgive me. I did not mean—"

She put her hand on his arm. "I understand. Do you still hold out hope she will be found?" Pity filled her expression.

"I think there's very little chance of that." Something inside him did believe she was still alive, but he couldn't bring himself to admit that to Grethel.

CHAPTER FOURTEEN

Aladdin, Grethel, and Abu visited Lüneburg Heath every Sunday to get out of the city and enjoy the warm summer sun and the lovely wildness of the heather. They took long walks, at first reminding Aladdin of the walks he and Kirstyn had taken in the Hagenheim forests. But the more they visited the Heath, the less their walks reminded Aladdin of Kirstyn and Hagenheim. After all, the Heath was nothing like Hagenheim's deep forests and rocky hills and outcroppings. And Grethel, though a lovely, kindhearted maiden, was not Kirstyn.

Near the end of autumn, after a long day of running through the heather with Abu and Abu's new dog, a shaggy brown-and-white Wolfspitz named Wolfie, Herr Kaufmann sat down with Aladdin in the main room of the house. They both sipped a drink Hilde had made with cherries and currants and apples in front of the hearth. More and more, Herr Kaufmann required a fire "to ward off the slight chill in the air" that no one else seemed to feel.

"It has been months since Duke Wilhelm was here." Herr Kaufmann stared at the fire. "What have you heard from the duke? Is there any news?"

Aladdin sighed. "No news. The duke gave up searching for her, and all of his men who were searching have now returned to Hagenheim." Aladdin did not wish to talk about Kirstyn, but Herr Kaufmann had not asked in weeks. He could not deny the man anything, not after all he had done for Aladdin. He'd suffered financial losses while Aladdin was searching for Kirstyn, and even since then, while Aladdin was too distracted by grief and frustration to do his job well.

"Truly, I am sorry, my boy. I am sorry."

Aladdin nodded.

"I remember when my Alice died in childbirth. I mourned for a while, but I finally realized that my mourning would not bring her back or make anything better. So I made the decision to live my life—and to concentrate on loving the family I had. I think that was a good decision."

Aladdin stiffened. Would Herr Kaufmann tell him it was time to stop mourning Kirstyn? That he should forget about her? His stomach churned.

"I poured myself into being a father, and I was glad and content. My son—Little Cedric, we called him—was such a joyful child. We enjoyed each other's company. He would rather sit next to me than anywhere else. He ran to me when he was injured or when he was proud of himself. I've never been happier than in those days—until he turned thirteen years old. Everything changed. Can you believe he was already chasing the young maidens in town, maidens who were two and three years older than he was? He had always been a bit precocious, and my mistake was that I foolishly indulged him."

Herr Kaufmann shook his head, staring down at the floor.

"When he demanded, I gave in. I started trying to check him when he was fourteen or fifteen, but by then it was too late. He thought he was an adult, smarter than his pathetic old father. He even tried to molest Grethel—can you imagine? She was still only a child, was growing up in our house, and he tried to . . . But I thank God that I caught him in time, before he did any harm to her. After that I never knew where he was. He stole things. He threatened people. He threatened me most of all. It was a terrible time. I pleaded with him to turn from his wicked ways. I promised him things . . . when I should have been stern with him. I was still too lenient with him. I know that now . . . now that it's too late.

"Two years ago I thought he was reforming. He pretended to want to help me in the business. But he only took the money I gave him and abandoned the goods he was supposed to fetch at the port—those which he did not steal. I was heartbroken, and I was angry. The bitterness was so strong in me, I could taste it on my tongue, believe it or not." He shook his head. "I had given him everything, tried everything to make him happy, and he betrayed me, his own father. I expected to be sad and bitter for the rest of my days."

Herr Kaufmann looked up, meeting Aladdin's gaze. "Then something happened, something I had not expected. And that something was you. I know I've said this before, but you restored my faith in people, and you even made me stop hating myself for causing my son's lack of self-control and integrity. You gave me back the joy I thought I'd lost forever."

"God is to thank for that," Aladdin was quick to say. "I am grateful to God for bringing me to you."

"Yes, yes, it was God. And God will bring someone to you now, to help you in your grief. In fact, I hope you will consider the possibility that . . . God has already brought you that person."

Aladdin shifted in his seat. "I appreciate your concern for me, but I am well. God has given me you, Abu, everyone in your household, and enough work to fill my time. My heart may be broken, but only God can heal that."

"Perhaps, but don't shut yourself away from the love of a woman the way I did. I don't want to see you make that mistake."

Aladdin rubbed his cheek. "I'm just not ready for that, but I thank you for caring. And now I believe I will go up to bed. I'm very tired."

He hurried away before Herr Kaufmann could say anything else. When he reached his room, he closed the door and bent over, gasping at the pain in his chest. It was as if he suddenly saw Kirstyn before him, so innocent and joyful. *O God, how could You let those evil men touch her?*

He fell to the floor on his knees. Tears dripped from his eyes, and he clenched his fists. He rested his forehead on the Turkish carpet and groaned. "Forgive me, God, for blaming You. But it hurts so much, and I miss her. Kirstyn . . ."

He remembered another time when she had coaxed him into going to the woods to explore. Sir Conrad was waiting to accompany them as they crossed the castle bailey. Kirstyn started skipping, and she glanced over her shoulder at Aladdin. "Come and skip with me!"

Aladdin managed a laugh, his heart tripping at the way her eyes glinted in the sun.

Somehow he couldn't accept that she was gone. She couldn't be dead or he would feel it. And yet the fact that Duke Wilhelm believed she was dead and had stopped searching for her . . .

A fresh wave of pain ripped through him and he let himself feel it, more than he ever had before, until it overwhelmed him.

"God, I cannot bear this pain."

Cast your pain on Me. Let Me bear it.

Aladdin imagined Jesus hanging on the cross, in horrible

pain. Yes, Jesus knew about pain and betrayal. Aladdin's pain might not go away completely, but he could let God carry his pain, this overwhelming sense of the violence that had happened to Kirstyn, how Aladdin had not been there to stop it, the pain of missing her and being told he'd never see her again.

God would bear the pain for him if he would cast it on Him.

Aladdin lay across his bed and felt a strange sense of peace wash over him.

The air became cooler, and they all went to the Heath for what might be the last outing before it grew too cold to enjoy.

When they reached home, everyone scattered to their separate rooms for the night. While Aladdin was finishing his nightly prayers, his mind went back to when he was about sixteen and Kirstyn had just celebrated her fourteenth birthday.

She was running up the gentle hill toward the woods, throwing her arms out and lifting her face to the sun. He let her get almost to the edge of the trees and then caught up with her. Together they found their walking sticks where they had left them, propped against an oak tree, and moved more slowly through the trees, Sir Conrad not far behind.

Aladdin had stopped at a spot between two beech trees, memories flooding his mind.

"That's where the bear attacked you," Kirstyn said.

He glanced back at her and nodded.

"Does your leg pain you anymore?"

He shook his head.

Suddenly she threw her arms around him and buried her face in his chest.

His heart thumped hard. Sir Conrad would no doubt report this back to the duke. He should push her away. Instead, he patted Kirstyn's shoulder.

He was aware of her hands on his back as she stood perfectly still. No one had ever held him like this. Perhaps if his mother hadn't died, if he'd stayed in the Holy Land with her, he might have experienced many embraces. But could any of them have been as sweet as this one?

He let his hand rest on her thin shoulder as he stared down at her blonde head, the hair fraying from its braids.

She pulled away from him, and her blue eyes caught his. "You're my dearest friend, Aladdin. I want you to be happy."

He opened his mouth, not sure what to say.

"And I want you to know that we will always be close. I won't ever leave Hagenheim and get married, as Margaretha intends to do. I want to stay here and go on walks with you in the woods."

Her words stole his breath. She seemed to sense that her presence in his life soothed the ache of not having a family. But she was too innocent still to understand that her parents would never allow them to remain as they were—the closest of friends. And in truth, he wasn't sure he could be content with that. But it was the fact that she thought of his happiness, perhaps even more than her own, that touched him deeply.

Aladdin took a deep breath to try to dispel the pain the memory conjured up. He grabbed his water pitcher and hurried downstairs to refill it.

All the candles had been extinguished, but when he reached the kitchen, the light from a full moon was shining in through the windows, giving him just enough light to find the fresh water bucket. He filled his pitcher and was turning around to leave when he saw a light flickering in the stairwell.

The light grew brighter, and he heard the sound of soft shoes shuffling on the steps. Grethel appeared carrying a small lantern.

"Aladdin. I thought you had gone to bed."

"I just came to get some water."

She approached him, her eyes large and round, a solemn look about her closed lips. Something was definitely on her mind, but she didn't speak as she stopped a few feet from him.

The silence was uncomfortable, so he asked, "Did you enjoy yourself today? The weather was a little cool. It may be a long time before . . ."

Grethel moved toward him until she and her lantern were so close he could see every curve of her face.

She set her lantern on the trestle table behind him, brushing his sleeve with her arm.

"You were so good at teaching Abu archery today. Is there anything you don't do perfectly?"

"Many things, I assure you." *Perfect.* That's what Kirstyn had often called him. But inside he felt far from perfect. In the deepest part of him he still felt like that poor, frightened little boy who was bullied by Mustapha into stealing. He was far from perfect now too, and he feared if those he loved discovered that he wasn't perfect, they would cease to love him—including Kirstyn.

And she'd said he pushed himself. He did, but only because he needed to prove he wasn't just a poor, unlovable thief. A rat, Mustapha had called him. Those memories brought him so much shame, even now.

"I always have a wonderful time with you, Aladdin. You are so kind to Abu and to my father. And even though I know you will never love me, you are always kind to me."

He couldn't help but stare into her eyes. She was so close.

And now that the lantern was behind him, the moonlight was shining on her face, lending her such a tender glow. Her eyelids dropped, and she was no longer looking at him.

"I imagined my father would find someone for me to marry. But I know he still hopes you . . . well, that you will marry me. He loves you like a son, and I . . . I have fallen in love with you too." She raised her eyes, and they seemed to pierce him through.

His heart stuttered. Grethel was a sweet girl. She was not mean-spirited or wrathful or petty. And if he married her, it would greatly please Herr Kaufmann. He could please the one man who had been ready to do anything to help Aladdin achieve what he wanted, even if it meant Herr Kaufmann would not get what he wanted. And wouldn't Aladdin be ensuring his own success? If he could marry someone who was good and kind and who truly loved him, what more could he ask for? He would surely come to love her, in time. He'd finally have a real family.

Perhaps this was how God intended to take away the awful aching pain of losing Kirstyn. And after so many months of hearing nothing from her, his head told him it was extremely unlikely she was still alive—even if his heart refused to believe it.

They stared into each other's eyes. He felt himself giving in and accepting that Kirstyn was never coming back. Could he really feel it if she died? Surely that was only wishful thinking. And it made practical sense that he should marry Grethel.

She placed her fingertips against his chin. "Could you ever love me, Aladdin?" she whispered. "Would you take away my pain of feeling unloved and unwanted? Because I believe I could take away your pain. Would you let me love you?"

Aladdin opened his mouth, but the words stuck in his throat. So he put his arms around her and pulled her to his chest, resting his cheek against her hair.

She felt comfortable in his arms, but the ache in his heart grew. Perhaps that was only because he was thinking of Kirstyn now, the last vestiges of hope—hope that she was still alive and could still be his—clinging to his heart, even as Grethel held on to him.

"You should go," Aladdin croaked, almost pushing her away. "We shall talk more when we're not tired and . . . Go, now."

She stood staring at him, as if uncertain.

He reached out and caressed her cheek. "Go." He picked up her lantern and handed it to her.

With one last look, she hurried away.

Chapter Fifteen

Kirstyn lay in the bottom of the cart with the tarp over her head and things piled on top of her, but she kept the tarp lifted enough so she could see through the cracks in the wagon's sides. The sun was high, and they seemed to be traveling over a particularly flat area. Something purple caught her eye. It was all around on the ground, a vibrant color, some kind of flower, which was strange, since it was late autumn and the air was already cooler and hinting of winter.

Kirstyn had stopped speaking when Michael was around. He would never tell her anything, and when he was nearby, neither would Anna. But she wished she knew where they were. What place had such an abundance of purple flowers? It reminded her of Margaretha's descriptions in her letters of the countryside in England.

She still thought about escaping, but she had failed so many times. Planning her escape was the thing that kept her sane in the long, lonely stretches when Michael would lock her in a basement for twenty-four hours at a time. The hours crept by so slowly she nearly went mad when she had nothing to do except to yearn for home, her family, and Aladdin—and to plan her next escape.

But perhaps it was time to just stay quiet and do what her father had told her to do, which was to wait for him to rescue her. Trying to escape was not working, after all. It only gave Michael an excuse to manipulate Anna's emotions by telling her, "See how people treat me? Nothing ever goes right for me, so I'm forced to do bad things just to survive. Even my father doesn't care about me. He gave my inheritance to some Saracen orphan boy."

A few times lately, Kirstyn had even found herself feeling sorry for Michael, which terrified her and set her to reminding herself how Michael's behavior must look to the people who cared about her, like her mother and father. Looking through their eyes, Kirstyn was able to get clarity again about Michael's actions, to see that they truly were evil, to understand that his words revealed a very twisted way of thinking. It even helped Kirstyn stop thinking angry thoughts about her brothers Steffan and Wolfgang. They were just immature boys. She could hardly wait to tell them she forgave them for the way they had always teased her and Margaretha.

Dwelling on the protective way Aladdin had treated her also helped dispel the twistedness of Michael's words and actions. Aladdin had protected her many times, the greatest of which was when the bear had attacked them. When Aladdin had lain in bed after the attack, she visited him every day. Once, when she saw his leg without the bandage, she got light-headed and had to look away and take deep breaths. But if she ever tried to take the blame for his injuries, he would say, "Do you want me to remind you yet again that you saved my life? You ran *toward* an enraged bear with only a *stick* and beat her on the head with it."

Of course, she would always protest his praise—praise she little deserved. She'd only distracted the bear for a few moments until Sir Ruger arrived. But she could be grateful Aladdin was so gracious and did not hate her.

In less than a week he was getting around with only a walking stick to aid him. Frau Lena was amazed, but she would not let him stand upright for more than a few minutes, lest too much blood flow to his leg wounds. But always Aladdin was smiling and sure that his leg would be as good as ever very soon.

"Besides," he said, "what man wouldn't want these wonderful scars to show off his bravery?"

Kirstyn shook her head, then laughed.

One day she walked in on Frau Lena checking the injuries on his shoulder and chest. He would certainly have some scars there as well. And for some reason, her cheeks heated at seeing his bare chest.

He snatched up his shirt. Frau Lena asked her about her family while he pulled the garment over his head. That was when she began to realize it was uncommon for a girl her age to be such close friends with a boy his age. But Aladdin had never been anything less than chivalrous and kind to her—fierce in his protection of her, but gentle with her feelings—Michael's opposite in every way.

The cart hit a particularly deep hole, shaking her from her reverie.

Later in the day, the cart wheels rattled over what was obviously a cobblestone street. People conversed all around, some near and some farther away. There was also the sound of horses' hooves, a blacksmith's clanging hammer, and even children playing, shouting, and laughing. They were in a town, or possibly a village on market day.

The cart finally stopped, and Kirstyn was certain she smelled a river, along with the noises that accompanied one. The things that had been piled onto her legs and torso were lifted off of her. Finally she was dragged by her feet until she could stand, with the tarp still wrapped around her, and was hoisted over Michael's shoulder. She caught a glimpse of the tops of buildings and blue sky before she was carried into a building.

Inside, Michael yanked the tarp off of her and shoved her toward some steps leading down. "Tie her up," Michael barked to Anna.

Anna followed Kirstyn down the steps to the cellar of the building. Anna held a candle, but it was difficult to see even the steps they were treading on. Once Michael was behind them, Kirstyn whispered, "Where are we?"

"It's a warehouse on the river. Michael says we can stay here until . . . until he arranges to have you sold."

"Sold? What do you mean?"

"He plans to sell you to the highest bidder."

"But . . . sold as what? A slave?"

"I suppose so." Anna avoided looking at Kirstyn.

Instead of trying to reason with Anna, bribe her, or appeal to her sense of compassion, none of which had worked before, Kirstyn said, "I wouldn't have thought even Michael was capable of such evil."

Her knees shook as she grasped just how heinous it was, and how much danger she would be in if someone paid money for her. They could do anything they wished with her.

Michael was cruel, but he did not treat her as badly as he might have in the four or five months since he took her. He fed her enough to make sure she didn't die, and he had not molested her, besides hitting her a couple of times. Poor Anna was the one he yelled at and beat every time he drank too much wine or strong spirits. And yet she refused to leave him. It had been so maddening to Kirstyn in the beginning, but strangely, she had come to accept it and had all but stopped trying to convince Anna to leave. It was too disheartening to hear Anna defend him.

Anna said nothing and lit a few more candles in the dark cellar. But besides a few candle nubs and a few old tables and a broken chair, there was nothing in the cellar, and certainly no bed.

"Where will I sleep?" Kirstyn took hold of Anna's arm. "Please don't leave me down here." Tears stung her eyes. It was humiliating to beg, but she couldn't bear the thought of being left alone in this dark room with no windows and nothing to do when the sun was shining just outside the walls.

Anna took hold of the rope tied around Kirstyn's wrists. "Michael said to tie you here."

"I will cook and clean. I'll be the servant for you and Michael if you will not tie me here." Her hands started shaking.

"What's going on down there?" Michael's voice boomed from above.

"I want to work for you," Kirstyn said, talking fast. "I will do anything, but I cannot bear to be locked down here in the dark. I will go mad and I . . . I will do myself harm. You have driven me mad by leaving me in the dark too many times." It was not far from the truth.

A long silence followed as Anna waited for Michael to speak.

"Very well," he said, his voice cool and even. "Come up here."

Anna blew out the candle nubs on the tables and started up the stairs with Kirstyn. At the top, Michael took hold of Kirstyn's arm in a painful grip, pinching her flesh with his cruel fingers.

"Why should I believe you won't try to escape?"

"I never succeed, and I'm tired. I just want to see the sun." Had she finally lost all hope and self-respect after months and months of this abuse? No. She might pretend to have given up, but inside she would remain as defiant as ever.

Michael's expression was sullen. He seemed to be trying to cover the scar on his forehead with his brown hair, which had grown long and came across his brow in a swoop. As well he might. Her father was undoubtedly looking for him. Perhaps he had a description of him and was even now close on their trail.

Kirstyn said a quick prayer that Michael would say yes to her request.

"Very well. You can help Anna prepare supper. But I'll be watching you."

Kirstyn was so glad to be standing upright in the light of day. She set about helping Anna by washing the pot in which they would be cooking frumenty, then preparing the vegetables— peas and leeks and beans. They thickened it with a handful of dried oats and set it over the fire to boil. All the while Michael sat on a stool, watching her as he used his knife point to clean under his fingernails.

Look all you want, Michael. One day my father will hunt you down. You'll never know a day of peace for the rest of your pathetic life, and you'll know true fear just before he hangs you.

As usual, the thought gave her a moment of satisfaction.

She couldn't help wondering what Aladdin was doing and if he knew she'd been taken captive and held for ransom. Did he pray for her? Worry about her? Was he seeking her, as she was sure her father was? Did he still care as much for her as he did that last day she'd seen him a year and a half ago, when she kissed his cheek?

She loved him even more now than she did then, as she'd

had plenty of time to think about him these last months. And she didn't just love him as a friend. Not anymore. When she lay for hours in the dark, sometimes she imagined what it would be like to kiss him and be his wife. Would Aladdin be shocked and repulsed if he knew she thought such things?

She gazed out the window, watching people go by on the street outside. *God, please don't let Michael get angry and send me down to the basement.* She was so happy to be able to see the sun and people again.

Michael's face was red as he slammed the door behind him. Kirstyn was tied to a support beam where she stood kneading bread. She stopped, and a tremor rippled through her at the look on his face.

He turned and punched his fist into the wall, then left the room. Anna exchanged a glance with Kirstyn, then went back to shelling peas for the frumenty.

A few minutes later someone knocked on the door. Michael asked, "Who is there?"

A muffled voice answered, and Michael opened the door.

A tall, gaunt man with darting eyes and oily hair entered the room. "Where is she?"

Michael jerked his head in Kirstyn's direction.

The man looked her up and down and nodded, his thin lips curving into a smile that sent a shiver down Kirstyn's spine. It had been a long time since anyone besides Michael and Anna had looked directly at her. Why would Michael let this man see her?

The man turned back to Michael, and they sat on two stools

at the far side of the large, nearly empty room and talked in hushed tones.

Kirstyn did her best to listen. Were they discussing her?

Anna left the room to fetch more water. Kirstyn tried not to make a sound, hoping the men would forget she was there. And gradually, they did begin to speak a little louder.

"I know a sheik who would pay a lot of gold and spices for her," the almost skeletal man with the greasy hair said.

Raw fear flooded Kirstyn's middle like molten lead. Her arms lost their strength as the bread dough went limp in her hands. It must be very far to where sheiks lived. Would her father be able to find her so far away?

But they were still talking. She forced herself to listen.

"Your father's new partner is planning to marry your sister. Together they will inherit everything."

Michael's face twisted into something dark and ugly.

". . . name is something strange . . . Arabic. Aladdin."

"I remember. And now that I'm here, I shall break into the house and slit his throat while he sleeps. Or perhaps that would be too quick. I want him to know I'm selling his childhood love to the highest bidder."

Kirstyn's heart crashed into her throat, and she could hardly draw in a breath. If only her thoughts would quiet so she could listen.

"What are you doing to our bread?" Anna stood over her.

Kirstyn was so focused on eavesdropping that she hadn't noticed Anna enter.

"You've squished it to nothing." Anna pointed at the lump of bread dough. Kirstyn held it so tightly it was oozing between her fingers.

She worked to mold the dough back into a ball, but her heart was pounding. *Aladdin*. He must be here in this town! But he was in great danger.

She tried to continue listening as she reshaped the lump of dough. Oh, why wouldn't Anna be quiet? Didn't she know Kirstyn was desperate to hear what Michael was saying? But she couldn't let her become suspicious, so she looked at Anna and nodded, pretending to understand what sounded like only babble.

A minute later the bony man left. Michael sat with his hands clenched into fists and resting on his thighs while he stared broodingly at the floor.

O God, please don't let Michael harm Aladdin. I would give anything to see him again. I miss him so much. But I couldn't bear it if Michael hurt him. Would Aladdin even recognize her if he saw her? Her clothes were dirty and torn. She was thinner and probably looked gaunt and haggard. And her hair . . . She hadn't been able to comb it for months. She hadn't had the strength to care until now, when she imagined seeing Aladdin again.

She had to warn him that Michael was planning to kill him. But how?

Aladdin recorded figures in the ledger at Herr Kaufmann's desk in the warehouse. As the afternoon wore on, the sellers, overseers, and boat captains trickled in to report their numbers for the day.

"I don't want to upset Herr Kaufmann," one of the sellers said in a quiet voice, "but I have heard that his son has returned to Lüneburg."

A sudden coldness froze Aladdin. Would he be able to protect Herr Kaufmann from his son causing him even more pain?

He'd at least have to put his guards on high alert. "Do you know what he wants?"

"No doubt money. He is trouble."

"Say nothing to Herr Kaufmann." Aladdin would decide if and when to tell him. He'd like to make certain the rumor was true first, so he asked one of Herr Kaufmann's warehouse guards, Claus, to ask around town.

The next day Claus came into the office, and by the look on his face, his news was bad. "Herr Kaufmann's son is here. I saw him myself."

"What is he doing here?"

"Nothing good. The word is he's angry that Herr Kaufmann has decided to appoint you as his heir."

"Yes, that makes sense."

"And that you're marrying Herr Kaufmann's daughter."

"That is well known, is it?"

Claus shrugged. "It is known."

"Where is he staying?"

"It's best you do not confront him, Aladdin. He's a dangerous man, and nothing would please him more than to see you dead. You mustn't go near him."

"I understand. I'll be careful. Now tell me."

Claus frowned on one side of his mouth. "He goes by Michael now, but I still haven't discovered where he's staying."

"Michael?" Could it be? Could Herr Kaufmann's son be the man who had taken Kirstyn captive? Could she be with him even now?

Aladdin stood so quickly he knocked over the stool he'd been sitting on. "You must help me find him. Immediately. Take me to someone who knows him or who's talked to him. There's no time to lose."

Claus's face flushed. "Saints above! He could be the Michael we've been searching for."

Aladdin's own face heated, and he grabbed Claus by the arm. "Let us go, man." What was he waiting for?

"You must not confront him." Claus's jaw hardened. "I shall go now, but you must let me and the other guards find him."

"I'm going with you."

CHAPTER SIXTEEN

Aladdin arrived home just as it was getting dark. Grethel hurried forward to greet him.

"Welcome home, Aladdin." She smiled sweetly. "Let me take your coat."

"Thank you."

She helped him off with it, then hung it on a hook. "How was your day?"

This was the moment of every day that he should kiss her. After all, they were making plans to be married. But a memory of Kirstyn would always leap into his mind. It was what happened every time he thought about kissing Grethel. But today . . . he had an even better reason for not kissing her.

The look of hope on her face made him uneasy. "Is your father home? I need to speak with him."

"He's in the dining hall waiting for supper."

"I have some news you should probably hear as well."

Grethel took his arm, and together they made their way to the main room of the ground floor.

Herr Kaufmann sat at the head of the table. His eyes were closed, his hands folded and resting on his belly. Aladdin's heart squeezed at how much he was about to disturb his beloved mentor's tranquility.

Herr Kaufmann's eyes opened, and he sat up straighter in his chair. A smile spread over his face as he held out his hands to them. "My dear Grethel and Aladdin. How much pleasure it gives me to see you two. Come and let me kiss you."

Grethel leaned down and let him kiss her cheek. He squeezed Aladdin's shoulder and gave him a quick hug.

"Herr Kaufmann, there is something I must tell you and Grethel." Nervous energy still flowed through Aladdin's body. "And then I need to go out again."

"Oh?" Herr Kaufmann's bushy white brows drew together, and he leaned forward. "Sit down. You must have your supper, you know."

Aladdin took a deep breath. "Claus, a few of the town soldiers, and I have been looking all over town for the past few hours for a man named Michael."

Herr Kaufmann's face sagged. Grethel's eyes squinted closed, and a tiny groan escaped her lips.

"But we know who this man is." Aladdin leaned in to try to get their attention. "He's here in Lüneburg. It's your son, Herr Kaufmann."

Grethel made a sound like the squeal of a mouse.

Herr Kaufmann's eyes grew bigger and he leaned away. "Not Cedric."

"Yes, except he is using the name Michael."

"Oh no." Herr Kaufmann placed a hand over his heart. "Cedric Michael. That is what his godfather named him. But you said it was a rumor. Perhaps it isn't true. The Michael who took Lady Kirstyn had a scar on his forehead, and Cedric does not have a scar."

"He might have acquired the scar since you saw him last."

"Medium height, brown hair?"

"Claus saw him and recognized him."

Herr Kaufmann crossed himself, then slumped against the back of his chair.

"What do you think he wants?" Grethel looked stricken. Her lower lip trembled as she pressed the back of her hand against her cheek.

"We have been searching, as I said, but have not found where he is staying. We heard that he is holding a young woman captive. I believe it could be Lady Kirstyn." His heart leapt just saying the words aloud. "He is here trying to sell the captive maiden to whomever is able and willing to pay his price."

"Oh." Grethel covered her mouth with one hand.

Herr Kaufmann groaned and closed his eyes. It was a grave sin to sell a fellow human, a direct violation of Church law that could get a man excommunicated.

Just then Hilde and two other servants bustled into the room bearing the evening meal. After Hilde set down the enormous dish she was carrying, she turned to Herr Kaufmann.

"Whatever is the matter?" She glanced around at Aladdin and Grethel. "You all look as if you just heard the plague was in Lüneburg."

"Not the plague," Aladdin said softly.

"No, something worse. My son." Herr Kaufmann spat the words as if they tasted bitter.

"Oh dear." Hilde stood as still as a pillar of salt. She did not even blink. Finally she exclaimed, "What does he want? You will not let him in the house again, will you? Oh, Herr Kaufmann." She looked ready to burst out sobbing.

"He is not to set foot in this house." Herr Kaufmann was nearly shouting. "Aladdin, as soon as supper is done, we shall call all the male servants and set them on a schedule to stand watch over the house."

"I'll have to leave you to do that, Herr Kaufmann."

Not for the first time, Aladdin wondered how a man like Herr Kaufmann could have raised a son like this Cedric Michael.

Aladdin did not wait for the table to be set. He went upstairs to gather a few things, then rejoined the guards who were outside waiting for him. Hilde packed them a quick repast of cheese, sausage, and bread, and they were off.

The next day Kirstyn stirred the frumenty while waiting for the bread dough to rise. The rope around her wrist, which was tied to the wooden beam bracing the ceiling, was just long enough for her to reach the fireplace.

A knife blade caught Kirstyn's eye. Anna must have left it on the table when she went to the privy a few moments before. Her heart skipped a beat. She had to try again, didn't she?

Kirstyn lunged for the knife and sawed furiously at the rope around her wrist.

Her stomach flipped and tumbled. She *had* to escape this time, or else Michael would lock her in the pitch-black darkness of the cellar, not letting her see the light of the sun for days on end, never letting her out even to go to the privy, never allowing her to talk to Anna. She would surely go mad.

The knife was dull, but finally the tough fibers gave way.

Her eyes focused intently on the only door. It led directly to the street. Her paralysis wore off and she ran to it, turned the knob, and practically fell out, stumbling on the two steps that led to the cobblestones, then started running.

Her dress had been patched so many times she could hardly tell where the original fabric was, and her hair was messy and uncovered, but she didn't care. She was free.

She had rehearsed this over and over in her thoughts. She would try to locate the nearest church. *There.* A spire and cross rose above the roofs of the buildings. It was probably only a five-minute walk. Her heart thumped hard against her chest.

Several men traveled on the street. Would they grab her and try to hurt her?

Kirstyn walked as quickly as she could. Her pulse pounded. She felt so exposed. Was everyone looking at her?

A burly, middle-aged man made eye contact with her. He didn't look away but stared. Should she ask him for help? But what if he tried to harm her too? She could never defend herself against him, as big as he was.

A cold fear gripped her and she kept walking. She could make it to the church. She wasn't sure that man was safe, but there was no question of her safety at the church.

Her hands were shaking and her knees were weak. And yet she could walk for hours if it meant freedom.

Had Michael seen her leave? She couldn't resist the urge to look to the left, right. Then she glanced over her shoulder. A man who looked like Michael was just behind her. Her stomach clenched. She glanced again and realized it wasn't him. Still, she quickened her pace, eager to get out of the street.

Her eyes met those of a young woman, who looked down at

the rope dangling from her wrist. Kirstyn ducked her head and hid her wrist under her arm and kept walking.

Had someone moved the giant stone building? It was taking so long to reach the church. People were staring at her, some with expressions of horror, others pity, and others curiosity.

Finally the front of the church came into view. It was red brick, and she focused on the pointed arch door. She was so close. Just a few more steps. Her heart beat faster. She ran the last few steps, then pushed open the door and rushed inside.

Unused to so much exertion, she was gasping and her knees were shaking.

"*Junge Frau?*"

She turned to find a priest so close that she jumped back a step.

"Forgive me. I didn't mean to frighten you." The priest looked very young. He stood a respectful distance away. "Are you well? Can I offer any assistance?"

"I am well." No, that wasn't true at all. "I was a captive and I've just escaped." Her voice cracked and broke from her chest. She pressed her hand hard to her mouth. She sucked in a long breath to stop the tears. Then she started laughing. She was free!

"Who was holding you captive, junge Frau?" The priest was bending forward and trying to look into her face.

"Forgive me. I am just happy that I escaped. But I need your help. Will you please help me? My life and the life of someone I love . . . We are in great danger."

His mild green eyes blinked questioningly. "I will gladly help one of God's children. Will you tell me your name?"

"Kirstyn Gerstenberg of Hagenheim."

His mouth fell open as his eyes widened. "Someone has been looking for you."

Kirstyn kept her head down, her hood hanging low as she walked.

"Wouldn't you prefer to wait at the church?" The priest, who asked her to call him Francis, asked for the third time.

"Just take me to Aladdin." Kirstyn spoke under her breath, walking as fast as her weak knees would allow. She hadn't eaten all day—Michael had been punishing her for dropping his cup of wine as she handed it to him. But her desire to see Aladdin carried her along as if she rode on a cloud. "And thank you. Thank you so much."

Francis walked by her side. "I am not a priest yet. I have not been administered the rite of ordination. But I must help anyone in need as part of my preparation."

Kirstyn was certainly in need. She owned absolutely nothing but the dress she was wearing, which was torn and patched and stained. She'd had to borrow the long, hooded cloak from Francis to cover herself in case they met Michael on the street.

Oh, if only they could move faster! She just wanted to be safe with Aladdin. It was hard to believe she was truly free until she saw him.

"And your father is the Duke of Hagenheim?" Francis asked.

"Yes."

"He was here."

"Is he here now?" Her heart thudded inside her.

"No, I'm sorry."

"And where is here? Is this Lüneburg?"

"It is Lüneburg."

"But my father went elsewhere to look for me?"

"I . . . I believe . . . That is, it was my understanding that he went back to Hagenheim because he thought you were dead."

Her heart seemed to stop. Her father was no longer looking for her? He gave up? "Why would he believe me dead?"

"A bloody scarf was found—your bloody scarf. And then he searched but could find no trace of you. But here you are! You are well and whole and safe. Imagine your father's joy at being reunited with you again."

"Yes." That was a joyful thought indeed. Still . . . "Are you sure he stopped looking for me? And Aladdin? Did he give up as well?" Tears sprang to her eyes.

"I believe Aladdin kept searching for a while after the duke left. In fact, he was looking for you last night. I spoke to him myself when he came to the church to ask for help spreading the news that he was seeking a man named Michael and two women, one of whom was Lady Kirstyn."

Yes, of course. Aladdin would not give up searching for her. He had been looking for her all this time. Their hearts were so bonded, how could he ever give up on her? If either of them died, the other would surely feel it.

She could hardly wait to see him. "How much farther?"

"His home is near here, but he may be at the warehouse, the business where he and Herr Kaufmann work."

Soon they arrived at a large brick house. Francis knocked on the door while Kirstyn waited beside him. Still afraid of Michael walking by and seeing her, she kept her head down and her hood pulled low.

The door opened and Francis, in his quiet, humble voice, asked, "Is Aladdin home?"

"No, he's searching for Herr Kaufmann's son and Lady Kirstyn. Do you have information for him?"

"I do. Here is Lady Kirstyn." He turned around and held out a hand to Kirstyn.

"Oh my!" A large woman, very tall and wearing an apron, covered her mouth with her hands. "Come in! Come in, my dear." She motioned Kirstyn forward.

Kirstyn took one step closer. "Can you tell us where Aladdin is now? I need to see him."

"Bless you, child. We can send someone to fetch him, and you can rest while you wait for him." Her eyes seemed to take in Kirstyn's state and filled with pity and concern. No doubt Kirstyn looked pale and sallow and sunken.

"No, I thank you. I wish to go to wherever he is. He is not far, is he?"

"He may be at the warehouse, Lady Kirstyn, but he said he has been out searching for you."

"How far is this warehouse?"

"Not far. A ten-minute walk. But you come inside and let me give you something to eat. I'll send a servant to fetch Aladdin."

"Thank you, but I really should like to go myself."

"I'll fetch a guard to go with you. Otto!" She turned and shouted for the man, then gave the guard instructions. "Protect Lady Kirstyn and see her safely to the warehouse to find Aladdin."

"Lady Kirstyn!" A man appeared in the doorway and bowed. "Aladdin will be overjoyed to see you safe and well. Come."

The three of them set out down the street. Perhaps Kirstyn should have stayed at the house and waited for Aladdin. Her legs were getting weaker, and her stomach was beginning to feel sick. She had a vague and swimmy feeling in her head. But surely she could make it ten more minutes. If Aladdin was not at the warehouse, she would stay there and wait.

Aladdin had spent the morning in the company of two soldiers from the Lüneburg army, searching for Michael and Kirstyn. Now, together with Claus and two of Herr Kaufmann's other guards, he went back to the warehouse to regroup and allow them a few minutes to eat a midday meal.

Aladdin leaned against the wall and rested his head in his hands. He'd been so elated when he heard Michael was near. But in spite of all their searching, they still hadn't found him and possibly had caused him to go into hiding again. And Aladdin couldn't get rid of the thought that if they did find Michael, they might also learn the truth—and that truth might be too awful.

When their respite was over, the two soldiers strapped their swords on their backs and prepared to leave. Aladdin said a quick prayer, then looked up just as the door of the warehouse opened. The young novice, Francis, came in, and right behind him was a figure with a long black cloak. The hood fell back, and two large blue eyes fastened on him. The feminine face blossomed into a smile.

His breath went out of him in one great rush. His body seemed to advance toward her without his command. "Kirstyn. You're alive!"

She moved toward him as her face crumpled. When he reached her, he put his arms around her and she sagged against his chest.

He held her close, feeling her whole body shake with her sobs. She felt so small and frail. What had she been through? But she was alive! His heart soared. *God, You are so good. Thank You.* Still, the sound of her cries twisted his gut. He held her tighter, as if by wrapping her up in his arms he could fix what was broken.

Chapter Seventeen

Kirstyn saw Aladdin, and her heart flooded with warmth. His face showed shock, then he started toward her, his arms out, and when he embraced her, she knew she was finally safe from the horror, fear, and abuse.

His arms were so warm. Her knees buckled beneath her, but he held her up, almost lifting her off the floor. Did he know she loved him? She'd never told him. Did he still think of her as just a friend? No matter. She would enjoy his arms around her.

But she must look—and smell—terrible. She longed for a bath and fresh clothing. Her face burned. She couldn't stand here crying among all these strangers. She took a deep breath in, concentrating on forcing back the tears. Oh, Aladdin smelled good—his own smell that was familiar and reminded her of home mingled with the scent of herbal soap. And his shirt was so soft. Was it fine linen or silk? His chest was thicker than she remembered, and he seemed taller.

She pulled away and Aladdin loosened his hold, but a wave of dizziness came over her. She lifted her hand to her cheek, closing her eyes.

Aladdin's face hovered just above hers. "Do you need to lie down?"

"No, I am well. Aladdin, you're in danger. Michael wants to kill you." The urgency returned as the dizziness subsided. She gazed into Aladdin's eyes, even more gentle and warm than she remembered them. How handsome he was.

Aladdin was gazing at her as if she'd just told him a pleasant story, a slight smile curving his lips.

"You must listen. He intends to break into your house and slit your throat." Her stomach churned as she uttered the awful words.

His expression hardened. Finally. "My men and I shall go and capture him, and if he fights back, we shall kill him as he deserves. Where is he?"

"Oh." Did she even know how to get back to the place she had escaped from? "Truthfully, I don't know . . . I don't know how to get back there." At least a half-dozen men were staring at her, but she kept her gaze on Aladdin. "All I know is that he's staying in an old abandoned warehouse, and I could see water out of one of the windows."

How pathetic she was! She couldn't even help them find Michael. But the streets were so unfamiliar, and since she'd been following Francis, she didn't even know which direction to go.

"An abandoned warehouse near the water. Very good."

"I might be able to recognize it when I see it."

"Do not worry." Aladdin bent closer to her. The other men surrounding them were muttering excitedly amongst themselves. "We'll find it. And I shall take you to my home so you can rest."

"I should come with you to help you find it."

"Are you sure you want to?"

"Yes, yes. I want to help." She made her voice sound strong.

"Very well."

The men hefted weapons—swords, bludgeons, and daggers—and poured out the door with determined faces. Aladdin and Kirstyn went out last, his hand on her back. Did he know how comforting that was?

She was once again walking in the open. But she focused on the warehouses lining the side of the street. Which one was it?

Aladdin kept his arm around Kirstyn's shoulders as they walked. She was so thin and pale, but she'd insisted on coming with them.

Along with the two soldiers, Claus, Heinz, and Dietrich strode down the street carrying bludgeons and daggers, though their best weapon was their enormous breadth and strength. Aladdin was tall, but they were nearly twice as broad as he was. He was armed with a sword strapped across his back.

Aladdin and his small army rounded a bend in the street. Ahead lay the abandoned warehouse Aladdin had been thinking of, looking benign and quiet in the midday sun.

"Do you think that could be it?" Aladdin bent closer to Kirstyn.

They all stopped and she stared at it. "I think it is." She kept looking, then nodded. "I'm sure it is."

They were still at least a hundred paces away from the warehouse when Aladdin spotted a man emerging from a side street just ahead of them. He headed toward the warehouse.

The men froze, all watching the rather nondescript, short, brown-haired man walk up to the door, open it, and go inside.

"That's him." Kirstyn grabbed Aladdin's shirt and pressed her body against his. Her blue eyes gazed up at him. "Please stay with me. I don't want you near him."

Part of him wanted to charge ahead of the other men and pound his fist into Michael's face. But Kirstyn was more important.

Aladdin gave the signal and stayed at Kirstyn's side while the soldiers and guards ran to the door and burst in. Aladdin imagined Michael's look of terror at the men and their weapons. Soon they were hauling him back outside as if he weighed no more than a rag doll.

At last. Michael was caught and Kirstyn was safe, whole, and alive. But she had no idea how much he loved her.

Kirstyn clung to Aladdin as she watched the men drag Michael out the door while he kicked and yelled obscene words. Her stomach twisted in fear. *He can't get me now, and he can't hurt Aladdin.* But in spite of her argument, the fear continued to constrict her throat.

They also brought out Anna, holding her hands behind her. She probably tried to defend Michael, and they realized she was not a captive but an accomplice.

As the men passed with Michael and Anna, Michael glared at her and then at Aladdin. "You! How dare you take advantage of my foolish old father and take my inheritance." He kept kicking as the two guards had to half carry, half drag him down the street. And Anna simply kept her eyes straight ahead.

One of the guards looked at Aladdin. "Take them to the Rathous?"

He nodded. Then he turned back to Kirstyn. "You need rest and food. Can you make it back to Herr Kaufmann's house?"

"Yes, of course."

They started walking, but she began to feel even weaker. *Not now.* Her vision spun, and she began to lose her grip on Aladdin. The strangers walking by them, staring, grew blurry and dark. She felt herself being picked up and carried, her head resting against Aladdin's upper arm. She could still smell his shirt even if she couldn't see.

Gradually, her vision returned as she floated in and out of consciousness. She should feel embarrassed. Perhaps that would come later. For now she would just enjoy Aladdin's closeness and pray he was taking her to a bath . . .

CHAPTER EIGHTEEN

Aladdin caught Kirstyn, picking her up in his arms. Was she dying? Or had she only fainted? She couldn't die. He quickened his pace.

Her eyes fluttered and his breath quickened.

"Kirstyn? Can you hear me?"

"I think I can walk." But her voice was groggy and her eyes were still mostly closed.

He could feel her ribs as he held her, could feel her collarbone against his chest. Poor girl, so thin. When had she last eaten? His heart stuttered inside him as joy warred with heartbreak at what she must have suffered.

Holding her close, he walked fast. He wanted to get her home in case he needed to send someone for a doctor.

Hilde would feed her until she couldn't eat another bite. And Herr Kaufmann would give her the softest bed in the house. And Grethel would . . . *Grethel*.

No, no, no. His stomach sank. What would Kirstyn think of him when she discovered he'd promised to marry Grethel? Once, when she'd wanted him to go walking in the woods with her, she found him practicing swordplay with Valten. She said, "Do you really need to be a good swordsman too? You're already perfect at everything else."

His gut twisted at the thought of her finding out that he'd agreed to marry Grethel, that he'd given up on her still being alive. She would never again say he was perfect. If only he could keep her from finding out, to keep that a secret. How could she ever forgive him for being so faithless?

He would have to tell Grethel and Herr Kaufmann that he couldn't marry Grethel. How could he bear to lose their love and admiration?

For now he'd push that from his mind. Kirstyn deserved his attention. He would focus on taking care of her and, in every way he could, making up for the terrible ordeal she had been through. But the fear that Kirstyn would be disappointed in him . . .

"Aladdin?" She opened her eyes again.

"Yes?" They weren't very far from home now. "Are you in pain? You aren't injured, are you?" Then he noticed the rope dangling from her wrist. What had that man done to her?

"No." She seemed more alert now, and she nestled against his chest. "He didn't hurt me, not as he might have. But I'm afraid my wrist will be scarred."

He looked down at her hand, resting against him. Scabs, along with raw, weeping flesh, ringed her wrist. He was hollowed out by the sight. If only he could have protected her.

Kirstyn drank in every facet of Aladdin's face as he stared at her wrist, the pained look in his half-closed eyes, his parted lips. *Thank You, God. He must still care for me.* But could he love her?

And what would he think when he found out she loved him? She was ragged and pathetic, thin and pale, and she hadn't had a bath in a long time, while he wore the clothes of a wealthy merchant—a blue turban with silver-and-gold stitching and a long flowing cloak of blue velvet trimmed in fur.

"We're here." He turned into the doorway of a large four-story home. "Will you knock? My hands are full." He looked down at her in such an endearing way, it made her heart skip.

It was the same woman who had opened the door before.

"Oh, thank heavens! Are you unwell? Aladdin, is she unwell? Come in."

"Kirstyn"—Aladdin brushed past the woman—"this is Hilde."

"Lady Kirstyn, oh, my dear. You will want a good, hot meal and a soft bed. You poor thing. Come."

Kirstyn opened her mouth to speak, then bit her lip as Aladdin carried her through the entryway.

"What is it?"

She whispered, "Do you think I could have a bath?"

"Of course." He called over his shoulder to Hilde, "Could you please prepare a bath for Lady Kirstyn?"

"Of course. The poor dear."

"You can put me down now." Kirstyn suddenly felt shy, unable to look him in the eye as he complied. "I'm so sorry you had to carry me."

"I'm not sorry. That is . . . it wasn't your fault, and I didn't mind."

They exchanged a glance as Hilde hurried her away for her bath.

CHAPTER NINETEEN

K irstyn sighed as she stepped out of the small wooden tub of warm water and dried herself. She hadn't felt so relaxed in a very long time. But the thought that Aladdin was nearby, waiting for her, kept her from lingering in the comforting bath.

Once again she recalled the way Aladdin had looked at her since he had found her an hour ago, and she melted inside. Her sweet, thoughtful, generous Aladdin. Now she could finally have him back. And she could see her family again. She missed them so much. Tears stung her eyes at the thought of her mother's hugs and her father's powerful presence.

She shivered and quickly drew the clean white chemise over her head.

Would Aladdin go with her back to Hagenheim? Of course not. His business and his fortune were here in Lüneburg.

She didn't want to worry about that now. She would be joyful and anticipate being next to Aladdin again—and following through with the promise she had made herself during the lonely hours of her captivity, the promise to tell Aladdin how she felt about him.

The curtain parted, and Frau Hilde poked her head in the tiny space near the fire that had been sectioned off for Kirstyn and the tub. "Heavens above! I didn't know you'd be finished already. Let me get you dressed before you catch a chill." Hilde lifted a long-sleeved kirtle of deep blue silk over Kirstyn's head. It flowed over her shoulders and down her body to her feet with a satisfying rustle.

"Thank you. It's a beautiful dress. Whose is it?"

"Oh, this is Fräulein Grethel's dress—or it was, but she hasn't been able to fit in it since she was thirteen."

"Oh. I am smaller than I was. I did not eat so much when I was . . . when I was with Michael and Anna." She hadn't considered how it would feel to talk to strangers about where she had been for the past half year. Her face flushed.

"You poor dear."

Hilde said the words so tenderly, tears rushed to Kirstyn's eyes again.

"It is a terrible thing that has happened to you, but you are among good people here in this house. No one will harm you in any way, even . . . Well, we are very glad you are alive and well, my dear. Most of all Aladdin, poor thing. He mourned you with all his heart, he did."

"He thought I was dead?" Her heart sank. Had everyone given her up for dead? She thought at least Aladdin would have kept the faith that she was alive.

"Ja. None of us thought you could have survived. After all, your father found your scarf with blood all over it, and there seemed to be no other trace of you."

"Oh." Pain squeezed Kirstyn's heart. She'd prayed and believed that they were searching for her. It was one of the things that had kept her sane and kept her from complete despair. How could they have given up on her?

"'Tis a good thing for you that Michael was foolish and prideful enough to return to Lüneburg, thinking he could kill Aladdin and take Herr Kaufmann's business. Yes, you are a very fortunate young lady, after all."

"Yes." *After all.* After all that she had suffered at Michael's hands, undeservedly suffered, while those she loved had given her up for dead and gone on with their lives. Was she so insignificant to them? The fear that if she disappeared her family wouldn't even miss her swept over her like water, rushing over her head and submerging her. Had they been well on their way to forgetting about her completely? Her father and mother had eight children. But Aladdin? She was the most important person in his life, wasn't she? How could he believe she was dead and stop searching for her?

The pain in her chest intensified, like a knife twisting deeper.

Of course, she knew she was being ungracious. They had surely mourned for her. Their pain must have been terrible. But it didn't lessen her own heartache.

She made an effort to push these thoughts aside and focus on what Hilde was saying as she helped her on with her clothing and put a towel around her dripping hair.

"I only hope Grethel and Herr Kaufmann . . ." Hilde's voice trailed away, then she bit her lip.

"You hope they . . . what?"

"Nothing." Hilde shook her head and turned away, no longer meeting her gaze.

By the time Hilde had finished tying the laces at the sides of the dress, all Kirstyn could think about was seeing Aladdin again. Surely his words, his manner toward her, and the expression on his face would reassure her and help assuage this pain inside.

"Let me attend to that wrist." Hilde lifted Kirstyn's left hand to examine it, as Michael had always tied the rope around that wrist, then went to fetch something. She returned with a small pot and smeared yellow salve on all the open sores, then quickly wrapped Kirstyn's wrist with a cloth bandage.

Next Hilde helped her dry her hair as she sat on a stool before the fire. She closed her eyes. She might have been back home at Hagenheim Castle, her mother combing out her hair. Pleasantly warm, she nearly fell asleep as Hilde continued to prepare her coiffure, braiding two tiny plaits on either side of her head and wrapping them around the rest of her hair.

"You don't have to go to any trouble," Kirstyn said as Hilde reached for some ribbon.

"Nonsense. I am enjoying dressing the hair of the Duke of Hagenheim's daughter. Besides, you are so beautiful, and after all you have suffered, it is a pleasure to take care of you."

Being reminded of "all she had suffered" kept her from closing her eyes. She wished her hair was done so she could see Aladdin.

"Anyone in there?" His voice came from just outside the curtain.

"Patience," Hilde said. "She is nearly perfect."

"Are you hungry?" Aladdin asked.

"Yes!" Perhaps she sounded too eager.

"The servants say they have prepared you a feast."

"I am very grateful."

"Hilde, I hope you are not playing with her hair. She is beautiful without it."

"Hush, you," Hilde said with mock irritability. "I will not be rushed."

Kirstyn's heart had raced at hearing Aladdin's voice, but Hilde's declaration made it slow again. She couldn't think of a polite way to tell Hilde she didn't care about her hair. She just wanted to be with Aladdin—and to eat. Her stomach growled at the thought of food.

"I'm almost done," Hilde mumbled for Kirstyn's ears only. A tug here and a tuck there, then, "It is finished." She held out a small looking glass.

Kirstyn took it from her and gazed at herself. It had been a long time since she'd seen herself, as she and Anna had no looking glass. Kirstyn recoiled from her own image. Her skin was white and pasty from not being out in the sun. Her cheekbones jutted out, hollowing her cheeks. She'd never been so thin.

"I look . . . bad."

"You don't like your hair? I can rearrange it."

"Oh, no, you did a very good job with it. Thank you so much. I just . . . I don't look the same as I did before . . . before they . . . well, before." Could Aladdin possibly still think she was pretty? Or was he secretly as horrified as she was at how altered she looked? He was too kind to say so.

Her stomach suddenly was fluttering like birds' wings at seeing him again.

"If you are sure you like your hair, you can join Aladdin and the others."

Kirstyn stood on shaky legs, reminding her how hungry she was and that she was not used to so much activity. She stepped to the curtain and Hilde pushed it aside for her.

Aladdin stood at the end of the dimly lit corridor. He turned as she walked toward him.

"There you are." He met her halfway and held out his arm. "Are you feeling better?"

"Yes, thanks to Hilde. The bath was wonderful, and I believe I have Grethel to thank for this lovely gown."

He smiled down at her. It was so good to see his smile, Kirstyn felt the tears threaten. *Dear Lord of heaven, help me not to make a fool of myself. I am so weepy. Help me overcome.*

Aladdin led her into the main room of the house. Three people sat at a table in the center of the room, and all three turned to look at her.

Her stomach fluttered even more as she smiled and nodded at them, but none of them smiled back.

Herr Kaufmann seemed to recover himself somewhat. He stood and motioned with his hand. "Please, sit down, Lady Kirstyn."

A young boy stared at her with his mouth open and eyes wide. And the third person was a pretty young woman with dark hair. She must be Grethel.

"Please allow me to present my daughter, Grethel, and this is Abu. Grethel and Abu, we have visiting with us Lady Kirstyn, the daughter of the Duke of Hagenheim."

"Thank you so very much for your hospitality, Herr Kaufmann. I am grateful. And it is a pleasure to meet your family." She smiled again at Grethel and then Abu.

Kirstyn had used her smile many times to make people like her. It always seemed to work. Until now. Grethel stared at her as if Kirstyn had just slapped her. And Abu's eyes told her he was afraid she was about to steal his favorite person.

Aladdin seated her beside Abu and across the table from Grethel and him. At least she would have one friendly face to look at. But what did Aladdin really think when he looked at her skinny, sickly pale face?

The servants brought out bowls of soup and bread. Kirstyn immediately dipped her beautifully carved and polished wooden spoon into the soup. She probably should have been embarrassed at the "*Mmm*" sound she made as the flavors burst on her tongue, but she simply kept eating. The soup tasted of broth, bits of beef, leeks, carrots, and quinces, among other things. Delicious!

When she was spooning up the last bite, she noticed how quiet everyone else at the table was—and how bad her manners were, as she was just now glancing up from her food.

Herr Kaufmann, Aladdin, Grethel, and even Abu were all looking at her.

She set down her spoon. "That was the best soup I've ever tasted."

Aladdin smiled. "It is very good." He raised his spoon to his mouth.

Abu said, "Hilde makes sweet pies and cakes and fruit pasties. She is the best!"

Kirstyn could appreciate his enthusiasm, as well as his list of favorite foods. Now Grethel was the only one not smiling. She was staring down at her soup, her lips pursed together and her jaw set.

A frisson of foreboding rippled through Kirstyn. What could she have done to make Grethel angry?

"Thank you, Grethel, for allowing me to borrow your gown. It is very generous of you."

"That dress never fit me anyway." Grethel sat up straighter, as if to draw attention to her figure, which was fuller than Kirstyn's had been even before her abduction.

"I do thank you. The color is beautiful, and since I seem to have gotten thinner, it fits me very well."

Kirstyn knew that having a fuller figure was considered more attractive and conducive to bearing children, and therefore more desirable. She stared down at her clasped hands in her lap, again blinking back tears.

Frau Hilde entered the room with a large platter of roasted pheasant swimming in a delicious-smelling gravy. A large helping was spooned onto her trencher of bread. It was enough to cheer anyone, and when everyone had been served, Kirstyn began to eat. But this time she remembered to look up at the others between bites.

"Abu, what have you accomplished today?" Aladdin asked.

Abu slumped a bit and stared at his food. "The teaching master is forcing me to learn arithmetic."

"Not *forcing* you. You must think of it as *helping* you to learn it."

Abu did not answer, but he sighed. "I will learn it because you and Herr Kaufmann want me to learn it." But his expression was quite sad.

Aladdin smiled and Herr Kaufmann said, "Thank you. And you may come to enjoy learning someday. Like Aladdin."

Abu heaved another sigh.

The pheasant and its accompanying spicy gravy were quite delicious, and Kirstyn ate the dish with one of the wheat rolls. But before she was finished with her helping, she began to feel as if all the food might come back up. She stopped eating and sipped the fruit drink she had asked for in place of wine. It had been so long since she had drunk wine, she did not think it would sit well with her.

The meal went on for two more courses, but Kirstyn was only able to eat a few more bites. The conversation eventually turned to her parents.

"I am eager to see them." She forced herself to downplay her emotions and speak calmly.

"When the time comes," Herr Kaufmann said, "I shall send my guards to accompany you home."

"Thank you. That is very generous." Her stomach sank. Wouldn't Aladdin also accompany her?

"I wrote to your father while you were getting ready for supper." Aladdin drew out a rolled piece of parchment from inside his waistcoat. "You can read it and add anything you wish."

"Oh. But . . . can we not leave in the morning? We'll arrive the same time as my letter."

Aladdin's expression was gentle. "We will need you to remain here long enough to tell your story to the town council so they can judge your abductors. I am sorry. I hope it will only be two or three days at most."

"Of course." But she felt as if a huge boulder had been dropped on her. She stared at the table and took deep breaths, needing a few moments to overcome her distress. If only she and Aladdin were alone and these strangers were not staring at her.

"The letter will reach your parents before we ever could, and we will follow it on our way to Hagenheim very soon."

We. He said "we" would go to Hagenheim. The heavy feeling lifted a little.

When she looked up, Grethel's expression arrested Kirstyn's attention. Grethel's eyes narrowed, and she turned to glare at Aladdin. Then she stood and stalked out of the room.

Aladdin's jaw twitched and he swallowed hard.

"Grethel?" her father called after her. But then the corners of his mouth drooped and he gave an almost imperceptible shake of his head. "Will you excuse me? I shall see what is the matter." He pushed himself back from the head of the table and slowly left the room.

"May I go play?" Abu asked.

"Yes, you may," Aladdin answered.

Abu ran out, and she and Aladdin were alone in the dining hall.

"Is something wrong?" Kirstyn asked softly. "I sense that my presence is not entirely . . . wanted."

Aladdin got up from his seat, came around the table, and sat beside Kirstyn.

"I want you here. Very much." He gazed deeply into her eyes, his expression intense. "Herr Kaufmann and his daughter are kind people. There is nothing for you to be anxious about."

She drank in his features, so familiar to her, and yet there were subtle changes since she'd last seen him. He was a bit darker—he must have been in the sun more since he left Hagenheim. His face had filled out a bit, and he had more black stubble on his cheeks and chin. He was no longer the orphan boy. He was a very handsome, powerful man.

Aladdin picked up the parchment from the table and held it in front of her. "Will you write something in the letter for your parents?"

"Yes."

He fetched an ink pot and quill while she unrolled the letter and read it. She couldn't help imagining how her parents would feel when they saw it. She had to take a deep breath.

She took the pen from Aladdin and wrote,

> I love you, Mother and Father. I want you to know I am well and that Aladdin is taking care of me. I will be coming home to you very soon, and I want many hugs and kisses from my family when I arrive. Your loving daughter, Kirstyn.

Aladdin rolled it up and sealed it with an unfamiliar seal. "I shall be back in a moment. A servant will deliver this letter to the courier. He'll leave with it tonight."

Aladdin hurried out and came back only a minute later and

resumed his place beside her. Meanwhile, with her stomach so full, she had become rather drowsy.

She leaned into him, and he put his arm around her. They had always been friends, but they'd never allowed themselves to touch each other much. But now . . . it felt natural to lean on him, letting him place his hand on her upper arm and pull her closer while she rested her head on his shoulder. How good it felt to be with someone she trusted. After all the terror, pain, and abuse she'd been through the past year, she just wanted to be with her friend.

"Do you remember the time when we were little," Kirstyn said, "and we were playing blindman's buff behind the orphanage? It was the first time I ever saw you, and one of my earliest memories."

"I remember."

"A boy grabbed my arm, and you grabbed him."

"I thought he was about to hurt you."

"You were determined to protect me, even though that boy was much bigger than you were."

Aladdin gently squeezed her shoulder.

"I used to dwell on that and all the other memories I have of you."

"Do you remember when you saw that poisonous snake I was about to step on and screamed at me? You probably saved my life."

"I like to think so." Kirstyn almost laughed. "Do you remember the time you picked me up and held my feet on your shoulders so I could look into that squirrel's nest?"

"That squirrel almost bit your nose." A smile lightened his tone.

"I fell and you caught me. You were always there to protect me."

"I only wish . . ."

"What?"

"That I could have protected you when it counted most, when those kidnappers came."

Her stomach clenched. *I wish it too. So very much.* "It's all right. He had Anna, so he did not molest me, and he beat her more than he did me."

"It is so strange to me that Anna would stay with such a man."

"Yes. I hated her sometimes, knowing she could have set me free but chose instead to do Michael's bidding. But part of me pities her. She thinks what Michael feels for her is love and if she loses him, no one else will ever love her."

"I'm so glad you're safe from them. How overjoyed I was to see you alive." He rested his cheek on top of her head for a moment.

She also felt moments of joy, but she couldn't shake the feeling that all was not well. Perhaps it was only the strange way Grethel had reacted to her. But Herr Kaufmann had also reacted a bit strangely to her presence. Her body relaxed in Aladdin's embrace, but after her long ordeal . . . safety still seemed just out of her grasp.

CHAPTER TWENTY

Aladdin felt warm to his fingertips at Kirstyn sleeping against his shoulder. He'd dreamed of moments such as this.

Unfortunately, at least two people in the house would not feel the same. If either Grethel or Herr Kaufmann were to walk by and see them . . . He prayed they would not.

Aladdin didn't move, not wanting to wake Kirstyn, and let his mind wander.

He had hardly been able to eat, could hardly take his eyes off Kirstyn. It had been so long since he'd seen her, he just wanted to drink her in with his eyes. She was even more beautiful than he remembered, even though she was obviously weakened by her ordeal. And though he had told the truth when he said he was overjoyed to have her alive and well, some things kept surfacing to mar his joy.

He had to tell Grethel he couldn't marry her. *Dear God, don't let her and Herr Kaufmann hate me for that.* He felt a stab of pain at the thought of disappointing and hurting them. But, of course, he couldn't marry her. His feelings for Kirstyn were overwhelming, eclipsing anything he might feel for Grethel. It wouldn't be fair to marry her.

Would he also have to tell Kirstyn that he had agreed to marry Grethel? He felt sick just thinking about it. He also hoped she never found out that he had stopped searching for her, as her father had. She had called him her dearest friend. And though she knew he wasn't *actually* perfect, it still filled an empty place inside his heart to hear her say it.

If only Grethel would stay silent, Kirstyn need never know he'd agreed to marry a woman he didn't love.

It was wrong of him, cowardly to think like that. He nearly groaned aloud. He should be completely honest with Kirstyn. And Grethel. Tonight, with Kirstyn exhausted and still getting used to being safe, was not the right time.

Another thought tempered his joy—Kirstyn's scars. Those scars on her wrist would fade with time, but what kind of scars would she carry in her thoughts and her heart? She was obviously eager to get home to her mother and father, but in the meantime, would she allow him to comfort her? Would she let him love her? Marry her?

He mustn't get ahead of himself. It was too soon to talk about marriage. She probably didn't think of him that way. He was the Saracen orphan boy she had adopted, just like those ten orphans she wanted to adopt someday.

His stomach sank yet again at the thought of having to disengage himself from Grethel. But neither did he want to marry someone else when he was in love with Kirstyn. If he was honest with himself, he always had been in love with her. Making his fortune would not be enough to secure his happiness. Being "adopted" by Herr Kaufmann, saving Abu from the streets—none of that was enough. They were his family. But he wanted Kirstyn to be the most important part of that family.

The terrifying thing about wanting her was . . . she might reject him. And he might lose Herr Kaufmann too.

Kirstyn made a sound in her sleep and lolled her head on his shoulder. She opened her eyes. "Aladdin? Where am I?"

"You're in Herr Kaufmann's home."

"Is it nighttime? Or morning?"

"Nighttime. Come. I will help you to your room. Can you walk?"

"Yes, of course." She drew in a deep breath as she stood.

Aladdin guided her out from the bench and kept his arm around her as they made their way to the staircase. They ascended the steps slowly. Her hand rested against his chest as she snuggled her head against his shoulder. So trusting. His heart filled, swelling almost painfully.

"Aladdin?"

"Yes?"

"I'm glad you were here to help me."

"I'm glad too."

They stopped in front of the door of the room Hilde had prepared for her.

"I'll send Hilde up to help you get ready for bed. She can get you anything you need."

"Thank you, Aladdin." She gazed into his eyes as she opened the door.

"Of course." He turned and hurried down the steps. He found Hilde, then he went in his room and pressed a hand to his forehead.

The right thing to do would be to go now in search of Herr

Kaufmann and Grethel to beg their forgiveness. But didn't they know already? Both of them had guessed that he loved Kirstyn. Wouldn't they know that he simply couldn't marry Grethel now that Kirstyn had been found? She shouldn't even want to marry him. There was no need for him to go and tell her what she must already assume. Besides, they'd probably already gone to bed.

No, there was no need to tell them now.

Aladdin awoke while it was still dark outside. As he lay there, he became aware of a sound. He strained to hear, suddenly realizing it was coming from the room next to him. Kirstyn!

He leapt out of bed, tangling his legs in his covers. He fell to the floor on his knees, then sprang up and hurried to pull on some hose and a long, loose shirt. He went out and stopped outside her door. Nothing. Should he knock? It wasn't proper to go into her room while she slept, and now he wasn't even sure he'd heard anything. Perhaps he'd imagined it. He'd lain awake for hours, thinking about how he would tell Grethel he couldn't marry her and also thinking about Kirstyn.

He didn't wish to wake her. He stood listening, waiting. He finally sank to the floor, his back against her door. If he heard the sound again, he would knock.

Kirstyn was running from Michael. She could see the church just ahead. Her legs were so heavy. She forced them to move, but it was as if she were trying to run through a lake of thick, sticky honey. She pushed herself harder. Every time she glanced behind her, Michael was closer.

She reached the door of the church. It opened and she entered.

A priest stood in front of her. His face was hidden till he turned and looked at her. Michael. He smiled and leapt toward her, grabbing her arm.

Kirstyn tried to scream but no sound came.

She awoke and sat up, gasping, and let out a sob. She lay back down and covered her mouth. "It was only a dream," she whispered. "I'm safe here in this house. Aladdin is nearby." In the darkness, the only thing she could make out was the outline of a window.

She tried to calm her breathing. How would she get back to sleep now? She forced her mind to think thankful thoughts. *God, thank You for saving me from Michael. Thank You that Aladdin is here with me. Thank You, God, that I will see Mother and Father very soon, and that Aladdin sent them that letter so they will know I'm alive and not be sad. Thank You for Aladdin.*

She felt herself begin to drift off to sleep again.

It was morning. The sun was shining outside as Kirstyn entered the dining room. Aladdin and Grethel were standing there, their heads together. They looked up, their eyes focusing on Kirstyn. Aladdin looked sad, but Grethel smirked. She pulled Aladdin into her arms.

"Aladdin is marrying me," she said.

Aladdin frowned, shrugged his shoulders, and turned away from Kirstyn.

Grethel pointed to the door. "You have to go. Nobody wants you here."

Aladdin would not even look at her.

Kirstyn turned around to find Herr Kaufmann with a sullen expression. He also pointed at the door, mimicking his daughter.

Kirstyn stumbled toward it, blinded by her tears.

She was pushing herself up on her hands in bed as she blinked awake.

How could Aladdin do that to her? *O God, does he love Grethel?*

Grethel was very pretty. And the way she had looked at Kirstyn . . . She must be in love with Aladdin. How could she not be? He was handsome and kind and good and living in her house.

She lay back down on the bed. "It was only a dream," she whispered. But it had seemed so real. When she closed her eyes, she was back in that room with Aladdin shrugging and turning away from her, while Grethel smirked and ordered her to leave. A physical pain shot through her chest.

Aladdin had never said he loved her. She'd always imagined he did, had believed she was the most important person in his life. He was the orphan boy who sacrificed himself and let the bear maul him to protect her. He was her friend who went on walks with her in the woods, who did whatever she wanted—until the day he left her to go make his fortune.

What if she was never able to overcome her trembling fear every time she saw a stranger? What if she couldn't stop the weepiness? What if she had nightmares about Michael every night? How could she go through life, get married, and adopt orphans the way she'd always dreamed of if she was scarred and fearful and damaged?

Aladdin awoke in front of Kirstyn's door when he heard the servants downstairs. He went to his own room and got dressed for the day.

On his way down he passed Grethel's door, feeling even less inclined to speak to her about breaking their marriage agreement than he had the night before. She probably was not dressed yet anyway. He continued down the stairs.

Herr Kaufmann was sitting in his cushioned armchair in the solar. "Aladdin, my son. Did you sleep well?" He greeted him the same way nearly every morning, but this morning he did not seem as cheerful. Would their relationship change now?

Herr Kaufmann sighed. "I can guess what you are thinking. You no longer wish to marry my daughter."

"Well . . . yes. I am still in love with Kirstyn. I never wanted to hurt Grethel. I hope you understand. It is so painful to me—"

"As it is to me." Herr Kaufmann's tone and expression were the closest to anger directed at Aladdin he had ever experienced from his mentor. "If you had been lawfully betrothed in the Church, I would not so quickly accept your excuse of loving someone else."

Aladdin's heart raced. Would Herr Kaufmann be unwilling to forgive him?

"But I don't think Grethel will want to marry a man who's in love with another woman." Herr Kaufmann folded his arms across his chest, letting them rest on his belly as he stared at the wall.

"I hope you both will be able to forgive me in time. I'm so sorry."

"Yes, yes." Herr Kaufmann waved his hand in the air. "A heart is a fickle thing with a mind of its own."

Fickle? Aladdin had never really loved Grethel. He'd only agreed to marry her because . . . well, he wanted to please his mentor. And it was an attempt to stop his pain over Kirstyn's apparent death.

Herr Kaufmann's chin quivered, then locked in place. "Did you know that Cedric has admitted to seizing and carrying away Lady Kirstyn? He says he had a good reason that he will only reveal when the town council questions him publicly. Can you imagine? He expects us to believe that he could have an excuse for carrying off a woman and holding her against her will." He pressed his lips together and rubbed his forehead.

Aladdin placed a hand on his shoulder. Herr Kaufmann heaved a sigh and mumbled, "I should not be surprised at anything he would say or do. But to know that this was my son . . . It is a heavy, heavy blow."

Aladdin's heart ached at seeing Herr Kaufmann's grief. And it was even harder knowing his mentor might not welcome his comfort at the moment. Aladdin sat with him anyway, listening when he spoke and offering what sympathy he could, until the morning meal was ready.

Aladdin and Herr Kaufmann were joined at the table by Grethel and, just behind her, Kirstyn.

If possible Kirstyn was even lovelier than the night before. She smiled tentatively at him and his heart soared. But one glance at Grethel, the way her gaze was fastened on him—accusing, hurt, angry—brought his heart crashing back down again.

The mood at the table was somber, but it was sinking into his mind that Kirstyn was truly alive and whole—resurrected, as it were, from the dead. It was not a dream; he couldn't help feeling the joy of it.

"Where is Abu?" Aladdin asked.

"He had his breakfast early and is with his tutor." Herr Kaufmann's voice was slow and shaky, and he did not look Aladdin in the eye. "Perhaps I should send the lad away. Apparently I'm not very good at raising boys into decent, God-fearing men."

Both Grethel and Kirstyn stopped eating and stared at Herr Kaufmann. Aladdin sent up a wordless prayer and said, "You cannot take the blame on yourself. Each man is responsible for his own actions. Abu is a good boy, only playful."

"That is true, Papa." Grethel reached out and placed a hand on Herr Kaufmann's arm. "Michael's wickedness is not your fault. You did your best."

"Humph. Who is there to blame if not me? I am his father."

"Blame the devil, who tempted him to do wrong," Aladdin said. "Perhaps now Michael will repent." It would soon be too late.

Rather than looking mollified, Herr Kaufmann banged his fist on the table, then leaned forward, covering his face with his hands. A few moments later he arose and walked out of the room without a word.

Grethel sat unmoving, her gaze focused on the table. Kirstyn sent a questioning look at Aladdin, who gave her a slight shake of his head.

"Excuse me." Grethel stood and left the room without looking at either of them.

"What was that about?" Kirstyn asked.

"As strange as it sounds, Michael, the man who kidnapped you, is Herr Kaufmann's son."

"Oh." She pressed a hand to her heart. "How very . . . terrible."

"Yes."

"Well . . . what happens next?"

"We should receive word from the town council soon,

summoning you to give your testimony. Then Michael will have to defend himself. Most likely he will be hanged, but since your father is the Duke of Hagenheim, they may want to hear from him before they carry out his punishment. They may even allow him to take Michael back to Hagenheim to carry out his own judgment and sentence."

"You will go with me to the town council meeting, won't you?"

"I will be there with you." His heart pounded with how much he wanted to show her he would stand by her and support her.

"Well, since we will have to wait until I am summoned, perhaps you could show me around Lüneburg today. I want to see the place where you've been living and working for the past year and a half."

"I would be more than pleased to show you my new town."

Kirstyn hated how needy she had sounded as she said, "You will go with me to the town council meeting, won't you?" But when Aladdin looked so concerned and came around the table and held out his arm to her, she took a deep breath. *It's all right to ask for Aladdin's help. He cares about me.*

"Today is market day," Aladdin said. "I shall buy you a warm cloak and shoes so you won't have to borrow Grethel's."

Kirstyn glanced down at the dress. Truly, it was beautiful, but Kirstyn felt strange wearing it given Grethel's previous coldness.

Her chest ached. *Aladdin, do you love Grethel and not me?* She was very pretty. Perhaps he had fallen in love with her, living in her father's house, seeing her day after day. Perhaps now that Kirstyn was so thin and damaged and needy, he would not want her.

"I hope she doesn't mind that I'm wearing her things."

"I don't think she minds." But Aladdin's smile faltered.

They were soon out on the street, and Aladdin was pointing out different buildings. "This is St. Nikolai's Church, where we attend on Sundays. But later I shall show you the older St. John's Church."

At the marketplace Kirstyn chose a cloak made of black wool and trimmed with colorful embroidery. "It is expensive, isn't it? My father will pay you for it."

"It doesn't matter." Aladdin smiled as he paid the seller from a small bag of money he carried on his belt.

"I've never known what it was like to be in need and have no money and no one to help me. Until this year."

Aladdin squeezed her shoulder and drew close. His look was so sympathetic and interested, she went on.

"I think it has taught me compassion for others."

"You were already compassionate."

"But now I understand more and can empathize." Her throat tightened. She stared at Aladdin's face. Had he always had such a masculine jawline?

"I'm so sorry for what you went through." His voice was soft and gravelly.

"You are so brave, leaving Hagenheim and not knowing where you would go or what you would do. I can appreciate even more now just how courageous you were."

They turned and continued strolling, their arms linked. It felt a bit daring since they'd never done that before when her father's guards used to accompany them on their walks. But he *had* carried her in his arms after she fainted the day before.

"But at the time, I was a little angry with you for leaving me. Very selfish, wasn't I? Only thinking of what I wanted instead of wanting you to achieve your dream."

"You were not selfish at all. You could have ordered me to stay or said any number of things to force me. But you let me go."

How kind he was. She gazed up at him, not paying attention to where they were going, trusting Aladdin to lead her. He had such a handsome face, such beautiful brown skin and thick black hair. If only it were permissible to kiss his cheek, or even his lips.

But that was not the way she had planned to tell him she loved him. So many times she had imagined the words she would say to him as she lay awake in the dark with Michael's rope around her wrist.

Aladdin just seemed so much older and manlier now, in a way that made her stomach flip. It made her long to hear him say he wanted her to be his wife. But perhaps he only loved her as a friend. The new fear, which was becoming familiar, gripped her again. She might not be as important to him as he was to her.

Being held against her will and failing to escape for so long had robbed her of her confidence. She knew this. So she had to force herself to stop feeling the fear. For now she would enjoy being in Aladdin's company. Besides, they were on a public street. It was not the time to reveal her true feelings, or to ask him about his.

"This is the saltworks." Aladdin pointed to a high thick wall. "Herr Kaufmann is a salt master and owns the rights to four salt pans—a highly profitable position to be in."

"I'm sure it is. Salt is nearly as valuable as gold. And he trusts you to run his affairs?"

"Yes, he . . . well, he has told me he will make me his heir since his son, Michael, turned out so badly. He has given Michael so many chances to redeem himself, but he always does something evil instead, such as what he did to you."

He stopped walking and faced her. "I can hardly bear to think of him harming you. It makes me want to kill him." His voice was raspy. "Forgive me. After all you've been through, you shouldn't have to hear me spew my anger."

"It feels rather . . . healing to hear you say that."

He let out a breath, and one side of his mouth went up. He touched her cheek with the back of his gloved hand. "We can go into St. John's Church to get out of the cold for a few minutes."

He took her hand and pulled her in through the doors of the old church.

Just as they always were in Hagenheim, people were kneeling in prayer at the chancel and the crucifix, in front of the burning candles at the other end of the nave.

Aladdin and Kirstyn sat at the back of the church on a little bench. She rested her head on his shoulder. He put his arm around her and nestled her against his chest.

Her heart pounded. Surely he loved her as more than a friend.

"Do you want to talk about what happened to you?" he said softly, his breath teasing her hair on top of her head.

"I will talk a little, and then you tell me about your life here."

He agreed. So she told him about the mind-numbing feeling of never being allowed to talk to anyone, of never seeing the sun, and of having her every movement controlled. She could do nothing without Michael's permission. And while she spoke, Aladdin would sometimes make a sound in his throat or gently squeeze her shoulder.

When she told him about the times she had tried to escape and how despair always gripped her when she didn't succeed, that old feeling of helplessness crept over her again. She closed her eyes and reveled in the warmth of Aladdin's chest against her side.

"But now I want to hear about you." She turned her body so she was looking up at him.

He told her a little bit about his work on a typical day, then said, "But that is uninteresting. I shall tell you about Abu and how he came to live with us."

When he finished the tale, she said, "I'm so glad Abu has a family now. It reminds me of how my little brother Toby came to live with us."

Aladdin nodded. He knew the story, how her sister Margaretha had found Toby, a little orphan boy whose master mistreated him and didn't even give him a proper place to sleep. She brought him home to Hagenheim, and her parents adopted him.

While they had been talking, they had gotten warm, taken off their gloves, and laid them aside. No one had come into the church since they'd been sitting there, and it was very quiet. Aladdin picked up her hand and turned it over, as if examining it.

"Do you remember the time you got your hand stuck in that knothole?" he whispered.

"Yes. You said you might have to chop it off."

"I was only teasing you." Aladdin smiled.

"I like it when you smile. You were usually so solemn and thoughtful when we were children. Are you still so?"

He let his eyes leave her hand to gaze into her eyes. "Most would probably say so. But I do try to make time to play with Abu. I taught him archery."

"Did he like that?"

"Very much." Aladdin smiled again at her hand, caressing her fingertips one at a time, skimming over the nails, which were broken and jagged from her last escape attempt.

These kinds of caresses were not how friends related to one another, were they? But she tried not to let it show, how much his touch affected her.

"I remember I was as good at hitting the target as you were," Kirstyn said.

"Yes, but only at a certain distance."

"It isn't very chivalrous of you to remember that." She playfully swatted at his arm with the hand he had not captured in his larger one. She was beginning to feel breathless again. But he was only holding her hand, playing with it in the most innocent way.

"You must be getting hungry." He let go of her hand and reached for their gloves. "We should probably head home. The town council could send for you."

As Kirstyn pulled on her gloves, her hands shook just a bit. Her cheeks heated, as she had hoped he would kiss her hand.

The fact that they were in a church made her even more glad he couldn't read her thoughts.

CHAPTER TWENTY-ONE

Aladdin was almost sorry he had suggested they go back. But he didn't want her to get too tired. She needed rest and food to recover from her ordeal. She didn't need a lovesick man keeping her talking until she fainted—a lovesick man who couldn't stop thinking about kissing her. She had spoken about being selfish, but he was the selfish one.

They were walking back toward Herr Kaufmann's home when he caught a whiff of something that made his stomach rumble. A woman was sitting on a stool at the outskirts of the marketplace with a large basket covered with a linen cloth.

"Sausage and rolls!" she called out to them.

"May I have one?" Kirstyn's eyes were bright as she turned to him.

"Of course." He paid the woman, and she gave him two long bread rolls and two sausages about the length of his hand. He gave one of each to Kirstyn.

"How are you supposed to eat it?"

"Any way you like, but I put them together, like this." He

pressed the sausage into the roll so when he took a bite, he bit through both of them.

Kirstyn did the same with hers. "Mmm." She closed her eyes and chewed. "That is very good. I can almost taste sauerkraut."

"That's because sauerkraut's cooked inside the bread."

She looked down at her roll. "That is tremendous! I must have our cooks make these." She took another bite.

They walked toward the fountain in front of the Rathous in the town center. By the time they reached it, they had eaten their sausages and rolls. Aladdin fetched a dipper and caught some water flowing through the fountain. He gave the first dipperful of cold water to Kirstyn, and they took turns taking a drink.

"That was better than some five-course meals I've eaten." Kirstyn laughed. The sound was as high and melodious as he remembered. When he was a child, he imagined angels had given her that sound.

"Are you not cold?"

"Not very. I have this new warm cloak and my—Grethel's—gloves. And you? Are you cold?"

He shook his head.

They sat on the side of the fountain—a massive stone structure that reached as high as three men. It was even larger than the one in Hagenheim's Marktplatz.

"How are you feeling?"

Her cheeks were red from the cold, but the rest of her face was pale. He hoped it was from lack of sun, not from ill health.

"I feel well. But I'm glad to sit for a few minutes." She leaned against his shoulder.

He kept expecting someone to walk by and recognize him and ask who Kirstyn was, but so far no one had. They would no doubt wonder why he was sitting so close to another young woman besides Grethel. And yet his heart soared at having her so near.

"Aladdin?"

"Yes?"

"Do you think the courier has made it to Hagenheim yet?"

"He should be arriving tonight or tomorrow."

"Do you think my father will come to Lüneburg when he gets our letter?"

"I think he will take only enough time to gather provisions for himself and his men and saddle the horses."

That made Kirstyn smile. It was good to see her familiar smile and white teeth. What was it Song of Solomon said? *Thy teeth are like a flock of sheep that are even shorn, which came up from the washing; whereof every one bear twins, and none is barren among them.*

"I am feeling a bit tired," Kirstyn admitted.

"We shall go, then." He jumped down from the wall around the fountain and placed his hands on either side of her waist, the circumference so small his fingertips touched. She put her hands on his shoulders as he lifted her off the wall and set her feet on the ground.

"I'm sorry to cut our outing short." She kept her hands on his shoulders, gazing into his eyes. "I was enjoying spending the day with you . . . only the two of us."

His heart stuttered a few beats. "Kirstyn, I . . ."

"Yes?"

He swallowed. "The truth is, finding you and being able to be with you and talk to you and hold your hand—" He pulled her to his chest and whispered next to her ear, "These have been the best two days of my life."

She sniffed, and her hands tightened on his back.

"But now I need to get you home." He pulled away. "Are you well enough to walk?"

"Yes." She wiped her eyes with her hands, then held on to his arm. They walked through the marketplace and then the street toward Herr Kaufmann's, and soon they were home.

The town council had not sent for Kirstyn, so she went up to her room to rest, and Aladdin fell asleep in a chair.

When it was time for the evening meal, Grethel was away. "Staying with her friend Sybel," Herr Kaufmann said.

Aladdin still needed to speak to Grethel, to explain, but he was relieved she was away from home. It did dampen his joy to see Herr Kaufmann looking so gloomy. The poor man had received a blow, learning that Aladdin and Grethel's marriage, which he had hoped for and counted on, was not to be and learning of his son's latest nefariousness, which would likely lead to his execution.

Once Herr Kaufmann had finished eating, he excused himself and went to bed.

Aladdin and Kirstyn sat together at the table for at least an hour, talking about their days as children. When they ceased hearing the servants at their work, they went up to their rooms.

On the stairs Kirstyn said, "Sleep well, Aladdin. I shall see you in the morning."

The look on her face made him trip over his own feet. Perhaps he was just daft. But daft or not, he'd never been so full of joy.

Kirstyn sat opposite Aladdin, watching as he moved his knight over and across the chessboard.

"You shouldn't have done that." She immediately captured his knight with her bishop.

Aladdin sighed. "How did I miss that?"

"I suppose I'm just too clever for you." She grinned at him. But she had caught him staring at her instead of at the board. "You're not concentrating on the game."

He lowered his brows at her, twisting his mouth in a half frown. "We shall see."

He studied the board and chess pieces while she studied him. His face was endearing, even when he was intently staring at a chess game. His cheekbones were high and chiseled, but not in a harsh way. She liked that he kept his hair slightly longer, curling in the most beguiling way against his neck. A tiny scar snaked up his shoulder from underneath his fine white linen shirt, the start of much worse scars he had acquired when he saved her from the mama bear.

Finally he made his next move—setting out with his king.

"Are you sure you want to do that?" But Kirstyn didn't wait for him to change his mind. She put his king in check with her knight.

Aladdin slapped his hand to his forehead and made an unintelligible sound.

Finally, after studying the board, he made a move.

Kirstyn glanced down at the board, and suddenly it looked unfamiliar. Instead of gawking at Aladdin and letting her mind wander, perhaps she should have been planning her next move.

She made a poor move, and Aladdin captured two of her pawns. Then he went on to capture her knight, her bishops, and finally her queen.

"How did I let you win?" she moaned, but she knew how. She'd become distracted by him.

"You were defeated by the master. No one has beaten me at chess the entire time I've been in Lüneburg."

"Just you wait. I shall defeat you yet."

Aladdin's expression softened as he reached for her hand. "You defeat me every day just with your . . ." His gaze rested on her lips. "Your smile."

He leaned over the little chess table, his eyes capturing hers the way he'd captured her chess pieces.

"Aladdin!" Hilde called from the kitchen.

Aladdin let go of her hand as Hilde's footsteps sounded on the stone floor, getting closer. She stuck her head in the doorway. "Herr Kaufmann said you were coming to his office later today to help him with some work. Would you and Kirstyn like to take him his midday meal?"

"Of course," Aladdin said, then looked at Kirstyn. "Do you feel well enough to go? You might have to wait for an hour or so while I work."

"I am well and I don't mind. I want to get out in the sun every chance I can."

They retrieved the small basket, which contained enough food for all three of them, Hilde said, and set out.

"I think it's warmer today." Kirstyn walked very close to Aladdin's side, holding on to his arm.

Aladdin told her little bits of town history as they walked. Was it her imagination, or did his voice sound softer, more intimate than the day before as he leaned his head toward hers every time he spoke? Her eyes kept fastening on his lips. Her cheeks heated, even in the brisk winter air, at where her gaze—and thoughts—kept going.

At the warehouse they greeted Herr Kaufmann. Was it her imagination, or was he sad to see her? It must have something to do with Grethel being in love with Aladdin. Perhaps Kirstyn should have stayed home instead of accompanying Aladdin here.

They sat and ate together as the two men discussed business and numbers and those in their employ. Aladdin seemed so mature and intelligent. This was his domain. He was good at what he did. He had helped a wealthy man become even wealthier. Everything Aladdin did was successful. He never seemed to lose, and not just at chess. He'd even succeeded when he'd tangled with a bear. Though he did come away with some terrible scars, he'd survived.

But when he looked at her, he still had a vulnerable glint in his eye. She could still see that orphan boy who was so determined to do well in life, yet well aware that he was not only a fatherless orphan but also a foreigner, maligned and pushed around, literally sometimes, because of his Arabic origin and dark skin.

When they had finished eating, Herr Kaufmann called a man over.

"Take Lady Kirstyn around the warehouse. Show her the new shipments that just arrived from the Orient and Flanders."

Kirstyn followed her guide, Otto, as he led her to bags and bundles of silk cloth, embroidered slippers, and pungent and beguiling spices. Kirstyn looked through them all. It wasn't often that goods as fine as these came into Hagenheim. Though her people were well fed and content, she knew very few of them could afford luxury goods, except perhaps for the spices, which many considered essential.

Kirstyn browsed among the wares, staying out of the way of the men who came and went, carrying things out to be sold. Everyone knew exactly where they were going and what they were doing. Everything was labeled with a number, and guards stood nearby, watching over it all.

Aladdin came toward her. "Sorry I was so long."

"Has it been an hour already?" She had been looking through

some mechanical clocks that fascinated her. She'd never seen one outside of a monastery, and before that she had examined bright silk scarves, picking out the prettiest ones.

"More than. Take some of these scarves for your mother and sisters and yourself." He lifted a handful of them.

"May I? Are you certain it is all right?"

"Of course. Take as many as you like. I shall reconcile it in the books later."

She chose one scarf each for herself, her mother, her sisters-in-law, and her sisters. Aladdin had them carefully wrapped and sent back to the house by one of the young men working in the warehouse.

"If you are not too tired, I'd like to take you for a walk along the river."

"I would like that."

They set out, and by the time they reached the river, they were walking closer than ever, her arm through his. They came to a stone bridge and strolled over it, then stopped in the middle to lean on the side and look down at the slow-moving water.

"You are doing so well." Kirstyn turned her head to look at him. "You have everything you wanted—wealth, respect, and power. And you have people who love you—Herr Kaufmann and Abu." She purposely avoided mentioning Grethel.

"Those are the things I thought I wanted." He stared out over the water, his brows low over his eyes.

"Has that changed?" Her heart stuttered inside her. She had a feeling a lot had changed.

He turned toward her. "I thought if I made my fortune, I could make sure that I would never be poor and helpless again. I never wanted to feel the way I had when I was a child, overcome by the shame of stealing just to survive."

He almost never mentioned how he felt about his childhood before he came to Hagenheim. Vulnerability shone in his brown eyes, and it made her insides melt. She rested her hands on his chest and wished she had the courage to kiss him.

"But I also went through life gathering people, forming my own family of sorts—Priest, my friends at the orphanage, Herr Kaufmann, Abu, you . . . especially you."

"Do you still want me in your family?"

"More than anything."

Then why didn't he ask her to marry him? Or at least kiss her? Perhaps he would. He looked as if he wanted to.

"You look tired." His expression changed, and he pulled back from her. "We should go back. I don't want to exhaust you."

"You're not exhausting me." But the moment had obviously passed, and the breath she'd been holding rushed out of her.

Chapter Twenty-Two

Aladdin couldn't think about anything but kissing Kirstyn. But was it right to kiss her when she was still very much suffering the effects of a cruel, traumatic event? When her father was a duke and he did not know if he'd ever give his permission for them to marry?

He forced himself to take a step back and suggest they go home. Her expression changed, like a cloud covering the sun. But he needed to be wise, now more than ever.

His gaze was arrested by a stork's nest on a house nearby. The stork had flown to warmer climes, but the nest was still there, abandoned and empty. *Before that stork returns, let me be free to kiss Kirstyn.* It was a prayer he could feel good about.

He still needed to tell Grethel he couldn't marry her. But surely Herr Kaufmann would tell his daughter. They had not set a date and the banns had not been announced, after all.

Was he that much of a coward? Coward or not, if he could keep from revealing his marriage agreement with Grethel to Kirstyn, he would.

Kirstyn sat at the supper table with Aladdin and his family. Grethel was very quiet and hardly looked at anyone. Herr Kaufmann was also rather quiet. But Abu chattered away to Kirstyn about all the times they had all gone to Lüneburg Heath.

"When we competed in footraces, Aladdin always ran so fast, no one could beat him. I did catch him a few times, but I think he let me do it."

"You are very fast too," Aladdin told him. "Someday you'll be faster than I am."

Abu eyed him with a bit of suspicion. "Perhaps. If I grow to be taller than you."

Aladdin smiled and shook his head.

"And someday I will beat you at chess," Abu said.

"Never."

Kirstyn laughed. "He is very vain about his ability to win at chess."

Grethel made a slight noise, like a snort. Kirstyn glanced at her, but Grethel was taking a sip of her wine and looking down.

No one spoke for a few minutes as they were all enjoying the roast pheasant. Kirstyn had a thought.

"My father could be here tomorrow, could he not?" Kirstyn looked to Aladdin, who knew just how long it took to travel from Hagenheim to Lüneburg.

"It is feasible for him to arrive tomorrow."

"Oh?" Grethel suddenly seemed interested. "I suppose you will want to go back to Hagenheim immediately after he arrives, to be with your family."

"Yes, I suppose I will."

"She will have to wait until she speaks with the town council," Herr Kaufmann said with a rather severe look on his face. "She cannot leave until then."

"But shouldn't they talk to me soon? I thought they would have sent for me before now."

"It should be any day now." Aladdin met her gaze, but only for a moment.

She had been so hopeful Aladdin might kiss her when they'd stood on the bridge, only to be disappointed. But neither that thought nor Herr Kaufmann's and his daughter's obvious unhappiness could dampen her spirits. She was too full of joy that she would soon see her father.

The next morning Aladdin entered the dining hall to find Herr Kaufmann sitting there sipping his warm compote.

"Good morning." Aladdin smiled.

"Good morning, Aladdin."

Herr Kaufmann's expression made Aladdin's step falter. His voice was heavy, and he stared down into his cup.

"Here we are." Hilde entered carrying a platter. "Hot raspberry pasties, cream, and comfits and wafers."

"You have outdone yourself, Hilde." Aladdin could at least get a smile from Hilde.

Aladdin was just finishing a rolled-up wafer that he filled with cream and preserved cherries when he heard Kirstyn's light footfalls.

Kirstyn smiled as she entered the room. "Good morning, Herr Kaufmann. Good morning, Aladdin." Instead of sitting on the bench beside Aladdin, she sat across from him.

He was glad, for two reasons. He could look at her without drawing as much attention, and he would not have to fight the temptation to hold her hand as he would have if she'd sat beside him.

"Did you sleep well, Lady Kirstyn?" Herr Kaufmann was ever the polite host.

"Yes, I thank you. I'm so grateful for the soft bed. And you? Did you sleep well?"

"As well as can be expected, I suppose. I am thankful to God for sleep of any amount at my age."

"Oh, you are still young enough to enjoy life," Kirstyn said.

"I am thankful for the life I have," Herr Kaufmann said. He turned to Aladdin. "I shall take care of business today. You may stay with Lady Kirstyn again, since I expect the town council will be sending for her today."

"Have you spoken with them?" Aladdin had heard nothing.

"I spoke with Herr Reynart yesterday." Herr Kaufmann's expression became even gloomier.

The poor man. To have a son like Cedric. Aladdin wished he could comfort his mentor, but he couldn't think of anything to say. No one spoke. Aladdin sipped his compote and tried not to stare too much at Kirstyn while she ate. But every time she caught him, she smiled.

"I shall go." Herr Kaufmann rose from the table. "Good day, Lady Kirstyn. Aladdin."

They bid him a good day, and Kirstyn wiped her lips with her napkin. "I suppose we cannot go for a walk today. Perhaps we will play chess?"

Aladdin strode to Kirstyn's side. She stood and reached out to him. The next thing he knew, he was holding her close. He would never tire of holding her in his arms.

Kirstyn closed her eyes, putting everything else out of her mind except the tender way Aladdin held her. He was so tall and strong and warm. She tightened her arms around him. "You make me feel so safe."

He stroked her hair and his breathing quickened. Did her words affect him so much?

He pulled away and gazed into her eyes.

A strangled cry came from the doorway. They both turned to see Grethel. Her lip trembled, but then her eyes narrowed.

Aladdin's arms loosened, and they both took a step away from each other.

"How could you?" Grethel's voice shook as she pierced Aladdin with her eyes. "You are betrothed to *me!*"

Kirstyn went numb.

"Grethel, I'm so sorry. Please don't be angry, but we are not—"

"You horrible, hateful man!" Grethel stabbed her forefinger at Aladdin as tears flowed down her face. "Don't come near me again." She turned and ran.

Aladdin took one step toward Grethel, then stopped and turned to Kirstyn. His face was stricken. Her own pain stifled a momentary twinge of pity.

"Are you betrothed to Grethel?"

He shook his head. "We are not betrothed."

"Did you promise to marry her?"

"Only after I thought you were gone forever. But it can be undone. There was no betrothal."

"Why didn't you tell me?" Had he forgotten her so quickly? Did she mean so little to him after all? The numbness was replaced by a sharp pain that spread from her chest through her body.

"Kirstyn, please." He held out his hands to her. "I'm sorry."

"I think you should go and beg forgiveness from that young woman." Kirstyn turned and walked out of the room, holding her head high. Aladdin called to her, but she barely heard him through the beating of a hundred birds' wings in her ears.

She grew dizzy walking up the stairs to her bedchamber. She made it inside and closed the door, then sank to the floor.

He'd promised to marry another woman. Aladdin. Her Aladdin. What did this mean? That he never loved her? Did he love this woman? The pain was so overwhelming she gasped.

A few moments later a knock sounded at the door.

"Lady Kirstyn?"

She forced the breath back into her lungs. "Yes, Hilde?"

"Two of the town soldiers are here to escort you to the town council."

The veneer of toughness and strength that had served her through months of being held captive fell over her like a familiar shield.

"I'll be out in a moment."

She took several deep breaths, wiped her nose, and opened the door. Hilde walked down the stairs with her and at the bottom squeezed her hand. "Now, do not be afraid. All will be well."

"Yes, of course."

The soldiers bowed to her. "Please come with us," one of them said.

Kirstyn walked between them as they exited the house and started down the street.

What was it Aladdin had said when she asked him if he would come with her to the town council? *I will be there with you.* Yet here she was, alone, and he was probably off apologizing to the woman he had promised to marry.

No matter. She did not need him or anyone else. Her father would soon arrive to personally punish whoever had hurt his daughter.

She would dwell on that. She could not think about Aladdin now.

Aladdin called after Kirstyn. His heavy heart followed her footsteps from the dining hall and up the stairs. He reeled from how quickly his euphoria at having Kirstyn in his arms had changed to cold, sinking horror at Grethel's tears and Kirstyn's refusal to even look at him.

What should he do now? Go after Kirstyn or beg Grethel's forgiveness?

Oh, the wretchedness of what he had done. He could have at least told Grethel the truth—that he couldn't marry her because he was in love with Kirstyn.

He'd always prided himself on doing the right thing, behaving honorably, earning the admiration of everyone around him. It was as if night had become day and day night. And he was to blame.

"Grethel?" He called her name as he slunk through the house's corridors. He found her in the kitchen, sobbing in Hilde's arms.

Hilde looked up at him. She patted Grethel's shoulder. "You had best talk it over with him, my child."

Grethel spun around, her eyes red and her face blotchy and wet. "What do *you* want? I told you I never wanted to see you again."

"Please forgive me, Grethel. I know I should have told you. It was wrong of me. When I found out that Kirstyn was alive, I knew . . . I'm so sorry."

Grethel stared at him as if he were the most loathsome creature she had ever beheld.

Someone was knocking at the front door. Hilde hurried to see who was there.

"So you don't want to marry me? I want to hear you say it."

Three of the servants were watching and listening, their eyes as big as chickens' eggs. Better to have awakened Grethel two nights ago and told her then, in private, than to do it here in front of the servants.

"I hope you will forgive me someday. I didn't mean to hurt you."

Her face contorted. "Didn't mean to hurt me? No, you've only humiliated me, rejected me, and the whole town will know. They'll laugh at me, scorn me." A tear dripped from her eye and she angrily swiped at it. "You've ruined me forever."

"I'm sure that's not true."

"How dare you say that to me."

"I'm only saying that no one could disrespect you over this. Your father is wealthy and powerful. You are beautiful in every way. Every man in town will want you."

"Don't patronize me. I hate you."

She stepped toward him and shoved his shoulder. "Stay away from me." She stalked out.

A beating would have been preferable. He closed his eyes and leaned against the wall. And yet, in spite of his guilt, he felt a weight lifted off him at knowing that he would not be marrying Grethel.

When he opened his eyes, the servants were still staring at him, motionless as stones.

He tried to appear humble and remorseful, but the servants' looks were baleful. After all, they'd known Grethel all her life.

"Don't let it get you down," Albrecht said with a half frown, finally breaking their silence. "It's hard to love two women. Every man I know who's tried it has come out the worse for it."

"It isn't like that," Aladdin said, but perhaps he should stop there. Better if he didn't tell them he'd never actually loved their mistress, not enough to truly wish to marry her.

"Take a tankard of wine to help you lick your wounds, sir."

"No, thank you." He nodded to them and walked away.

His heart was thumping hard as he took the steps two at a time to Kirstyn's room. He knocked on the door and waited. No answer. "Kirstyn?" Still no answer.

"Aladdin," Hilde called from the bottom of the staircase.

He came halfway back down. "Yes?"

"Lady Kirstyn is gone with the soldiers to the Rathous."

"The town council."

"Yes."

"Thank you, Hilde." He ran the rest of the way down the stairs, grabbed his cloak from the peg near the door, and raced out.

Kirstyn stood before a group of ten men seated in a row behind a table in an enormous room. The ceiling was frescoed and so were the walls, framed between intricately carved wooden beams, reminding her a bit of the Great Hall in Hagenheim Castle.

One of the men rose from his seat. "Lady Kirstyn."

Just then, the heavy door at the side of the room opened and several men entered, but Kirstyn only had eyes for the first man in.

"Father!" Kirstyn ran to him and threw her arms around him. He was still wearing his traveling clothes and smelled like horse, but she didn't mind. Her father was here, and he wouldn't let anyone hurt her.

When she pulled away, tears glinted in his blue eyes. Rarely had she seen tears on her father's face. It made the salt drops start in her own eyes.

"You're alive. I thank God." Her father seemed to choke on the words. He swallowed, his smile wobbling, and laid a hand on her head. "My beautiful girl." He hugged her again.

"Is Mother well? All my sisters? How is everyone?"

"They are all well and overjoyed to hear you were found." His brown hair was full of gray. It surely wasn't that gray before she left.

"I missed you so much." Tears stung her eyes again as the nights of longing for her family flooded her mind.

"I missed you too, precious girl." He gently squeezed her chin. "And now I hear the town council is starting. Let us see this fiend from hell who stole you from us. Come."

She took his arm, and he led her straight up to the council members.

Aladdin had told her how the town had fought the nobles who once owned and controlled Lüneburg and its wealth and how they expelled them from their midst. They subsequently established their own town council to govern Lüneburg. They naturally would not be as impressed by meeting a duke, but each of them did stand and bow to the Duke of Hagenheim.

"Forgive me, Your Excellencies, for interrupting your proceedings," Father said. "I am here to take my daughter home as soon as possible and to see you enact justice, or if you prefer, you may turn the prisoner over to me and I shall take him back to Hagenheim to make certain he is duly punished for his crimes."

Power exuded from his broad shoulders, and she had never

felt prouder that he was her father. But honestly, she just wanted to sit at his knee and let him place his comforting hand on her head and listen to him tell her about home. How blessed she was to have him.

From the corner of her eye she saw Aladdin rush in. He moved through the people present to take a position near Herr Kaufmann at the front.

"Lady Kirstyn," the white-haired man on the town council began. "Because you are the daughter of Duke Wilhelm of Hagenheim, you do not have to speak about what the accused has done. You will be allowed to write it out and give it to the council, and no one else need hear it. But if you wish to, you may give us your story now and we will be able to rule more quickly in the matter."

"I have nothing to hide. I certainly have done nothing wrong, so I do not mind speaking freely here and now."

"As you say. Then will you kindly tell us what happened at the warehouse on *Schlachthous Strasse*?"

"I was attacked and taken forcibly from the Marktplatz of Hagenheim on the first day of May, 1415, by a man named Michael and another man."

She told them in as few words as possible all that had happened to her, forcing herself to speak about those horrifying, painful events in a monotone, determined to state only the facts as if she felt nothing.

Some of the men on the town council did not look at her, others were expressionless, while others wore looks of concentration. They asked her a few questions, and then they turned toward each other, saying a few quiet words and motioning with their hands.

The leader finally addressed her. "Thank you, Lady Kirstyn.

Now we will bring out the man and woman who were captured when you were freed."

Kirstyn turned on her heel to walk the short distance back to her father, but as soon as she did, her gaze met Aladdin's.

Part of her wanted to run to him and let him wrap her in his arms. But she remembered Grethel's words—and Aladdin's guilty, remorseful expression—and she felt the painful rush all over again.

Kirstyn pretended not to see him and instead stood by her father's side, flanked by several of his mightiest knights. One of the men nearby, probably a clerk of some kind at the Rathous, fetched a small chair and brought it to her. She thanked him and sat down, holding her chin up as they escorted Michael into the room.

Aladdin's heart ached as he listened to Kirstyn tell her story.

His precious Kirstyn. This never should have happened to her. She had been so innocent and sweet when he left Hagenheim, and now her mind was filled with painful memories of the cruelties done to her. The ache changed to a stabbing pain when she refused to acknowledge him. Now *he* had also hurt her with his inconstancy. He should have listened to his spirit, which had told him all along that she was still alive. He should have had more faith.

He had to win Kirstyn's favor again. He simply had to. The thought that she might not forgive him was unbearable.

Michael clomped into the room with chains on his ankles and rope around his wrists. *How does it feel?* Aladdin burned to confront the man himself, to be on the town council so that he could make Michael feel small, the way he had done to Kirstyn.

The council leader asked him, "Did you forcibly seize and carry away this woman, Lady Kirstyn, from Hagenheim?"

Michael stood straight and tall, as if proud of himself instead of ashamed.

"I did carry away this woman." He turned and pointed at Kirstyn, and Aladdin wanted to punch his smug face. "But I only kidnapped her because that man asked me to."

Michael turned and pointed straight at Aladdin.

Chapter Twenty-Three

Kirstyn watched as Michael pointed to Aladdin. Aladdin's face went slack, then hardened as his jaw flexed.

"That is a lie." Aladdin raised his voice above the crowd.

Kirstyn's mind raced. What Michael said made her sick to her stomach. But why would Aladdin have told Michael to kidnap her? It must surely be one of Michael's cruel lies.

"Explain yourself," the town councilman said in a stern voice.

"It is simple. Aladdin of Hagenheim was in love with Kirstyn, the Duke of Hagenheim's daughter. He thought if he could have her kidnapped, then rescue her after a long time of captivity, she—and her father—would be so grateful to him, her father would allow her to marry him."

"That is not true." Aladdin's face paled. "Kirstyn, you mustn't believe him! I would never do such a thing."

A loud murmur swept through the room. Kirstyn's knees went weak. Surely it wasn't true. But what if it was?

"And while I was away doing his bidding," Michael went on, "Aladdin was here, endearing himself to my father and stealing my inheritance."

She suddenly felt light-headed, her vision spinning. Father placed a gentle hand on her shoulder. Her forehead burned as darkness closed in around her.

She pulled on her father's arm. He leaned down to her. She whispered, "I don't feel well. I need to go."

He put his arm around her and helped her up. She walked toward the door of the town hall while leaning on her father. Her vision was clearing, and she glanced at Aladdin.

He turned to look at her at the same moment. His angry expression changed to one of pleading just before he was blocked from her view by the crowd.

Aladdin's heart sank as he watched Kirstyn leave. *O God, don't let her believe this lie!* She already thought him faithless and deceitful, as well she should. But he was certainly not guilty of this.

When the town council and their guards were able to shush everyone into silence, the head of the council asked, "Do you have any proof of this accusation?"

Michael said, "Aladdin did not want to put anything in writing that could be used against him, but perhaps my old partner, Rutgher, is still in the dungeon in Hagenheim. He will tell the truth about the matter. He was there when Aladdin approached us both."

Aladdin's breath came fast, heat boiling inside him. If he said Michael was lying and his accusation was absurd, his protestations would only make him seem guilty.

Aladdin forced himself to listen to the proceedings.

The town council addressed one of Duke Wilhelm's guards. "Where is this partner in the crime of kidnapping Lady Kirstyn?"

"He was released a month ago—after he cooperated and told us everything he knew. Duke Wilhelm doesn't normally keep prisoners long term. He forbade Rutgher from ever setting foot in Hagenheim again. We don't know where he is."

Wouldn't the town council see through Michael's lies? That this was only a desperate attempt to blame someone else? Surely they wouldn't believe him. But when Aladdin looked around, sidelong glances of suspicion were aimed at him by the townsmen.

The council spoke amongst themselves.

Should Aladdin stay and see how this hearing would go? Or should he run out and find Kirstyn? If she believed Michael's lies, how could he change her mind? It was his word against Michael's. And the seed of doubt had been planted in the minds of everyone here.

With dread hanging over him, he watched as they dismissed Michael and brought in Anna.

She seemed sad and defeated, her voice low and her head even lower. She told her version of the kidnapping, but she glossed over what Michael had done and failed to mention her role in luring Kirstyn into the dark alley where the kidnappers were waiting for her.

"Was anyone else involved in seizing and holding Lady Kirstyn captive besides you, Michael, and Rutgher?" one of the councilmen asked. "Perhaps someone who hired Michael to kidnap the duke's daughter?"

Anna looked confused. "No."

Aladdin breathed a relieved sigh. It was not solid proof that he was not involved, but it certainly cast doubt on Michael's accusation.

What would the town council do with Anna? Aladdin was appalled that she would participate in kidnapping Kirstyn and keeping her tied up against her will. But she might be willing to repent and renounce her loyalty to Michael. Still, what she had done would be difficult to forgive.

Perhaps it was Herr Kaufmann he should be worried about. When Aladdin looked back at him, he had such a pained look on his face. And even though the town council would probably want to question him, Aladdin left to go to the warehouse and fetch a guard to take care of Herr Kaufmann and make sure he made it safely home.

Kirstyn let her father take her to the Salty Boar Inn, where he secured a room for them as well as space for his knights and guards to sleep. Then they sat down to a meal in the main room downstairs.

"My men will tell us what was said at the hearing."

"Father"—she still held on to his arm—"I don't believe Aladdin had anything to do with the kidnapping. Michael invented that to shift the blame off himself."

"How can you be sure?"

Kirstyn sat up. "Surely you can't believe Aladdin capable of such a thing."

"Is that the only reason you don't think he did it? Because you don't think him capable of it?"

"No. Michael is so cruel, he would have thrown that at me at some point if it were true. If Aladdin promised him money to let him rescue me, he surely wouldn't have let him keep me for so long, and besides that, Michael would not have been trying to sell me. Also, there is another reason."

Kirstyn hesitated, her heart weighed down with pain as she

remembered Grethel's face as she spoke the words that had so hurt her that morning.

"What is it?"

"If Aladdin had hired Michael to kidnap me in some desperate scheme to get me to marry him, he would not have asked Herr Kaufmann's daughter to marry him."

Father raised his brows.

"I only just heard about it this morning. Grethel was angry that Aladdin and I . . . were spending so much time together, and he admitted it was true—that he had promised to marry Grethel." She wasn't ready to tell her father that they had been tenderly embracing each other and probably appeared to be kissing.

Father stared at the scarred wooden table in front of them. "Does it bother you that he wanted to marry Grethel?"

"I felt so hurt."

"Did he promise to marry you? Did you have an agreement?"

Kirstyn shook her head. "No."

"Did he say he loved you or wanted to marry you?"

"No, but . . . I thought he loved me." Maybe she was wrong. Maybe he only cared about her as a friend.

"Do you love him?"

Kirstyn huffed out a breath and crossed her arms over her chest in an effort to rid herself of the tears that were threatening. "Perhaps I do, but even if I didn't, and even if he only loves me as a friend, how could he decide to marry someone else so quickly after thinking I'd been killed? I thought I meant more to him than that."

She also thought her father wouldn't give up searching for her so quickly, but she wasn't ready to confront him with that. She might end up telling him that she'd always felt as if she wasn't as important to him as her siblings were, and then she'd be sobbing in this inn in front of a lot of strangers.

"Do you have reason to think he has decided not to marry Grethel, now that he knows you are alive?"

Did she? There was the fact that he never mentioned being in love with Grethel. Also, the way he held her and looked at her. "Perhaps, but . . . he had not told Grethel he no longer wanted to marry her, apparently. And she was upset."

Her father said nothing for a few moments. "It sounds like Aladdin was hoping neither of you would discover the truth. That surprises me. I've never known him to deceive anyone."

"I always thought Aladdin was perfect."

"No one is perfect."

She knew that, of course. Perhaps she had been unfair to Aladdin. She knew how hard he pushed himself to learn and do everything better, working harder than anyone else. She'd thought she was the most important person in the world to him, that he would never hurt her. Still . . . she wasn't sure what to feel anymore.

"We can either stay here and sort all this out with Aladdin, or we can go home right away. Your mother will not rest until she sees you are well."

Kirstyn hesitated. "I want to see Mother, but I want to talk to Aladdin first."

Father was silent. Finally he said, "Then we shall wait until you are ready. If we leave before the town council is ready to turn Michael over to me, I can return to bring him back to Hagenheim to be executed."

Kirstyn nodded. She pushed the thought of Michael's execution from her mind. Her father would never allow Michael to go free after what he had done. But her stomach sank at the prospect of leaving Aladdin, her last sight of him with that pleading, sad look. Hopefully she would see him tonight and he would apologize for not telling her of his betrothal to Grethel—though, in all fairness, he had never spoken to Kirstyn about love or marriage.

She didn't want to leave Aladdin, but during her long ordeal she had yearned for her mother's voice telling her all would be well. She had imagined her pain at thinking her daughter was dead, and she couldn't bear to delay her return to Mother. She didn't like to draw out her mother's pain and worry for even an hour more than necessary.

After sending a guard to stay with Herr Kaufmann, Aladdin sat down to tend to some business that had been neglected the last few days since Kirstyn had escaped from Michael. The books were in a tangle, the numbers not updated. One of the assistants had miscalculated, but Aladdin had nearly finished straightening it out when two men entered and approached him. They were Lüneburg soldiers.

"Aladdin, the councilmen have sent us to fetch you. They have some questions."

He stood and went with them. As he walked, his head suddenly free of business, his thoughts turned again to Kirstyn.

O God, let this not take long. He needed to find her and explain himself to her. Surely she would believe him.

Once at the Rathous he stood before the town council. Everyone else had gone, including the prisoners, Michael and Anna, who were taken back to their cells.

"What have you to say?" Herr Ackermann asked him. Every one of the councilmen pinned him with an intense stare.

"Surely you don't believe the accusation of a lawless man like Michael? I am innocent. He is only trying to deflect blame from himself. I have never had any contact with Michael Kaufmann. None whatsoever. I never would have subjected the woman I love to such an ordeal."

"And you are speaking of Lady Kirstyn?"

"Yes. We were good friends in Hagenheim since we were children." He swallowed, praying she still returned his love—if not as a husband, then at least as a friend.

"Very well." Herr Ackermann gave Aladdin a long, grave look. "You have a good reputation in Lüneburg for being a man of integrity—and that isn't often said of a merchant. So without any evidence against you, we will not detain you longer, but I do want to warn you." He paused. "Some people will give credence to Michael's claims. And one of those people seems to be Herr Kaufmann."

Aladdin's breath caught in his throat. How could Herr Kaufmann believe Michael over Aladdin? Was it possible Herr Kaufmann had felt so much pain over Michael's betrayals because he loved his son so much?

"Has Herr Kaufmann been to see his son? Has he spoken privately with him?"

Herr Ackermann sighed. "I didn't think it could do any harm, so we allowed it. But his son always did have such power over him. They spoke for some time before the hearing began. Cedric Michael must have persuaded him, because now Herr Kaufmann is demanding that we release Michael and apprehend you."

Again, the feeling of numbness in mind and heart and body washed over him like a bucket of cold water. Would this destroy everything he had worked for? Everything his heart had longed for?

"There is no evidence against you, so you are in no danger from us," Herr Ackermann said, "but . . . I wanted to warn you."

"Thank you." Aladdin turned to leave. What would he do if Herr Kaufmann turned against him? How painful to think that the man who often called him "son" could believe him to be a liar capable of something so evil as kidnapping.

He stumbled out of the Rathous and onto the street. Was it his imagination, or were people looking at him differently? He refused to care. He had to talk to Kirstyn—and Herr Kaufmann.

The last time Duke Wilhelm and his men had been in Lüneburg they stayed at Herr Kaufmann's house and stables, but would they have presumed on him this time? Aladdin quickened his step until he was near home. One glance at the quiet facade and he was fairly sure Duke Wilhelm and his men, and therefore Kirstyn, were not there.

He hesitated. Should he go inside or walk past and go in search of Kirstyn and her father? Since Aladdin was here . . . he went inside.

Grethel froze in the entryway, staring at him, then coldly turned away.

"*Guten Tag*, Grethel," he said anyway.

"My father doesn't want to see you." Her tone was cool and even.

His heart crashed against his chest. He did his best to ignore it. "Is he here?"

"He doesn't want to see you." She faced him and spoke more forcefully.

"Well, I want to see him." Aladdin brushed past her in the narrow passageway. He stuck his head in the dining hall. No one was there. He searched through the ground floor but found only servants. Then he went upstairs, taking the steps two at a time.

Aladdin knocked on Herr Kaufmann's chamber door.

"Who is it?"

"Aladdin. May I come in?" His stomach churned like a boiling cauldron as he waited for Herr Kaufmann to speak.

His mentor opened the door. His expression was one of embarrassment and almost fear, which caught Aladdin off guard.

"I suppose you have heard . . ."

"I heard you demanded the town council release Michael and imprison me, even though you must know I would never hire someone to abduct Lady Kirstyn."

"Truthfully . . ." Herr Kaufmann let out a long sigh. "I cannot lie to you, Aladdin. I know you didn't do that. But Michael threatened me. He said he had friends whom he had instructed to do terrible things to Grethel if I did not appear to support his claim. He told me I had to cut you off and cast you out."

Aladdin thought for a moment, then shook his head. "Michael has no power to do such a thing. Duke Wilhelm surely plans to take him to Hagenheim and execute him as soon as the councilmen release him to the duke."

Herr Kaufmann nodded. "Yes, I know. But I was afraid and I told the council . . . But you know. For a moment, I confess—just for a moment—I believed Michael. After all"—he pinned Aladdin with an accusatory lift of his brows—"I thought you would never hurt my daughter and deceive her."

Aladdin's face grew hot. "I did not deceive her. I agreed to marry her because I thought Kirstyn was dead. You know this."

"But not telling her that you had changed your mind was not the action of a man of integrity."

The words cut him to the heart because they were true. How could he explain? He hardly understood it himself.

"I never would have thought you would go back on your

word. But I forgive you. And I believe Grethel will also forgive you, in time. But the truth is, I need your help. This thing with Michael has me unable to think straight." Herr Kaufmann put a hand to his head and sank down in a chair.

"You know I will help you any way I can."

"I need you to pretend with me, just for a little while, so I will know Grethel and my business are safe. He threatened to have his friends burn down all my warehouses and destroy everything I own. I need you to pretend that I have cast you out and you are on your own. Just until I am sure Michael has no more power." Herr Kaufmann leaned toward him and laid his hand on his shoulder. "I know it isn't fair to ask it of you, but will you do it? Will you help us?"

Herr Kaufmann's hand on his shoulder was like a cold, heavy weight. If people thought Herr Kaufmann believed Michael over Aladdin . . .

"Are you so afraid of Michael? With all your guards? This is madness, if you will forgive me for saying so."

"You don't understand what he's capable of." Herr Kaufmann leaned in, his eyes full of fear. "He has the devil on his side. It's as if Satan himself is protecting him and giving him favor. He has the most uncanny ability to get what he wants and wreak havoc."

"But we need not fear him. 'Greater is he that is in you, than he that is in the world.'"

Herr Kaufmann's expression hardened. "I need your support now, Aladdin. I cannot risk Grethel's life and well-being. I would do anything to keep my daughter safe."

An ache started under his ribs and spread to his chest. He felt as if he were losing a father, his friends, not to mention his reputation and his share of the business he'd worked so hard for.

"Will you help me by cooperating with me in this?"

"Very well. I will do as you wish."

"I had it in mind that you could stay at the Salty Boar Inn and tomorrow put on a long, hooded cloak to disguise yourself. I'll send one of my guards to fetch you and escort you to the warehouse. The business has been suffering since Lady Kirstyn came." He shrugged. "I am glad she was found and is safe and that we could help her, but it is true. Things have been rather chaotic again since you've been spending so much time with her."

Aladdin's heart sank even lower. "Very well."

Herr Kaufmann nodded. "Thank you. You can come by later and get your things." Then he stepped out into the corridor and yelled, "Send for one of my guards!"

Herr Kaufmann cleared his throat, and his gaze flitted everywhere except on Aladdin. "You must go now."

Aladdin imagined Michael's face as he told his lies and made his threats, spreading his evil in the world. If only Aladdin could choke him until the coward begged to be able to tell the truth.

Aladdin moved past Herr Kaufmann and started down the stairs. He could barely see the steps in front of him as he left the house that had been his home for a year and a half.

Perhaps he deserved this. After all, he had hurt Grethel and made her feel rejected.

After a while, hardly knowing where he was heading, he came to the Salty Boar Inn. The sky was growing dark. Not only was the sun setting, but rain clouds were rolling in, blotting out what light was left.

As he approached, he saw two of Duke Wilhelm's knights standing outside talking. The duke and Kirstyn must be staying there.

Aladdin had to talk to Kirstyn, but first he had to gather his thoughts. He headed toward St. John's Church and went inside.

He stood at the back of the nave, staring at the stained glass depiction of the snake deceiving Eve into eating the fruit of the Tree of Knowledge of Good and Evil in the garden of Eden. He made his way toward the altar and knelt in front of the chancel.

God, I have hurt Kirstyn and I have hurt Grethel, and Herr Kaufmann has cast me out of his house . . . But I must at least convince Kirstyn that I care for her and would never hurt her again. Help me.

He covered his face with his hands, then leaned forward until his forehead touched the floor.

Chapter Twenty-Four

Kirstyn and her father walked to Herr Kaufmann's home in the twilight and the threat of rain. When they arrived, they were welcomed into the main room, the dining hall. Hilde smiled at them, but she kept glancing away, her smile faltering, and she hurried away to fetch Herr Kaufmann.

Normally Herr Kaufmann was in this room at this time of day, sitting in his favorite chair and enjoying the fire, talking with Abu and Grethel and Aladdin. Where was everyone?

She and Father sat down to wait.

A few minutes later Herr Kaufmann entered the room. He approached them with outstretched hands, but his smile was absent.

"Duke Wilhelm. Lady Kirstyn. How good it is to see you. Won't you sup with us tonight?"

"Thank you for your kind offer," Father said. "But we came because we wanted to thank you for your kindness and hospitality to Kirstyn after her ordeal."

She was a little surprised her father didn't accept his offer to dine with him, but he, too, must have sensed that something was amiss—not to mention that Grethel would not exactly be happy to see her. And of course, Herr Kaufmann had just seen his son confess to kidnapping her and heard that son raise doubts as to Aladdin's character. Though she could hardly conceive that he would believe such accusations about Aladdin.

But of a surety, it must be a painful time for Herr Kaufmann. She wished she could do something for him. He had been so kind to Aladdin.

Her father stood. "We had better get back to the inn before the rain starts."

"You are more than welcome to stay here," Herr Kaufmann said, but the invitation sounded lukewarm.

"I thank you, but my men are waiting for us there."

Hilde stood in the doorway. "Herr Kaufmann?"

"Excuse me just for a moment." He went to talk with Hilde, then came back moments later. "Please take these things." He held out a tapestry bag to Kirstyn. "These are the things Grethel loaned to you. She wishes you to keep them."

Kirstyn took it. "I am very grateful. Please tell her thank you for me." She wanted to ask if Aladdin was here, but surely if he was he would come and greet them.

Later, with her father carrying the bag, they walked back toward the inn. A stiff wind blew down the cobblestone street as a raindrop fell on her head, sending a shiver down her back.

They reached the inn, and a dark figure stood in front of the door. He was tall and had his arms wrapped around himself, as he was not wearing a cloak.

"Aladdin?"

He turned and faced her. "Kirstyn. May I speak to you?"

"Not for very long," Father said. "She needs her rest." Then his expression softened. "Come inside out of the cold."

They stepped into the inn, and while her father ordered food, Aladdin and Kirstyn sat at a table in the corner.

"Kirstyn, I want you to know that I had nothing to do with your abduction." His face was drawn and sadder than she had ever seen it. His eyes pleaded with her as he leaned close.

"I do believe you. Michael is just the sort of evil schemer to make up such a lie."

Aladdin expelled a breath. "Thank you. And I'm . . . sorry I believed you were dead, sorry I agreed to marry Grethel, and sorry I didn't tell you, or her, right away."

He gazed intently into her eyes. But his words brought back the feeling of betrayal, and it still stung.

"When your father said you were dead," he went on, "I was in so much pain, thinking my hope of seeing you again, of marrying you, was over. I agreed to marry Grethel to please Herr Kaufmann, and because I thought it might make the pain go away. But I don't think I could have married her, when the time came. And Grethel wouldn't have wanted to marry me knowing how I felt about you."

Kirstyn said quietly, "I suppose I shouldn't be angry with you. But it hurt that you seemed to forget about me so quickly."

"It was daft of me." Aladdin sighed. "The truth is . . . I was hurting so badly. I wanted to believe you were still alive, but after we searched for so long and never found you, and your father found that bloody scarf . . . I just wanted to ease my heartache. But it didn't help. I felt like I would never get over your death, but I was not being fair to Grethel."

Was he saying he was in love with her? Her heart expanded in her chest. But this didn't explain everything.

Aladdin squirmed inwardly if not outwardly. The look on Kirstyn's face was one he had never seen directed at him before.

"But why didn't you tell Grethel you didn't want to marry her once I returned?"

"I . . . I don't know." He ran his fingers through his hair.

"You could have told me all this. You should have told me. Surely you weren't afraid of my anger."

"I didn't want you to be angry, but it was more that I . . . I couldn't bear for you to think less of me. I didn't want you to know that I hadn't kept searching for you."

"You could have been honest with me. Why weren't you?"

Aladdin closed his eyes, then slowly reopened them. He rubbed his hand over his cheek, staring down at the table. "You always jested that I was perfect. The truth is, I wanted you to think I was perfect, even though I knew I wasn't. I tried so hard to impress everyone—especially you. I was afraid you would stop . . . caring about me if you learned about Grethel."

Kirstyn's mouth opened, but a serving maid came and set down food and drink in front of them. Kirstyn's father was right behind her. He sat beside Kirstyn.

They ate together, talking of childhood days back in Hagenheim. He felt as though there was still a lot left unsaid between them, but nothing they could say in front of her father. Would she go back to Hagenheim before he knew how she felt about him? Now that he'd found her again, how could he let her go?

After they finished their meal, Duke Wilhelm stepped outside to speak to his knights.

Kirstyn reached across the table and took Aladdin's hand in hers and lifted it to her cheek.

Her soft skin was like silk. His breaths came fast, but she

quickly put his hand down and cleared her throat. "I don't want to be separated from you again, but I have to go back home to see my mother. I know it isn't fair for me to ask you, but would you consider coming back to Hagenheim with me, just for a while?"

Aladdin's heart clenched painfully. How could he bear to tell her no? But how could he leave Lüneburg? To have any chance of marrying Kirstyn—which was what he wanted more than anything—he had to ensure he had a fortune with which to take care of the Duke of Hagenheim's daughter, and he'd made a commitment to Herr Kaufmann.

She leaned closer. How he wanted to kiss her, to caress her cheek. But he had no right to.

Her father was approaching, a scowl on his face. Aladdin and Kirstyn leaned away from each other. She ducked her head, pressing her lips together.

"Well, Aladdin, we shall see you soon, I am sure." Her father stood there waiting.

It was Aladdin's hint to leave. His heart beat erratically, and a cold sweat broke out on the back of his neck. He wanted to go back to Hagenheim with her, but he might be severing all ties with Herr Kaufmann if he did.

"Farewell, Kirstyn."

Chapter Twenty-Five

Kirstyn wasn't ready to let him go yet. She said quietly, so her father couldn't hear, "Come back to Hagenheim with Father and me. I'm sure Father would be glad to have you take over as steward."

But even as she said the words, a guarded look descended over him. Was she wrong to ask that of him? But she couldn't help it. She needed Aladdin to be near.

"I will think about it." His openness and emotion had vanished.

"I know you don't want to be just a steward after your success as a merchant, but don't you wish to be near me? You may have what you've always wished for, but I need you, Aladdin." Her voice hitched and tears burned her eyes.

He bent his head slightly toward hers. "I will come, then. I must get some things settled here, then I will come."

Her heart leapt. "Oh, thank you."

He lifted his hand, as if to touch her cheek, then let his hand fall.

She wanted to grab his hand and pull it to her lips, but when she glanced at her father, he was frowning.

Aladdin's heart was breaking as he gazed into Kirstyn's beautiful face. She had been through so much. And when she said he needed him . . . he would do anything to be there for her. At least his fear that Kirstyn would believe Michael's lies about him was put to rest.

What would the Duke of Hagenheim say when he learned Aladdin was back in Hagenheim and expecting him to give him a job as his steward? But Aladdin knew how to buy and sell. He knew what people wanted and what they would pay for it. He could start his own business in Hagenheim. Though it might take some time.

Aladdin left the inn and strode down the wet street, a light rain falling on his head and shoulders.

He walked to Herr Kaufmann's four-story house beside the Ilmenau River, sandwiched in between two other homes, as the houses were lined up one after the other, with a slight space between. He often wondered—if one of them fell, would they all fall?

What kind of reception would Aladdin find there? What about Abu? He could imagine how confusing this all would be for him, poor boy. He certainly didn't deserve this turmoil in his life.

Aladdin just wanted to walk and relive the intimate looks in Kirstyn's eyes. He'd felt so humbled with gratitude at God's merciful kindness, allowing her to be found. He'd proudly showed her how successful he was, how rich and influential he was in town. All his dreams had come true.

It was dark now. Hardly anyone was on the street, and those who were hurried home to their warm fires and their families. It seemed every man had a wife and family. But Aladdin would be sleeping at the inn tonight.

"Aladdin."

He glanced up to see Claus, one of Herr Kaufmann's guards.

"What has happened? Heinz told me Herr Kaufmann sent for him to escort you from his house. Surely that cannot be true."

"I'm afraid it is." Apparently the guards weren't in on the pretense.

Claus scowled. "That Cedric Michael is nothing but trouble. I don't know how Herr Kaufmann could believe anything he says after all he's done."

"It must be difficult to lose all hope for one's child." Aladdin thought of how much Duke Wilhelm loved his children and could well imagine him having trouble giving up on one of them. But he couldn't imagine the duke's children ever deceiving and hurting their father the way Michael had.

"I suppose, but I could forgo hope if my child were Michael." He raised an eyebrow and frowned. "But I have to get to Herr Kaufmann's and relieve Heinz. In fact, I believe they are waiting for you to come and gather your belongings." His expression faltered as he no doubt remembered that Aladdin was no longer welcome at Herr Kaufmann's home. "I'm sorry, Aladdin. We could go there now, if you haven't already taken your things."

"Very well." He may as well get it over with.

"Forgive me," Claus said, "but would you mind coming in behind me so they don't know I was talking to you? I don't want him to ask me questions about . . . well . . ."

"I understand." Aladdin stopped and waited for Claus to precede him. "Don't worry. I won't tell him that you talked with me or that you think his son is evil."

Claus gave a half smile. "You are a good man, Aladdin."

Aladdin stood in the cold, misty rain and shivered. At least perhaps he could get his warm cloak. After waiting a few moments, Aladdin plodded on.

When he arrived, Herr Kaufmann was standing in the entryway talking with Claus. His gaze landed on Aladdin and he stepped back.

"Claus will show you where your possessions are." Herr Kaufmann kept his head up but averted his eyes from Aladdin's.

Aladdin followed the burly guard. He tried to catch Herr Kaufmann's eye, but he would not look at him.

Aladdin found two bags stuffed full, one tapestry bag with a short handle and the other a cloth bag with a longer handle. He slung the latter over his shoulder. Claus walked him out.

As he passed Herr Kaufmann again, he stopped. "May God bless you."

Herr Kaufmann said nothing, only glancing at Aladdin's face for a moment before looking away again.

Outside, night had closed in, making it difficult to see, although the lights from people's windows illuminated the watery streets enough that he wouldn't stumble.

Which way should he go? Since he did not want Kirstyn or her father to see him looking like a man who was just cast out of his home, carrying all he owned in two bags, he turned in the opposite direction, toward the warehouse and marketplace.

Aladdin had a few marks, along with some more valuable gold pieces, in the leather pouch on his belt. He could afford to pay for a room somewhere, but not for very many nights, especially if he hoped to buy food—and start a business of his own. But surely Herr Kaufmann had put some of his wages into one of the bags.

While he had worked for Herr Kaufmann, Aladdin had

safeguarded his wages in Herr Kaufmann's underground strong room in his own locked chest alongside his benefactor's. He'd had little need for money as long as he lived with Herr Kaufmann, and it was understood he was a part owner in the business, although Herr Kaufmann had not yet signed legal documents to that effect.

Aladdin trudged down the street. Icy fingers of sadness clutched his throat. But he needed to think about where he would go.

He was passing by the abandoned warehouse where Michael had kept Kirstyn before she had escaped. For that reason alone, it was almost a sacred place to him.

When he reached it, the door was unlocked. He went inside.

The large room was pitch-black. He left the door open and searched inside his bags, first the tapestry one, then the cloth. Finally, at the very bottom of the bag, his hand closed around the nub of a candle. At the same time his hand bumped a purse of money, or that was what it felt like. He pulled them both out.

He managed to light the candle. Then he opened the pouch, holding his breath as he dumped some of its contents into his hand—gold, silver, and marks. The money was a fraction of what was in Aladdin's stored wages.

He closed the door shut on the rain and the deserted street outside. He lay on the cold, hard floor of the nearly empty warehouse, pillowing his head on the smaller of the two bags, and stared into the darkness.

He'd thought God had been good to him when he was working for Herr Kaufmann, making greater profits than any of the other merchants and salt masters in town. He'd thought God was making a way for him to be with Kirstyn. And then when Aladdin thought she was dead . . . the profits had made no sense to him. What good was a fortune without Kirstyn?

Memories swept over him . . . lying on a foul-smelling pallet with six or seven children piled up like puppies. Stealing food. Stealing a merchant's purse. Mustapha calling him a rat. The look of desperation in Zuhayr's eyes.

Why would Kirstyn want to marry him? He wasn't good enough for a duke's daughter. He had no family name, didn't even have his own home.

He started shivering and sat up. Once again he searched through his bags. Not finding any blankets, he pulled out some dry clothing along with his cloak and changed out of his wet garments.

He lay listening to the cold rain hitting the roof of the warehouse until late into the night, then awoke several times to silence. Finally, when some light filtered in through the tiny window, Aladdin jumped up and looked around.

Various items were scattered over the floor. Food and a few cooking utensils lay strewn near the fireplace. But the thing that caught his eye was a bit of rope lying on the floor. Was it the same rope that had been used to tie Kirstyn by the wrist?

He picked it up and examined it, feeling the pain she must have endured during her long captivity. How she must have suffered. His own pain had been washed away when he saw her again, held her in his arms, and looked into her eyes. Though her trial must have seemed endless, was she glad she had the pain to compare with her joy?

Perhaps it was too soon for that.

He pulled his cloak tighter around himself and noticed there was a bright whiteness outside, even though the sun was just coming up. Everything outside was covered in fluffy white snow. The falling rain must have turned to snow at some point during the night.

Now he just had to help Herr Kaufmann balance the accounts and get the business out of its current chaos—secretly, while Aladdin's reputation was ravaged—before leaving for Hagenheim.

Chapter Twenty-Six

Kirstyn read through the letter she had just written.

My dearest friend Aladdin,

I have only been home a few days, but I am longing to see you again. Please don't forget your promise to come to Hagenheim. I hope you don't resent me for asking it of you. My family is being very kind to me, but I need my dearest friend.

My mother was overjoyed to see me. She cried so much. She still cries sometimes when she embraces me and feels how thin I am. But I am doing my part to fatten back up. I described those rolled wafers with the cream and preserved red fruit to Cook, and she makes them almost as well as Hilde.

The orphans were so kind and made me cry to see their joyful smiles when I visited them for the first time. The little ones cling to me and I can't stop hugging them. I used to dream about adopting all of them. It seems you and I have the same thoughts, as you already adopted one—in a sense—when you brought Abu home with you. It's easy to see how much he loves and admires you.

Perhaps it is foolish of me, but I feel as if I miss Lüneburg, even though I was only there for a few days. I fell in love with the beautiful buildings there, particularly the doors and doorways. Such color and creativity! It's my favorite thing about Lüneburg—besides the fact that you are there.

Please write to me and tell the courier when you are coming to Hagenheim before you send him away.

> I am, as ever, your loving
> friend
> Kirstyn Gerstenberg

She sealed the letter with wax and one of her family's seals. When the wax had cooled, she kissed the letter. It still hurt to think he had thought she was dead and was planning to marry someone else. But she truly loved him, enough to forgive him and not hold him to a standard of perfection.

Several days later the courier returned, entering the solar where Kirstyn was reading with Adela, while Toby and Mother were playing chess. Kirstyn jumped up and hurried toward him.

He only stared at her with a sad expression.

"What is it?" Kirstyn's heart stuck in her throat.

"I could not find Aladdin. It seems he . . . well, he is not living with Herr Kaufmann anymore. No one seems to know where he went, but no one had seen him in Lüneburg for several days. Word is that Herr Kaufmann is trying to get his son released from the gaol, blaming Aladdin for the kidnapping."

Kirstyn clutched at her throat as the courier handed her back her letter.

"I could have continued looking for him, but I thought you would want to know the news."

Kirstyn's mind raced. What could have happened to Aladdin?

Mother came up beside her and embraced her. "I'm sure we will hear from Aladdin soon."

Kirstyn spent the next few days alternately praying in the chapel and wandering around the castle. She wrote Aladdin another letter but kept it in her room. But why did he not come to Hagenheim as she had asked?

He had always made friends easily, whether they admired him for his brilliance or his integrity or his hard work. Perhaps he was already making his fortune elsewhere. But not knowing was haunting her. She lay awake most of the night, wondering if he was safe.

A few days later the snow melted and Aladdin had straightened out the accounts and given specific instructions, training one of the assistants to do Aladdin's job. He spoke privately to Herr Kaufmann.

"I need to go back to Hagenheim to be with Lady Kirstyn."

"What is the meaning of this? Go back to Hagenheim? I need you here, to help me with the business."

"The people of Lüneburg think you believe me guilty of paying your son to abduct Lady Kirstyn. But I have remained faithful to you, preparing everyone for my departure."

"So this is about your anger with me?" Herr Kaufmann lifted his chin, a wheedling note in his voice. "You are hurt that

I have tried to make certain Michael doesn't send his evil friends to hurt Grethel and my business?"

"No." Aladdin closed his eyes for a moment and let out a breath. He needed to tell the truth. "I am hurt that you forced me out of the house and are pretending to believe Michael's lies about me."

Herr Kaufmann's face scrunched. "That is only temporary. You know—"

"But that is not why I'm going to Hagenheim. I promised Kirstyn I would go and be with her. After the terrible thing that happened to her, she needs me there, and I want to be there . . . for her."

"My dear boy." One side of Herr Kaufmann's mouth went down in a sympathetic half frown. "I know you love her, but . . . she has a family to take care of her needs. And though I can't imagine anyone not admiring you for all your good qualities, I'm afraid . . ." He lowered his head and looked up at Aladdin with a baleful expression. "Duke Wilhelm will never let you marry his daughter."

A heavy hand of dread grabbed Aladdin's middle. Did Herr Kaufmann have to voice his own fear?

"And why is that? Because I am an orphan? Or because I am a Saracen? No, don't answer that. It doesn't matter. The truth is, I will go and be there for her, be her friend and support her, even if there is no chance of my marrying her."

"You would do this in spite of the fact that your life is here? The fact that you are making your fortune here in Lüneburg, more riches than you could ever hope to make in Hagenheim? Don't you know you have become like a son to me?"

They both knew their relationship had been damaged by Aladdin breaking his promise to marry Grethel, even if Herr

Kaufmann wouldn't admit it. And being forced to pretend Herr Kaufmann didn't trust him was even further damage, though he did still love the man.

"And you are like a father to me, but that does not change the way I feel about Lady Kirstyn. I'm sorry, but this is something I have to do."

Herr Kaufmann's face was drawn, his wrinkled eyes drooping more than usual. "I do not agree that this is a good plan. I need you here, and it pains me that you would abandon me, especially after all Cedric Michael has done."

He could feel the mantle of guilt his mentor was trying to place on his shoulders, but he also knew he was not responsible for Michael's sins. "So you will not give me your blessing?"

Herr Kaufmann huffed out a breath as he turned his head away. "You ask too much."

The hurt weighed on Aladdin, preventing him from asking his mentor and employer for his wages that were stored underground in the strong room. No doubt he would think that was also asking too much.

Aladdin bought a horse and left Lüneburg early the next morning. Instead of hard-packed dirt, the Salt Route was paved with stones, and the stones made a sharp sound with every strike of his horse's hooves. He'd been traveling for hours. The sun's position in the sky showed it was well past noon.

He wanted to marry Kirstyn. How could he be so near her, in the same town, and not think about it every minute? But he did not have enough money to buy a house big enough for all the orphans she dreamed of adopting. Besides, as Herr Kaufmann had pointed out, Duke Wilhelm might never approve of Aladdin marrying his daughter.

When Aladdin reached Hagenheim, he asked around and found a shop he was able to rent from Herr Goteken.

"If you don't have a place to stay," he said, "I have an extra bed in my servants' quarters. You can sleep there and I won't charge you any extra."

Wanting to save as much as possible, Aladdin accepted the offer, though it made him feel as if he could not sink much lower.

Aladdin sat blowing on his fingers in the cold shop, surrounded by the wares he had bought with the money he found in his bag.

He tried to concentrate on the numbers in front of him, but the cold air only reminded him of times when he and Kirstyn would go exploring the forest in winter, or when she would visit the orphanage with her mother and they would play outside in the snow.

A customer entered. The wind blew in with her, making his eyes water, blurring the tiny lines and numbers in front of him.

"The anise and the cinnamon are much less than what they sell them for at the market," the middle-aged woman said, looking over her shoulder at Aladdin. "Is this the correct price?"

"It is. Please tell your friends, because that price will go up eventually."

She gave a slow nod and had him measure out some of

each, also making several other purchases before saying, "Are you not the Saracen boy who grew up in the Hagenheim orphanage?"

"I am."

She smiled. "You have done very well for yourself. God bless you, and a good day to you."

"Thank you, and you as well."

The cold blew in again as she left. Fresh pain attacked him. *This* was "doing very well"? To him it looked like failure. It *felt* like failure to have Kirstyn seem even more out of reach. But he needed to remember that he was here to offer support to Kirstyn. But couldn't he love and support her more if he was married to her? He had to earn more, enough to buy a house, if he even had a chance to marry her. His striving to increase his wealth and reputation in Lüneburg was only a means to an end, and now he had walked away from them.

At least he wasn't on the street, being used as someone's pawn, stealing and being beaten. But even that thought left him hollow.

Aladdin cupped his hands over his mouth, trying to focus on the numbers in the ledger. But his mind went again to Kirstyn. What would she think when she read the letter he had just sent? He had written and rewritten it several times. What could he say? He no longer had the means to marry her.

He longed to see her, but to what purpose? He should probably wait until she sent for him. After all, as Herr Kaufmann had said, she had her family to care for her.

The next day Herr Goteken, the owner of his shop, entered with a grin. "I have found out who you are."

"Oh?"

"You are the orphan from the Holy Land that Priest

brought back. And then I found out from my friend over in Lüneburg that you are the golden boy with the Midas touch who was working with Herr Kaufmann and made him wealthier than the pope."

Aladdin had no response to that.

"What were your duties when you were with Herr Kaufmann? Did you choose the goods to sell? How much to buy? The prices? Were you underselling the other merchants, or just selling superior goods?"

"Some of everything." Aladdin was cautious in how he replied, not wishing to give away any secrets that might harm Herr Kaufmann in any way.

Aladdin forced a smile. Herr Goteken must have been handsome when he was younger, and at forty years old, he still had a strong face with hardly any wrinkles and was tall without the slightest stoop to his shoulders, but his stomach was paunchy and his hair was mostly white.

"I don't know if I told you, but I have a few shops in town, and I have sellers who go around to towns in the area to sell in the marketplaces on market day. Perhaps you could work some of your magic with my business—whatever it is you did for Herr Kaufmann—and even help me with my books. They're in a terrible tangle since I don't have time to keep up with them. I would pay you well."

"Are you not afraid we'll be in competition with each other since I have this shop?"

"No, no, your little shop cannot affect me. And I also want you to take your meals at my home—since you're sleeping there as it is—as part of your payment." He quoted a salary. "What do you say? Will you help me with my account books at least?"

Aladdin was pleasantly surprised at the amount. "I will take a look and help if I can."

"Very good." Herr Goteken's smile grew even broader. "I'll bring my ledgers to you tonight."

CHAPTER TWENTY-SEVEN

Kirstyn caught her father early in the morning as he was breaking his fast. "I am very worried about Aladdin. Could we not send a couple of soldiers to Lüneburg to find him? Surely someone knows where he went."

Her father's expression softened on a sigh, and he placed his hand gently on her head. "I'm a little concerned for him too. Let us wait another day or two, and if we haven't heard from him by then, I shall send two men to Lüneburg to look for him."

"Oh, thank you, Father." But the fact that he was also concerned about Aladdin added to her own anxiety.

She hurried to the chapel, where a few candles burned. She knelt and bowed her face to the floor. "O God," she whispered, "I cannot bear the thoughts that whirl around in my mind. I need You to take care of Aladdin. Don't let him go hungry or without a warm place to sleep." Tears dripped to the flagstones under her.

If he hadn't wanted to make his fortune, he'd probably be safe and warm in Hagenheim, working for her father as his steward. But he had always tried so hard to prove himself, to win people over, to impress everyone he met. Why? Was he wounded, deep inside, because of having no parents? Perhaps that was why she loved him so much. She wanted to heal his wounds, to save him from whatever thoughts were driving him so hard.

"But that's not my job, is it, God? You're the only One who can heal a soul wound." Kirstyn lifted her head to gaze at the crucifix in front of her. Jesus was wounded so He could heal others. "By Your stripes we are healed."

Could Jesus heal her soul wounds too? Being taken and held against her will for half a year had wounded Kirstyn. She had so many nightmares she had to have someone sleeping in her room with her. She woke up wondering where she was, imagining she could still feel the rope around her wrist. She would look around to see where Michael was, to see if she had a hope of escaping.

She and Aladdin were both wounded. "Please heal us, God, but please also let me love him."

She stayed and prayed for an hour, perhaps two. Then she heard footsteps. She didn't turn around until they entered the chapel.

Her father crossed himself and stood silently before the crucifix. Then he motioned to her with his hand.

Kirstyn quickly finished her prayer, lit another candle, and bowed herself out.

In the corridor outside the chapel, her father said, "A letter from Aladdin has just arrived." He held it out to her.

She clutched it to her chest.

"It seems that Aladdin is in Hagenheim."

"He is?" Her heart leapt, then crashed. If he was in Hagenheim, why hadn't he come to see her? Why was he sending her a letter instead of visiting her in person? Tears pinched the back of her eyes.

It was dark in the corridor, so she ran to her bedchamber. Inside her room, she threw open the shutters to let in more light and opened the letter.

My most precious friend, Lady Kirstyn,

I pray this letter finds you well and content. I am imagining your joyful reunion with your mother and siblings and all the little ones at the orphans' home. It fills my heart with warmth knowing you are loved and cared for. I pray every day that you will have no lasting effects from your harrowing ordeal. I know God cares for you very much, as do I.

I have come to Hagenheim as I promised and am here at your disposal. I want to support you in any way that I can, so please tell me in what ways I may serve you. I now have a small shop on White Stone Street, and you may send for me there.

Your faithful servant forever,
Aladdin

How could he write such a short, cool, emotionless letter? And how long had he been in Hagenheim without telling her?

Kirstyn read the letter again, then a third time. The fact that he was near but could stay away from her . . . Hot tears fell and splashed on the open letter.

She wadded it up and threw it on her bed. How dare he treat her this way?

Her door opened and Mother walked toward her. "Your father told me you received a letter from Aladdin." She came close to Kirstyn and placed her hand on her shoulder. "Is it bad news?"

"He is in Hagenheim and hasn't come to see me. He told

me where his new shop is, that I can send for him, but . . . why didn't he come here himself?" How could he stay away? Didn't he understand how much she loved him and wanted to see him?

"But that is good, isn't it? He's here, as you wanted."

"I love him, Mother. I think I've always loved him. But if he loved me the way I thought he did . . ." She stopped and shook her head, unable to go on. She flicked away the tears that fell onto her cheeks.

"Perhaps you should go and talk to him. I'll come with you if you wish. Father won't let us leave the castle without a guard to escort us, but I could make the guards wait outside."

"If he can bear to stay away from me, then I can stay away from him."

Mother took a deep breath and let it out slowly. "I understand how you feel, but it would be good to try to understand Aladdin's feelings. To go to him and talk."

Kirstyn shook her head again. "Perhaps I will later, but for now I'm too angry."

"And hurt, I would imagine." Mother put an arm around her. "Love can call forth a multitude of emotions, especially when things are not going smoothly. Perhaps Aladdin is staying away because he knows he needs to be able to give you things, not the least of which is a house, before he can marry you."

"It just hurts so much that he didn't come to see me." Kirstyn buried her face in her mother's shoulder.

"I know." Mother patted Kirstyn's back.

Kirstyn's chest hurt, a physical pain much like the one she experienced when she was held captive by Michael and he would force her to lie covered by a tarp or blanket, still and quiet, when people were around. She'd thought that pain was gone forever when she had escaped. But she was wrong. Only now she was feeling it when she thought about Aladdin. How could that be right?

Kirstyn sat at supper in the Great Hall with the rest of the family. Her brothers Steffan and Wolfgang were being loud and arguing about who was the better swordsman. One of Father's knights approached and spoke close to Father's ear. Adela was almost in tears while talking to Mother about losing her favorite gold ring.

I was kidnapped and treated violently only a few weeks ago. She looked around at her family. But her family members were all oblivious.

A loud crash sounded behind her. Kirstyn screamed and covered her head with her arms. Her heart pounded in her throat and her hands shook. Was Michael coming after her? Had the town council released him?

"Kirstyn?"

"Don't let him get me!"

All was quiet, but her whole body was on high alert. When she got the courage to move her arms and open her eyes, her father and mother were beside her, staring down at her.

"What is it?" Mother's eyes were big, her mouth open. "What is wrong?"

Kirstyn's hands shook even more as she realized Michael wasn't there. "Wh-what was that loud noise?"

"It was only one of the servants dropping a pitcher of water."

The servants had stopped what they were doing to stare at her. Even Steffan and Wolfgang were motionless and quiet, their gazes fastened on her.

She made an effort to straighten her shoulders. "I'm all right."

Mother put her arms around her, and Father patted her shoulder and stood very close.

I will not cry. I will not cry. Kirstyn put her hand over her mouth to stifle the sob that bubbled up. Only a few tears leaked out, and she brushed those away while Mother's body and arms shielded her from view.

"You're safe now, my precious *liebling*," Mother mumbled.

"I'm going to Lüneburg soon," Father said, "to bring Michael here to be hanged. You will never have to be afraid of him again."

Was it evil that the thought of Michael being hanged was actually comforting? She knew as a Christian she was required to forgive him, and she would . . . someday . . . but she also never wanted to worry about seeing him again.

Chapter Twenty-Eight

The next day Kirstyn retrieved a book from the library. She hoped she might see her father working at his desk, but he wasn't there.

She was on her way up to her bedchamber when someone hurried up behind her. She spun around. Wolfgang smiled at her.

"Kirstyn! I know something that will make you happy. Aladdin is back in Hagenheim."

She tried not to glare at her brother. "Why would that make me happy?"

Wolfgang's mouth fell open. "Because he's your friend."

"He was my friend. Now . . . I don't know what he is. Just a shopkeeper, I suppose."

"That's unkind. Didn't Aladdin help rescue you from Michael?" Wolfgang's brown eyes looked confused.

"I escaped. Aladdin was only there when Herr Kaufmann's men came and arrested Michael and Anna." She knew she was being unjust and peevish, but anger felt almost good, powerful, and much better than the pain it was blocking.

Kirstyn turned away from her brother and started up the

steps to the next floor, holding her book to her chest with her right hand.

"Do you mean you're not even going to go see him?"

"No, I'm not." Honestly, she thought she might, as soon as she stopped feeling so . . . angry.

"Even after he saved you from the bear when you were children?"

Kirstyn's step faltered, then she continued climbing the stairs.

"Kirstyn!"

Something caught her left wrist and held on.

Kirstyn screamed and spun around on the steps, dropping her book.

Wolfgang let go of her wrist as if it were a burning cinder. "You didn't have to scream. I wasn't going to . . ." He stared at her wrist, and his face went white. "Kirstyn, I'm sorry."

Her heart was thumping hard and her hands shook, just like last night after the loud crash. Her brother must think she had gone completely mad. She did her best to breathe, but memories of Michael's face kept leaping before her—the cruel blackness of his eyes, the twist of his lips when he was shouting at her. She could feel the rope around her wrist, chafing and pulling.

Every time Michael pulled on the rope . . . Kirstyn heard herself sobbing before she felt the tears.

Wolfgang was kneeling beside her on the steps. "I'll go get Mother."

"No, I'm all right." Kirstyn pressed a shaking hand over her mouth. "I know you must think me crazed. Sick in my mind." She tried to laugh but couldn't quite manage it.

"No, I don't."

She stared at her wrist. No rope. She was home. She was well, and her brother was sitting beside her on the step.

Kirstyn took a deep breath. She was all right. She took another deep breath. The tears were drying, and her hands were not shaking as much. Wolfgang held out his hand. She took it and let him pull her to her feet.

"Let me help." He went down a few steps to retrieve her book, which had taken quite a tumble, then hurried back up. "I'm sorry for grabbing your wrist, Kirstyn. I'm so sorry."

She couldn't remember him ever apologizing to her before, but his brown eyes were wide and attentive to her.

"It's all right. I shouldn't have screamed." She shook her head at her foolishness.

"Father explained that you are reacting similarly to some men after they've been in several battles, because of that evil man kidnapping you. It's hard to separate what's real from the memories, he said. I'm sorry I reminded you . . . of what happened."

They walked slowly up the steps, with Wolfgang close at her elbow but not touching her.

"It's not your fault. I am well."

"And you don't have to go see Aladdin if you don't want to. In fact, if he mistreated you in any way, I'll go and beat him up for you."

"No, he hasn't mistreated me. Not really. I just . . . I feel hurt he hasn't come to see me."

"I shall go and tell him. I'll make him come and see you."

"No, no, please don't do that, Wolfie." She sighed. "Truly, he hasn't done anything wrong. He . . . Well, it's a long story. I probably shouldn't even be angry with him. The truth is, I do want to go visit him."

She missed him so much it made her chest ache again.

"I'll go with you if you'd like."

"I'm not ready just yet." She didn't want him to see her crying and falling apart at every loud noise and unexpected touch.

Wolfgang nodded and handed her the book as they reached her door.

"Thank you, Wolfgang."

One corner of his mouth quirked up in a crooked smile. "You're my *schwester.*"

"You're so much kinder now that you're thirteen."

"I'm fourteen."

"Oh. I guess I missed your last birthday." Tears stung her eyes again, but she blinked them away.

"I'm glad you're home."

"Thank you. It's good to be home." She wanted to hug him, but she wasn't sure his new gentleness would extend that far.

"And I'll go with you to see Aladdin anytime you wish. Just tell me."

"But perhaps the kindness is because Steffan is not around." She raised her brows at him.

He looked sheepish. "We were very childish and mean-spirited sometimes. I'm sorry we teased you and Margaretha too much."

"I forgive you."

Kirstyn hugged him before he could protest, then went into her bedchamber.

Herr Goteken delivered the ledgers as promised. Within a few days Aladdin had mostly figured out the mistakes and gaps in Herr Goteken's record keeping. The problem he still had not deciphered was that the ledger listing the inventory in the warehouse did not reconcile with what was actually there. He might have expected there to be fewer goods than what was listed, but there were actually more goods in the warehouse—almost twice as many. He had thought it merely an error in the arithmetic, but it was beginning to appear that much of the inventory showed no known origin.

That evening he went to his sleeping quarters. The two-story building was behind Herr Goteken's home and was where his household servants slept. Aladdin's tiny bed stood against the wall, the farthest from the fireplace. The fire had burned out the night before, long before dawn, because Herr Goteken had not given them enough wood to keep it burning.

Aladdin checked the woodpile beside the hearth. It was even colder tonight, but they had less wood than the night before.

Friedrich, one of Herr Goteken's servants, was staring balefully at the small pile of wood. Aladdin's chest squeezed in pity.

"I'm going to ask for more wood." Aladdin walked toward the door.

Friedrich's eyes were wide. "Herr Goteken doesn't like us coming back to the big house after we've gone for the night. It's forbidden."

"Not for me." Aladdin went out the door, closing it quickly to let in less cold air, and tramped across the snowy ground to the back door of an added-on guardhouse, storage room, and entry-way to the back of the house. He knocked.

Tomas, the tall servant whose job it was to protect the house at night, opened the door and growled, "What do you want?" Then, more mildly, "Is that you, Aladdin?"

"Tomas, the other servants and I would like more wood so our fire doesn't burn out."

Tomas motioned him inside while holding up a lamp. He

closed the door against the cold. "Master says I've been giving you too much wood. He rations it out himself now. Perhaps if *you* asked him . . ."

"Where is he? I'll ask him now."

"Oh no, he mustn't be disturbed this late at night."

"Very well. I will take more wood now and will ask him tomorrow."

Tomas scratched his head. "That would not please the master. He may throw you out."

"I shall pay him for the extra wood, then." Aladdin went to the stack in the corner of the room and started gathering wood into his arms. "If he throws me out, it will be for the best. The Holy Writ says, 'And we know that all things work together for good to them that love God, to them who are the called according to his purpose.'" Although there had been times in the last year when he questioned whether he truly understood that portion of Scripture.

Aladdin hefted the wood and carried it to the door. He looked at Tomas, who reluctantly opened the door and closed it behind him.

Aladdin carried the wood into the servants' quarters and dropped it next to the fireplace. Then he proceeded to add some to the fire.

The servants around him cheered. Aladdin carried some wood up the stairs to where some of the female servants slept. They were all smiles too. "How did you ever manage to get Herr Goteken to give you so much wood?"

Aladdin just shrugged. As he hurried back down the stairs, he called, "*Gute Nacht*, ladies."

"Won't Herr Goteken be angry with you?" Friedrich asked.

Aladdin began removing his clothing to get ready for bed. "I shall find out tomorrow."

Aladdin entered the kitchen anteroom where he and the servants ate their meals. Cook looked up and saw him. "Aladdin! You mustn't eat with the servants. Master wishes you to go to the big house and eat with him and his wife and children." Her eyes were round as she wiped her hands on her apron.

"Did he give a reason?"

"No, sir." She glanced at the servant boy standing in the corner and shooed him with her hand. He took off running and darted out the door.

"Well, I shall take my usual breakfast that you always wrap up for me." Every morning Cook gave him a fruit pasty or a fresh roll along with a wedge of cheese and an apple and he would take his bundle with him and eat it when he arrived at the shop.

Cook's mouth opened as she stared at him, then she turned and started gathering his breakfast.

The door banged open and Herr Goteken stepped in.

Cook spun around and her hands fluttered at the sight of him.

"Aladdin!" Herr Goteken said, far louder than necessary, ignoring Cook and the rest of the kitchen servants. "Come to the big house. I have something to say to you."

He had no choice but to go with his landlord.

Herr Goteken strode quickly across the small space between the house and the kitchen. Tomas watched them walk by. Other servants stopped their work to watch them as well. When they had entered the house, Herr Goteken turned to Aladdin in the corridor where everyone on the ground floor would hear what he said.

"Aladdin, you did something last night that is forbidden—you took more wood for the servants' fire. Everyone in my household knows it is forbidden." His brows were lowered as he stared down at him, his face a mere foot from Aladdin's in the dimly lit corridor. "Did you know that?"

"Yes, Herr Goteken. I was told as much." A sense of wariness and dread filled him, and he wondered absently where else he might find a shop to rent and a place to sleep. He had thought about going to Hamburg. He still had that recommendation letter Duke Wilhelm had written. Perhaps Hamburg's grand burghers, who ruled the town, would hire him as a financial clerk. But he didn't want to be that far from Kirstyn.

Silence hovered as they stared each other in the eye. Suddenly Herr Goteken smiled and leaned away from him. "That's what I like about you, Aladdin. Courage!" He laughed so loud the sound vibrated inside Aladdin's ears.

Herr Goteken clapped him on the shoulder. "From now on you are to eat with me in my dining hall." He kept his hand on Aladdin's shoulder and led him into a large room. "Have I introduced you to my family? This is my wife, Berta, and my children, Heinrich and Schroder and little Sofia."

Aladdin nodded to them each in turn. They sat down as Herr Goteken sat at the head of the table and motioned for him to sit across from Frau Goteken.

Aladdin pretended not to be uncomfortable and talked with Herr Goteken, who dominated the conversation, and Aladdin occasionally spoke a few words to Frau Goteken and the children, who seemed rather fascinated by him.

"Aladdin once worked for the Duke of Hagenheim," Herr Goteken told his children.

"Did he live in the castle?"

"Why do you ask me? Ask him yourself."

"Did you?" The little boy turned his eyes on Aladdin.

"I worked in the castle and slept with the other servants in the servants' quarters outside the castle, much as I do here."

"Aladdin made Herr Kaufmann of Lüneburg a very wealthy man," Herr Goteken said. "I'm hoping he shall do the same for me."

"Herr Kaufmann was already a very wealthy man when I went to work for him," Aladdin protested, "partially due to his being a *Sülfmeister.*"

"Oh yes! A master salter." Goteken narrowed his eyes at Aladdin. "I don't suppose you can help me get a lease on a few salt pans."

"I'm afraid I have no control or authori—"

"No matter. That was not your expertise, was it? No, you know efficiency and strategy, heh? I suppose you had Herr Kaufmann buying expensive silks and spices from the Orient and the Holy Land. Is that the secret of your success? Did you travel to the Holy Land to trade with your own people there?" Herr Goteken had that half-amused look that meant ridicule.

"I never traveled to the Holy Land. And the secret to success is giving people what they need, and then what they want, according to what they can afford."

"Ah." Herr Goteken narrowed his eyes again. "Not a lot of silks, gold, ivory, and jade?"

"We imported those goods too, but most of our inventory was more practical and not brought from so far away as the Orient or the Holy Land."

Herr Goteken stared at him as if trying to decide something.

The children and Goteken's wife excused themselves from the table. Aladdin also rose. "I should be getting to the shop."

Herr Goteken waved his hand to dismiss him.

Aladdin put on his warmest cloak and headed out into the cold day. As he walked he thought about how he'd almost solved the mystery of the discrepancies in the ledger. But he didn't want to reveal anything until he was certain of his findings.

He was nearly to the shop when someone called, "Aladdin!"

Hereford, a buyer for Herr Kaufmann, came hurrying toward him. "I thought that was you!" He slapped him on the shoulder. "What are you doing in Hagenheim?"

"I opened my own shop." He smiled at the jovial man who had always been friendly to him. "How are things in Lüneburg?" He hadn't realized how much he longed to hear from the man he had loved as a father, and from the household he had lived with for a year and a half.

"Things are good. Except that Herr Kaufmann seems to believe in the reform of that evil imp of a son of his. He's even been visiting him in the Rathous gaol." Hereford frowned and shook his head. "How he can believe a word that man says is beyond my understanding. The love of a father, I suppose. But I was heartily sorry that he sent you away, Aladdin. No one believes the man's lies about you."

Some did, but Aladdin decided not to point that out. "Thank you for your confidence in me."

"Oh, and something else is afoot."

Aladdin raised his brows to encourage him to go on.

"Johann has come back from Florence."

"Johann?"

"You were not in Lüneburg when he left, were you? Well, it was generally known that he was in love with Grethel Kaufmann, but Herr Kaufmann disapproved of him since he was an artist with no interest in business. Grethel was brought very low by his

leaving. It was thought she might marry you, Aladdin, but . . ."
He frowned again, obviously not wanting to voice the rest of his
thoughts. "But now Johann is returned, and he has asked Herr
Kaufmann to allow him to marry her."

"How did he answer?"

"No one is entirely sure, but it seems he has not said yes or
no. Johann comes to the house but is not allowed to be alone
with Grethel. I believe Herr Kaufmann will soften and let her
marry him, especially since she was . . . well, she was disappointed, as you know, when you told her you couldn't marry her
because you were in love with Lady Kirstyn of Hagenheim."

"So everyone knows that?"

"Well . . ." He shrugged. "Those who are acquainted with
the family, certainly. But it's not my intention to cause you any
pain."

"No, it's all right. I am very glad to hear that Grethel's first
love has returned. I'm happy for her."

Hereford smiled. "It is good to see you, Aladdin. Very good
to see you. How is Herr Goteken treating you? He's not always
the kindest employer or landlord, I hear."

"He treats me well enough. I cannot complain."

"When I come back to Hagenheim, shall I look for you?"

"I hope you do."

They parted ways, and Aladdin felt a lightness of heart at
hearing that Grethel's old love had returned. But not hearing
from Kirstyn had weighed him down over the last several days.
She must be angry with him. If she wanted to see him, wouldn't
she send for him as he had asked? He'd inquired of one of the
knights if she was well and he'd said yes.

The longer he waited, the harder it was to actually go to the
castle and request to see her.

A week went by. Aladdin had been sitting on the unfortunate information about the extra goods in Herr Goteken's warehouse that were not listed in his books. He had prayed many times but still was unsure what to do. But his conscience wouldn't let him go on any longer. He had sent word to Herr Goteken to meet him at the end of the workday.

Aladdin had hired a young man to watch his shop and wait on customers while he set up a second shop near the Marktplatz. Upon his return, he worked on the numbers from Herr Goteken's ledgers while he waited for his landlord to arrive. At least it was not so cold today. He couldn't even see his breath and had stopped having to blow on his fingers to unfreeze them.

"What is it, Aladdin?" Herr Goteken stood in the office doorway, his body half turned toward Aladdin.

Since no one else was around, Aladdin began. "I've noticed some discrepancies in the book of records and the actual inventory of goods in your warehouse."

"You can see that just from looking at the ledgers?"

"Yes, if I also examine the warehouse's inventory."

"Oh, well, I don't need you to examine the warehouse's inventory. That is not your job."

Aladdin stared at him a moment. "So you are not concerned about there being extra goods that are unaccounted for?"

"Aladdin, your job is to straighten out my books and help me increase my profits. Why should you be concerned about extra goods? If my warehouse contained less inventory than was listed, then I would be upset." His face broke into a brittle smile. "It is nothing you need to worry about."

"But I have been examining your inventory, and more extra goods appear nearly every day—or perhaps every night."

Herr Goteken scrunched his face and pursed his lips as though he was giving it great thought. "I shall have my guards look into it. Thank you, Aladdin."

Aladdin was nearly certain now that Herr Goteken's men were stealing other merchants' wares and bringing them here. And not only did Herr Goteken know about it, he was ordering them to do it. But how were they getting away with it?

Herr Goteken began walking away, then turned around. "Just remember, you work for me. I'll tell you what concerns you and what doesn't. And if you prove yourself loyal and useful, who knows? There might be a fortune in it for you." His tone was flat and even.

Aladdin nodded even as his mind was churning.

He needed evidence. Facts. He needed to know whom Goteken was stealing from and how. And then . . . what would Aladdin do then?

Aladdin couldn't let the thieving go on. It wasn't right for those Goteken was stealing from. But he would have to trust that God would show him what to do.

CHAPTER TWENTY-NINE

Aladdin had decided the only way to find out exactly who was thieving was to spend the night at Herr Goteken's warehouse.

On Saturday Aladdin worked at his new shop all day, then went to bed as usual. He sometimes sat and wrote a letter to Kirstyn by candlelight—letters he had yet to send—while Herr Goteken's other servants drank wine and strong spirits. Aladdin would be asleep well before they were in bed. He'd simply roll over and go back to sleep when they woke him with their noise.

But tonight Aladdin stuffed his bed with old clothing to look like he was sleeping in it, then he slipped out with a large flask of strong spirits under his cloak and made his way under the cover of night to the warehouse.

Herr Goteken's men guarded the warehouse. But Aladdin had heard them talk and knew they liked to drink when they were on duty.

When he reached the warehouse, he heard quiet voices before he saw the two guards sitting on stools outside the one door to the warehouse.

He had to get them away from the door.

He stood behind a nearby building, occasionally peeking around the side to see if they were still there. He watched them, listening to their voices, but was unable to make out their words from his hiding place. Would they eventually get up and walk away? But the longer he waited, the more convinced he was that they would stay right where they were all night.

Aladdin moved carefully around to the side of the warehouse. The guards didn't see him, so he slipped around the back. Then, when he was at the other end, he listened.

The men were still talking. A small group of people were walking down the street, approaching Aladdin. He ducked behind the warehouse until they had passed. Then he saw a boy, probably around twelve years old, wandering down the street. He recognized him as one of the boys who sometimes stole food at the market but was too clever to get caught.

Aladdin covered his face as much as he could with a scarf he wore around his neck and went out to meet the boy. "Would you like to make some money?"

The boy's eyes grew wide. He stepped closer to Aladdin.

"Take this flask over there to those men in front of the warehouse. Tell them you'll give it to them if they will help you get your little sister out of a hole she fell into."

"What hole?"

"There is no hole. Just get them to walk with you over there." Aladdin pointed to the other side of the street where the buildings cast a heavy shadow. "Then, when they start to ask you where it is, just tell them she must have gotten free on her own. Then give them the flask and run home."

The boy looked confused, but he shrugged and took the flask. Aladdin pressed the two marks in his other hand and watched him head toward the guards.

Aladdin waited while the boy spoke to the guards. After they walked away toward the river, Aladdin carefully hurried to the warehouse door, glancing constantly at the boy and the guards. He took the key he had "borrowed" from Herr Goteken's desk when he was not looking and unlocked the door. The boy and the guards were nearly to the river. Aladdin snuck inside and closed the door almost all the way, spying through the crack until the boy shoved the flask into their hands and ran away.

Aladdin quietly closed the door, then hurried to a corner where he had already set up a tented pile of blankets to hide in. He crawled inside. All was quiet, and it was too dark to see anything, so, leaving a small opening at eye level, he closed his eyes and fell asleep.

Aladdin was awakened by a light shining in his eyes. Why was his bed so hard? Then he remembered he was sleeping on the floor in the warehouse.

He tried to focus on whatever was shining the light. Through the gap in his makeshift tent, he saw two men, each carrying a lantern. Soon they put their lanterns down and began bringing in full wooden crates and setting them down. Aladdin concentrated on their faces and recognized two of Herr Goteken's guards. He listened as they brought in crate after crate. Finally, when they paused to rest, one of the guards laughed.

"Herr Bingen will never miss those spices."

"Yeah, but Herr Schlossmann has already been complaining that someone is stealing his silk cloth. I told Herr Goteken, but he said to keep taking a little at a time. He was going to make it look like one of Schlossmann's workers was the culprit."

"He's a sly one."

"But he pays well." They both laughed. After they finished bringing in the stolen goods, they left.

Aladdin lit his own candle and examined the goods—much of them just ordinary items similar to what Herr Goteken sold every day in the shops he owned and distributed to various other markets in the area.

Aladdin blew out his candle, cleaned up his makeshift bedding, and waited until it was time for the guards to leave for their morning meal. Aladdin would have a minute or two before the next shift of guards came, so he sat by the window and never took his eyes off the guards at the door after dawn began to break. Finally they left, walking off down the street.

Aladdin hurried out the door, locking it behind him and praying no one saw him, then kept his scarf around the lower part of his face and his hood drawn low as he walked back.

On Monday Aladdin awoke feeling unsettled and anxious. He sat up and realized he'd slept late. All the servants had arisen and gone. Then he remembered the dream he'd had, of Kirstyn crying and turning away from him. Then the dream shifted to the front steps of the town cathedral. Kirstyn and a richly dressed man were standing in front of the priest saying their marriage vows. She turned and gave Aladdin a baleful look, then went inside the church to take the Holy Eucharist with her new husband.

Aladdin's heart seemed to weigh a hundred stones. Why hadn't Kirstyn sent for him or at least written to him?

His shops were doing well, and he now had three people

working for him. He no longer worried he might be poor enough to steal, but his success was not enough to fill the need inside him for a family. The need for a friend. The need for Kirstyn.

If Kirstyn would wait for him, he'd travel to Flanders and the Orient, buy goods there, and bring them back to Germany to sell. He might settle somewhere like Lübeck or another Hanseatic town to the north and trade with the Norwegians and Pomeranians. It wouldn't take that long before he would be wealthy enough to feel worthy of marrying Kirstyn. But he was tired of missing her. And it wasn't fair to make her wait for him.

First he needed to clear his conscience, do the right thing by getting to the bottom of Herr Goteken's nefarious activities.

Aladdin went down to the warehouse in the hope that the two guards he'd seen moving goods into Herr Goteken's warehouse would be there. Aladdin milled about the area outside the warehouse, but there was no activity anywhere around it. He was about to give up looking when he spotted the two guards a little way down the street. They were laughing with two other men, who abruptly turned and went in the other direction.

This was the moment he had come for. Aladdin strode up to the guards. "Good morning." Aladdin introduced himself.

"Herr Goteken's new account keeper, are you? I'm Giese," the larger one said, "and this is Matthias."

"I wonder if I might ask you a question or two."

"We're not busy at the moment."

"Very good. I only wished to ask you about the cargo I saw you bringing into Herr Goteken's warehouse two nights ago."

Giese drew back, while Matthias seemed to choke on his own saliva and began coughing.

"What are you speaking of?" Giese demanded.

"I watched you and Matthias bring in the crates. I know Herr

Goteken didn't pay money for those goods. I want to know where you got them."

"Who are you to ask us that?" Matthias suddenly stepped forward, his nose only a handsbreadth from Aladdin's.

The man was no taller than Aladdin, but he was much wider. He could break Aladdin's face with one blow of his fist.

Aladdin's heart skipped a few beats, but he stood his ground. "I only ask because Goteken suspects you of cheating him, but I can help you fool him. You know Goteken would sell you to a slaver for half your worth if he thought he could get away with it."

Apprehension flickered over the guard's face, but then he nodded. "Has Herr Goteken told you he suspects we are cheating him? Well, he would cheat his mother to make half a mark. And if you'll help us keep our secret, we will cut you in. There's a shipment of pearls, jade, and ivory stored in a warehouse not far from here. If you keep your mouth shut, I'll give you a share of it—enough to make you a wealthy man." Giese stepped forward and tapped Aladdin's chest and winked.

Aladdin's mind churned. Did these men just offer him the chance to have everything he'd wanted, or at least get closer to it?

"How much are you offering in exchange for helping you fool Herr Goteken?"

"Come back tonight after dark. We'll show you."

"So Goteken knows nothing about this shipment? But he knows about all the other shipments you've been thieving from?"

"He sends us to take a small amount from each of the warehouses on Saturday night, when all the guards are drinking."

"How do you get away with it? Are you bribing all those guards?"

"A few of them. You are a curious one."

"I want to know if I'm a man among many—easily discarded by Herr Goteken."

"You? No, Herr Goteken values you, even if it's only because you are well known as the Golden Boy of Lüneburg and a friend of the Duke of Hagenheim and his daughter. But Goteken doesn't pay you what you're worth, and now you can get your revenge on him." He leaned closer to Aladdin. "Wouldn't you like to be rich? Rich enough to marry the duke's daughter? Who deserves it more than you, eh?"

A sick feeling in Aladdin's stomach reminded him how he would feel if anyone found out he had profited from stolen property. But the sick feeling was also there because . . . he actually was tempted to do it. Aladdin could buy a house for Kirstyn. He could finally marry her and have the family he'd always wanted.

But it wouldn't be honestly gained. He would not be able to respect himself if he did it. And self-respect and peace of mind were two things he wasn't willing to give up.

Besides, God would not bless a lack of integrity.

However, if he flatly refused Giese's offer, they might kill him to keep him from telling the authorities—or Herr Goteken.

"Perhaps I will come tonight," Aladdin said.

A smile overspread Giese's weather-beaten face. "I thought you would come around to my thinking."

"But whether or not I do, you can be certain I will not tell Herr Goteken. There is no love between us."

"I thought as much."

When Aladdin arrived back at his sleeping quarters in Herr Goteken's home, he packed up his few belongings, placing Kirstyn's letters in the leather pouch that hung close to his side. Without speaking to anyone, he simply walked out of the house, not knowing where he would sleep.

Aladdin saddled his horse and rode toward Hagenheim Castle. He already knew what he would say to her brother Valten, Lord Hamlin.

His thoughts were of Kirstyn as he guided his horse toward the gray stone castle whose five towers were visible over rooftops at the other end of town.

He longed to see her. His breath hitched at the prospect. But he couldn't marry her now, and she had not answered his letter. She must surely be angry. It had been weeks. He had half hoped, half feared she would come and visit him in his little shop. What would she think of him, now just a lowly shopkeeper? Seeing her would only make him feel the full weight of his failure.

He found Lord Hamlin where he'd hoped he would be, in the practice field training the other knights. Valten was one of the few people as tall as Aladdin. And he seemed broader in the shoulders every time Aladdin saw him. He kept his hair cut short and he walked with strength and confidence, though Aladdin knew him to be quite humble when he wasn't giving orders or reprimanding someone.

After he dismounted from his horse, Kirstyn's oldest brother greeted him with one of his elusive almost-smiles and clapped him on the shoulder. "I heard you were living in Hagenheim again. It is good to see you."

At least Kirstyn's brother didn't hate him.

"I have a matter to discuss with you, about someone who I've discovered is stealing from other merchants."

Valten leaned closer. "Tell me about this."

So Aladdin explained everything he knew about Herr Goteken's and his guards' thieving.

"I shall deal with this," Valten said, his brows lowered in that severe look of his.

"Do you need anything else from me?"

"No. Better for you to stay out of sight for a while. Did you say you were sleeping in Herr Goteken's servant barracks? Best not to go back there. You can stay here. There's always room in the knights' barracks."

"Thank you, but I'm not sure Lady Kirstyn would appreciate having me so near." Aladdin winced at the admission.

"I'm certain that is not true." Valten gazed harder at Aladdin. "Kirstyn has you to thank for saving her from that bear, and she would rather go walking in the woods with you than do anything."

"Perhaps at one time, but . . . we're not children anymore."

"You wanted to marry her, but she doesn't want to marry you," Valten said with his usual forthrightness. He was a man of few words, but he was concerned about his sister.

"No. That is . . . I don't know what her feelings are, exactly."

Valten stared at him with a quizzical look.

"I don't know if your father would allow me to marry her even if I were rich enough to buy a house worthy of her."

"You said you have two shops. Buy her a house and I'm sure Father will allow her to marry you."

It filled his lungs with air to hear him say that. "I'm not sure Kirstyn will want to wait. In fact, I think she must be angry with me. She may not wish to marry me."

"Have you talked to her?"

"I sent her a letter a few weeks ago and she has not responded."

"If there's one thing I know about women, it's that they hate it when we don't talk to them."

Valten might be right. Pride, fear, and excessive work had kept him away. His breath came faster at the thought of seeing her again. He had promised to be there for her. Perhaps if he apologized, she would forgive him.

"She is well, then?" Aladdin asked.

Valten hesitated and frowned almost imperceptibly.

"What is it? Is something wrong with Kirstyn?"

"She is well enough. Only . . . you should let her tell you."

Valten wished him well and went to take care of the trouble with Herr Goteken. And Aladdin strode back toward the castle.

CHAPTER THIRTY

K irstyn climbed up the keep tower to the very top. When she
was a child, she wasn't allowed up here without a parent
or another adult, since the crenellations made it tempting for a
child to climb onto them to get a better view—and then fall to
the ground far below.

Kirstyn pulled her cloak tighter around her shoulders to
block the brisk wind. From here she could see everything around
the castle—the fruit tree orchard to the north, the stables, the
gatehouse, the town to the south, and the meadow and forest to
the east.

She turned to the west to look out over the fields where
Valten and his men often practiced their fighting skills, jousting,
and war games. And indeed, Valten was there. He seemed to
notice something, stopped what he was doing, and strode toward
a rider on a horse who dismounted and came to meet him.

Her heart pounded and her breath grew shallow. Aladdin.

She trembled as Aladdin and Valten greeted each other like
old friends, probably because of the sword-fighting training Valten

had given him. Then they talked as if they had business—a lot of business, apparently. And the longer she watched them talk, the angrier she became. If Aladdin could come to the castle and talk to Valten, why could he not come and talk to her? If Valten was like an old friend, how much more was she?

She watched until they parted and went in opposite directions.

She had to see him, had to look Aladdin in the eye and ask him why he had avoided her for weeks.

She turned and raced down the steps. By the time she reached the bottom, she was breathing so hard she stopped and bent forward. Would she be able to catch Aladdin before he left? If not, she would grab a guard and force him to go with her, to follow Aladdin to his shop. She would demand to know what she had done to make him avoid her.

How dare he behave as if she meant nothing to him?

She strode toward the door that led to the courtyard outside, and just as she reached it, it burst open. A guard stood there with Aladdin.

Her gaze met Aladdin's, and they stood staring at each other.

The guard cleared his throat. "Lady Kirstyn, Aladdin wishes to see you." He shuffled his weight from one foot to the other.

"You may go." Kirstyn nodded at the guard.

Aladdin stepped inside. "Kirstyn, please forgive me for not coming to see you sooner. How are you? Are you well?"

He was so contrite, his expression so gentle, the fire inside her turned to ashes. She crossed her arms in an effort to bring it back. When she didn't say anything, he continued.

"I wrote you a letter."

The fire flamed up again. "What kind of letter was that to write to me?"

Two guards entered through the door Aladdin had just come

through, forcing them to move out of the way. The guards stared curiously.

"Is there someplace we could go to talk privately?" Aladdin leaned close. His eyes reminded her of her old, sweet Aladdin.

No. She couldn't think like that. She was angry with him.

They could go up to the top of the keep tower. "Come." She spun on her heel and headed toward the stairs. When she had gone up enough steps that no one below could see them, Aladdin brushed her fingers with his. It was a clear invitation to hold his hand. She shivered. Her fingers tingled. But she continued up the steps without looking back and without taking his hand.

When they reached the top and were out in the open air, Kirstyn faced Aladdin. "Why did you not tell me you were in Hagenheim? Why shun me for weeks and then send me that short, impersonal letter? Do you think I have no feelings? That I wouldn't feel pain?"

Her words were hitting their mark by the look in his eyes, but she wanted him to feel her hurt.

"I did not mean to shun you. Kirstyn, I'm sorry. I thought you would send for me after I sent you that letter. I also wasn't sure . . . That is, I would never presume—"

"You should have. You should have presumed. I told you I wanted you here."

"You're right, of course. I'm sorry. Fear and pride prevented me from coming to the castle right away to see you."

She kept her arms crossed in front of her, protecting herself. Tears pricked her eyes.

"Will you forgive me, Kirstyn? I'm here now." He gave her the tiniest smile.

Truly he was so handsome, and his face held such an endearing look, it took her breath away. "I forgive you. But I . . ."

"What? Is something else wrong?"

She pressed her fingers over her lips. She didn't want him to see her cry. She took a deep breath and let it out before finally saying, "I needed you, but you stayed away."

Aladdin moved closer to her. She leaned toward him, and he wrapped his arms around her. She rested her head on his chest, and he gently rubbed her shoulders.

"I'm sorry. I'm here, and I'm not going away." His voice was ragged as he spoke next to her ear. "Tell me what's wrong."

She took a deep breath and spoke with her cheek resting against his chest. "I have felt as if I'm losing my mind. Loud noises terrify me beyond reason. Wolfgang grabbed my wrist and I screamed. My heart beat so hard I couldn't breathe. It feels as if Michael is right there, hurting me. The memories come back and it's as if I'm trapped again with him and Anna."

Aladdin caressed her back. "You aren't losing your mind. It's only because the ordeal was so recent and is still so fresh in your mind. When you get used to feeling safe, you will get beyond this fear, Kirstyn. I know you will."

His words were kind, and they made sense, being similar to what her mother and father had said to her. But the truth was . . . "I needed you. But you didn't come."

He expelled a breath. "I'm sorry."

"And I just want to be angry with you a little bit longer." It sounded silly when she said it out loud. She looked up at him.

Aladdin nodded. He frowned and sighed. "Then I want you to hit me."

"What?"

"Hit me right here." He pointed to his left cheek. "It will make your anger go away."

"I will not hit you."

"Do it. I don't want you angry with me forever."

"You're teasing me."

"I'm not."

But amusement glimmered in his eyes. It rekindled her anger, so she clenched her fist and punched his shoulder.

"That wasn't hard enough. Hit me harder."

She drew her fist back but hesitated, staring at his shoulder. He seemed to be bracing for the blow. She grabbed his face to hold it still. She pressed her lips to his.

It hardly took a moment for him to wrap his arms around her and kiss her back. She threw all her pent-up feelings into the kiss. She would make sure he never forgot her again, and never forgot this kiss.

A shudder went through Aladdin's body. When they finally stopped kissing, Kirstyn whispered, "Just hold me," and buried her face in his chest.

He held her as tenderly as he could. His heart was still pounding after that kiss. His arms encircled her shoulders, his cheek pressed against the top of her head. *O God, how can I give her up, even if I can't buy her a house? She needs me.*

It seemed obvious now: Kirstyn needed his nearness, his comfort. Riches meant very little to her. If he had let go of his fear of being poor and unworthy, let go of his desire to be rich, he could have been here for her, and he could have admitted something to her.

He whispered against her hair, "I need you too."

She tightened her arms around him and spoke, her breath against his neck. "We were always meant to be together."

"But I still feel I failed you. Not only by not being here, but in other ways. And I'm sorry."

Kirstyn had her parents' example to reassure her that even when she failed or did something wrong, they still loved her. Aladdin had depended on the approval of teachers and caregivers. He didn't know the unfailing love of a doting mother or father, and she wanted to give that to him. She had this feeling whenever she was around the orphans, but with Aladdin, it was even stronger.

"I forgive you, and hearing you confess your imperfect thoughts makes me feel more connected to you, since I am not perfect either. You don't have to be perfect for me to care about you. In fact . . ." She smiled. "It's a relief to find out you're not perfect."

She leaned away and looked up at him. His lips, at least, were perfect, and so near.

"Thank you for forgiving me." Aladdin let out a long sigh. "The truth is, Herr Kaufmann was so afraid of some threats Michael made against his business and Grethel that he asked me to leave his house. He pretended to believe Michael's lies about me so Michael's friends wouldn't harm Grethel and burn down his warehouses. But he still wanted me to stay and take care of his accounts and the business. He wasn't very pleased when I told him I was coming to Hagenheim."

"That's so unfair! How could he expect you to comply with that? And how does Michael have so much power when he's locked up in the Rathous?"

"He still has evil friends, apparently, who will do his bidding. But when Herr Kaufmann planned to give his business to me and make me his heir, it meant nothing to me . . ."

Kirstyn gazed into his gentle face. He looked so intense, she was afraid to say anything lest she drive away the tender look in his eyes.

"It meant nothing because you were not with me. I know I have no right to ask you, but will you marry me, Kirstyn?" His voice was breathless. "I love you so much."

"Yes." A wave of warmth and peace rolled through her.

He leaned forward until his forehead was resting on hers. "I so much want to kiss you. May I kiss you?"

She thought he'd never ask.

Aladdin's heart was beating nearly out of his chest as Kirstyn's mouth curved into a gentle smile.

"Yes." She lifted her chin, bringing her lips closer to his.

He brushed his lips against hers as his fingers reverently held her face. He opened his eyelids a slit as he stared back at her, then closed them as his mouth again caressed hers, kissing her with all the fervor welling up inside him. She kissed him back just as eagerly.

Kirstyn pressed her face to his chest and wrapped her arms around his back.

They stood holding each other for several minutes. How good God had been to him. Aladdin almost felt guilty, as if he'd received so much more than his share of good things in life. And in this moment, every other pain he'd ever felt was as if it had never existed.

She lifted her head and cupped his face again. But instead of kissing him, she looked him in the eyes. "Will you let me be your family now?"

He knew she was waiting for his response, so he nodded. "Yes." Then she kissed him gently on the lips.

Oh, what he'd been missing. She was right—he should have come to see her much sooner.

But there was still the problem of being able to provide for Kirstyn. It was hard to let go of the desire to make his fortune and prove himself. Would it be enough to have a family of his own with Kirstyn if they had to live off of Duke Wilhelm's charity?

CHAPTER THIRTY-ONE

Aladdin stood in the doorway of one of his shops when a man he recognized rode by. "Georg, is that you?"

The man turned and broke into a smile. "Aladdin!"

Georg, one of Herr Kaufmann's guards, rode over to him and dismounted. "You are the man I came to find. Let's go over to the Marktplatz fountain so we can talk."

Aladdin's curiosity was piqued, but he tried not to speculate. They both sat on the outside edge of the fountain. Aladdin ignored the people milling about, as no one was near enough to hear their conversation, and focused on what Georg was saying.

"Michael has escaped from gaol."

"Escaped? He is free?" Aladdin's face heated.

"Everyone is speculating whether Herr Kaufmann helped him. But Herr Kaufmann is so afraid of him, I can't imagine he did."

"Do the people of Lüneburg believe I was responsible for Lady Kirstyn's kidnapping?"

Georg shook his head. "I think most people know what an evil liar Michael is. They realize Herr Kaufmann is terrified of his son. It seems likely that Michael threatened him with something dire. I don't know what, perhaps that he would hurt Grethel. I don't suppose anyone knows for sure. In the meantime, Johann has wed Herr Kaufmann's daughter, and he gave me this letter and sent me to find you."

Georg handed the letter to Aladdin. He opened it and read:

To Aladdin of Hagenheim, from Johann Botelsdorf, husband of Grethel Kaufmann,

Greetings. I hope you will forgive me for writing to you, since you do not even know me. But as I have heard much about your good character, I pray you will give heed to my entreaties.

I am writing to you to ask if you could get a message to Duke Wilhelm of Hagenheim that Michael has escaped. We believe he is still in Lüneburg and is planning to, at the very least, steal from Herr Kaufmann, who is so afraid of Michael that he hardly even leaves the house, and never without at least two guards accompanying him.

If the duke would come and apprehend Michael and take him back to Hagenheim for punishment, we would be eternally grateful, and I believe Herr Kaufmann would be overjoyed to see you again. I have been trying to help with the business, but alas, I am no businessman. I fear there will be little left of it if you do not help us.

Your servant,
Johann Botelsdorf

Aladdin stood. "Come. We must find Duke Wilhelm."

Aladdin's heart jumped into his throat as he entered Herr Kaufmann's home for the first time since he was asked to leave.

Frau Hilde hurried into the entryway while wiping her hands on her apron.

"Aladdin. Dear, dear Aladdin." A tear slipped from her eye and she caught it with her apron.

Aladdin embraced her, and when they parted, she was wiping her eyes again.

"Good morning, Aladdin," a young man greeted him. "I'm Johann Botelsdorf. Thank you very much for coming."

"It is my pleasure," Aladdin said as Hilde went quietly back to the kitchen. "And Duke Wilhelm, Lord Hamlin, and several of their knights came with me to find and apprehend Michael."

"That is very good to hear. And now, will you follow me?"

He was a soft-spoken young man with dark hair and eyes. Johann led him into the dining hall, where they sat in cushioned chairs against the wall.

"As you have probably heard, Herr Kaufmann has been ill."

"I had not heard." Aladdin sat on the edge of his chair.

"Michael broke into the house three nights ago. Herr Kaufmann encountered him in the kitchen, it seems, as Michael was coming up the steps carrying a chest from the strong room. Michael attacked him and hit him in the head. The guards came and prevented the theft, but he escaped."

Aladdin's heart crashed against his chest. "How badly was he hurt?"

"Herr Kaufmann was on the floor and did not open his eyes for a few minutes. He has been in bed ever since."

"And Abu? Is he well? He was not hurt, was he?"

"No, Abu is well. He was asleep in his bed when it happened."

"Is Herr Kaufmann well enough that I might speak to him?"

"I believe he would like that. But first, I would like to tell you that we all regret that you were cast out of the house. I hope you will forgive Herr Kaufmann."

"Of course. I don't hold any grudge against Herr Kaufmann."

"That is very gracious of you." Johann's fingernails bore the stains of dark paints, and his hair was rather unkempt. "We are grateful for your forgiving nature, because now I, Herr Kaufmann, and all the family are hoping you will help us."

Aladdin leaned forward, waiting for the quiet man, who was pausing in his speech.

"I have been trying to take care of Herr Kaufmann's business affairs during his illness—from which, the physicians say, he may never recover—and I am doing a very poor job of it." His thick brown brows rose to meet the hair that hung down on his forehead. "I am an artist. I love my work. But I have no mind for business, buying and selling and numbers. I came back here to see if Grethel would marry me. I am willing to stay in Lüneburg as long as Grethel's father needs her, but if the business is entrusted to me, I'm afraid there will be nothing left of it in six months.

"Which is why I am imploring you to return here to Lüneburg, to help Herr Kaufmann with his business affairs. He is willing and eager to make you his full partner, both legally and in every other way. Would you be willing to help us?" Johann waited, never taking his eyes off Aladdin's.

"I . . . I would have to speak with Lady Kirstyn before I could agree to stay permanently. But I can help."

Johann let out a sigh and smiled for the first time. "I am most grateful to you. Now I can go back to painting and Herr Kaufmann can rest instead of trying to teach me how to run things."

"May I see Herr Kaufmann?"

"Of course. I shall take you to him."

Aladdin climbed the stairs behind Johann as they made their way to Herr Kaufmann's bedchamber.

"Herr Kaufmann." Johann approached the bed. "Aladdin is here to see you. Are you able to speak with him now?"

"Aladdin? Aladdin is here?"

"I am, Herr Kaufmann." Aladdin couldn't see him yet, as the bed curtains blocked his view.

Johann moved aside and Aladdin stepped forward.

Herr Kaufmann's face was pale and gray, and his eyes were hollow. He reached out, and Aladdin took his hand in both of his.

"Aladdin, my son." Tears welled up in his eyes and his lower lip and chin trembled.

Aladdin's own eyes filled with tears.

"How are you feeling? I have heard you've been sick."

Herr Kaufmann drew in a raspy breath. "I have wronged you, Aladdin. I treated you poorly, you who had been so faithful to me. Will you forgive me?" A tear slipped from the corner of his eye and ran down to his pillow.

"I do, Herr Kaufmann. Of course I forgive you. Please don't upset yourself. I love you too well to hold anything against you."

Herr Kaufmann squeezed his hand. "But Michael . . . He is out there on the streets again. The town's guards haven't been able to find him."

"Duke Wilhelm is here, and he and his knights and soldiers will find him, I have no doubt."

"That is comforting."

"And while we wait for him to be captured . . . I want to see you well and healthy again. What do the doctors say is the matter?"

"Thank you, dear boy. You always were kind and good, and God's favor rests on you." He took a deep breath and let it out. "As for me, I am old, and my physician says my heart is weak. The shock of seeing Cedric and the blow to my head must have brought on the bad humors." He waved his hand in the air. "But it is no matter. I am old and my life has run its course."

"You mustn't say such a thing. Length of life is God's business. He will decide."

"That is true. And you always do me good." Herr Kaufmann's eyes twinkled as he made an effort to sit up. Aladdin and a nearby servant helped pull him up and arranged his pillows so he could sit higher.

"Has Johann told you?" Herr Kaufmann motioned for Aladdin to lean in. "We need your help, Aladdin. No one knows the business better than you, and no one is so competent as you. Won't you come back and take over the business? I shall have papers drawn up so that everything will belong to you and Grethel. We all miss the days when you were here."

"I will need to speak to Lady Kirstyn, as we are hoping to be married soon. If she agrees to come to Lüneburg, we will wish to have our own house."

"Of course, of course. I will make it so you have complete control over the business. You may have the money to buy any house you wish. You will visit me, won't you? A few times a week?"

"I will."

"You are faithful to your word. You always were." A sorrowful expression swept over his face, and Aladdin imagined he was thinking of Cedric Michael.

The visit was soon over. Aladdin stepped out of the room and into the corridor with Johann, and they were joined by Grethel, who took Johann's arm and smiled up at him. Then she turned her eyes on Aladdin.

"Thank you for coming."

"Grethel. I am glad to see you." After all, she was like a sister to him. And he was very glad to see that *she* was glad to be with Johann.

"Aladdin! You're home!" Abu came running up the stairs.

Aladdin embraced the boy and then held him out by his shoulders so he could look him over. "I believe you've grown half a foot since I left."

"And I'm faster too! Shall we have a race?"

Aladdin couldn't help laughing. "We shall, when I'm wearing something more suitable for racing, and when we go out to the Heath again."

They talked of what Abu had been studying with his tutor and how Herr Kaufmann had promised to get Abu a larger boat and go sailing with him when the weather was warmer—but that was before Herr Kaufmann had fallen sick.

"I don't like to ask him for anything now," Abu said softly. "But now that you are here, I think he will get well again."

Aladdin smiled and tousled Abu's hair. "I hope so."

CHAPTER THIRTY-TWO

Aladdin worked late every evening. Herr Kaufmann's books were in chaos. In addition to the mess in the ledgers, Michael's old childhood friends had been stealing from the warehouse and from the cogs that carried the salt from Lüneburg to Hamburg. By the end of one week, two of the thieves had already been captured.

Meanwhile, Duke Wilhelm and his men were working with the town council to find Michael. They agreed to release Anna and see if she would lead them to Michael. Duke Wilhelm's men were following her.

Aladdin made time every midday to go to Herr Kaufmann's house and visit him, and soon he was even getting out of bed, letting the servants help him down the stairs so he could have his midday meal with Aladdin in the dining hall.

And no matter how tired he was at the end of the day, Aladdin still managed to write to Kirstyn every night and send the letters by courier.

Would you be willing to live in Lüneburg? he wrote to her. *There are many orphans here, much more than in Hagenheim, who live on the streets and are sometimes beaten for stealing food. They need someone to help them, to start an orphanage, or even to adopt them.* She wouldn't be able to resist that.

He had only been in Lüneburg about a week when he found a house. It was large, made of brick and half timbers, with five floors and a beautiful, decorative doorway of variegated brick. The previous owner had died after a forty-year marriage to his wife, who preceded him in death by only a few weeks. They had been very content, by all accounts, a generous couple who helped their neighbors.

The house's interior was in very good condition, and the heirs were even selling most of the furniture. Aladdin imagined bringing Kirstyn there. Would she like it after living at Hagenheim Castle all her life? It was one of the best houses in town, but it was no castle.

While still thinking it over, Aladdin stepped outside and looked up. There, on the flat surface made by a row of windows that jutted out from the fifth story, a stork was building its nest.

Aladdin bought the house that same day.

"Aladdin."

Aladdin looked up as he sat in the warehouse going over the accounts. He turned around on his stool, and a young woman was standing in the doorway. "Anna."

"Greetings, Aladdin." Her eyes looked hollow and her clothes were dirty. "I'm sorry to disturb you, but I thought you would like to know where Michael is hiding."

Aladdin sprang from his seat and grabbed his sword from where he kept it under his desk. Then he followed Anna outside.

She glanced over her shoulder at him. "He's in an old building near the town gate."

"Why are you telling me this?" Aladdin walked fast to keep up with her.

Anna didn't answer, she just kept walking.

They hurried down the street as they wove their way through the people and animals. Finally Anna went down a small alley.

"I'll wait for you to tell him I'm here." Aladdin stopped just at the entrance of the narrow side street.

She disappeared. A few minutes later Michael emerged from behind a dilapidated building. His face was twisted into a sneer. He was holding a battle-ax.

"You thought you could take my father's business." Michael advanced a step.

"You thought you could take my inheritance." He advanced another step. "You even thought you could take my sister as your wife." As he stepped out into the sunlight, the blade of his battle-ax gleamed and glinted.

"But I took Lady Kirstyn, and there was nothing you could do about it. And now . . ." Michael swung the ax to the left, then the right as he advanced more quickly. "I shall take your life."

Aladdin had never fought anyone with a battle-ax, but he parried his first strike the same as he would have a man with a sword. Michael was slow to recover, the battle-ax heavier and slower than Aladdin's sword. Aladdin took advantage by striking out, going on the offensive, quickly beating Michael back to the entrance of the alley.

Michael's face grew redder and fiercer. Finally Aladdin lunged, aiming his sword at Michael's ribs, a moment before Michael swung the ax at Aladdin's head.

Aladdin sidestepped and ducked. The ax blade whooshed

past Aladdin's ear just as his sword point sank into Michael's side.

Michael let out a scream of fury. He lifted the ax with another cry. Aladdin waited for him to bring down the ax, leaping back to avoid the blade. Then he plunged his sword into Michael's chest.

Michael sank to his knees, then fell over on the ground, lifeless.

Only then did Aladdin realize Duke Wilhelm's men were behind him, watching.

Anna ran forward and fell at Michael's side. She turned him over and screamed at his lifeless face.

Chapter Thirty-Three

Kirstyn sat at her desk writing a letter to Aladdin.

> I miss feeling your arms around me. I miss talking to
> you and seeing you. I know it will take some time for you to
> find a house for us, and I may not see you for many weeks, but

Footsteps came down the hall toward her room at a rapid pace. Suddenly Adela burst into the room. "It's Aladdin and Father." She was breathing hard, her eyes big and round.

"What? What about Aladdin and Father?" Kirstyn stood, her heart pounding.

"They're here!"

Kirstyn ran out of the door and Adela followed her.

"A guard came and said they're on their way home, just outside of town. They'll be at the castle in minutes."

Kirstyn hurried down the stairs. "Is this dress becoming enough? Perhaps I should change." She put her hands to her hair. Was it in place?

"You look very pretty," Adela said, nudging her with her hands. "He doesn't care about your dress or your hair. Come!"

Kirstyn's heart was bursting as she ran the rest of the way to the front door and outside into the hazy sunshine. She strained her eyes but did not see him. She passed through the castle gatehouse. Adela stopped, but Kirstyn kept going. One of the guards shouted at her, then followed close behind her as she ran.

She hurried to the town gate that she and Aladdin always exited through to go walking in the woods. Just as she reached it, Aladdin came into view, sitting atop a cream-colored horse. His eyes locked on hers. He halted his horse and dismounted. They ran to each other, and she threw herself into his arms.

She held him tight, afraid to let go, because if she did, she might forget that there were people watching them, including her father and his knights, and kiss him right here. But when he started talking, his breath near her ear, it was almost as good as a kiss.

"Oh, Kirstyn," he said in a ragged whisper. "It feels so good to hold you."

"Have you come to take me back to Lüneburg with you?" she asked, not loosening her grip on him.

"Yes, and if your father won't give his permission, I'm prepared to steal you away and marry you without his consent."

She pulled away and looked up into his face. What a wonderful face it was. Dark skin that stood out against the cream-colored shirt under his cloak, the warm brown eyes that told her he wished he could kiss her lips. But he leaned down and kissed her cheek instead.

He held her hand and his horse's reins, and they started walking back. "I bought us a house," Aladdin said with a shy smile.

A shiver of pleasure rippled through her. "What does it look like?"

Aladdin described the house in detail, then said, "And it has a stork's nest."

"Oh!" Kirstyn hugged his arm. "It's a sign from God." They both laughed.

When they entered the castle gates, many people called out and waved to Aladdin, some coming to slap him on the back and say a few words of greeting. He was so well loved. From the lowliest servant to the highest-ranking knight, everyone seemed glad to see him.

The next hour was a blur of talking with Mother, Adela, and Toby, as well as eating and drinking and showing Aladdin to the room where he would be staying. Kirstyn wished to be alone with him, but to be near Aladdin, to look upon him, and to hear his voice was enough—for now.

When her father came in, he talked with the group for a few minutes, then he and Aladdin excused themselves and went to talk privately.

Kirstyn laughed and talked with her mother and siblings, though her thoughts were often on what Aladdin and her father were saying.

Valten went to his home a half hour's ride away and brought back Gisela and their children. So many of her family members were there that they made a lively group. Everyone looked at Kirstyn with such strange expressions, as if they were pleased and glad but a bit sad at the same time, for it was no secret that she and Aladdin were planning to marry and leave Hagenheim.

Finally Father and Aladdin returned and joined them. Aladdin smiled and came straight to Kirstyn to whisper in her ear, "Your father says we may marry as soon as we like—and I am in favor of soon, as I need to get back to Lüneburg and the business. But you may set the date."

"May we get married here?" Kirstyn asked. The noise around them actually gave them a bit of privacy, as no one else could hear them.

"Yes, here at the castle. You say when."

"Rapunzel and Gerek should be able to get here in only a few days, but I don't think I can bear to wait for Sophie and Gabe. Besides, they won't be able to come for months. Sophie could give birth at any time."

"So, in a few days? Four days? Five days?"

"Five days." Kirstyn couldn't help smiling and staring at his lips. For a moment she thought he would kiss her, but again, he only leaned down and kissed her cheek.

A courier was dispatched to Keiterhafen Castle with an invitation to the wedding for Rapunzel and Sir Gerek. Meanwhile, the servants prepared a betrothal feast for Aladdin and Kirstyn, and afterward there was music and dancing. Aladdin and Kirstyn danced all the dances for nearly an hour before going back to the table to sit.

While no one seemed to be paying them any attention, Aladdin leaned in, his face very close to Kirstyn's.

"I want you to know, I'm so grateful you love me. I feel like the most blessed man alive."

She caressed his hand, then lifted it to her face, brushing the back of it against her cheek.

"I tried so hard to never make a mistake, to be the best at everything, so you would love me, and so your father would allow me to marry you. But I know that God—and you—will love me in spite of my imperfections."

"I am very happy to hear that, because I've learned that I don't have to have some extraordinary talent for God—and you—to love me. And I had to get kidnapped to realize how much my family loves me."

He brought her hand up to his lips and kissed her fingers. She caressed his cheek, the prickly stubble of his three-day growth of beard rasping against her fingertips.

"I would like all orphans to know that they don't have to feel as if no one loves them, and I'm particularly thinking about Abu. Do you think Herr Kaufmann would allow us to adopt Abu? And do you think Abu would like that?"

Aladdin's throat bobbed as he swallowed. "I don't know, but we can ask."

"You would like that, would you not?"

"I would indeed." He brushed her neck with his fingertips. "I love you, Kirstyn. My heart is yours forever." He leaned in, and this time he kissed her lips—the kiss she'd been waiting weeks for. But they kept it brief, as people were all around them.

Someday soon they'd have all the privacy they wished for. So, for now, she was content to gaze into his eyes while he pressed her hand against his chest.

Kirstyn had accepted that she would not be able to have a conversation alone with Aladdin before the wedding, as they were always surrounded by family members. So when Aladdin sat with her in the Great Hall two evenings before the wedding, she gladly let him hold her hand under the table. Then he leaned over and said, "Will you let me read the letters you wrote while I was away?"

Her heart quickened. "Only if you let me read all the letters you wrote to me."

"I shall bring them to you tonight."

After the meal, everyone was hurrying to make final arrangements for the wedding, preparing for extra guests to arrive the next day. While no one seemed to be watching them, she and Aladdin went up the back stairs, first to Kirstyn's room to fetch her letters—a rather tall stack she'd written but never sent—and then to Aladdin's room to fetch his. She waited for him in the corridor outside.

Aladdin exited holding a stack of folded letters—almost as big as the stack she had written for him. Her eyes filled with tears at the sight of them. She took them and reverently pressed them to her heart. "Thank you."

Suddenly it occurred to her that they were alone. It had apparently occurred to Aladdin a moment before it did to her because he brushed his cheek against hers, inching his lips around to hers. Then he kissed her sweetly and tenderly, the action infused with so much longing and promise.

When the kiss ended, he pressed his forehead to hers. "Sleep well. I can hardly wait to read my letters."

She was still a little breathless as she said, "Yes. Thank you for my letters."

"You haven't read them yet."

"No, but I know I shall enjoy them, because you wrote them to me." She might have leaned in for another kiss if she hadn't heard someone coming up the stairs toward them. So she slipped into her room and closed the door.

A lamp was burning in her room, as Adela was preparing for bed. Kirstyn hurried over to it and opened Aladdin's first letter.

My beloved Kirstyn,

I saw a stork today. It flew over Lüneburg, flapping its great wings, and of course, I thought of you. I thought of the day we climbed up and watched the stork feed its chicks. How amazed I am that that beautiful little girl who seemed to me to be a golden angel from heaven has grown up and now—unless I am wrong—actually loves me.

But then I thought about how I have failed her. I have failed to make my fortune, and now that I'm back in Hagenheim, I'm hardly better off than when I left Hagenheim. You are willing, but I am unable. It is one of the worst realizations I've ever had.

If you are reading this letter, it means that we are together again and all is well. It's hard to imagine how that will ever come about, seeing my situation as it is right now. But God would not wish me to be hopeless or discouraged. So I shall do as David did—"David encouraged himself in the Lord"—and continue on. You are more beautiful and loving than I deserve, but I am so grateful for the memories I have of you.

Your loving servant,
Aladdin

Kirstyn nearly burst into tears. But Adela said, as she yawned, "I'm so tired."

"I'll put out the lamp in a little while."

"Are those all letters from Aladdin?"

"Yes." Kirstyn opened the next one.

"It will be more than a little while if you read all those. Go ahead. I'll just turn and face the wall."

"Thank you, Adela."

"I have to be kind to you. You'll be leaving me, just like all my other sisters, after one more night."

Kirstyn was already reading the next letter.

My most beautiful Kirstyn,

By the time you read this letter, you will have already heard that I arrived back in Lüneburg with Herr Kaufmann and his family. Thankfully, he is recovering from his illness, and Abu and I are doing our best to cheer him. Grethel is joyful and content now that she and Johann are married, and that is also helping his spirits, no doubt. It does not seem to bother Herr Kaufmann anymore that Johann is an artist. But perhaps that is because he is a rather successful one, having painted portraits of several wealthy men between here and Florence. And I am very glad for him. He is a good sort of fellow, though he is terrible at running a business. He was not exaggerating when he said he would have ruined Herr Kaufmann's business in six months. I suppose it is difficult to be good at both business and art.

I have just received another of your letters. They fill my heart with both joy and longing—longing to see you and speak face-to-face with you. Longing to hold you and kiss you, though I have no right as of yet. But my hope is fully renewed, now that God has given me this miracle of reconciliation with Herr Kaufmann.

I will tell you, since I know you will be wondering, that Anna is well. She hurt you by not helping you escape from Michael, but I know you will agree that she was hurt more than anyone by his cruelty. She was quite broken after Michael's death. But after a day or so of crying, she admitted to me, still with tears, that she knew Michael was the worst thing that had happened to her, and she was ashamed for having helped him hold you against your will. She had found a group of pilgrims who were traveling to Köln who wished to take her with them on their pilgrimage to see the relics of the Three Wise Men. I gave her some money, not knowing if what she said was true, and we haven't seen her since. I hope I did the right thing.

I think I may have found a house for us. I go tomorrow to look at it. I feel such joy imagining us in our own home together. You fill my thoughts so much, sometimes I am distracted from my work. Do you think I shall be more distracted when you are here with me? Or less? I am eager to find out.

Kirstyn held the letter to her face and kissed it. What joy to be able to read Aladdin's thoughts about her when he was in high spirits and anticipating their marriage. What was he thinking as he was reading her letters? She blushed as she remembered some of the things she had written. Would he think her too shameless in her longing for him? That she was too honest about her feelings? She might find out tomorrow. But in the meantime, she would savor all of Aladdin's letters by the light of the oil lamp.

The next morning Aladdin went in search of Kirstyn. He'd hardly slept at all after reading her letters. He took the risk of someone seeing him at her bedchamber, and he knocked on the door. Kirstyn's youngest sister, Adela, opened it.

"She isn't here. She got up early."

Aladdin thanked her and hurried down the stairs. He looked

for her in the Great Hall and even the kitchen, but she was not in either place. Would she be in the solar? While he was downstairs, he decided to check the library.

He went in and there she was, standing by the window, looking out. She turned and saw him. She stood there staring at him as he crossed the room, which seemed empty, lit only by the cloudy sky outside the window.

He pulled her to him and kissed her, letting the words of her letters flit across his memory. Could she feel from his kisses how much he reciprocated her longing? He held her close, one hand on her back and the other cradling the back of her head.

When they were both out of breath, she laid her head on his shoulder. "You enjoyed my letters, I believe?"

"I did."

"I enjoyed yours too." She squeezed him tighter, one hand gripping his shoulder.

"I'm not sure it's wise for us to be alone together."

"It's good the wedding is tomorrow." Gazing into his eyes, she smiled. "Perhaps we could get one of the guards to accompany us on a walk in the woods."

"I would enjoy that."

The sun chased away the clouds while Kirstyn's female relatives were making her ready for her wedding. They dressed her elaborately, complete with a veil, and finally she was allowed to go downstairs to join her future husband in their walk to the church.

Never had there been a handsomer bridegroom. Aladdin's black hair set him apart from everyone else in the room, along with his dark skin and beautiful dark eyes. But it was what was in his heart and his mind that she loved the best—the kindness and gentleness, love, loyalty, tenacity, and integrity. Her Aladdin had all the characteristics of a prince among men.

She walked down the street toward the cathedral with her hand on his arm, feeling as if she were floating through a haze of joy that dulled her sight. When they reached the door of the cathedral and stood on the steps, she couldn't see anyone except the priest—and Aladdin.

When they had said their vows on the front steps of the church in front of God, the priest, and all the people gathered there, they went inside the church, leading the rest of the people, including her family, all their friends, and as many of the towns-people as would fit inside. Afterward, the people parted and she and Aladdin walked through the middle of them and led them all outside into the sunshiny street.

People drifted in and out of her consciousness, but mostly she saw Aladdin's smile and sincere expressions, heard his gracious words to all the well-wishers, and felt his gentle attentiveness to her. And when he whispered in her ear, "I have everything I ever wished for," she knew she would remember those words for the rest of her life.

CHAPTER THIRTY-FOUR

Aladdin watched Kirstyn's face as he said, "Here's our house. Do you like it?"

She covered her mouth with her hands and drew in a loud breath. "I love it." She turned to her husband and threw her arms around him. "It looks like home."

"I'm so glad it pleases you."

Since Aladdin had arranged to have the house cleaned and furnished, with a few servants already employed, they were able to stay their first night in Lüneburg at their new home.

The next day, while Abu was at one of his tutoring sessions, Aladdin and Kirstyn met with Herr Kaufmann. He stood up to greet them when they walked in.

"You're looking quite well," Kirstyn said. Truly, he had a lot more color in his cheeks.

"I feel much better." Herr Kaufmann motioned for them to sit. They chatted about sundry things before Herr Kaufmann said, "I have a notion what it is you would like to talk about, but please, do tell me."

Aladdin's gaze met Kirstyn's, and he said, "We would like to adopt Abu—if he is willing, of course."

Herr Kaufmann nodded thoughtfully. "I think that is a very good thing. You are both young and will give Abu a wonderful home. I am old and don't know how much longer I will be here. Abu looks up to you so much, Aladdin, and I know he will come to love you, Lady Kirstyn."

An hour later Abu came downstairs from his tutoring session. "Aladdin! Lady Kirstyn! I'm so glad you're here. Now we can go to the Heath and have races and practice archery and have picnics again."

Aladdin gave him a big hug, then noticed the tears in Kirstyn's eyes. She held out a hand to Abu, who walked more calmly to her and gave her a quick hug.

"Abu," Herr Kaufmann said, "Aladdin and Lady Kirstyn have something to talk over with you."

Abu's eyes grew cautious as he looked from Kirstyn to Aladdin.

Aladdin smiled at him and rested a hand on his shoulder. "Abu, Lady Kirstyn and I have our own house now, and we'd like for you to come and live with us. Herr Kaufmann will always love you, and Grethel and Johann will as well, and you can come and visit them anytime you wish. But Lady Kirstyn and I would like to adopt you as our son. We want to love you and be a family together. What do you think? Would you like that?"

Abu's lips parted. He kept looking from the floor to Aladdin and back to the floor. "Would you . . . be my . . . father, then?"

"Yes, and Lady Kirstyn would be your mother."

Abu's head was bowed, and when he lifted his eyes, they were filled with tears. He threw himself into Aladdin's chest, and Aladdin enfolded him, squeezing him tight.

"Is that a yes?" Aladdin asked through the emotion that was clogging his own throat.

Abu nodded. Kirstyn came over and put an arm around each of them. Finally, after a few quiet sniffs from every person in the room, Abu took a step back. "It might take me a little while to get used to calling you Father." He looked shyly at Kirstyn. "And you Mother."

"That is quite all right." Kirstyn smiled through the tears. "We promise to love you always."

"Yes," Aladdin added, "and you don't have to be perfect."

Kirstyn tucked Abu into his bed and kissed his cheek. "Good night, Abu. I'll let your father pray with you."

Aladdin knew his wife wanted to be as close to Abu as he was, but she was also trying to give him time to become more comfortable with her. She smiled and left the room.

"Abu?"

"Yes?" Abu was looking up at Aladdin with those large, round eyes.

"To be our son by law, you have to be baptized in the Church and have my name added to yours. Are you ready to declare that you believe in the God of the Christians?" Compassion for the boy rose inside Aladdin. "I was very young when Priest and Sir Meynard rescued me from the streets, but I grew to love Jesus just as Priest did. Do you think you can do that too?"

"Why do you believe this Jesus can save us when we die?"

"If Jesus had the power to create us, then He has the power to save us."

Abu's little-boy face relaxed a bit as he stared up at the

canopy that stretched over his bed. Finally he said, "Do you believe it?"

"Yes."

"But why?"

"Why do I believe? That is difficult to answer. Faith is—"

"No, I mean, why would Jesus die to save us?"

"The Holy Writ says God is love." Aladdin felt a helplessness to explain all of this. But his love for Abu was growing with every word.

Abu lifted his hand and rubbed his cheek. "If Jesus and God love me, then . . . I want to be a Christian. Like you, Aladdin. I mean, Father." He smiled as if he were agreeing to play a game of chess or blindman's buff.

Aladdin let out a breath he hadn't known he was holding. "Will you vow to follow Jesus and have no other gods before Him? Will you be baptized in the Church?"

"I will."

A week later Aladdin was standing at the back of the nave of St. Nicholas Church with Kirstyn, Herr Kaufmann, Hilde, and a few others. They all watched as Abu was baptized by a priest in the stone font. With his hair dripping, he turned and looked at those standing around him.

Aladdin was seeing Abu for what he was—a vulnerable child with painful memories. It was suddenly written all over his face. But the hope and peace of finally being in a family were also there, the joy of believing in a God who was powerful enough to love him and save him—and give him a family.

Kirstyn and Aladdin surrounded him with their arms, embracing him. Herr Kaufmann, Grethel, Johann, and Hilde moved in and embraced him as well. Aladdin was not the only one blinking rapidly, sniffing, and wiping his eyes.

The priest said the last part of the sacrament of baptism. "Depart in peace, and the Lord be with you. Amen." Then he took out a handkerchief from inside his sleeve to wipe the tears from his face.

They all went back to Aladdin and Kirstyn's home, where the servants had prepared a feast. Herr Kaufmann stood to make an announcement.

"It was God's good will to grant me, in my old age, not one but two blessings—a son in Aladdin and a grandson in Abu—to replace what the devil had stolen from me." His eyes misted over, and he had to clear his throat before continuing. "God is truly good. I am blessed beyond measure with a wonderful daughter, a prosperous business, and two young men to help me. Abu, I hope you will come to visit me often."

"I will." Abu nodded.

Aladdin, who was sitting next to him, squeezed his shoulder.

They all raised their glass goblets. Even Abu was given a bit of watered-down wine in his cup.

"To Abu of Lüneburg. May he always remember fondly this, the day of his baptism into Christ and the Church."

They all drank to that.

"And may he always have family and friends who care for him as much as we do."

That night, when Aladdin and Kirstyn tucked Abu into his bed, Abu smiled and said sleepily, "This has been the best day of my life."

EPILOGUE

Two Years Later

Kirstyn and Aladdin sat on the benches around the table that had been set up in the backyard of the new Lüneburg orphanage. Children ran around, laughing and squealing, playing with ribbons that had been attached to the ends of long sticks. Three little girls about Abu's age of eleven were practicing the show they had prepared, waving their ribbons in unison, twirling, weaving in and out, then ending with a flourish.

Abu watched them, his eyes focused on one little girl in particular with big blue eyes and hair the color of newly cut hay. Kirstyn's breath caught as she was reminded of another little boy with eyes that had watched her in just the same way.

"All right, children." The mistress of the orphanage clapped. "Come to the table. Abu's birthday feast is ready."

While the children enjoyed the feast, the Meistersingers sang and played Abu's favorite songs. Kirstyn fed their two-month-old baby, then handed her off to Aladdin, who patted her back and talked to her in his soft but proud father voice.

When everyone had eaten their fill, Abu came over to kiss his baby sister's cheek, then sat quickly to watch as the three girls performed their ribbon-stick show. Abu was all attention. He applauded most enthusiastically, and when the blonde-haired girl smiled at him, Abu's cheeks turned bright red.

Afterward the children started a game of blindman's buff, and Aladdin leaned over and whispered in Kirstyn's ear, "Does this remind you of anything?"

Kirstyn smiled. "The time you defended me from Hanns? You were always my hero."

Making sure not to jostle the sleeping baby on his shoulder, Aladdin leaned over and kissed her. "You were always my lady."

"Mother, Father, do you have to do that in front of my friends?" Abu grimaced and shook his head.

"Sorry, son." Aladdin gave Abu his best contrite expression. "We shall try to refrain."

Abu ran off, and Aladdin winked at Kirstyn.

She glanced around. This was always her dream, her purpose, and exactly what she had hoped for. All the times she'd gone on walks with Aladdin, sharing her thoughts with him and their friendship as children, even then it was as if she'd foreseen this very scene of love, joy, and family.

Acknowledgments

This story needed, and received, lots of input from people who helped me realize my vision of an Aladdin story. I want to thank all those people for their help. I want to particularly thank Julee Schwarzberg and Jocelyn Bailey for their very insightful editorial feedback, which was spot on. I also want to thank Natasha Kern for her diligence, going above and beyond in helping with the editing process as well, opening my eyes to areas I had not paid enough attention to, which proved invaluable. Thanks also for Kimberly Carlton and her insight and helpfulness. This book, perhaps more than any of my others, truly benefitted, and would not have been complete, without all of these great editing minds. Though its shortfalls are definitely mine.

I want to thank all my friends who have been so supportive—Regina Carbulon, with her indomitable positivity, support, and encouragement; Mary Freeman, for always being willing to provide me with tea and a listening ear; Kathy Bone, for her friendship, humor, and petit fours; Grace and Faith Dickerson, for their brainstorming help and feedback; Suzy Parish, for praying for me; Terry Bell, for brainstorming with me; and Julie Mouvery, for being a great prayer warrior.

Thanks to all my readers—for encouraging e-mails and messages, writing and posting reviews, telling your friends about my books, and for all the other ways you bless me. I pray this story has special meaning to you, as it did for me. God bless!

DISCUSSION QUESTIONS

1. Even as a small child, Aladdin knew stealing was wrong. He grew up feeling shame over this part of his life. What about your childhood, either positive or negative, has become ingrained in your identity and how you see yourself?
2. Why did Aladdin and Lady Kirstyn form such a bond? Was there something in each of them that met a need in the other?
3. Why did Aladdin leave Kirstyn and Hagenheim? Why didn't Kirstyn have her father order him to stay?
4. What was it that Aladdin wanted out of life? What was driving him to seek his fortune and to try to gain the approval and admiration of those around him?
5. What roles did Herr Kaufmann play in Aladdin's life? If this was a parallel to other versions of the Aladdin story, who would Herr Kaufmann be?
6. Why did Lady Kirstyn believe she wasn't talented or

extraordinary? How was she different from her brothers and sisters? Was her estimation of herself accurate?

7. Why did Michael kidnap Lady Kirstyn? Whom did he want revenge against?

8. What do you think of Anna's decision to stay with Michael? Was she also desperate for acceptance, just as Aladdin was? In what ways did they handle this desire differently? What would you do if your desire for acceptance ever lured you into a toxic relationship?

9. How did Kirstyn deal with her captivity? What were the emotional scars she dealt with after it was over?

10. Why did Aladdin agree to marry Grethel, even though he didn't love her? Have you ever done something you didn't want to do just to please someone else?

11. Aladdin once said, "I'm not perfect. But I wish I was." Do you ever feel this way? In what ways did Aladdin's wish to be perfect affect his life? Was he afraid God wouldn't love him if he wasn't perfect?

12. Why was Kirstyn so angry with Aladdin for not coming to see her right away after he came back to Hagenheim? What were the fears that kept Aladdin away?

13. What does the Bible say about how we should treat orphans and foreigners?

14. Aladdin's wish was to make his fortune. In what ways did he accomplish this goal?

She lost everything to the scheme of an evil servant. But she might just gain what she's always wanted . . . if she makes it in time.

Available in print, e-book, and audio!

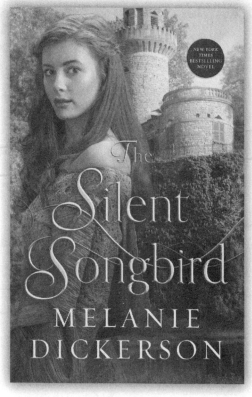

The
GOLDEN BRAID

The one who needs rescuing isn't always the one in the tower.

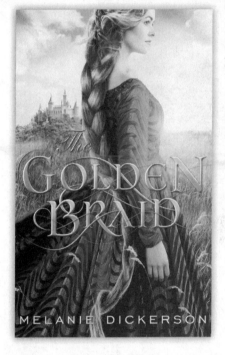

Rapunzel can throw a knife better than any man around. And her skills as an artist rival those of any artist she's met. But for a woman in medieval times, the one skill she most desires is the hardest one to obtain: the ability to read.

Available in print, e-book, and audio!

Don't miss the Medieval Fairy Tale novels also available from Melanie Dickerson!

Available in print, e-book, and audio!

An Excerpt from
The Huntress of
Thornbeck Forest

I

*The year 1363, in the northeast German reaches of the
Holy Roman Empire, the Margravate of Thornbeck*

The tip of the arrow found its mark, a perfect shot through the
deer's heart and lungs. The animal took two steps forward, then
a side step, and fell over.

Odette's five men—more boys than men, as they were around
thirteen or fourteen years old—darted out of the cover of the

bushes and ran toward the animal that would feed at least four families. They began to cut it apart and prepared to carry it, and all evidence of it, away in their leather game bags.

But far more than four hungry families and many orphaned children inhabited the town of Thornbeck, so Odette motioned to the two boys looking to her. They set off deeper into the forest that was the margrave's game park. The only one reaping the good of Thornbeck Forest, rightfully, was the margrave. He could spare a few deer to feed the poor. He could spare them quite well.

Odette moved through the trees and undergrowth, trying to step as quietly as possible. The two boys stayed behind her. The moon was full, the night sky was clear of clouds, and enough light filtered through the trees to help her find her way to another of the harts' favorite feeding spots. Either a salt deposit was there or the grass was particularly sweet, because that was where she often found her most desired prey—fully grown red deer—with their necks bowed low as they ate.

Odette came within sight of the spot and crouched to wait, holding her longbow and an arrow at the ready. Soon, a hind moved soundlessly into the small clearing. Odette's fingers twitched in anticipation of the meat that would assuage the hunger of many people, but the twinge of pity that pinched her chest kept her from raising her bow and taking aim. It was summer, tomorrow being St. John the Baptist Day, and the hind no doubt had at least one newborn fawn, possibly two or three, hidden away somewhere, waiting for her to come back and nurse them.

Creating more orphans, even of the animal kind, went against everything Odette strove for, so she resisted taking the shot. Instead, she sat waiting and watching. After a few minutes, her breath stilled as a large stag with huge antlers stepped up beside the hind. He kept his head high as he seemed to be listening.

Odette swiftly raised her bow and pulled the arrow back. She pressed her cheek close to take aim and let the arrow fly.

Just at that moment, the stag must have caught wind of her or heard a noise because he turned and leapt away in one fluid movement, and the hind was less than a moment behind him. Odette's arrow missed them and disappeared in the night.

With the boys behind her, she went to search for the arrow. She did not want the margrave's forester finding it. She was careful to poach only one or two large animals a night, and it was important to take away all evidence that they had been there.

Where was that arrow? Odette went to the spot where it should have landed, beyond where the deer had been standing. She hunted around the bush, then parted the leaves to peer inside and underneath, searching for the white feather on the end. She felt around on the ground. No white feather and no arrow.

Her men were searching a little farther away. Suddenly, she heard laughter. She lifted her head, much like she had seen the deer do many times, and listened. Her two men looked at her, their eyes wide.

Voices drifted toward them, too far away for her to make out the words, but they seemed to be growing nearer. She clenched her teeth. Why couldn't she find that arrow? With reluctance, she motioned for the young men to follow her and moved away, back toward the town. She couldn't let anyone see her here, not with a longbow and a quiver of arrows on her back. The penalty for poaching was imprisonment, being fastened in the pillory in the town square, or having one's hand or ear cut off.

The voices likely belonged to people looking for special herbs and flowers to burn in the Midsummer bonfire the next night. Tomorrow even more people would be out in Thornbeck Forest, wandering into the margrave's game park. It would be too dangerous to go out hunting at all. If only she had not missed that stag.

She backtracked toward the three men she had left to take the hart she had killed earlier. They were hoisting the various pieces of meat over their shoulders and across their backs to carry out of the forest. They paused to kick the leaves and dirt over the bloody evidence of their kill.

As Odette approached, they turned and froze.

"It's me," she whispered. "We need to leave. People are coming this way."

They nodded as one of them dragged a tree limb over the ground to further disguise the evidence of their kill.

Just before they reached the edge of the forest, Odette pulled an old gray cloak out of her pouch and used it to cover her longbow and arrows, tucking them under her arm. She called to the young men, "Wait."

They stopped and looked at her.

"Give me one of those bags. I will deliver it."

They exchanged glances. Then the tallest boy said, "Rutger said we should deliver all the game to his storehouse, for him to distribute."

"I will tell him that I delivered this bag." She lifted a heavy haunch of venison off his shoulder. "He will not mind."

The boys continued on, but Odette, dressed as a boy with a long dark tunic and hose, her blond hair hidden inside her hood, went in a different direction.

She headed for the little hut just outside the town wall, a place where many of the poorest people lived in makeshift shelters. She knocked on the house that was leaning to one side and held up with sticks, and little Hanns opened the door, peeking around the side and rubbing his eyes with his fist.

"I'm sorry for waking you, Hanns."

"Odette!"

"Shh." She put her finger to her lips, then whispered, "I brought you something. In the morning you will have some fried venison for breakfast. How does that sound?"

Hanns stopped rubbing his face, his mouth fell open, and his eyes got round. As Odette held out the leather bag, the air rushed out of him with an excited, "Oh!"

"Don't wake your mother now. You can surprise her in the morning."

"I will!" Without closing the door, he turned and, straining to carry the heavy meat, disappeared inside the dark one-room, dirt-floor house.

Odette closed the door and turned to hasten home while it was still dark.

The story continues in *The Huntress of Thornbeck Forest* by Melanie Dickerson.

ABOUT THE AUTHOR

Jodie Westfall Photography

Melanie Dickerson is a *New York Times* bestselling author and a Christy Award winner. Her first book *The Healer's Apprentice* won the National Readers' Choice Award for Best First Book in 2010, and *The Merchant's Daughter* won the 2012 Carol Award. Melanie spends her time daydreaming, researching the most fascinating historical time periods, and writing stories at her home near Huntsville, Alabama, where she gathers dandelion greens for her two adorable guinea pigs between writing and editing her happily ever afters.

www.MelanieDickerson.com
Twitter: @MelanieAuthor
Facebook: MelanieDickersonBooks